D0950738

THE
SOULFORGE

Margaret Weis

THE SOULFORGE
©1998 TSR, Inc.
©2003 Wizards of the Coast, Inc.

Distributed in the United States by Holtzbrinck Publishing. Distributed in Canada by Fenn Ltd.

Distributed to the hobby, toy, and comic trade in the United States and Canada by regional distributors.

Distributed worldwide by Wizards of the Coast, Inc. and regional distributors.

DRAGONLANCE and the Wizards of the Coast logo are registered trademarks of Wizards of the Coast, Inc., a subsidiary of Hasbro, Inc.

All Wizards of the Coast characters, character names, and the distinctive likenesses thereof are trademarks of Wizards of the Coast, Inc.

Printed in the U.S.A.

Cover art by Larry Elmore
First Printing: January 1998
Library of Congress Catalog Card Number: 98-8779

9 8 7 6 5

US ISBN: 0-7869-1314-2
620-86512-001-EN

U.S., CANADA,	EUROPEAN HEADQUARTERS
ASIA, PACIFIC, & LATIN AMERICA	Wizards of the Coast, Belgium
Wizards of the Coast, Inc.	T Hosfveld 6d
P.O. Box 707	1702 Groot-Bijgaarden
Renton, WA 98057-0707	Belgium
+1-800-324-6496	+322 467 3360

Visit our web site at **www.wizards.com**

Dedicated with love and friendship to

Tracy Raye Hickman

ACKNOWLEDGMENTS

This is to gratefully acknowledge the help of the friends of Krynn on the alt.fan.dragonlance newsgroup. They have walked that magic land more recently than I and were able to supply me with invaluable information. Thank you all.

I would like to acknowledge the work of Terry Phillips, whose original Adventure Gamebook, *The Soulforge*, was the inspiration for my story.

FOREWORD

t's been over ten years since we gathered in my little apartment for a game session. Dragonlance was known only to a handful of us then, an infant full of promise not yet realized. We were playing the first adventure of what would eventually prove to be a wonderful experience for millions—but on that night, as I recall, we mostly didn't know what we were doing. I was running the game from my own hastily assembled design notes. Both my wife and Margaret were there among a host of others who were struggling to find their characters from the thin shadowy outlines we had given them. Who were these Heroes of the Lance? What were they really like?

We were just settling in to the game when I turned to my good friend Terry Phillips and asked what his character was doing. Terry spoke . . . and the world of Krynn was forever changed. His rasping voice, his sarcasm and bitterness all masking an arrogance and power that never needed to be stated suddenly were real. Everyone in the room was both transfixed and terrified. To this day Margaret swears that Terry wore the black robes to the party that night.

Terry Phillips happened to choose Raistlin for his character and in that fated choice gave birth to one of Dragonlance's most enduring characters. Terry even wrote an Adventure Gamebook on Raistlin's tests which bore the same title as the book you hold in your hands. Krynn—not to mention Margaret and myself— owe no small debt of gratitude to Terry for bringing us Raistlin.

Other characters in Dragonlance may belong to various creators, but Margaret, from the very outset, made it clear to all concerned that Raistlin was hers and hers alone. We never begrudged her the dark mage—she seemed to be the only one who could comfort his character and soothe his troubled mind. The truth is that Raistlin frightened the rest of us into distance. Only Margaret knew how to bridge that abyssal gulf.

Now you hold the story of Raistlin as told by Margaret—the one person who knows him best of all. The journey may not always be comfortable but it will be a worthy one. Margaret has always been a master storyteller. Here, now, is the story that she has longed to tell.

And if Terry is reading this now—wherever he is—I wish him peace.

Tracy Hickman
October 10, 1997

The Creation of Raistlin Majere

Margaret Weis

'm often asked, "Who's your favorite character?" This is tantamount to asking a mother to name her favorite child! We love our children for themselves, a love individual as each child.

It is true, however, that a writer comes to know and like some characters better than others. Some I know better than I know my own friends and family! The innermost recesses we hide from the world are clearly visible to our Creator. Playing God with my characters, I see their weaknesses, their strengths, their inner doubts and turmoil, and their dark and secret parts. Raistlin Majere was such a character.

When I first met Raistlin, he was a name on a Character Sheet. I knew his "stats," developed for the Dragonlance role-playing game. I knew he was a third-level mage in his early twenties. I knew he was slight in build, wore red robes, and that he was known among his friends as "The Sly One." I knew he had a strong, well-built, powerful twin brother named Caramon. But he was just one of a number of characters—Tanis, Sturm, Flint, Tasslehoff—until I read the passage that said Raistlin had "golden skin and hourglass eyes."

"Why does he have golden skin and hourglass eyes?" I asked, puzzled.

"Because the artists think he would look cool!" was the reply.

This intrigued me. I had to know the reason Raistlin had golden skin and hourglass eyes. In trying to solve this mystery, I was led to an understanding of the true nature of Raistlin's character.

That he would be jealous of his good-looking, stronger twin brother was a natural feeling to which every person who has ever grown up with a sibling could relate. That he was not generally trusted or well liked by his peers was obvious. If his friends called him "The Sly One," what would his enemies term him? Naturally he would be the target of bullies, which would lead his brother to protect him. It seemed to me that Raistlin would grow dependent on his brother for such protection, but that he would, at the same time, resent Caramon for it. Thus Raistlin would constantly struggle against a love as smothering as it was nurturing.

The fact that Raistlin was of slight build and physically weaker than his brother seemed to indicate a sickly youth, which might also be indicative of an introspective nature, particularly if he was forced to spend time cooped up in a sickbed. Such a childhood would have contributed to his feeling of alienation from his peers but would later give him empathy for others in like circumstances.

That Raistlin would turn to the study of magic was again obvious. Of course, it would be his elder half-sister, the restless and ambitious Kitiara, who would lead his thoughts in that direction. In a rough and dangerous world her younger brother lacked physical strength to wield a weapon. He needed some way to defend himself. Magic was the answer, especially since he already showed some talent in that area. Raistlin soon came to realize that magic was also the means by which he could gain power and ascendancy over others.

All very intriguing, but it didn't explain the golden skin and hourglass eyes. Certainly he wasn't born with them. His twin brother and his elder half-sister were perfectly normal-looking humans. Perhaps his study of magic had caused this transformation. He must have had to take a test to prove his abilities to the wizards who lived in the Towers of High Sorcery.

What sort of magical test would they give young wizards? A difficult test, probably extremely difficult. Otherwise anyone with a bit of talent could declare himself a wizard. What if the Test required that a mage stake his or her very life on the outcome? And what if something happened during the Test that caused Raistlin's skin to acquire a golden tinge and to give him eyes that would see the ravages of time upon all living things? Thus the Test in the Tower of High Sorcery came into existence. It was during that Test that Raistlin had the fateful meeting with the lich, Fistandantilus.

I became so fascinated with Raistlin that I wrote a short story about his journey to the Tower to take the Test. I also came to know a lot about Caramon on that trip. I saw Caramon's great inner goodness that to his friends would seem a weakness but that in the end would be the rock on which he would build a successful and happy life.

I'm still learning about Raistlin. With every book I write about him and his twin and their adventures in the world, I discover something new. Raistlin is, and continues to be, a favorite of all the many different characters it has been my privilege and my joy to know.

—Margaret Weis
August 1998

The alloys produced by early iron workers . . . were made by heating a mass of iron ore and charcoal in a forge or furnace having a forced draft. Under this treatment, the ore was reduced to the sponge of metallic iron filled with a slag composed of metallic impurities and charcoal ash. This sponge of iron was removed from the furnace while still incandescent and beaten with heavy sledges to drive out the slag and to weld and consolidate the iron. . . . Occasionally this technique of ironmaking produced, by accident, a true steel . . .[1]

[1]"Steel Production" Microsoft® Encarta® Encyclopedia, 1993–1995.

Book 1

A mage's soul is forged in the crucible of the magic.

—Antimodes of the White Robes

I

He never wore his white robes while traveling.

Few mages did, in those days, the days before the great and terrible War of the Lance spilled out of its caldron like boiling oil and scalded the countryside. In those days, just fifteen or so years before the war, the fire beneath the pot had been lit, the Dark Queen and her minions had struck the sparks that would start the blaze. The oil was cool, black, and sluggish in the caldron. But at the bottom, the oil was beginning to simmer.

Most people on Ansalon would never see the caldron, much less the bubbling oil inside, until it was poured on their heads, along with dragonfire and the countless other horrors of war. At this time of relative peace, the majority of people living on Ansalon never looked up, never looked from side to side to see what was going on in the world around them. Instead, they gazed at their own feet, plodding through the dusty day, and if they ever lifted their heads, it was usually to see if it was likely to rain and spoil their picnic.

A few felt the heat of the newly kindled fire. A few had been watching closely the turgid black liquid in the caldron. Now they could see that it was starting to simmer. These few were uneasy. These few began to make plans.

The wizard's name was Antimodes. He was human, of good middle-class merchant stock, hailing from Port Balifor. The youngest of three, he had been raised in the family business, which was tailoring. To this day, he still displayed with pride the scars of the pinpricks on the middle finger of his right hand. His early experience left him with a canny business sense and a taste for, and knowledge of, fine clothing, one reason he rarely wore his white robes.

Some mages were afraid to wear their robes, which were a symbol of their calling, because that calling was not well loved in Ansalon. Antimodes was not afraid. He did not wear his white robes because white showed the dirt. He detested arriving at his destination mud-splattered, the stains of the road upon him.

He traveled alone, which in those uneasy days meant that he was either a fool, a kender, or an extremely powerful person. Antimodes was not a fool, nor was he a kender. He traveled alone because he preferred his own company and that of his donkey, Jenny, to that of almost all others of his acquaintance. Hired bodyguards were generally loutish and dull, not to mention expensive. Antimodes could adequately and handily defend himself, should need arise.

The need had rarely arisen, in all his fifty-plus years. Thieves look for prey that is timid, cowering, drunk, or heedless. Though his finely made dark blue woolen cloak with its silver clasps showed him to be a man of wealth, Antimodes wore that cloak with an air of confidence, riding with his back straight on his daintily stepping donkey, his head held high, his sharp-eyed gaze taking notice of every squirrel in the trees, every toad in the ruts.

He displayed no weapon, but his long sleeves and tall leather boots could easily conceal a poignard; the bags that dangled from his hand-tooled leather belt almost certainly contained spell components. Every thief worth his lock-picking tools recognized that the ivory case Antimodes wore on a leather thong looped around his chest contained magical scrolls. Shadowy figures lurking in the hedgerows slunk out of his way and waited for likelier victims.

Antimodes was journeying to the Tower of High Sorcery in Wayreth. He was taking the long way around, for he could have easily walked the corridors of magic in order to reach the tower from his home in Port Balifor. He had been requested to make the journey overland. The request had come from Par-Salian, head of the Order of White Robes and head of the Wizards' Conclave, and therefore, strictly speaking, Antimodes's master. The two were fast friends, however, their friendship dating back to the day when both were young and had arrived at the Tower at the same time to take the exacting, grueling, and occasionally lethal test. Both had been kept waiting in the same antechamber in the tower, each had shared his trepidation and fear with the other, each had found much-needed comfort, consolation, and support. The two White Robes had been friends ever since.

Thus Par-Salian "requested" that Antimodes take this long and tiresome journey. The head of the conclave did not order it, as he might have done with another.

Antimodes was to accomplish two goals during his journey. First, he was to peer into every dark corner, eavesdrop on every whispered conversation, peep through the shutters of every window that was locked and bolted. Second, he was to look for new talent. The first was a bit dangerous; people do not take kindly to snoops, especially if said people have something to hide. The second was tedious and boring, for it generally meant dealing with children, and Antimodes had an aversion to children. All in all, Antimodes preferred the spying.

He had written his report in his neat and precise tailor's handwriting in a journal, which he would turn over to Par-Salian. Antimodes reread in his mind every word in that journal as he trotted along on his white donkey, a present from his eldest brother, who had taken over the family business and was now a prosperous tailor in Port Balifor. Antimodes spent his time on the road pondering all he had seen and heard— nothing significant, everything portentous.

"Par-Salian will find this interesting reading," Antimodes told Jenny, who gave her head a shake and pricked her ears to indicate her agreement. "I look forward to handing the journal over," her master continued. "He will read it and ask questions, and I will explain what I have seen and heard, all the while drinking his most excellent elven wine. And you, my dear, will have oats for dinner."

Jenny gave her hearty approval. In some places in which they'd stayed, she'd been forced to eat damp, moldy hay or worse. Once she'd actually been offered potato peelings.

The two had nearly reached their journey's end. Within the month, Antimodes would arrive at the Tower of High Sorcery in Wayreth. Or, rather, the tower would arrive at Antimodes. One never found the magical Tower of Wayreth. It found you, or not, as its master chose.

This night Antimodes would spend in the town of Solace. He might have pushed on, for the season was late spring, and it was only noon, with plenty of daylight left for travel. But he was fond of Solace, fond of its famous inn, the Inn of the Last Home, fond of Otik Sandath, the inn's owner, and especially fond of the inn's ale. Antimodes had been tasting that chilled dark ale with its creamy head in his imagination ever since he had swallowed his first mouthful of road dust.

His arrival in Solace went unnoticed, unlike his arrival in other towns in Ansalon, where every stranger was taken to be a thief or plague-carrier, a murderer or kidnapper of children. Solace was a different town than most on Ansalon. It was a town of refugees, who had fled for their lives during the Cataclysm and had only stopped running when they came to this location. Having once been strangers on the road themselves, the founders of Solace took a kindly view toward other strangers, and this attitude had been passed down to their descendants. Solace had become known as a haven for outcasts, loners, the restless, the adventuresome.

The inhabitants were friendly and tolerant—up to a point. Lawlessness was known to be bad for business, and Solace was a town with a sharp eye for business.

Being located on a bustling road that was the major route from northern Ansalon to all points south, Solace was accustomed to entertaining travelers, but that was not the reason few noticed the arrival of Antimodes. The main reason was that most of the people of Solace never saw him, due to the fact that they were high above him. The major portion of the town of Solace was built in the vast, spreading, gigantic branches of the immense and wondrous vallenwood trees.

The early inhabitants of Solace had literally taken to the trees to escape their enemies. Having found living among the treetops to be safe and secure, they had built their homes among the leaves, and their descendants and those who came after them had continued the tradition.

Craning his neck, Antimodes looked up from the donkey's back to the wooden plank bridges that extended from tree to tree, watching the bridges swing and sway as the villagers hastened across on various errands. Antimodes was a dapper man, with an eye for the ladies, and though the women of Solace kept their flowing skirts firmly in hand when crossing the bridges, there was always the possibility of catching a glimpse of a shapely ankle or a well-turned leg.

Antimodes's attention to this pleasant occupation was interrupted when he heard sounds of shrill yelling. He lowered his gaze to find that he and Jenny had been overtaken by a brigade of bare-legged, sunburned boys armed with wooden swords and tree-branch spears and giving battle to an army of imaginary foes.

The boys had not meant to run down Antimodes. The swirl

of battle had carried them in his direction; the invisible goblins or ogres or whatever enemy the boys chased were in full retreat toward Crystalmir Lake. Caught up in the shouting, yelling, sword-thwacking melee, Antimodes's donkey, Jenny, shied and danced, wild-eyed with fright.

A mage's mount is not a war-horse. A mage's mount is not trained to gallop into the noise and blood and confusion of battle or to face spears without flinching. At most, a mage's mount must accustom herself to a few foul-smelling spell components and an occasional lightning show. Jenny was a placid donkey, strong and hale, with an uncanny knack for avoiding ruts and loose stones, providing her rider with a smooth and comfortable journey. Jenny considered that she'd put up with a great deal on this trip: bad food, leaky accommodations, dubious stablemates. An army of stick-wielding boys was simply too much to bear.

By the twitch of her long ears and the baring of her yellow teeth, Jenny was obviously prepared to strike back by bucking and kicking at the boys, which would have probably not damaged the boys much but would certainly dislodge her rider. Antimodes endeavored to control the donkey, but he was not having any luck. The younger boys, maddened with battle lust, did not see the man's distress. They swirled about him, lashing out with their swords, shrieking and crowing in shrill triumph. Antimodes might well have entered Solace on his posterior, when, out of the dust and noise, an older boy—perhaps about eight or nine— appeared, caught hold of Jenny's reins, and, with a gentle touch and forceful presence, calmed the terrified donkey.

"Go around!" the youth ordered, waving his sword, which he had shifted to his left hand. "Clear out, fellows! You're frightening the donkey."

The younger boys, ranging in age from six upward, good-naturedly obeyed the youth and continued on their rowdy way. Their shouts and laughter echoed among the enormous trunks of the vallenwood trees.

The older boy paused and, with an accent that was definitely not of this part of Ansalon, spoke his apology as he soothingly stroked the donkey's soft nose. "Forgive us, good sir. We were caught up in our play and did not notice your arrival. I trust you have taken no harm."

The young man had straight, thick blond hair, which he wore bowl-cropped around his ears in a style that was popular in Solamnia, but nowhere else on Krynn. His eyes were gray-blue, and he had a stern and serious demeanor that belied his years, a noble bearing of which he was extremely conscious. His speech was polished and educated. This was no country bumpkin, no laborer's son.

"Thank you, young sir," Antimodes replied. He carefully took stock of his spell components, checking to make certain that the buffeting he had taken had not loosened any of his pouches he wore on his belt. He was about to ask the young man's name, for he found himself interested in this youth, but, on looking up, he found the young man's blue eyes fixed upon the pouches. The expression on the youthful face was one of disdain, disapproval.

"If you are certain you are well, Sir Mage, and have taken no harm from our play, I will take my leave." The youth made a stiff and rigid bow and, letting loose the donkey's halter, turned to run after the other boys. "Coming, Kit?" he called brusquely to another older boy, who had halted to study the stranger with interest.

"In a minute, Sturm," said the other youth, and it was only when she spoke that Antimodes realized this curly-haired boy, wearing pants and a leather vest, was actually a girl.

She was an attractive girl—now that he studied her closely—or perhaps he should say "young lady," for though only in her early teens, her figure was well defined, her movements were graceful, and her gaze was bold and unwavering. She studied Antimodes in her turn, regarding him with an intense, thoughtful interest that he found difficult to understand. He was accustomed to meeting with disdain and dislike, but the young woman's interest was not idle curiosity. Her gaze held no antipathy. It seemed as if she were making up her mind about something.

Antimodes was old-fashioned in his attitude toward women. He liked them soft and perfumed, loving and gentle, with blushing cheeks and properly downcast eyes. He realized that in this day of powerful female wizards and strong female warriors his attitude was backward, but he was comfortable with it. He frowned slightly to indicate his own disapproval of this young hoyden and clucked at Jenny, urging her in the direction of the public stables, located near the blacksmith's shop. The stables, the blacksmith's, and the baker's shop, with its immense ovens, were three of the few buildings in Solace situated on the ground.

Even as Antimodes passed by the young woman, he could feel her brown-eyed gaze focused on him, wondering, considering.

2

Antimodes saw to it that Jenny was comfortably established, with an extra measure of feed and a promise from the stableboy to provide the donkey with extra attention, all paid for, of course, in good Krynn steel, which he laid out with a lavish hand.

This done, the archmage took the nearest staircase leading up to the bridge walks. The stairs were many, and he was hot and out of breath by the time he finished the climb. The shadows of the vallenwoods' thick foliage cooled him, however, providing a shady canopy under which to walk. After a moment's pause to catch his breath, Antimodes followed the suspended walkway that led toward the Inn of the Last Home.

On his way, he passed numerous small houses perched high in the tree branches. House designs varied in Solace, for each had to conform to the tree in which it stood. By law, no part of the living vallenwood could be cut or burned or in any other way molested. Every house used the broad trunk for at least one wall, while the branches formed the ceiling beams. The floors were not level, and there was a noticeable rocking motion to the houses during windstorms. Such irregularities were considered charming by the inhabitants of Solace. They would have driven Antimodes crazy.

The Inn of the Last Home was the largest structure in Solace. Standing some forty feet above ground level, it was built around the bole of a massive vallenwood, which formed part of the Inn's interior. A veritable thicket of timbers supported the inn from beneath. The common room and the kitchen were on the lowest level. Sleeping rooms were perched above and could be reached by a separate entrance; those requiring privacy were not forced to traipse through the common room.

The inn's windows were made of multicolored stained glass, which, according to local legend, had been shipped all the way from Palanthas. The stained glass was an excellent advertisement for the business; the colors glinting in the shadows of the leaves caused the eye to turn in that direction, when otherwise the inn might have been hidden among the foliage.

Antimodes had eaten a light breakfast, and he was therefore hungry enough to do full justice to the proprietor's renowned cooking. The climb up the stairs had further sharpened Antimodes's appetite, as did the smells wafting from the kitchen. Upon entering, the archmage was greeted by Otik himself, a rotund, cheerful middle-aged man, who immediately remembered Antimodes, though the mage had not been a guest in perhaps two years or more.

"Welcome, friend, welcome," Otik said, bowing and bobbing his head as he did to all customers, gentry or peasant. His apron was snow-white, not grease-stained as with some innkeepers. The inn itself was as clean as Otik's apron. When the barmaids weren't serving customers, they were sweeping or scouring or polishing the lovely wooden bar, which was actually part of the living vallenwood.

Antimodes expressed his pleasure in returning to the inn. Otik proved he remembered his guest by taking Antimodes to his favorite table near one of the windows, a table that provided an excellent view, through green-colored glass, of Crystalmir Lake. Without being asked, Otik brought a mug of chilled dark ale and placed it before Antimodes.

"I recall how you said you enjoyed my dark ale last time you were here, sir," Otik remarked.

"Indeed, Innkeep, I have never tasted its like," Antimodes replied. He also noted the way Otik carefully kept from making any reference to the fact that Antimodes was a user of magic, a delicacy Antimodes appreciated, though he himself scorned to hide who or what he was from anyone.

"I will take a room for the night, with luncheon and dinner," said Antimodes, bringing out his purse, which was well stocked but not indecently full.

Otik replied that rooms were available, Antimodes should have his pick, they would be honored by his presence. Luncheon today was a casserole of thirteen different types of beans simmered with herbs and ham. Dinner was pounded beef and the spiced potatoes for which the inn was famous.

Otik waited anxiously to hear his guest say that the bill of fare was perfectly satisfactory. Then, beaming, the barkeep bustled fussily off to deal with the myriad chores involved in running the inn.

Antimodes relaxed and glanced about at the other customers. It being rather past the usual luncheon hour, the inn was relatively empty. Travelers were upstairs in their rooms, sleeping off the good meal. Laborers had returned to their jobs, business owners were drowsing over their account books, mothers were putting children down for afternoon naps. A dwarf—a hill dwarf, by the looks of him—was the inn's only other customer.

A hill dwarf who was no longer living in the hills, a hill dwarf living among humans in Solace. Doing quite well, to judge by his clothes, which consisted of a fine homespun shirt, good leather breeches, and the leather apron of his trade. He was not more than middle-aged; there were only a few streaks of gray in his nut-brown beard. The lines on his face were uncommonly deep and dark for a dwarf of his years. His life had been a hard one and had left its mark. His brown eyes were warmer than the eyes of those of his brethren who did not live among humans and who seemed to constantly be peering out from behind high barricades.

Catching the dwarf's bright eye, Antimodes raised his ale mug. "I note by your tools that you are a metal worker. May Reorx guide your hammer, sir," he said, speaking in dwarven.

The dwarf gave a nod of gratification and, raising his own mug, said, speaking in Common, "A straight road and a dry one, traveler," in gruff return.

Antimodes did not offer to share his table with the dwarf, nor did the dwarf seem inclined to have company. Antimodes looked out the window, admiring the view and enjoying the pleasant warmth seeping through his body, a refreshing contrast to the cool ale that was soothing his dust-parched throat. Antimodes's assigned duty was to eavesdrop on any and all conversation, and so he listened idly to the conversations of the dwarf and the barmaid, though it did not appear to him that they were discussing anything sinister or out of the ordinary.

"Here you go, Flint," said the barmaid, plunking down a steaming bowl of beans. "Extra portion, and the bread's included. We have to get you fattened up. I take it you'll be leaving us soon?"

"Aye, lass. The roads are opening up. I'm behind time as it is, but I am waiting for Tanis to return from visiting his kin in Qualinesti. He was supposed to be back a fortnight ago, but still no sign of his ugly face."

"I hope he's all right," the barmaid said fondly. "I don't trust them elves, and that's a fact. I hear he doesn't get on with his kin."

"He's like a man with a bad tooth," the dwarf grumbled, though Antimodes could detect a note of anxiety in the dwarf's gruff tone. "He has to keep wiggling it to make sure it still hurts. Tanis goes home knowing that his fine elf relatives can't stand the sight of him, but he keeps hoping maybe this time matters will be different. But no. The blasted tooth's just as rotten as it was the first time he touched it, and it's not going to get better till he yanks it out and has done with it."

The dwarf had worked himself up into red-faced indignation by this time, topping off his harangue with the somewhat incongruous statement of, "And us with customers waiting." He took a swig of ale.

"You've no call to call him ugly," said the barmaid with a simper. "Tanis looks like a human. You can't hardly see any elf in him at all. I'll be glad to see him again. Let him know I asked about him, will you, Flint?"

"Yes, yes. You and every other female in town," the dwarf returned, but he muttered the words into his beard, and the barmaid, who was heading back to the kitchen, did not hear him.

A dwarf and a half-elf who were business partners, Antimodes noted, making deductions about what he'd heard. A half-elf who had been banished from Qualinesti. No, that wasn't right. A banished half-elf could not go back home. This one had done so. He'd left his elven homeland voluntarily, then. Not surprising. The Qualinesti were more liberal-minded about racial purity than their cousins, the Silvanesti, but a half-elf was half-human in their eyes and, as such, tainted goods.

So the half-elf had left his home, come to Solace, and joined up with a hill dwarf, who had himself probably either left his thane and his clan or had been cast out. Antimodes wondered how the two had met, guessed it must be an interesting story.

It was a story he was not likely to hear. The dwarf had settled down to shoveling beans into his mouth. Antimodes's own plate arrived, and he gave the meal his full attention, which it well deserved.

He had just finished and was sopping up the last bit of gravy with his last bite of bread when the door to the inn opened. Otik was there to greet the new guest. The innkeeper appeared nonplussed to find a young woman, the same curly-haired young woman Antimodes had met earlier on the road.

"Kitiara!" Otik exclaimed. "Whatever are you doing here, child? Running an errand for your mother?"

The young woman cast him a glance from her dark eyes that might have sizzled his flesh.

"Your potatoes have more brains than you do, Otik. I run errands for no one."

She shoved past him. Her glance swept the common room and fixed on Antimodes, much to his astonishment and annoyance.

"I've come to speak to one of your guests," the young woman announced.

She ignored Otik's fluttering, "Now, now, Kitiara. I'm not sure you should be bothering the gentleman."

Kit strode up to Antimodes, stood beside his table, gazed down on him.

"You're a wizard, aren't you?" she asked.

Antimodes indicated his displeasure by not rising to greet her as he would have done to any other female. Expecting either to be made sport of or perhaps propositioned by this ill-mannered hoyden, he set his face in stern lines of disapproval.

"What I am is my own affair, young lady," he said with sardonic emphasis on the last word. He shifted his gaze deliberately out the window, indicating that the conversation was ended.

"Kitiara . . ." Otik hovered anxiously. "This gentleman is my guest. And this is really not the time or the place to . . ."

The young woman put her brown hands on the table and leaned over it. Antimodes was now starting to be truly angered by this intrusion. He shifted his attention back to her, noting as he did so—he would have been less than human if he had not noticed—the curve of her full breasts beneath the leather vest.

"I know someone who wants to become a wizard," she said. Her voice was serious and intense. "I want to help him, but I don't know how. I don't know what to do." Her hand lifted in a gesture of frustration. "Where do I go? Who do I talk to? You can tell me."

If the inn had suddenly shifted in its branches and dumped Antimodes out the window, he could not have been more astonished. This was highly irregular! This simply wasn't done! There were proper channels. . . .

"My dear young woman," he began.

"Please." Kitiara leaned nearer.

Her eyes were liquid brown, framed by long, black, thick lashes. Her eyebrows were dark and delicately arched to frame the eyes. Her skin was tanned by the sun; she'd led an outdoor life. She was well muscled, lithe, and had grown through the awkwardness of girlhood to attain the grace, not of a woman, but of a stalking cat. She drew him to her, and he went willingly, though he was old enough and experienced enough to know that she would not permit him to come too close. She would allow few men to warm themselves at her inner fire, and the gods help those who did.

"Kitiara, leave the gentleman to his dinner." Otik touched the girl's arm.

Kitiara rounded on him. She did not speak, she merely looked at him. Otik shrank back.

"It is all right, Master Sandath." Antimodes was quick to intervene. He was fond of Otik and did not want to cause the innkeeper trouble. The dwarf, who had finished his dinner, was now taking an interest, as were two of the barmaids. "The young . . . um . . . lady and I have some business to transact. Please, be seated, mistress."

He rose slightly and made a bow. The young woman slid into the chair opposite. The barmaid whisked over to clear the plates—and to try to satisfy her curiosity.

"Will there be anything else?" she asked Antimodes.

He looked politely at his young guest. "Will you have something?"

"No, thanks," said Kitiara shortly. "Be about your business, Rita. If we need anything, we'll call."

The barmaid, offended, flounced off. Otik cast Antimodes a helpless, apologizing glance. Antimodes smiled, to indicate he wasn't the least concerned, and Otik, with a shrug of his fat shoulders and, wringing his pudgy hands, walked distractedly away. Fortunately the arrival of additional guests gave the innkeeper something to do.

Kitiara settled down to business with a serious intensity that drew Antimodes's approval.

"Who is this person?" he asked.

"My little brother. Half-brother," she amended as an afterthought.

Antimodes recalled the scathing look she'd given Otik when he mentioned her mother. No love lost there, the archmage guessed.

"How old is the child?"

"Six."

"And how do you know he wants to study magic?"

Antimodes asked. He thought he knew the answer. He'd heard it often.

He loves to dress up and play wizard. He's so cute. You should see him toss dust into the air and pretend he's casting a spell. Of course, we assume it's a stage he's going through. We don't really approve. No offense, sir, but it's not the sort of life we had in mind for our boy. Now, if you could talk to him and tell him how difficult . . .

"He does tricks," said the girl.

"Tricks?" Antimodes frowned. "What sort of tricks?"

"You know. Tricks. He can pull a coin out of your nose. He can throw a rock into the air and make it disappear. He can cut a scarf in two with a knife and give it back good as new."

"Sleight-of-hand," said Antimodes. "You realize, of course, that this is not magic."

"Of course!" Kitiara scoffed. "What do you think I am? Some yokel? My father—my real father—took me to see a battle once, and there was a wizard who did some true magic. War magic. My father's a Solamnic knight," she added with naive pride that made her suddenly seem a little girl.

Antimodes didn't believe her, at least the part about her father being a Solamnic knight. What would the daughter of a Solamnic knight be doing running around like a street urchin in Solace? He could well believe that this tomboy was interested in military matters. More than once, her right hand had rested on her left hip, as if she were either accustomed to wearing a sword or accustomed to pretending that she wore one.

Her gaze went past Antimodes, out the window, and kept going. In that gaze was yearning, longing for distant lands, for adventure, for an end to the boredom that was probably about to stifle her. He was not surprised when she said, "Look, sir, I'm going to be leaving here sometime soon, and my little brothers will have to fend for themselves when I'm gone."

"Caramon will be all right," Kitiara continued, still gazing out at the smoky hills and the distant blue water. "He's got the makings of a true warrior. I've taught him all I know, and the rest he'll pick up as he goes along."

She might have been a grizzled veteran, speaking of a new recruit, rather than a thirteen-year-old girl talking of a little snot-nosed kid. Antimodes almost laughed, but she was so serious, so earnest, that instead he found himself watching and listening to her with fascination.

"But I worry about Raistlin," Kitiara said, her brows drawing together in puzzlement. "He's not like the others. He's not like me. I don't understand him. I've tried to teach him to fight, but he's sickly. He can't keep up with the other children. He gets tired easily and he runs out of breath."

Her gaze shifted to Antimodes. "I have to leave," she said for the second time. "But before I go, I want to know that Raistlin is going to be able to take care of himself, that he'll have some way to earn his living. I've been thinking that if he could study to be a wizard, then I wouldn't have to worry."

"How old . . . how old did you say this boy was?" Antimodes asked.

"Six," said Kitiara.

"But . . . what about his parents? Your parents? Surely they . . ."

He stopped because the young woman was no longer listening to him. She was wearing that look of extreme patience young people put on when their elders are being particularly tedious and boring. Before Antimodes could finish, she had twisted to her feet.

"I'll go find him. You should meet him."

"My dear . . . " Antimodes started to protest. He had enjoyed his conversation with this interesting and attractive young person, but the thought of entertaining a six-year-old was extremely unwelcome.

The girl ignored his protests. She was out the door of the inn before he could stop her. He saw her running lightly down the stairs, rudely shoving or bumping into anyone who stood in her way.

Antimodes was in a quandary. He didn't want to have this child thrust upon him. Now that she was gone, he didn't want to have anything more to do with the young woman. She had unsettled him, given him an uneasy feeling, like the aftereffects of too much wine. It had been fine going down, but now he had a headache.

Antimodes called for his bill. He would beat a hasty retreat to his room, though he realized with annoyance that he would be held a virtual prisoner there during the rest of his stay. Looking up, he saw the dwarf, whose name he recalled was Flint, looking back.

The dwarf had a smile on his face.

Most likely Flint was not thinking at all about Antimodes. The dwarf may have been smiling to himself over the delicious meal he had just enjoyed, or he may have been smiling at the taste of the ale, or just smiling over the pleasantness of the world in general. But Antimodes, with his customary self-importance, decided that Flint was smirking at him and the fact that he, a powerful wizard, was going to run away from two children.

Antimodes determined then and there that he would not give the dwarf any such satisfaction. The archmage would not be driven out of this pleasant common room. He would remain, rid himself of the girl, deal quickly with the child, and that would be an end of it.

"Perhaps you would care to join me, sir," Antimodes said to the dwarf.

Flint glowered and flushed red and ducked his head into his ale. He muttered something about rather having his beard boiled before he'd share a table with a wizard.

Antimodes smiled coldly to himself. Dwarves were notorious for their distrust and dislike of wielders of magic. The archmage was now certain that the dwarf would leave him alone. Indeed, Flint quaffed his ale in a hurry and, tossing a coin on the table, gave Antimodes a curt nod and stumped out of the inn.

And here, on the dwarf's heels, came the girl, hauling along not one child but two.

Antimodes sighed and ordered a glass of Otik's finest two-year old mead. He had a feeling he was going to need something potent.

3

The encounter was likely to prove more unpleasant than Antimodes had feared. One of the boys, the one Antimodes assumed was the elder, was an attractive child, or would have been had he not been so extremely dirty. He was sturdily built, with thick arms and legs, had a genial, open face and a gap-toothed smile, and he regarded Antimodes with friendly interest and curiosity, not in the least intimidated by the well-dressed stranger.

"Hullo, sir. Are you a wizard? Kit says you're a wizard. Could you do some sort of trick? My twin can do tricks. Would you like to see him? Raist, do the one where you take the coin out of your nose and—"

"Shut up, Caramon," said the other child in a soft voice, adding, with a frowning glance, "You're being foolish."

The boy took this good-naturedly. He chuckled and shrugged, but he kept quiet. Antimodes was startled to hear the two were twins. He examined the other boy, the one who did tricks. This child was not in the least attractive, being thin as a wraith, grubby, and shabbily dressed, with bare legs and bare feet and the peculiar and distasteful odor that only small and sweaty children emit. His brown hair was long, matted, and needed washing.

Antimodes regarded both children intently, and made a few deductions.

No loving mother doted over these boys. No loving hands combed that tangled hair, no loving tongue scolded them to wash behind their ears. They did not have the whipped and hangdog air of beaten children, but they were certainly neglected.

"What is your name?" Antimodes asked.

"Raistlin," replied the boy.

He had one mark in his favor. He looked directly at Antimodes while speaking. The one thing Antimodes detested most about small children was their habit of staring down at their feet or the floor or looking anywhere except at him, as though they expected him to pounce on them and eat them. This boy kept his pale blue eyes level with those of the adult, held them fixed and unwavering on the archmage.

These blue eyes gave nothing, expected nothing. They held too much knowledge. They had seen too much in their six years—too much sorrow, too much pain. They had looked beneath the bed and discovered that there really were monsters lurking in the shadows.

So, young man, I bet you'd like to be a mage when you grow up!

That was Antimodes's standard, banal line in these circumstances. He had just sense enough not to say it. Not to say it to those knowing eyes.

The archmage felt a tingling at the back of his neck. He recognized it—the touch of the fingers of the god.

Tamping down his excitement, Antimodes spoke to the older sister. "I'd like to talk to your brother alone. Perhaps you and his twin could—"

"Sure," said Kitiara immediately. "C'mon, Caramon."

"Not without Raistlin," Caramon said promptly.

"Come on, Caramon!" Kitiara repeated impatiently. Grasping him by the arm, she gave him a yank.

Even then, the boy held back from his sister's strong and impatient tug. Caramon was a solid child. It seemed unlikely that his sister would be able to budge him without resorting to a block and tackle. He looked at Antimodes.

"We're twins, sir. We do everything together."

Antimodes glanced at the weaker twin to see how he was taking this. Raistlin's cheeks were faintly flushed; he was embarrassed, but he seemed also smugly pleased. Antimodes felt a slight chill. The boy's pleasure in his brother's show of loyalty and affection was not that of one sibling's pleasure in the love of another. It was more like the pleasure a man takes in exhibiting the talents of a well-loved dog.

"Go on, Caramon," Raistlin said. "Perhaps he'll teach me some new tricks. I'll show them to you after supper tonight."

Caramon looked uncertain. Raistlin cast his brother a glance from beneath the thatch of lank, uncombed hair. That glance was an order. Caramon lowered his eyes, then, suddenly cheerful again, he grabbed hold of his sister's hand.

"I hear Sturm's found a badger hole. He's going to try to whistle the badger out. Do you think he can do it, Kit?"

"What do I care?" she asked crossly. Walking off, she smacked Caramon a blow on the back of his head. "Next time do as I tell you. Do you hear me? What kind of soldier are you going to make if you don't know how to obey my orders?"

"I'll obey orders, Kit," said Caramon, wincing and rubbing his scalp. "But you told me to leave Raistlin. You know I've got to watch out for him."

Antimodes heard their voices arguing all the way down the stairs.

He looked back at the boy. "Please sit down," he said.

Silently Raistlin slid into the chair opposite the mage. He was small for his age, his feet did not reach the floor. He sat perfectly still. He didn't fidget or jitter. He didn't swing his legs or kick at the legs of the chair. He clasped his hands together on the table and stared at Antimodes.

"Would you like something to eat or drink? As my guest, of course," Antimodes added.

Raistlin shook his head. Though the child was filthy and dressed like a beggar, he wasn't starving. Certainly his twin appeared well fed. Someone saw to it that they had food on the table. As for the boy's excessive thinness, Antimodes guessed that it was the result of a fire burning deep down in the inner recesses of the child's being, a fire that consumed food before it could nourish the body, a fire that left the child with a perpetual hunger he did not yet understand.

Again Antimodes felt the sanctifying touch of the god.

"Your sister tells me, Raistlin, that you would like to go to school to study to be a mage," Antimodes began, by way of introducing the topic.

Raistlin hesitated a moment, then said, "Yes, I suppose so."

"You suppose so?" Antimodes repeated sharply, disappointed. "Don't you know what you want?"

"I never thought about it," Raistlin replied, shrugging his thin shoulders in a gesture remarkably similar to that of his more robust twin. "About going to school, I mean. I didn't even know there were schools to study magic. I just thought magic was a . . . a—" he searched for the phrase—"a part of you. Like eyes or toes."

The fingers of the god hammered on Antimodes's soul. But he needed more information. He had to be sure.

"Tell me, Raistlin, is anyone in your family a mage? I'm not prying," Antimodes explained, seeing a pained expression contort the child's face. "It's just that we've found that the art is most often transmitted through the blood."

Raistlin licked his lips. His gaze dropped, fixed on his hands. The fingers, slender and agile for one so young, curled inward. "My mother," he said in a flat voice. "She sees things. Things far away. She sees other parts of the world. She watches what the elves are doing and the dwarves beneath the mountain."

"She's a seer," said Antimodes.

Raistlin shrugged again. "Most people think she's crazy." He lifted his gaze in defiance, ready to defend his mother. When he found Antimodes regarding him with sympathy, the boy relaxed and the words flowed out, as if a vein were cut open.

"She forgets to eat sometimes. Well, not forgets exactly. It's like she's eating somewhere else. And she doesn't do work around the house, but that's because she's not really in the house. She's visiting wonderful places, seeing wonderful, beautiful things. I know," Raistlin continued, "because when she comes back, she's sad. As if she didn't want to come back. She looks at us like she doesn't know us sometimes."

"Does she talk about what she's seen?" Antimodes asked gently.

"To me, a little," the boy answered. "But not much. It makes my father unhappy, and my sister . . . well, you've seen Kit. She doesn't have any patience with what she calls Mother's 'fits.' So I can't blame Mother for leaving us," Raistlin continued, his voice so soft that Antimodes had to lean forward to hear the child. "I'd go with her if I could. And we'd never come back here. Never."

Antimodes sipped his drink, using the mead as an excuse to keep silent until he had regained control of his anger. It was an old story, one he'd seen time and again. This poor woman was no different from countless others. She had been born with the art, but her talent was denied, probably ridiculed, certainly discouraged by family members who thought all magic-users were demon spawn. Instead of receiving the training and discipline that would have taught her how to use the art to her benefit and that of others, she was stifled, smothered. What had been a gift had become a curse. If she were not already insane, she soon would be.

There was no longer a chance to save her. There was yet a chance to save her son.

"What work does your father do?" Antimodes asked.

"He's a woodcutter," Raistlin answered. Now that they had shifted topics, he was more at ease. His hands flattened on the table. "He's big, like Caramon. My father works really hard. We don't see him much." The child didn't appear overly distressed by this fact.

He was silent a moment, then said, his brow furrowed with the seriousness of his thought process, "This school. It isn't far away, is it? I mean, I wouldn't like to leave Mother for very long. And then there's Caramon. Like he said, we're twins. We take care of each other."

I'm going to be leaving sometime soon, the sister had said. *My little brothers will have to fend for themselves when I'm gone.*

Antimodes clasped hands with the god, gave Solinari's hand a deal-clinching shake. "There is a school quite close by. It is located about five miles to the west in a secluded wood. Most people have no idea it is even there. Five miles is not a long walk for a grown man, but it is quite a hike for a small boy, back and forth every day. Many students board there, especially those who come from distant parts of Ansalon. It would be my suggestion that you do the same. The school is only in session eight months out of the year. The master takes the summer months off to spend at the Tower of Wayreth. You could be with your family during that time. I would have to talk to your father, though. He is the one who must enroll you. Do you think he will approve?"

"Father won't care," Raistlin said. "He'll be relieved, I think. He's afraid that I'll end up like Mother." The child's pale cheeks were suddenly stained red. "Unless it costs a lot of money. Then I couldn't do it."

"As to the money"—Antimodes had already made up his mind on that point—"we wizards take care of our own."

The child didn't quite understand this. "It couldn't be charity," Raistlin said. "Father wouldn't like that at all."

"It's not charity," Antimodes said briskly. "We have funds set aside for deserving students. We help pay their tuition and other expenses. Can I meet with your father tonight? I could explain this to him then."

"Yes, he should be home tonight. The job's almost finished. I'll bring him here. It's hard for people to find our house sometimes after dark," Raistlin said apologetically.

Of course it is, Antimodes said silently, his heart wrenched with pity. A sad, unhappy, slovenly kept house, a lonely house. It hides among the shadows and guards its dark secret.

The child was so thin, so weak. A good strong gust of wind would flatten his frail frame. Magic might well be the shield that would protect this fragile person, become the staff upon which he could lean when he was weak or weary. Or the magic might become a monster, sucking the life from the thin body, leaving a dry, desiccated husk. Antimodes might well be starting this boy on the path that would lead to an early death.

"Why do you stare at me?" the child asked curiously.

Antimodes gestured for Raistlin to leave his chair and come stand directly in front of him. Reaching out, Antimodes took hold of the boy's hands. The youngster flinched and started to squirm away.

He doesn't like to be touched, Antimodes realized, but he maintained his hold on the boy. He wanted to emphasize his words with his flesh, his muscle, his bone. He wanted the boy to feel the words as well as hear them.

"Listen to me, Raistlin," Antimodes said, and the boy quieted and held still. He realized that this conversation was not that of an adult talking down to a child. It was one equal speaking to another. "The magic will not solve your problems. It will only add to them. The magic will not make people like you. It will increase their distrust. The magic will not ease your pain. It will twist and burn inside you until sometimes you think that even death would be preferable."

Antimodes paused, holding fast to the child's hands that were hot and dry, as if he were running a fever. The archmage was ranging about mentally for a means of explanation this young boy might understand. The distant ringing tap of the blacksmith's shop, rising up from the street below, provided the metaphor.

"A mage's soul is forged in the crucible of the magic," Antimodes said. "You choose to go voluntarily into the fire. The blaze might well destroy you. But if you survive, every blow of the hammer will serve to shape your being. Every drop of water wrung from you will temper and strengthen your soul. Do you understand?"

"I understand," said the boy.

"Do you have any question for me, Raistlin?" Antimodes asked, tightening his grip. "Any question at all?"

The boy hesitated, considering. He was not reluctant to speak. He was wondering how to phrase his need.

"My father says that before mages can work their magic, they are taken to a dark and horrible place where they must fight terrible monsters. My father says that sometimes the mages die in that place. Is that true?"

"The Tower is really quite a lovely place, once you become accustomed to it," said Antimodes. He paused, choosing his words carefully. He would not lie to the child, but some things were beyond the understanding of even this precocious six-year-old. "When a mage is older, much older than you are now, Raistlin, he or she goes to the Tower of High Sorcery and there takes a test. And, yes, sometimes the mage dies. The power a mage wields is very great. Any who are not able to control it or to commit their very lives to it would not be wanted in our order."

The boy looked very solemn, his eyes wide and pale. Antimodes gave the hands a squeeze, the boy a reassuring smile. "But that will be a long, long time from now, Raistlin. A long, long time. I don't want to frighten you. I just want you to know what you face."

"Yes, sir," said Raistlin quietly. "I understand."

Antimodes released the boy's hands. Raistlin took an involuntary step backward and, probably unconsciously, put his hands behind his back.

"And now, Raistlin," said Antimodes, "I have a question for you. Why do you want to become a mage?"

Raistlin's blue eyes flared. "I like the feeling of the magic inside me. And"—he glanced at Otik, bustling about the counter; Raistlin's thin lips parted in a pallid smile—"and someday fat innkeepers will bow to me."

Antimodes, taken aback, looked at the child to see if he were joking.

Raistlin was not.

The hand of the god on Antimodes's shoulder suddenly trembled.

4

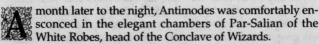 month later to the night, Antimodes was comfortably ensconced in the elegant chambers of Par-Salian of the White Robes, head of the Conclave of Wizards.

The two men were very different and probably would not have been friends under ordinary circumstances. Both were about the same age, in their fifties. Antimodes was a man of the world, however. Par-Salian was a man of books. Antimodes liked to travel, he had a head for business, he was fond of good ale, pretty women, comfortable inns. He was nosy and inquisitive, fussy in his dress and his habits.

Par-Salian was a scholar, whose knowledge of the art of magic was undeniably the most extensive of any wizard then living upon Krynn. He abhorred travel, had little use for other people, and was known to have loved only one woman, a misguided affair that he regretted to this day. He took little care of his personal appearance or physical comfort. If absorbed in his studies, he often forgot to come to meals.

It was the responsibility of some of the apprentice magic-users to see to it that their master took sustenance, which they did by surreptitiously sliding a loaf of bread beneath his arm as he read. He would then absentmindedly munch on it. The apprentices often joked among themselves that they could have substituted a loaf of sawdust for the bread and Par-Salian would have never known the difference. They held him in such awe and reverence, however, that none dared try the experiment.

This night, Par-Salian was entertaining his old friend, and therefore he had left poring over his books, though not without a pang of regret. Antimodes had brought as a gift several scrolls of dark magic, which the archmage had acquired by chance on his travels. One of their black-robed sisters, an evil wizardess, had been slain by a mob. Antimodes had arrived too late to save the wizardess, which he would have at least made a halfhearted attempt to do, all mages being bound together by their magic, no matter to which god or goddess they pledged their allegiance.

He was, however, able to persuade the townspeople, a set of superstitious louts, to allow him to remove the wizardess's personal effects before the mob set fire to her house. Antimodes had brought the scrolls to his friend, Par-Salian. Antimodes had kept for himself an amulet of summoning undead spirits. He could not and would not have used the amulet—the undead were a smelly, disgusting lot, as far as he was concerned. But he intended to offer it in trade to some of his black-robed brethren in the tower.

Despite the fact that Par-Salian was of the White Robes, completely dedicated to the god Solinari, he was able to read and understand the scrolls of the evil wizardess, though at some pain to himself. He was one of the very few wizards ever who had the power to cross allegiances. He would never make use of them, but he could take note of the words used to perform the spell, the effects of the spell, the components needed to cast it, the spell's duration, and any other interesting information he came across. His research would be recorded in the annals of the Tower of Wayreth. The scrolls themselves would then be deposited in the tower's library, with an assigned valuation.

"A terrible way to die," said Par-Salian, pouring his guest a glass of elven wine, nicely chilled and sweet, with just a hint of woodbine, which reminded the drinker of green forests and sunlit glens. "Did you know her?"

"Esmilla? No." Antimodes shook his head. "And you could say that she asked for it. The mundane will overlook the snatching of a child or two, but start passing bad coins and they—"

"Oh, come now, my dear Antimodes!" Par-Salian looked shocked. He was not noted for his sense of humor. "You're joking, I think."

"Well, perhaps I am." Antimodes grinned and sipped his wine.

"Yet I see what you mean." Par-Salian struck the arm of his high-backed wooden chair in impatience. "Why do these fool mages insist on wasting their skills and talents in order to produce a few poor quality coins, which every shopkeeper between here and the minotaur islands can tell are magicked? It just doesn't make any sense to me."

Antimodes agreed. "Considering the effort one expends on producing only two or three steel coins, a mage could do manual labor for less effort and make far more. If our late sister had continued to sell her services to rid the town of rats, as she had been doing for years, she would no doubt have been left in peace. As it was, the magically created coins threw everyone into a panic. First, most people believed that they were cursed and were terrified to touch them. Those who didn't think the money was cursed feared that she was about to start minting coins at a rate to rival the Lord of Palanthas and would soon own the town and everything in it."

"It is precisely for this reason that we have established rules about the reproduction of coins of the realm," said Par-Salian. "Every young mage tries it once. I did and I'm sure you probably did yourself."

Antimodes nodded and shrugged.

"But most of us learn that it simply isn't worth the time and effort, not to mention the serious impact we could have on Ansalon's various economies. This woman was certainly old enough to know better. What was she thinking?"

"Who knows? Gone a bit daft, maybe. Or just greedy. She angered her god, however. Nuitari abandoned her to her fate. Whatever defensive spells she tried to cast fizzled."

"He is not one to permit the frivolous use of his gifts," said Par-Salian in stern and solemn tones.

Antimodes shifted his chair a bit nearer the fire that crackled on the hearth. He always felt extremely close to the gods of magic when visiting the Tower of High Sorcery—close to all the gods of magic, the light, the gray, and the dark. This closeness was uncomfortable, as if someone was always breathing down the back of his neck, and was the main reason Antimodes did not live in the tower but chose to reside in the outside world, no matter how dangerous it might be for magic-users. He was glad to change the subject.

"Speaking of children . . ." Antimodes began.

"Were we?" Par-Salian asked, smiling.

"Of course. I said something about snatching children."

"Ah, yes. I remember. Very well, then, we were speaking of children. What have you to say about them? I thought you didn't like them."

"I don't, as a rule, but I met a rather interesting youngster on my trip here. He's one to take note of, I think. In fact, I believe three already have." Antimodes glanced outside the window toward the night sky, where shone two of the three moons sacred to the gods of magic. He nodded his head knowingly.

Par-Salian appeared interested. "The child has innate gifts? Did you test him? How old is he?"

"About six. And, no. I was staying at the inn in Solace. It wasn't the time or the place, and I've never put much stock in those silly tests anyway. Any clever child could pass them. No, it was what the boy had to say and how he said it that impressed me. Scared me, too, I don't mind telling you. There's more than a bit of cold-blooded ambition in that boy. Frightening in one so young. Of course, that could come from his background. The family is not well off."

"What did you do with him?"

"Enrolled him with Master Theobald. Yes, I know. Theobald is not the Conclave's greatest teacher. He's plodding and unimaginative, prejudiced and old-fashioned, but the boy will get a good, solid grounding in the basics and strict discipline, which won't hurt him. He's been running wild, I gather. Raised by an older half-sister, who is something special in her own right."

"Theobald is expensive," said Par-Salian. "You implied the boy's family was poor."

"I paid for his first semester." Antimodes waved away any acknowledgment that he'd done something laudable. "The family must never know, mind you. I made up some tale about the tower having established funds for deserving students."

"Not a bad idea," said Par-Salian thoughtfully. "And one we might well put into practice, especially now that we're seeing some of the unreasoning prejudice against our kind starting to die off. Unfortunately, fools like Esmilla keep putting us in a bad light. Still, I believe that people are in general more tolerant. They're starting to appreciate what we do for them. You travel abroad openly and safely, my friend. You could not have done so forty years ago."

"True," Antimodes admitted, "although I believe that in general the world is altogether a darker place these days. I ran into a new religious order in Haven. They worship a god known as Belzor, and it sounds very much to me as if they're planning on cooking and serving up that same old tripe we heard from the Kingpriest of Istar before the gods—bless their hearts—dropped a mountain on him."

"Indeed? You must tell me about it." Par-Salian settled back more comfortably in his chair. Taking a leather-bound book from the table at his side, he opened it to a blank page, dated it, and prepared to write. They were about to get down to the important business of the evening.

The main part of Antimodes's job was to report on the political situation of the continent of Ansalon, which, as was nearly always the case, was done up in a confused and tangled knot. This included the new religious order, which was discussed and summarily dismissed.

"A charismatic leader out of Haven," Antimodes reported. "He has only a few followers and promises the usual assortment of miracles, including healing. I didn't get a chance to see him, but from what I heard he is probably a rather highly skilled illusionist with some practical knowledge of herb lore. He's not doing anything in the way of healing that the Druids haven't been practicing for years, but it's all new to the people of Abanasinia. Someday we may have to expose him, but he's not doing any harm at the moment and is, in fact, doing some good. I'd recommend that we not start trouble. It would look very bad for us. Public sympathy would be all on his side."

"I quite agree." Par-Salian nodded and made a brief note in his book. "What about the elves? Did you go through Qualinesti?"

"Only the outskirts. They were polite, but they wouldn't permit me to go farther. Nothing's changed with them in the last five hundred years, and provided the rest of the world leaves them alone, nothing will change. As for the Silvanesti, they are, as far as we know, hiding out in their magical woods under the leadership of Lorac. I'm not telling you anything you don't already know, however," Antimodes added, pouring himself another glass of elven wine. The topic had reminded him of the excellence of its taste. "You must have had a chance to talk to some of their mages."

Par-Salian shook his head. "They came to the Tower this winter, but only on business, and then they were close-lipped and spoke to us humans only when absolutely necessary. They would not share their magic with us, though they were quite happy to use ours."

"Do they have anything we would want?" Antimodes asked with a faintly amused smile.

"So far as scrollwork, no," Par-Salian replied. "It is shocking how stagnant the Silvanesti have become. Not surprising, considering their terrible distrust and fear of change of any sort. The only creative mind they have among them belongs to a young mage known as Dalamar, and I'm certain that as soon as they discover what he's been dabbling in, they'll throw him out on his pointed ear. As to their top White Robes, they were quite eager to obtain some of the new work being done on evocation spells, particularly those of a defensive nature."

"They wanted to pay in gold, which is worthless these days. I had to be quite firm and insist on either hard steel, which, of course, they don't have, or barter. Then they wanted to palm off on me some moldy magical spells that were considered old-fashioned in my father's day. In the end, I agreed to trade for spell components; they grow some quite lovely and unusual plants in Silvanesti, and their jewelry is exquisite. They traded and left, and I haven't seen them since. I wonder if they're not facing some threat in Silvanesti or if they've divined that some threat is approaching. Their king, Lorac, is a powerful mage and something of a seer."

"If they are, we'll never know about it," Antimodes said. "They would rather see their people wiped out before they would lower themselves to ask any of us for help."

He sniffed. He hadn't any use at all for the Silvanesti, whose white-robed wizards were part of the Conclave of Wizards, but who made it clear that they considered this a tremendous condescension on their part. They did not like humans and indicated their dislike in various ways, such as pretending they could not speak Common, the language of all races on Krynn, or turning away in contempt when any human dared to desecrate the elven language by speaking it. Incredibly long-lived, the elves saw change as something to be feared. The humans, with their shorter life spans, more frenetic lives, and constant need to "improve," represented everything the elves abhorred. The Silvanesti elves hadn't had a creative idea in their heads in the last two thousand years.

"The Qualinesti elves, on the other hand, keep a close watch on their borders, but they do permit people of other races to enter, provided they have permission from the Speaker of the Sun and Stars," Antimodes went on. "Dwarven and human metalsmiths are highly regarded and encouraged to visit— though not to stay—and their own elven artisans do occasionally travel to other lands. Unfortunately, they frequently meet with much prejudice and hatred."

Antimodes knew and liked many of the Qualinesti and was

sorry to see them misused. "Several of their young people, particularly the eldest son of the speaker—what's his name?"

"The speaker? Solostaran."

"No, the eldest son."

"Ah, you must mean Porthios."

"Yes, Porthios. He's said to be thinking that the Silvanesti have the right idea and that no human should enter Qualinesti land."

"You can't really blame him, considering the terrible things that happened when the humans entered Qualinesti land after the Cataclysm. But I don't think we need worry. They'll bicker over this for the next century unless something pushes them one way or the other."

"Indeed." Antimodes had noted a subtle change in Par-Salian's voice. "You think something is likely to push them?"

"I've heard rumblings," said Par-Salian. "Distant thunder."

"I haven't heard thunder," Antimodes said. "The few Black Robes I meet these days are a little too smooth. They act as if bat guano wouldn't ignite in their hands."

"A few of the more powerful have quietly dropped out of sight," said Par-Salian.

"Who's that?"

"Well, Dracart, for one. He used to stop by on a regular basis to see what new artifacts had come in and to check on possible apprentices. But the only wizards of the Black who have come by lately have been those of low ranking, who wouldn't be invited to share the secrets of their elders. And even they seem a bit edgy."

"I take it, then, you have not seen the fair Ladonna," Antimodes said with a sly wink.

Par-Salian smiled faintly and shrugged. That fire had died years ago, and he was too old and too absorbed in his work to be either pleased or annoyed by his friend's teasing.

"No, I have not spoken to Ladonna this past year, and what is more, I believe that whatever she is doing she is deliberately hiding from me. She refused to attend a meeting of the heads of the orders, something which she's never done before. She sent a representative in her name—a man who said exactly three words the entire time and those were 'pass the salt.'" Par-Salian shook his head. "Queen Takhisis has been quiet too long. Something's up."

"All we can do is watch and wait, my friend, and be prepared to act when necessary." Antimodes paused, sipped his elven wine. "One bit of good news I have is that the Solamnic knights are finally beginning to pull themselves together. Many have reclaimed their family estates and are rebuilding their holdings. Their new leader, Lord Gunthar, is a keen politician who has the ability to think with his head, not his helmet. He's endeared himself to the local populace by cleaning out a few goblin strongholds, mopping up some bandits, and sponsoring jousts and tourneys in various parts of Solamnia. Nothing the rabble likes more than to see grown men hammer on each other."

Par-Salian looked grave, even alarmed. "I don't consider this good news, Antimodes. The knights have no love for us. If they stop at hunting goblins, that is one thing, but you can be certain that it will be only a matter of time before they add sorcerers to their list of enemies, as they did in the old days. Such is even written into the Measure."

"You should meet with Lord Gunthar," Antimodes suggested, and he was amused to see Par-Salian's white eyebrows nearly shoot off his head. "No, I'm quite in earnest. I'm not suggesting you should invite him here, but—"

"I should think not," Par-Salian said stiffly.

"But you should make a trip to Solamnia. Visit him. Assure him that we have only the good of Solamnia in mind."

"How can I assure him of that when he could point out, with considerable justification, that many in our order do not have the good of Solamnia in mind? The knights distrust magic, they distrust us, all of us, and I must tell you that I'm not particularly inclined to trust them. It seems to me wise and prudent to keep out of their way, to do nothing to draw attention to ourselves."

"Magius was the friend of Huma," prodded Antimodes.

"And if I recall the legend correctly, Huma was not greatly respected by his fellow knights for that very reason," Par-Salian returned dryly. "What news of Thorbardin?" He changed subject abruptly, indicating that the matter was closed.

Antimodes was diplomatic enough not to continue to press the issue, but he decided privately that he would visit Solamnia, perhaps on the way back, though that would mean going a considerable distance out of his way to the north. He was as curious as a kender about the Solamnic knights, who had long been held in disrespect and even antipathy by people who had once looked upon the knighthood as law-givers and protectors. Now it appeared as if the knighthood was regaining something of its old standing.

Antimodes was eager to see this for himself, eager to see if somehow he might be able to profit from it. He would not mention this junket to Par-Salian, of course. The Black Robes were not the only members of the conclave to keep their doings secret.

"The dwarves of Thorbardin are still in Thorbardin, we presume, mainly because no one has seen them leave. They are completely self-sufficient, with no reason to take any interest in the rest of the world, and I really don't see why they should. The hill dwarves are expanding their territory, and many are starting to travel to other lands. Some are even taking up residence outside their mountain homelands." Antimodes thought of the dwarf he'd met in Solace.

"As to the gnomes, they are like the dwarves of Thorbardin, with one exception—we assume the gnomes still reside in Mount Nevermind because no one has seen it explode yet. The kender appear to be more prolific than ever; they go everywhere, see everything, steal most of it, misplace the rest, and are of no use whatsoever."

"Oh, I think they are of use," said Par-Salian earnestly. He was known to be fond of kender, mainly so (Antimodes always said sourly) because he remained isolated in his tower and never had dealings with them. "Kender are the true innocents of this world. They remind us that we spend a great deal of time and energy worrying about things that are really not very important."

Antimodes grunted. "And so when may we expect to see you abandon your books, grab a hoopak, and take off down the road?"

Par-Salian smiled back. "Don't think I haven't considered it, my friend. I believe I would be a deft hand at hoopak flinging, if it came to that. I was quite skilled with a slingshot when I was a child. Ah, well, the evening grows long." This was his signal to end the meeting. "Will I see you in the morning?" he asked with a faint anxiety, which Antimodes understood.

"I would not dream of interfering in your work, my friend," he answered. "I will have a look through the artifacts and scrolls and the spell components, especially if you have some elven merchandise. There's one or two things I want to pick up. Then I'll be on my way."

"You are the one who would make a good kender," said Par-Salian, rising in his turn. "You never stay in one place long enough for the dust to settle on your shoes. Where do you go from here?"

"Oh, round and about," Antimodes said lightly. "I'm in no

hurry to return home. My brother is capable of running the business quite well without me, and I've made arrangements for my earnings to be invested, so that I make money even when I'm not there. Much easier and far more profitable than chanting spells over a lump of iron ore. Good night, my friend."

"Good night and safe journeying," Par-Salian said, taking his friend by the hand and giving it a hearty shake. He paused a moment, tightened his grasp.

"Be careful, Antimodes. I don't like the signs. I don't like the portents. The sun shines on us now, but I see the tips of dark wings casting long shadows. Continue sending me your reports. I value them highly."

"I will be careful," said Antimodes, a little troubled by his friend's earnest appeal.

Antimodes was well aware that Par-Salian had not told all he knew. The head of the conclave was not only adept at seeing into the future, he was also known to be a favorite of Solinari, the god of white magic. Dark wings. What could he possibly mean by that? The Queen of Darkness, dear old Takhisis? Gone but not forgotten. Not dare forgotten by those who studied the past, by those who knew of what evil she was capable.

Dark wings. Vultures? Eagles? Symbols of war? Griffins, pegasi? Magical beasts, not seen much these days. Dragons?

Paladine help us!

All the more reason, Antimodes determined, why I should find out what's happening in Solamnia. He was heading out the door when Par-Salian again stopped him.

"That young pupil . . . the one of whom you spoke. What was his name?"

It took Antimodes a moment to shift his thoughts to this different tack, another moment to try to remember.

"Raistlin. Raistlin Majere."

Par-Salian made a note of it in his book.

5

I t was early morning in Solace, very early. The sun had not yet dawned when the twins awoke in their small home that lurked in the shadows of a vallenwood. With its ill-fitting shutters, shabby curtains, and straggling, half-dead plants, the house looked nearly as forlorn and neglected as the children who inhabited it.

Their father—Gilon Majere, a big man with a broad and cheerful face, a face whose natural placidity was marred by a worry line between his brows—had not come home that night. He had traveled far from Solace on a job for a lord with an estate on Crystalmir Lake. Their mother was awake, but she had been awake since midnight.

Rosamun sat in her rocking chair, a skein of wool in her thin hands. She would wind the wool into a tight ball, tear it apart, and then rewind it. All the while she worked, she sang to herself in an eerie low-pitched voice or sometimes paused to hold conversations with people who were not visible to anyone except her.

If her husband—a gentle, caring man—had been at home, he would have persuaded her to leave off her "knitting" and go to bed. Once in bed, she would continue to sing, would be up again in an hour.

Rosamun had her good days, her lucid periods, when she was cognizant of much of what was going on around her, if not particularly interested in participating in it. The daughter of a wealthy merchant, she had always relied on servants to do her bidding. Now they could not afford servants, and Rosamun was inept at running a household herself. If she was hungry, she might cook something. There might be enough left over for the rest of the family, provided she didn't forget about the food completely and leave it to burn in the kettle.

When she fancied she was doing the mending, she would sit in her chair with a basket of torn clothes in her lap and stare out the window. Or she might put her worn cloak about her shoulders and go "visiting," wandering the shaded walkways to call on one of their neighbors, who generally kept an eye out for her and managed to be gone when Rosamun rang the bell. She had been known to forget where she was and would stay in someone's house for hours until her sons found her and fetched her home.

Sometimes she would recall stories about her first husband, Gregor uth Matar, a rogue and a rake, of whom she was stupidly proud and still loved, though he had abandoned her years before.

"Gregor was a Solamnic knight," she was saying, talking to her unseen listeners. "And he did so love me. He was the most handsome man in Palanthas, and all the girls were mad about him. But he chose me. He brought me roses, and he sang songs beneath my window and took me riding on his black horse. He is dead now. I know it. He is dead now, or he would have come back to me. He died a hero, you know."

Gregor uth Matar had been declared dead, at any rate. No one had seen or heard from him in seven years, and most believed that if he wasn't decently dead he should have been. His loss was not generally mourned. He might well have been a knight of Solamnia, but if so he had been banished from that strict order years ago. It was known that he, his new wife, and their baby daughter had left Palanthas by night and in a hurry. Rumor followed him from Solamnia to Solace, whispering that he had committed murder and had escaped the hangman only by means of money and a fast horse.

He was darkly handsome. Wit and charm made him a welcome companion in any tavern, as did his courage—not even his enemies could fault him on that—and his willingness to drink, gamble, and fight. Rosamun spoke truly about one of his traits. Women adored him.

An avowed fragile beauty, with auburn hair, eyes the color of a summer forest, and silken white skin, Rosamun had been the one to conquer him. He had fallen in love with her with all of his passionate nature, had remained in love with her longer than might have been expected. But when love died, it could never, for him, be rekindled.

They had lived well in Solace. Gregor made periodic journeys back to Solamnia, whenever money was running low. His highly placed family apparently paid him well to keep out of their lives. Then came the year he returned empty-handed. Rumor held it that Gregor's family had finally cut him off. His creditors pressing him hard, he traveled north to Sanction to sell his sword to whoever would have him. He continued to do so, coming back home at intervals but never staying long. Rosamun was wildly jealous, accused him of leaving her for other women. Their quarrels could be heard throughout most of Solace.

And then one day Gregor left and never returned. Rumor agreed that he was probably dead, either from a sword thrust in front or, more likely, a knife in the back.

One person did not believe him to be dead. Kitiara lived for the day when she would be able to leave Solace and set out in search of her father.

She talked of this as she did what she could, in her impatient way, to ready her little brother for his journey to his new school. Raistlin's few clothes—a couple of shirts, some trousers, and some oft-mended stockings—were done up in a bundle, along with a thick cloak for the winter.

"I'll be gone by spring," Kit was saying. "This place is too stupid for words." She lined her brothers up for inspection. "What do you think you're doing? You can't go to school dressed like that!"

Grabbing Raistlin, she pointed at his bare and dusty feet. "You have to wear shoes."

"In the summer?" Caramon was stunned.

"Mine don't fit me," Raistlin said. He'd had a small growth spurt that spring. He was now as tall as his twin, if only about half his weight and a quarter of his girth.

"Here. Wear these." Kit hunted out a pair of Caramon's old shoes from last winter and tossed them at Raistlin.

"They'll pinch my toes," he protested, regarding them glumly.

"Wear them," Kit ordered. "All the other boys in the school wear shoes, don't they? Only peasants go barefoot. That's what my father says."

Raistlin made no reply. He slid his feet into the worn shoes.

Picking up a dirty dishcloth, Kit dipped it in the water bucket and scrubbed Raistlin's face and ears so vigorously that he was certain at least half his skin must be missing.

Squirming free of his sister's grasp, Raistlin saw that Rosamun dropped her ball of wool on the floor. Her beauty had faded, like a rainbow fades when the storm clouds overtake the sun. Her hair was drab and lusterless, her eyes had too bright a luster, the luster of fever or madness. Her pale skin had a gray cast to it. She stared vaguely at her empty hands, as if she were wondering what to do with them. Caramon picked up the wool, handed it to her.

"Here, Mother."

"Thank you, child." She turned her vacant gaze to him. "Gregor's dead, do you know that, child?"

"Yes, Mother," Caramon said, not really hearing her.

Rosamun would often make incongruous statements like this. Her children were used to them and generally ignored them. But this morning Kitiara rounded on her mother in sudden fury. "He's not dead! What do you know? He never cared for you! Don't say things like that, you crazy old witch!"

Rosamun smiled and twined her wool and sang to herself. Her boys stood nearby, quiet, unhappy. Kit's words hurt them far more than they hurt Rosamun, who wasn't paying the slightest attention to her daughter.

"He's not dead! I know it and I'm going to find him!" Kitiara declared, her vow low and fervent.

"How do you know he's alive?" Caramon asked. "And if he is, how will you find him? I've heard there are lots of people in Solamnia. Even more than here in Solace."

"I'll find him," Kit replied confidently. "He told me how." She gazed at them speculatively. "Look, this is probably the last time you'll see me for a long while. Come here. I'll show you something if you promise not to tell."

Leading them into the small room where she slept, she produced from her mattress a crudely crafted, handmade leather pouch. "In here. This is my fortune."

"Money?" Caramon asked, brightening.

"No!" Kitiara scoffed at the notion. "Something better than money. My birthright."

"Let me see!" Caramon begged.

Kitiara refused. "I promised my father I would never show it to anyone. At least not yet. Someday, though, you will see it. When I come back rich and powerful and riding at the head of my armies, then you will see it."

"We'll be part of your army, won't we, Kit," Caramon said. "Raist and me."

"You'll be captains, both of you. I'll be your commander, of course," Kit said matter-of-factly.

"I'd like being a captain." Caramon was enthusiastic. "What about you, Raist?"

Raistlin shrugged. "I don't care." After another lingering

glance at the pouch, he said quietly, "We should leave now. I'll be late."

Kit eyed them, her hands on her hips. "You'll do, I suppose. You come straight back home, Caramon, after you drop Raistlin off. No hanging about the school. You two have to get used to being separated."

"Sure, Kit." It was now Caramon's turn to be glum.

Raistlin went to his mother, took her by the hand. "Good-bye, Mother," he said with a catch in his voice.

"Good-bye, dear," she said. "Don't forget to cover your head when it's damp."

And that was his blessing. Raistlin had endeavored to explain to his mother where he was going, but she had been completely unable to comprehend. "Studying magic? Whatever for? Don't be silly, child."

Raistlin had given up. He and Caramon left the house just as the sun was gilding the tips of the vallenwood leaves.

"I'm glad Kit didn't want to come with us. I have something to tell you," Caramon said in a loud whisper. He glanced back fearfully to see if his sister was watching them. The door slammed shut. Her duty for the morning done, Kitiara was going back to bed.

The children took the tree walkways as far as they could. Then, when the rope bridges came to an end, the twins ran down a long staircase to reach the forest floor. A narrow road, little more than two wheel ruts and a hard-baked footpath, led in the direction they were going.

The boys ate hunks of stale bread, which they had torn off a loaf that had been left out on the table.

"Look, there's blue stuff on this bread," Caramon noted, pausing between bites.

"It's mold," said Raistlin.

"Oh." Caramon ate the bread, mold and all, observing that it "wasn't bad, just sort of bitter."

Raistlin carefully removed the part of the bread with the mold. He studied the mold intently, then slipped the piece inside a pouch he carried with him everywhere. By the end of the day, that pouch would be filled with various specimens of plant and animal life. He spent his evenings studying them.

"It's a long walk to the school," Caramon stated, his bare feet scuffing up the dirt on the road. "Almost five miles, Father says. And once you get there, you have to sit at a desk all day and not move, and they don't let you go outside or nothing. Are you sure you're going to like that, Raist?"

Raistlin had seen the interior of the school only once. It consisted of a large room, with no windows, so that there were no outside distractions. The floor was stone. The desks stood high off the stone floor, so that the winter cold would not chill their feet. The students sat on tall stools. Shelves containing jars with various herbs and other things in them that ranged from the horrible and disgusting to the pleasant or mysterious lined the walls. These jars held the spell components. Other shelves held scroll cases. Most of the scrolls were blank, meant for the students to write upon. But some were not.

Raistlin thought of this quiet, dark room, the peaceful hours spent in study with no distractions from unruly brothers, and he smiled. "I won't mind it," he said.

Caramon had picked up a stick, was slashing about with it, pretending it was a sword. "I wouldn't want to go there. I know that. And that teacher. He has a face like a frog. He looks mean. Do you think he'll whip you?"

The teacher, Master Theobald, had indeed looked mean. Not only that, but their first meeting proved him to be haughty, self-important, and probably less intelligent than the majority of his pupils. Unable to gain their respect, he would almost certainly resort to physical intimidation. Raistlin had seen the long willow branch standing in a prominent place beside the master's desk.

"If he does," Raistlin said, thinking of what Antimodes had told him, "it will be just another blow of the hammer."

"You think he'll hit you with a hammer?" Caramon demanded, horrified. He halted in the middle of the road. "You shouldn't go to that place, Raist."

"No, that's not what I meant, Caramon," Raistlin said, trying to be patient with his twin's ignorance. After all, the statement had been somewhat bizarre. "I'll try to explain. You fight with a stick now, but someday you'll own a sword, a real sword, won't you?"

"You bet. Kit's going to bring me one. She'll bring you one, too, if you ask her."

"I already have a sword, Caramon," Raistlin said. "Not a sword like yours. Not one made of metal. This sword is inside me. It's not a very good weapon right now. It needs to be hammered into shape. That's why I'm going to this school."

"To learn to make swords?" Caramon asked, frowning with the mental effort. "Is it a blacksmith school, then?"

Raistlin sighed. "Not real swords, Caramon. Mental swords.

Magic will be my sword."

"If you say so. But anyhow, if that teacher does whip you, just tell me." Caramon clenched his fists. "I'll take care of him. This sure is a long walk," he repeated.

"It is a long walk," Raistlin agreed. They'd gone only about a quarter of the distance, and he was already tired, although he didn't admit it. "But you don't have to come with me, you know."

"Well, of course I do!" Caramon said, looking astonished at the idea. "What if you get attacked by goblins? You'd need me to defend you."

"With a wooden sword," Raistlin observed dryly.

"Like you said, someday I'll have a real one," Caramon answered, his enthusiasm undaunted by logic. "Kitiara promised. Hey, that reminds me of what I was going to tell you. I think Kit's getting ready to go somewhere. Yesterday I ran into her coming down the stairs from that tavern at the edge of town. The Trough."

"What was she doing there?" Raistlin asked, interested. "For that matter, what were you doing there? That place is rough."

"I'll say!" Caramon agreed. "Sturm Brightblade says it's a place where thieves and cutthroats hang out. That's one reason I was there. I wanted to see a cutthroat."

"Well," said Raistlin with a half-smile, "did you see one?"

"Naw!" Caramon was disgusted. "At least, I don't think so. All the men were pretty ordinary. Most didn't look any different from Father, only not as big."

"Which is exactly what a good assassin would look like," Raistlin pointed out.

"Like Father?"

"Certainly. That way, he can sneak up on his victim without the victim noticing him. What did you think an assassin would look like? Dressed all in black with a long black cape and a black mask over his face?" Raistlin asked mockingly.

Caramon pondered. "Well . . . yes."

"What an idiot you are, Caramon," Raistlin said.

"I guess so," Caramon replied, subdued. He stared down at his feet, kicked at the dirt for a few moments. But it wasn't in Caramon's nature to be depressed for long. "Say," he said cheerfully, "if they really are ordinary, maybe I did see a cutthroat after all!"

Raistlin snorted. "What you did see was our sister. What was she doing there? Father wouldn't like her going into places like that."

"That's what I told her," Caramon said, self-righteous. "She smacked me and said that what Father didn't know wouldn't hurt him, and I was to keep my mouth shut. She was talking to two grown-up men, but they left when I came. She was holding something in her hand that looked like a map. I asked her what it was, but she just pinched my arm real hard"—Caramon exhibited a blue and red bruise—"and took me away and made me swear on a grave in the graveyard that I'd never say a word to anyone. Otherwise a ghoul would come and get me one night."

"You told me," Raistlin pointed out. "You broke your promise."

"She didn't mean you!" Caramon returned. "You're my twin. Telling you is like telling myself. 'Sides, she knows I'll tell you. I swore for both of us, anyway. So if the ghoul comes and gets me, it'll get you, too. Hey, I wouldn't mind seeing a ghoul, would you, Raist?"

Raistlin rolled his eyes but said nothing. He saved his breath. He hadn't covered half the distance to the school yet and already he was exhausted. He loathed his frail body that seemed determined to thwart every plan he made, to ruin every hope, to wreck every desire. Raistlin cast a jealous glance at his well-built, stout, and healthy twin.

People said there had once been gods who ruled over mankind, but the gods had grown angry at man and had gone away. Before they left, the gods had cast down a fiery mountain on Krynn, shattering the world. Then they had abandoned man to his fate. Raistlin could well believe that this was so. No just and honorable god would have played such a cruel joke as had been played on him—splitting a single person in two, giving one twin a mind without a body, the other a body without a mind.

Yet it would be comforting to think that there was an intelligent reason behind the decision, a purpose; comforting to know that he and his twin were not just some freak of nature. It would be comforting to know that there were gods, if only so that one could blame them!

Kitiara often told Raistlin the story of how he had nearly died, how she had saved his life when the midwife had told her the baby was good as dead and to leave it alone to gasp out its pitiful life. Kit was always a little miffed that Raistlin was not properly grateful to her. She was never to know, being strong herself, that sometimes, when Raistlin's body burned with fever and his muscles ached beyond endurance, when his mouth was parched with a thirst he could never quench, he cursed her in the night.

But Kitiara had been responsible for his entry into the school of magic. She had made amends.

If only he could manage to reach that school without collapsing first.

A farm cart, trundling past, proved Raistlin's salvation. The farmer stopped and asked the boys where they were going. And although he frowned when Raistlin told him of their destination, he agreed to give them a lift. He gazed pityingly at the frail child, coughing in the dust and the wheat chaff blowing off the fields.

"You plan on making this walk this every day, lad?"

"No, sir," Caramon answered for his brother, who couldn't speak. "He's going to magic school to learn to make swords. And he's got to stay there by himself, and they won't let me stay with him."

The farmer was a kindly man who had small children of his own. "Look, boys, I come this way every day. If you met me at the crossroads of a morning, I could give you a lift. I'll meet you in the afternoon coming back. That way, you could at least be home with your family in the evenings."

"That'd be great!" Caramon cried.

"We can't pay you," Raistlin said at the same time, his face flushed with shame.

"Pshaw! I don't expect pay!" the farmer shot back, looking quite fierce. He glanced sidelong at the boys, especially the sturdy Caramon. "What I could use is help in the fields. My own young'uns are too little to be of much good to me yet."

"I could work for you," said Caramon promptly. "I could help you while Raist is in school."

"It's agreed, then."

Caramon and the farmer each spat on their palms, clasped hands on the bargain.

"Why did you agree to work for him?" Raistlin demanded after they had settled themselves at the back of the empty wagon, their feet dangling over the edge.

"So you could ride back and forth to school," Caramon said. "Why? What's wrong with that?"

Raistlin bit his tongue. He should thank his brother, but the words stuck in his throat like a bad-tasting physic.

"It's just . . . I don't like you working for me. . . ."

"Oh, heck, Raist, we're twins," Caramon said, and grinning happily, he nudged his brother in the ribs. "You'd do the same for me."

Thinking about it, as the cart rolled toward Master Theobald's School for Mages, Raistlin wasn't all that certain he would.

*   *   *   *   *

The farmer's cart was there to pick them up in the afternoon. Raistlin returned home to find that his mother had never missed him. Kitiara was surprised to see him back and demanded to know the reason. She was always angry when her plans were thwarted. She had made up her mind that Raistlin was to board at the school, and she was displeased to hear that he had decided to do otherwise.

She had to hear the story of the farmer twice, and even then was certain he was up to no good. The idea of Caramon working for the farmer further angered her. Caramon would grow up to be a farmer, she said in disgust. With manure instead of blood on his boots.

Caramon protested that he would not. They argued for a while; Raistlin went to bed with a headache. He awoke to find the argument settled. Kit appeared to have other things on her mind. She was preoccupied, more irritable than usual, and the boys were careful to keep out of the way of the flat of her hand. She did see to it that they were fed, however, frying up some dubious bacon and serving the remainder of the moldy bread.

Late that night, as Kitiara slept, small, deft hands lifted the pouch from her belt. Fingers, whose touch was delicate as the legs of a butterfly, removed the pouch's contents—a torn leaf of paper and a thick, folded piece of leather. Raistlin took them both to the kitchen, studied them by the light of the banked cooking fire.

Traced on the paper was a family crest picturing a fox standing victorious over a dead lion. The motto was "None too mighty" and beneath that was written "Matar." On the soft leather was a crudely drawn map of the route between Solace and Solamnia.

Swiftly Raistlin folded the paper, tucked it back into the pouch, and reattached the pouch onto Kit's belt.

Raistlin did not mention his find to anyone. He had learned early on that knowledge is power, especially knowledge of other people's secrets.

The next morning Kitiara was gone.

6

I t was hot in the mage school. A fire roaring on the hearth heated the windowless classroom to an almost unbearable degree. Master Theobald's voice droned through the heat, whose currents could be seen radiating from the fireplace. A fire spell was the one spell the master was truly adept at casting. He was pleased to show off his talent whenever he could.

Raistlin didn't mind the heat nearly as much as the other boys. He would have enjoyed it if it weren't for the fact that he would soon have to go out into the cold and the snow. Moving from one extreme to the other, venturing out into the chill in sweat-damp robes, took its toll on Raistlin's frail body. He was just now recovering from a sore throat and high fever that had robbed him of his voice for several days, forcing him to remain at home in bed.

He detested missing school. He was more intelligent than the master. And Raistlin knew in his soul that he was a better wizard than Master Theobald. Still, there were things he could learn from the master, things he must learn. The magic burned inside Raistlin like the fever, more pleasant yet just as painful. What Master Theobald knew and Raistlin did not was how to control the burning, how to make the magic serve the spellcaster, how to transmit the fever to words that could be written and spoken, how to use the fever to create.

Master Theobald was such an inept teacher, however, that Raistlin often felt as if he were lying in ambush, waiting to pounce upon the first bit of useful information that might accidentally wander in his direction.

The pupils of Master Theobald sat on their tall stools and tried desperately to stay awake, not easy to do in the heat after the heavy midday meal. Anyone caught dozing off would be awakened by the whip-snap of the lithe willow branch across his shoulders. Master Theobald was a big, flabby man, but he could move quickly and quietly when he wanted to. He liked nothing better than to catch a pupil napping.

Raistlin had spoken quite glibly to his brother about being whipped that first day of school. Since then his thin shoulders had felt the snap of the willow branch, a pain that cut more deeply into the soul than into the flesh. He had never before been struck, except for the occasional smack from his sister, slaps which were delivered in a spirit of sibling affection. If Kitiara sometimes hit harder than she'd meant, her brothers knew that it was the thought that counted.

Master Theobald hit with a gleam in his eye and a smile on his fat face that left no doubt he enjoyed meting out punishment.

"The letter *a* in the language of magic," Master Theobald was saying in his somnambulistic monotone, "is not pronounced 'aa' as it is in the Common vernacular, nor is it pronounced 'ah' as you will hear it in the elven, nor yet 'ach' as we find it spoken among the dwarves."

Yes, yes, thought Raistlin drearily. Get on with it. Quit showing off. You've probably never spoken to an elf in your life, you fat old dundering idiot.

"The letter *a* in the language of magic is spoken as 'ai.' "

Raistlin snapped to alertness. Here was information he needed. He listened attentively. Master Theobald repeated the pronunciation.

" 'Ai.' Now, you young gentlemen, say this after me."

A drowsy chorus of *ai*s sighed through the stifling room, punctuated by one strong *ai* spoken firmly by Raistlin. Generally his voice was the quietest among them, for he disliked drawing attention to himself, mainly because such attention was usually painful. His excitement at actually learning something useful and the fact that he was one of the few awake and listening had prompted him to speak more loudly than he'd intended.

He immediately regretted having done so. Master Theobald regarded Raistlin with an approving eye, at least what could be seen of that eye through the pouches of fat surrounding it, and gently tapped the willow branch upon the desk.

"Very good, Master Raistlin," he said.

Raistlin's neighbors cast him covert, malignant glances, and he knew he'd be made to pay for this compliment. The boy to his right, an older boy, almost thirteen, who had been sent to the school because his parents could not stand to have him around the house, leaned over to whisper.

"I hear you kiss his arse every morning, 'Master Raistlin.'"

The boy, known as Gordo, made vulgar smacking sounds with his lips. Those sitting nearby responded with smothered giggles.

Master Theobald heard and turned his eye on them. He rose to his feet and the boys immediately hushed. He headed for them, the willow branch in his hand, when he was distracted by the sight of a small pupil actually slumbering soundly, his head on his arms, his eyes closed.

Master Theobald smiled. Down came the willow branch across the small shoulders. The pupil sat bolt upright with a pained and startled cry.

"What do you mean, sir, sleeping in my class?" Master Theobald thundered at the young malefactor, who shrank before his rage and surreptitiously wiped away his tears.

During this commotion, Raistlin heard a flurry of activity behind him, a sort of scuffling, but he didn't bother to look around. The antics of the other boys seemed petty and stupid to him. Why did they waste their time, such precious time, in nonsense?

He said "ai" quietly to himself until he was sure he had it right, and even wrote down the vowel combination upon his slate in order to practice it later. Absorbed in his work, he ignored the muffled giggles and sniggers going on around him. Master Theobald, having completely demoralized one small urchin, returned to his desk well satisfied. Seating himself ponderously, he continued with the lesson.

"The next vowel in the language of the arcane is *o*. This is not pronounced 'oo,' nor yet 'och,' but 'oa.' Pronunciation is most important, young gentlemen, and therefore I suggest you pay attention. Pronounce a spell incorrectly and it will not work. I am reminded of the time when I was a pupil of the great wizard—"

Raistlin fidgeted in irritation. Master Theobald was off on one of his tales, stories that were dull and boring and served invariably to laud the mediocre talents of Master Theobald. Raistlin was copying down carefully the letter *o* with the phonetic pronunciation "oa" next to it when suddenly his stool shot out from underneath him.

Raistlin tumbled to the floor. The fall, completely unexpected, was a hard one. Stinging pain shot through his wrist, which he'd instinctively used to try to catch himself. The stool toppled to the floor with a loud clatter. His neighbors broke into guffaws, immediately silenced.

Master Theobald, his face purple against his white robes, sprang to his feet and stood quivering in rage like a mound of vanilla pudding.

"Master Raistlin! What is the meaning of this disruption to my lecture?"

"He went to sleep, sir, and fell off his stool," Gordo offered helpfully.

Crouched on the floor, nursing his injured wrist, Raistlin located the string that had been tied to the leg of his stool. As he reached to grab it, the string slithered across the floor to disappear up the sleeve of Devon, one of the Gordo's minions, who sat behind him.

"Sleeping! Interrupting me!" Master Theobald snatched up the willow branch and bore down upon Raistlin. Seeing the blow coming, he hunched his shoulders, and raised his arm to make himself as small a target as possible.

One cut of the willow sliced the flesh of Raistlin's upraised arm, narrowly missing his face. The master lifted his hand to strike again.

Rage, hot as a forge fire, burned through Raistlin. His anger consumed his fear, consumed his pain. His first wild impulse was to leap to his feet and attack his teacher. A trickle of common sense, icy cold, ran through Raistlin's body. He felt the idea as a physical sensation, a chill that tingled his nerve endings and set him shivering, even in the white heat of his fury. He saw himself attacking the master, saw himself looking the fool—a puny weakling with spindly arms shrieking in a high-pitched voice, flailing away impotently with his tiny fists. Worse, he would be the one in the wrong. Master Theobald would triumph over him. The other boys—Raistlin's tormentors—would laugh and gloat.

Raistlin gave a strangled gasp and went limp, lying on his back, his legs twisted at an angle, knees together. One hand slid nervelessly to the floor, the other lay flaccid across his thin chest. His eyelids closed. He made his breathing as quiet as he could manage, quiet and shallow.

Raistlin had been sick many times during his short life. He knew how to be sick, he knew how to feign illness. He lay, pale and shattered and apparently lifeless, on the floor at the master's feet.

"Cripes!" said Devon, the boy who had tied the string to the stool. "You've killed him!"

"Nonsense," said Master Theobald, though his voice cracked on the word. He lowered the willow stick. "He's just . . . just fainted. That's all. Fainted. Gordo"—he coughed, was forced to clear his throat—"Gordo, go fetch some water."

The boy ran off to do as he was told. His feet pounded on the stone floor; Raistlin could hear him fumbling at the water bucket. Raistlin continued to lie where he had fallen, his eyes closed, not stirring or making a sound. He was enjoying this, he discovered—enjoying the attention, enjoying their fear, their discomfiture.

Gordo ran back with the water dipper, slopping most of the water over the floor and the skirts of the master's robes.

"You clumsy oaf! Give me that!" Master Theobald cuffed Gordo, snatched the dipper from him. The master knelt down beside Raistlin, very gently dabbed the child's lips with water.

"Raistlin," he said in a soft, whining whisper. "Raistlin, can you hear me?"

Laughter bubbled up inside Raistlin. He was forced to exert an extraordinary amount of self-control to contain it. He lay still one more minute. Then, just as he could feel the master's hand starting to tremble in anxiety, Raistlin moved his head from side to side and made a small moaning sound.

"Good!" said Master Theobald, sighing in relief. "He's coming around. You boys back off. Give him air. I'll take him to my private quarters."

The master's flabby arms lifted Raistlin, who let his head loll, his legs dangle. He kept his eyes closed, moaning now and then as he was carried in state to the master's quarters, all the boys traipsing along after them, though Theobald ordered them angrily several times to remain in the schoolroom.

The master laid Raistlin down upon a couch. He drove the other boys back to the classroom with threats, not the willow branch, Raistlin noted, peering through a slit in his closed eyelids. Theobald shouted for one of the servants.

Raistlin allowed his eyes to flicker open. He kept them deliberately unfocused for a moment, then permitted his eyes to find Master Theobald.

"What . . . what happened?" Raistlin asked weakly. He glanced vaguely around, tried to lift himself. "Where am I?"

The exertion proved too much. He fell back upon the couch, gasping for breath.

Master Theobald hovered over him. "You . . . um . . . had a bad fall," he said, not looking directly at Raistlin, but darting nervous glances at him from the corner of his eyes. "You fell off your stool."

Raistlin glanced down at his arm, where an ugly red welt was visible against his pale skin. He looked back at Master Theobald. "My arm stings," he said softly.

The master lowered his gaze, sought the floor, looked up gladly when the servant, a middle-aged woman who did the cooking and cleaning and took care of the boys, entered the room. She was extremely ugly, with a scarred face, missing the hair on one side of her head. It had been burned off, purportedly because she'd been struck by lightning. This perhaps accounted for the fact that she was quite slow mentally.

Marm, as she was known, kept the place clean, and she'd never yet poisoned anyone with her cooking. That was about all that could be said of her. The boys whispered that she was the result of one of Master Theobald's spells gone awry, and that he kept her in his household out of guilt.

"The boy had a bad fall, Marm," said Master Theobald. "See to him, will you? I must return to my class."

He cast a final anxious glance backward at Raistlin, then swept out of the room, inflating himself with what was left of his pride.

Marm brought a cold, wet cloth that she slapped over Raistlin's forehead and a cookie. The cloth was too wet and dripped greasy water into Raistlin's eyes, the cookie was burnt on the bottom and tasted like charcoal. Grunting, Marm left him to recover on his own and went back to whatever it was she had been doing. Judging from the greasy water, she was washing dishes.

When she was gone, Raistlin removed the cloth and cast it aside in disgust. He threw the cookie into the fireplace with its ever-present fire. Then he lay back comfortably on the couch, snuggled into the soft cushions, and listened to the master's voice, which could be heard droning, in a somewhat subdued tone, through the open door.

"The letter *u* is pronounced 'uh.' Repeat after me."

" 'Uh,' " said Raistlin complacently to himself. He watched the flames consume the log and he smiled.

Master Theobald would never strike him again.

7

he lesson another day was penmanship.

Not only did a mage have to be able to pronounce the words of magic correctly, but the mage must also be able to write them down, form each letter into its proper shape. Words of the arcane must be penned with precision, exactness, neatness, and care on the scroll, else they would not work. Write the spell word *shirak*, for example, with a wobble in the *a* and a scrunch in the *k*, and the mage who wants light will be left in the dark.

Most of Master Theobald's students, true to the naturally clumsy characteristics of small boys, were fumble-fisted. Their quill pens, on which they had to carve the points themselves, either split or sputtered, bent or broke or leapt out of their clutching fingers. The boys invariably ended up with more ink on themselves than on the scrolls, unless they happened to upset the ink bottle, which accident occurred on a regular basis.

Any visitor entering the school on the afternoon of penmanship classes to find himself confronted by the inky faces and hands of innumerable small demons, might well have imagined that he'd wandered into the Abyss by mistake.

This thought crossed the mind of Antimodes the moment he walked through the door. This and a sudden swift memory of his own days in the schoolroom, a memory brought on mostly by the smell—small bodies overly warmed by the fire, the cabbage soup they'd choked down for lunch, ink and warm sheepskins—caused him to smile.

"The Archmagus Antimodes," announced the servant, or something approximating that, for she completely mangled his name.

Antimodes paused in the doorway. The flushed, inky, frustrated faces of twelve boys lifted from their work to stare at him with hope in their eyes. A savior, perhaps. One who would free them from their toil. A thirteenth face looked up, but not as quickly as the others. That face appeared to have been intent upon its work, and only when that work was completed did it lift to stare at the visitor.

Antimodes was pleased—quite pleased—to see that this face was almost completely devoid of ink, with the exception of a smudge along the left eyebrow, and that there was not an expression of relief on the face, but rather one of irritation, as if it resented being interrupted in its work.

The irritation passed swiftly, however, once the face recognized Antimodes, as Antimodes had recognized the face.

Master Theobald rose hastily from his chair, officious and ponderous, jealous and insecure. He did not like Antimodes, because the master suspected—and rightly so—that Antimodes had been opposed to Theobald's appointment as schoolmaster and had voted against him in the conclave. Antimodes had been outvoted, Par-Salian himself having presented very strong arguments in Theobald's favor: He was the only candidate. What else were they to do with the man?

Even his friends agreed that Theobald would never make more than a mediocre mage. There were some, Antimodes among them, who questioned how he had managed to pass the Test in the first place. Par-Salian was always evasive whenever Antimodes brought up the subject, and Antimodes was left to believe that Theobald had been passed on the condition that he accept a teaching assignment, a job no one else wanted.

Antimodes could offer no better suggestion. He himself, given the choice, would have preferred going to Mount Nevermind to instruct the gnomes in pyrotechnics to teaching snot-faced human children magic. He had grudgingly gone along with the majority.

Antimodes was forced to admit that Par-Salian and the others had been right. Theobald was not a particularly good teacher, but he saw to it that his boys—the girls had their own school in Palanthas, taught by a slightly more competent wizardess—learned the basics, and that was all that was necessary. He would never light any fires in the average student, but where the fire of greatness already burned, Master Theobald would stoke it.

The two mages met with a show of amicability in front of the children.

"How do you do, sir?"

"How do you do, my dear sir?"

Antimodes was gracious in his greeting and lavish in his praise of the classroom, which to himself he thought was unbearably hot, stuffy, and dirty.

Master Theobald was profuse in his welcome, all the time certain that Antimodes had been sent by Par-Salian to check up on him and bitterly resenting the fact that the archmage was carelessly wearing a luxurious cape made of fine lamb's wool that would have cost the teacher a year's salary.

"Well, well, Archmagus. Are the roads still snow-covered?"

"No, no, Master. Quite passable. Even up north."

"Ah, you've come from the north, have you, Archmagus?"

"Lemish," Antimodes said smoothly. He'd actually been much farther north than that quaint and woodsy little town, but he had no intention of discussing his travels with Theobald.

Theobald had no use for travel of any sort. He raised his eyebrows in an expression of disapproval, manifested his disapproval by turning away and ending their conversation. "Boys, it is my great honor to introduce to you Archmagus Antimodes, a wizard of the White Robes."

The boys sang out an enthusiastic greeting.

"We have been practicing our writing," said Theobald. "We were just about to conclude for the day. Perhaps you would like to see some of our work, Archmagus?"

Actually there was only one pupil in whom Antimodes was interested, but he solemnly walked up and down the aisles and regarded with feigned interest letters that were every shape except the correct shape, and one game of x's and o's, which the player made a vain attempt to cover up by overturning his ink bottle on top of it.

"Not bad," said Antimodes, "not bad. Quite . . . creative . . . some of these." He came to Raistlin's desk—his true goal. Here he paused and said with sincerity, "Well done."

A boy behind Raistlin made a noise, a rude noise.

Antimodes turned.

"Pardon, sir," the boy said, with apparent contriteness. "It was the cabbage for lunch."

Antimodes knew that noise hadn't been caused by cabbage. He also knew what it implied, and he immediately realized his mistake. He remembered the ways of small boys—he had been a bit of a troublemaker himself as a youth. He should not have praised Raistlin. The other boys were jealous and vindictive, and Raistlin would be made to suffer.

Trying to think of some way to rectify his mistake, prepared to point out a flaw—no one was perfect, after all—Antimodes looked back at Raistlin.

On Raistlin's thin lips was a pleased smile. One could almost call it a smirk.

Antimodes swallowed his words, with the result that he very nearly choked on them. Coughing, he cleared his throat and walked on. He saw nothing after that. His thoughts were turned inward, and it wasn't until he came face-to-face with Master Theobald that Antimodes realized he was still in the classroom.

He stopped short, looked up with a start. "Oh . . . er . . . very nice work from your pupils, Master Theobald. Very nice. If you wouldn't mind, I should like to speak to you privately."

"I really should not leave the class. . . ."

"Only for a moment. I'm certain these fine young gentlemen"—Antimodes gave them a smile—"will be content to study on their own in your absence."

He was fully aware that the fine young gentlemen would probably take advantage of the opportunity to play marbles, draw obscene pictures on their practice scrolls, and splatter each other with ink.

"Only a moment of your time, Master Theobald," Antimodes said with the utmost respect.

Scowling, Master Theobald stomped out of the classroom, leading his way into his private quarters. Here he shut the door and faced Antimodes.

"Well, sir. Please make haste."

Antimodes could already hear the uproar break out in the classroom.

"I should like to talk to each pupil individually, if you please, Master Theobald. Ask them each a few questions."

At this, Master Theobald's eyebrows nearly took wing and flew off his head. Then they came together over the puffy eyelids in a suspicious frown. Never before in all his years of teaching had any archmagus ever bothered to visit his classroom, much less demand a private chat with the students. Master Theobald could only jump to one conclusion, and he did, landing on it squarely with both feet.

"If the conclave does not find my work to be satisfactory . . ." he began in huffy tones.

"They do. Quite the contrary," Antimodes said, hastening to reassure him. "It's just some research I'm conducting." He waved his hand. "Investigating the philosophical reasoning that prompts young men to choose to spend their time in this particular course of study."

Master Theobald snorted.

"Please send them in to see me one by one," said Antimodes.

Master Theobald snorted again, turned on his heel, and waddled back into the classroom.

Antimodes settled himself in a chair and wondered what in the name of Lunitari he was going to say to these urchins. In reality, he wanted only to talk to one pupil, but he dare not single out Raistlin again. The Archmagus was still pondering things when the first, the eldest boy in the school, entered the room, abashed and embarrassed.

"Gordo, sir." The boy made an awkward bow.

"And so, Gordo, my boy," said Antimodes, embarrassed himself but attempting to conceal it, "how do you plan to incorporate the use of magic into your everyday life?"

"Well, s-sir," Gordo stammered, obviously baffled, "I don't rightly know."

Antimodes frowned.

The boy grew defensive. "I'm only here, sir, 'cause my ma makes me come. I don't want to have nothing to do with magic."

"What do you want to do?" Antimodes asked, surprised.

"I want to be a butcher," Gordo said promptly.

Antimodes sighed. "Perhaps you should have a talk with your mother. Explain to her how you feel."

The boy shook his head, shrugged. "I've tried. It's all right, sir. I'll stay here until I'm old enough to be apprenticed, then I'll cut and run."

"Thank you," Antimodes said dryly. "We'll all appreciate that. Please tell the next boy to come in."

By the end of five interviews, Antimodes's antipathy for Master Theobald had changed to the most profound pity. He also felt alarmed and dismayed. He had learned more in fifteen minutes talking to these five boys than he had in five months of traveling throughout Ansalon.

He was well aware—he and Par-Salian had often discussed it—that mages were viewed with suspicion and distrust by the general populace. That was as it should be. Wizards should be surrounded with an aura of mystery. Their spellcasting should inspire awe and a proper amount of fear.

He found no awe among these boys. No fear. Not even much

respect. Antimodes might blame Master Theobald and did blame the master for some of the problem. Certainly he did nothing to inspire his students, to lift them from the common everyday muck of ignorance in which they were wallowing. But there was more to it than that.

There were no children of nobles in this school. Insofar as Antimodes knew, there were few children of nobles in any of the schools of magic in Ansalon. Only among the elves was the study of the arcane considered suitable for the upper class, and even they were discouraged from devoting their lives to it. King Lorac of Silvanesti had been one of the last elves of royal blood known to have taken the Test. Most were like Gilthanas, youngest son of the Speaker of the Sun and Stars of Qualinesti. Gilthanas could have been an excellent mage, had he taken the time to study the art. But he merely dabbled in magic, refused to take the Test, refused to commit himself.

As to humans, these children were sons of middle-class merchants, most of them. That wasn't bad—Antimodes himself had come from such a background. He at least had known what he wanted and had been willing to fight for it, his parents having been completely opposed to the very idea of his studying magic. But these children had been sent here because their parents had no idea what else to do with them. They were sent to study magic because they weren't considered good enough to do anything else.

Were wizards truly held in such low regard?

Depressed, Antimodes huddled down in the overstuffed chair, as far from the fire as he could drag it, and mulled this over in his mind. The depression had been growing on him ever since his trip to Solamnia.

The knights and their families had been polite, but then they would always be polite to any well-to-do, fair-spoken traveling human stranger. They had invited Antimodes to stay in their dwellings, they had fed him roast meats, fine wines, and entertained him with minstrels. They had not ever once discussed magic, had never asked him to assist them with his spellcasting, or made reference to the fact that he was a wizard. If he brought it up, they smiled at him vaguely and then quickly changed the subject. It was as if he had some type of deformity or disease. They were too polite, too well bred to shun him or openly revile him for it. But he was well aware that they averted their glances when they thought he wasn't looking. In truth, he disgusted them.

And he disgusted himself. He saw himself for the first time through the eyes of these children. He had tamely gone along with the knights' cold-shouldered treatment, had even curried their favor in a most undignified manner. He had suppressed who and what he was. He had not unpacked his white robes once during the trip. He had removed his pouches of spell components and hidden the scroll cases under the bed.

"At my age, you'd think I would know better," he said to himself sourly. "What a fool I made of myself. They must have rolled their eyes and breathed sighs of relief when I left. It is a good thing Par-Salian doesn't know of this. I'm thankful I never mentioned my intention of traveling to Solamnia to him."

"Greetings again, Archmagus," said a child's voice.

Antimodes blinked, returned to the present. Raistlin had entered the room. The archmage had been looking forward to this meeting. He had taken a keen interest in the boy since the first time they'd met. The conversations with the other children had been merely a ruse, contrived in order to have the chance to talk privately with this one extraordinary child. But his recent discoveries had so devastated Antimodes that he found no pleasure in talking with the one student who showed any aptitude at all for magic.

What future lay ahead for this boy? A future in which wizards were stoned to death? At least, Antimodes thought bitterly, the populace had feared Esmilla, the black-robed wizardess, and fear implies a certain amount of respect. How much worse if they had merely laughed at her! But wasn't that where they were heading? Would magic end up in the hands of disappointed butchers?

Raistlin coughed slightly and shifted nervously on his feet. Antimodes realized that he'd been staring at the child in silence, long enough to make Raistlin feel uncomfortable.

"Forgive me, Raistlin," Antimodes said, motioning the boy to come forward. "I have traveled far and I am weary. And my trip was not entirely satisfactory."

"I'm sorry to hear that, sir," Raistlin said, regarding Antimodes with those blue eyes that were much too old and wise.

"And I am sorry that I praised your work in the schoolroom." Antimodes smiled ruefully. "I should have known better."

"Why, sir?" Raistlin was puzzled. "Wasn't it good, as you said?"

"Well, yes, but your classmates . . . I should not have singled you out. I know boys your age, you see. I was a bit of a rascal myself, I'm sorry to say. I'm afraid they'll be hard on you."

Raistlin shrugged his thin shoulders. "They're ignorant."

"Ahem. Well, now." Antimodes frowned, disapproving. It was all very proper for him, an adult, to think this, but it seemed wrong in the child to say it. Disloyal.

"They can't rise to my level," Raistlin continued, "and so they want to drag me down to theirs. Sometimes"—the blue eyes staring at Antimodes were as clear and brilliant as glare ice—"they hurt me."

"I . . . I'm sorry," Antimodes said, a lame statement, but then he was so completely taken aback by this child, by his coolness and astute observations, that he could think of nothing more intelligent.

"Don't be sorry for me!" Raistlin flared, and there was the flash of fire on the ice. "I don't mind," he added more calmly and shrugged again. "It's a compliment, really. They're afraid of me."

The populace had feared Esmilla, the black-robed wizardess, and fear implies a certain amount of respect. How much worse if they had merely laughed at her! Antimodes recalled his own thoughts. Hearing them repeated in this childish treble sent a shiver up his spine. A child should not be this wise, should not be forced to bear the burden of such cynical wisdom this young.

Raistlin smiled then, an ingenuous smile. "It's a hammer blow. I think about what you told me, sir. How the hammer blows forge the soul. And the water cools them. Except I don't cry. Or if I do," he added, his voice hardening, "it's when they can't see me."

Antimodes stared, amazed and confused. Part of him wanted to hug close this precocious child, while another part warned him to snatch the child up and toss him into the fire, crush him as one crushes the egg of a viper. This dichotomy of emotion so unsettled him that he was forced to rise to his feet and take a turn about the room before he felt capable of continuing the conversation.

Raistlin stood silently, waiting patiently for the adult to finish indulging himself in the strange and inexplicable behavior adults often exhibited. The boy's gaze left Antimodes and strayed to the book shelves, where the gaze focused and sharpened with a hungry edge.

That reminded Antimodes of something he'd meant to tell the boy and had, in the ensuing disturbing conversation, almost forgotten. He returned to his chair, sat forward in the seat.

"I meant to tell you, young man. I saw your sister when I was in . . . on my travels."

Raistlin's gaze darted back to the archmage, was alight with interest. "Kitiara? You saw her, sir?"

"Yes. I was quite astonished, I may tell you. One doesn't expect . . . a girl that age . . ." He paused, not quite certain where, under the light of the lad's blue eyes, to go from here.

Raistlin understood. "She left home shortly after I was enrolled in the school, Archmagus. I think she'd wanted to leave before that, but she was worried about Caramon and me. Me especially. She figures that now I can take care of myself."

"You're still only a child," Antimodes said sternly, deciding precociousness had gone far enough.

"But I can take care of myself," Raistlin said, and the smile—the smirk Antimodes had seen earlier—touched his lips. The smile widened when Master Theobald's loud, haranguing voice was heard booming through the door.

"Kitiara came home a couple of months after she left, before winter set in," Raistlin continued. "She gave Father some money to pay for her room and board. He said it wasn't necessary but she said it was; she wouldn't take anything from him ever again. She wore a sword, a real one. It had dried blood on it. She gave Caramon a sword, but Father was angry and took it away from him. She didn't stay long. Where did you see her?"

"I can't quite recall the name of the place," Antimodes said, carefully evasive. "These small towns. They all look alike after a while. She was in a tavern with some . . . companions."

Disreputable companions, he almost said, but he didn't, not wanting to upset the child, who seemed genuinely fond of his half-sister. He had seen her among mercenary soldiers of the very worst sort, the kind who sell their swords for money and are willing to sell their souls, too, if anyone happened to want the wretched things.

"She told me a story about you," Antimodes went on quickly, not giving the child time to ask more questions. "She said that when your father first brought you here, to Master Theobald's, you came into his library—this very room—sat down and began to read one of the books of magic."

At first Raistlin looked startled, then he smiled. Not the smirk, but a mischievous grin that reminded Antimodes that this boy really was only six years old.

"That wouldn't be possible," Raistlin said, with a sidelong

glance at Antimodes. "I'm only now learning to read and write magic."

"I know it's not possible," Antimodes replied, smiling himself. The boy could be quite charming when he chose. "Where would she have come by such a story, then?"

"My brother," Raistlin answered. "We were in the classroom, and my father and the master were talking about letting me enter the school. The master didn't want to admit me."

Antimodes raised his eyebrows, shocked. "How do you know? Did he say so?"

"Not in so many words. But he said I wasn't properly brought up. I should speak only when I was addressed, and I should keep my eyes down and not 'stare him out of countenance.' That's what he said. I was 'pert' and 'glib' and 'disrespectful.' "

"So you are, Raistlin," admonished Antimodes, thinking he should. "You should show your master and your classmates more respect."

Raistlin shrugged, dismissed them all with that shrug, and continued with his story. "I got bored listening to Father apologize for me, and so Caramon and I went exploring. We came in here. I pulled a book off the shelf. One of the spellbooks. Only a practice one. The master keeps the real spellbooks locked up in his cellar. I know."

The child's voice was cool, serious; the eyes glistened with longing. Antimodes was suitably alarmed and made a mental note to warn Theobald that his precious spellbooks may not be as safe as the master imagined.

Then suddenly the boy was a boy again. "I may have told Caramon the spellbook was real," Raistlin said, the mischievous grin returning. "I don't remember. Anyway, Master Theobald came dashing in, all huffing and puffing and mad. He scolded me for wandering off and 'invading his privacy,' and when he saw me with the book, he got madder still. I wasn't reading a spell. I couldn't read any of it.

"But"—Raistlin gave Antimodes a sly glance—"there's an illusionist in town. His name is Waylan, and I've heard him use magic and I memorized some of the words. I know the spells won't work, but I use them for fun when the other boys are playing at war. I said some of the words. Caramon was all excited and told father that I was going to summon a demon from the Abyss. Master Theobald got really red in the face and grabbed the book away from me. He knew I wasn't really reading the words," Raistlin added coolly. "He just wanted a chance to get rid of me."

"Master Theobald accepted you into his school," said Antimodes sternly. "He didn't 'get rid of you,' as you put it. And what you did was wrong. You should not have taken the book without his permission."

"He had to take me," Raistlin said flatly. "My schooling was bought and paid for." He stared very hard at Antimodes, who, having expected this, was prepared for it and returned the stare with bland innocence.

The child had met his match. He lowered his gaze, shifted it to the bookcase. One corner of his mouth twitched. "Caramon must have told Kitiara. He really did think I was going to summon a demon, you know. Caramon's like a kender. He'll believe anything you tell him."

"Do you love your brother?" Antimodes asked impulsively.

"Of course," Raistlin responded blandly, smoothly. "He's my twin."

"Yes, you are twins, aren't you," Antimodes said reflectively. "I wonder if your brother has a talent for magic? It would seem logic—"

He stopped, confounded, struck dumb by the look Raistlin gave him. It was a blow, as if the child had struck out with his fists. No, not with fists. With a dagger.

Antimodes recoiled, startled unpleasantly by the malevolence in the child's expression. The question had been idle, harmless. He had certainly not expected such a reaction.

"May I return to class now, sir?" Raistlin asked politely. His face was smooth, if somewhat pale.

"Uh, yes. I . . . uh . . . enjoyed our visit," said Antimodes.

Raistlin made no comment. He bowed politely, as all the boys were taught to bow, then went to the door, opened it.

A wave of noise and heat, bringing with it the smell of small boys and boiled cabbage and ink, surged into the library, reminding Antimodes of the tide coming in on the dirty beaches at Flotsam. The door shut behind the boy.

Antimodes sat quite still for long moments, recovering. This was difficult to do at first, because he kept seeing those blue poignard eyes, glittering with anger, sliding through his flesh. Finally, realizing that the day was winding on and that he wanted to reach the Inn of the Last Home before dark, Antimodes shook off the aftereffects of the unfortunate scene and returned to the schoolroom to make his farewells to Master Theobald.

Raistlin, Antimodes noted, did not look up as he entered.

The ride along the road on his placid donkey Jenny, past fields green with the early summer's first blooms, soothed Antimodes's soul. By the time he reached the inn, he could even laugh at himself ruefully, admit that he'd been in the wrong for asking such a personal question, and shrug off the incident. Putting Jenny up in the public stables, Antimodes wended his way to the inn, where he coated his troubles with Otik's honey mead and slept soundly.

*　*　*　*　*

That meeting was the last time Antimodes would see Raistlin for many years. The archmage maintained his interest in Raistlin and kept current on his advancement through his studies. Whenever a wizards' conclave was called, Antimodes made it a point to seek out Master Theobald and interrogate him. Antimodes continued paying for Raistlin's education as well. Hearing of the progress of the pupil, Antimodes considered it money well spent.

But he would not forget his question about the twin brother. Nor would he forget Raistlin's answer.

BOOK 2

I will do this. Nothing in my life matters except this. No moment in my life exists except this moment. I am born in this moment, and if I fail, I will die in this moment.

—Raistlin Majere

I

"Raist! Over here!" Caramon waved from the front of the farmer's cart, which he was driving. At the age of thirteen, so tall and broad and muscular that he often passed for much older, Caramon had become Farmer Sedge's top field hand.

Caramon's hair curled on his brow in soft auburn rings, his eyes were cheerful, friendly, and guileless: gullible. The children adored him, and so did every shyster, beggar, and con artist that passed through Solace. He was unusually strong for his age, also unusually gentle. He had a formidable temper when riled, but the fuse was buried so deep and took so long to burn that Caramon usually realized he was angry only when the quarrel had long since ended.

The only time his anger exploded was when someone threatened his twin.

Raistlin lifted his hand to acknowledge his brother's shout. He was glad to see Caramon, glad to see a friendly face.

Seven winters ago, Raistlin had decided that he must board at Master Theobald's school during the coldest months of the year, an arrangement that meant for the first time in their lives the twin brothers were separated.

Seven winters passed, with Raistlin absent from his home. In springtime, like this spring, when the sun melted the frozen roads and brought the first green and golden buds to the vallenwoods, the twins were reunited.

Long ago, Raistlin had given up secretly hoping that someday he would look into a mirror and see in himself the image of his handsome twin. Raistlin, with his fine-boned features and large eyes, his soft-to-the-touch reddish hair that brushed his shoulders, would have been the more handsome of the two but for his eyes. They held the gaze too long, stared too deeply, saw too much, and there was always the faint hint of scorn in them, for he saw clearly the shams and artifices and absurdities of people and was both amused and disgusted with them.

Jumping down from the cart, Caramon gave his brother a boisterous hug, which Raistlin did not return. He used the bundle of clothes he held in both arms as an excuse to avoid an overt show of affection, a show Raistlin found undignified and annoying. His body stiffened in his brother's embrace, but Caramon was too excited to notice. He grabbed the bundle, flung it in the back of the cart.

"C'mon, I'll help you up," Caramon offered.

Raistlin was beginning to think he wasn't as glad to see his twin as he'd first imagined. He had forgotten how irritating Caramon could be.

"I'm perfectly capable of climbing onto a farm cart without assistance," Raistlin returned.

"Oh, sure, Raist." Caramon grinned, not the least offended.

He was too stupid to be offended.

Raistlin pulled himself up onto the cart. Caramon bounded up into the driver's seat. Grasping the reins, he made clucking sounds with his tongue at the horse, turned the beast around, and started back up the road toward Solace.

"What's that?" Caramon jerked his head around, looked behind him at the school.

"Pay no attention to them, my brother," Raistlin said quietly.

Classes were over. The master usually took advantage of this time of day to "meditate," which meant that he could be found in the library with a closed book and an open bottle of the port wine for which Northern Ergoth was famous. He would remain in his meditative state until dinner, when the housekeeper would awaken him. The boys were supposed to use this time for study, but Master Theobald never checked on them, and so they were left to their own devices. Today a group had gathered at the back of the school to bid farewell to Raistlin.

"'Bye, Sly!" they were yelling in unison, the cry being led by their instigator, a tall boy with carrot-orange hair and freckles, who was new to the school.

"Sly!" Caramon looked at his brother. "They mean you, don't they?" His brows came together in an angry scowl. "Whoa, there!" He brought the cart to a halt.

"Caramon, let it pass," Raistlin said, placing his hand on his brother's muscular arm.

"I won't, Raist," Caramon returned. "They shouldn't call you names like that!" His hands clenched into fists that, for a thirteen-year-old, were formidable.

"Caramon, no!" Raistlin ordered sharply. "I will deal with them in my own time, in my own way."

"Are you sure, Raist?" Caramon was glaring back at the taunting boys. "They won't call you names like that if their lips are split open."

"Not today, perhaps," Raistlin said. "But I have to go back to them tomorrow. Now, drive on. I want to reach home before dark."

Caramon obeyed. He always obeyed when his twin commanded. Raistlin was the acknowledged thinker of the two, a fact that Caramon cheerfully admitted. Caramon had come to depend on Raistlin's guidance in most areas of life, including the games they played with the other boys, games such as Goblin Ball, Kender Keep Away, and Thane Beneath the Mountain. Due to his frail health, Raistlin could not participate in such exuberant sports, but he watched intently. His quick mind developed strategies for winning, which he passed on to his brother.

Minus Raistlin's tutelage, Caramon would mistakenly score goals for his opponents in Goblin Ball. He nearly always ended up being the kender in Kender Keep Away, and he constantly fell victim to the military tactics of the older Sturm Brightblade in Thane Beneath the Mountain. When Raistlin was there to remind him which end of the field was which, and to offer cunning ploys to outwit his opponents, Caramon was the winner more often than not.

Once again he clucked at the horse. The cart rolled down the rutted road. The catcalls ended. The boys grew bored and turned to other sport.

"I don't understand why you didn't let me pound them," Caramon complained.

Because, Raistlin answered silently, I know what would happen, how it would end. You would "pound them," as you so elegantly put it, my brother. Then you would help them to their feet, slap them on their backs, tell them you know they didn't mean it, and in the end you would all be the best of friends.

Except for me. Except for the "Sly One."

No, the lesson will be mine to teach. They will learn what it means to be sly.

He might have continued to sit, brooding and plotting and mulling over such wrongs, but for his brother, who was rattling on about their parents, their friends, and the fine day. Caramon's cheerful gossip teased his brother out of his ill humor. The air was soft and warm and smelled of growing things, compounded with horse and newly mown grass, much better smells than that of cooked cabbage and boys who bathed only once a week.

Raistlin breathed deeply of the soft, fragrant air and didn't cough. The sunshine warmed him pleasantly, and he found himself listening with keen enjoyment to his brother's conversation.

"Father's been gone these last three weeks and likely won't be back until the end of the month. Mother remembered that you were coming home today. She's been a lot better lately, Raist. You'll notice the change. Ever since the Widow Judith started coming to stay with her when she has her bad days."

"Widow Judith?" said Raistlin sharply. "Who's Judith? And what do you mean, stay with Mother when she has her bad days? What about you and Father?"

Caramon shifted uncomfortably on his seat. "It was a hard winter, Raist. You were gone. Father had to work. He couldn't take off or we would have starved. When Farmer Sedge was snowed in and didn't need me, I got a job in the stables, feeding the horses and mucking out. We tried leaving Mother alone, but—well, it wasn't working. One day she tipped over a candle and didn't notice. It nearly burned down the house. We did the best we could, Raist."

Raistlin said nothing. He sat on the cart, grimly silent, angry at his father and brother. They should not have left his mother in the care of strangers. He was angry at himself. He should not have left her.

"The Widow Judith's real nice, Raist," Caramon went on defensively. "Mother likes her a lot. Judith comes every morning, and she helps Mother dress and fixes her hair. She makes her eat something, and then they do sewing and stuff like that. Judith talks to Mother a lot and keeps her from going into her fits." He glanced uneasily at his brother. "Sorry, I mean trances."

"What do they talk about?" Raistlin asked.

Caramon looked startled. "I dunno. Female stuff, I guess. I never listened."

"And how can we afford to pay this woman?"

Caramon grinned. "We don't pay her. That's what's great about this, Raist! She does it for nothing."

"Since when have we lived off charity?" Raistlin demanded.

"It's not charity, Raist. We offered to pay her, but she wouldn't take it. She helps others as part of her religion—that new order we heard about in Haven. The Belzorites or some such thing. She's one of them."

"I don't like this," Raistlin said, frowning. "No one does something for nothing. What is she after?"

"After? What could she be after? It's not like we have a house crammed with jewels. The Widow Judith's just a nice person, Raist. Can't you believe that?"

Apparently Raistlin could not, for he continued to ask questions. "How did you come across such a 'nice person,' my brother?"

"Actually, she came to us," Caramon said after taking a moment to recollect. "She came to the door one day and said that she'd heard Mother wasn't feeling well. She knew we men-folk"—Caramon spoke the plural with a touch of pride—"needed to be out working and said that she'd be glad to sit with Mother while we were gone. She told us she was a widow lady, her own man was dead, her children grown and moved on. She was lonely herself. And the High Priest of Belzor had commanded her to help others."

"Who is Belzor?" Raistlin asked suspiciously.

By this time, even Caramon's patience was exhausted.

"Name of the Abyss, I don't know, Raistlin," he said. "Ask her yourself. Only be nice to the Widow Judith, all right? She's been real nice to us."

Raistlin did not bother to respond. He fell into another brooding silence.

He did not himself know why this should upset him. Perhaps it was nothing more than his own feelings of guilt for having abandoned his mother to the care of strangers. Yet something about this wasn't quite right. Caramon and his father were too trusting, too ready to believe in the goodness of people. They could both be easily taken in. No one devoted hours of her day to caring for another without expecting to gain something by it. No one.

Caramon was casting his brother worried, anxious glances. "You're not mad at me, Raist, are you? I'm sorry I snapped at you. It's just . . . well, you haven't met the widow yet, and—"

"You seem to be faring well, my brother," Raistlin interrupted. He did not want to hear any more about Judith.

Caramon straightened his back proudly. "I've grown four inches since fall. Father measured me on the doorframe. I'm taller than all our friends now, even Sturm."

Raistlin had noticed. He could not help but notice that Caramon was no longer a child. He had grown that winter into a comely young man—sturdy, tall for his age, with a mass of curly hair and wide-open, almost unbearably honest brown eyes. He was cheerful and easygoing, polite to his elders, fun-loving and companionable. He would laugh heartily at any joke, even if it was against himself. He was considered a friend by every young person in town, from the stern and generally morose Sturm Brightblade to the toddlers of Farmer Sedge, who clamored for rides on Caramon's broad shoulders.

As for the adults, their neighbors, especially the women, felt sorry for the lonely boy and were always inviting him to share a meal with the family. Due to the fact that he never turned down a free meal, even if he'd already just eaten, Caramon was probably the best-fed youngster in Solace.

"Any word from Kitiara?" Raistlin asked.

Caramon shook his head. "Nothing all winter. It's been over a year now since we heard from her. Do you think . . . I mean . . . Maybe she's dead. . . ."

The brothers exchanged glances, and in that exchange, the resemblance between the two, not usually noticeable, was quite apparent. Both shook their heads. Caramon laughed.

"All right, so she's not dead. Where is she, then?"

"Solamnia," said Raistlin.

"What?" Caramon was astonished. "How do you know that?"

"Where else would she go? She went to search for her father, or at least for his people, her kin."

"Why would she need them?" Caramon wondered. "She's got us."

Raistlin snorted and said nothing.

"She'll be back for us, at any rate," Caramon said confidently. "Will you go with her, Raist?"

"Perhaps," Raistlin said. "After I've passed the Test."

"Test? Is that like the tests Father gives?" Caramon looked indignant. "Miss one lousy sum and get sent to bed without any supper. A guy could starve to death! And what good is arithmetic to a warrior, anyway? Whack! Whack!"

Caramon slashed an imaginary sword through the air, startling the horse. "Hey! Oops. Sorry, there, Bess. I suppose I might need to know numbers for counting the heads of all the goblins I'm going to kill or how many pieces of pie to cut, but that's it. I certainly don't need twice-times and divisors and all that."

"Then you will grow up ignorant," said Raistlin coldly. "Like a gully dwarf."

Caramon clapped his brother on the shoulder. "I don't care. You can do all the twice-times for me."

"There might be a time when I am not there, Caramon," Raistlin said.

"We'll always be together, Raist," Caramon returned complacently. "We're twins. I need you for twice-times. You need me to look after you."

Raistlin sighed inwardly, conceding this to be true. And it wouldn't be so bad, he thought. Caramon's brawn combined with my brain . . .

"Stop the cart!" Raistlin ordered.

Startled, Caramon yanked on the reins, brought the horse to a halt. "What is it? You got to go pee? Should I come with you? What?"

Raistlin slid off the seat. "Stay there. Wait for me. I won't be long."

Landing on the hard-baked dirt, he left the road and plunged into the thick weeds and underbrush. Beyond him, a stand of wheat rippled like a golden lake, washed up against a shoreline of dark green pines. Pawing through the weeds, shoving them aside impatiently, Raistlin searched for the glint of white he'd seen from the cart.

There it was. White flowers with waxy petals, set against large, dark green leaves with saw-toothed edges. Tiny filaments hung from the leaves. Raistlin paused, inspected the plant. He identified it easily. The problem was how to gather it. He ran back to the cart.

"What is it?" Caramon craned his neck to see. "A snake? Did you find a snake?"

"A plant," Raistlin said. Reaching into the cart, he grabbed hold of his bundle of clothes, pulled out a shirt. He returned to his find.

"A plant . . ." Caramon repeated, his face wrinkling in puzzlement. He brightened. "Can you eat it?"

Raistlin did not reply. He knelt beside the plant, the shirt wrapped around his hand. With his left hand, he unclasped a small knife from his belt, and, moving cautiously, careful to keep his bare hand from brushing against the filaments, he snipped several of the leaves from the stem. He picked up the leaves with the hand protected by the shirt and, carrying them gingerly, returned to the wagon.

Caramon stared. "All that for a bunch of leaves?"

"Don't touch it!" Raistlin warned.

Caramon snatched his hand back. "Why not?"

"You see those little filaments on the leaves?"

"Fill-a-whats?"

"Hairs. The tiny hairs on the leaves? This plant is called 'stinging nettle.' Touch the leaves and they'll sting you enough to raise red welts on your skin. It's very painful. Sometimes people even die from it, if they react badly to it."

"Ugh!" Caramon peered down at the nettle leaves lying in the bottom of the wagon. "What do you want a plant like that for?"

Raistlin settled himself back onto the wagon's seat. "I study them."

"But they could hurt you!" Caramon protested. "Why do you want to study something that could hurt you?"

"You practice with the sword Kitiara brought you. Remember the first time you swung it? You nearly cut your foot off!"

"I still have the scar," Caramon said sheepishly. "Yeah, I guess that's true." He clucked at the horse and the cart lurched forward.

The brothers spoke of other matters after that. Caramon did most of the talking, relating the news of Solace—those who had newly moved into town, those who had left, those who had been born, and those who had died. He told of the small adventures of their group of friends, children with whom they'd grown up. And the truly remarkable news: A kender had taken up residency. The one who'd caused such a stir at the fair. He'd moved in with that grumpy dwarf metalsmith; much to the dwarf's ire, but what could you do about it, short of drowning the kender, whose untimely demise was expected daily. Raistlin listened in silence, letting his brother's voice flow over him, warming him like the spring sunshine.

Caramon's cheerful, mindless prattle removed some of the dread Raistlin felt, dread about going home and seeing his mother again. Her health had always been failing, it seemed to him. The winters drained her, sapped her strength. Every spring he returned to find her a little paler, a little thinner, a little farther removed into her dream world. As for this Widow Judith helping her, he would believe that when he saw it.

"I can drop you off at the crossroads, Raist," Caramon offered. "I have to work in the fields until sundown. Or you can come with me if you want. You can rest in the wagon until it's time go home. That way we can walk back together."

"I'll go with you, my brother," Raistlin said placidly.

Caramon flushed with pleasure. He started telling Raistlin all about the family life of Farmer Sedge and the little Sedges.

Raistlin cared nothing about any of them. He had staved off the hour when he must return home, he had insured that he would not be alone when he first encountered Rosamun. And he had made Caramon happy. It took so little to make Caramon happy.

Raistlin glanced back at the stinging nettle leaves he'd gathered. Noticing that they were starting to wilt in the sunshine, he tenderly wrapped the shirt more closely around them.

* * * * *

"Jon Farnish," said Master Theobald, sitting at his desk at the front of the class. "The assignment was to gather six herbs that may be used for spell components. Come forward and show us what you found."

Jon Farnish, red hair gleaming, his freckled face carefully arranged to appear solemn and studious—at least while it was in view of the master—slid off the high stool and made his way to the front of the classroom. Jon Farnish bowed to Master Theobald, who smiled and nodded. Master Theobald had taken a liking to Jon Farnish, who never failed to be immensely impressed whenever Master Theobald cast the most minor of spells.

Turning his back on Master Theobald, facing his classmates, Jon Farnish rolled his eyes, puffed out his cheeks, and pulled his mouth down at the corners, making a ludicrous caricature of his teacher. His classmates covered their mouths to hide their mirth or looked down hurriedly at their desks. One actually began to laugh, then tried to change it to a cough, with the result that he nearly choked himself.

Master Theobald frowned.

"Silence, please. Jon Farnish, do not let these rowdy individuals upset you."

"I'll try not to, Master," said Jon Farnish.

"Continue, please."

"Yes, Master." Jon Farnish thrust his hand into his pouch. "The first plant I gathered—"

He halted, sucked in a breath, gasped, and screeched in pain. Flinging the pouch to the floor, he wrung his right hand.

"Something . . . something stung me!" he babbled. "Ow! It hurts like fire! Ow!"

Tears streamed down his cheeks. He thrust his hand beneath his armpit and did a little dance of agony in the front of the room.

Only one of his classmates was smiling now.

Master Theobald rose to his feet, hastened forward. Prying loose Jon's hand, the mage examined it, gave a grunt. "Go into the kitchen and ask cook for some butter to put on it."

"What is it?" Jon Farnish gasped between moans. "A wasp? A snake?"

Picking up the pouch, Master Theobald peered inside. "You silly boy. You've picked stinging nettle leaves. Perhaps from now on, you'll pay more attention in class. Go along with you and stop sniveling. Raistlin Majere, come forward."

Raistlin walked to the front of the class, made a polite bow to the master. Turning, he faced his classmates. His gaze swept the room. They stared back at him in sullen silence, their lips compressed, eyes shifting away from his triumphant gaze.

They knew. They understood.

Raistlin thrust his hand into his pouch, drew forth some fragrant leaves. "The first plant I am going to talk about today is marjoram. Marjoram is a spice, named for one of the old gods, Majere. . . ."

2

The first few days of the summer of Raistlin's thirteenth year were unusually hot. The leaves of the vallenwoods hung limp and lifeless in the breathless air. The sun bronzed Caramon's skin, burned Raistlin's as the two made the daily trek back and forth from school to home in the farmer's cart.

In school, the pupils were dull and stupid from the heat, spent the days swatting at flies, dozing off, waking to the sting of Master Theobald's willow branch. Finally even Master Theobald conceded that they were accomplishing nothing. Besides, there was the Wizards' Conclave he wanted to attend. He gave his students a holiday for eight weeks. School would recommence in autumn, after the harvest.

Raistlin was thankful for the holiday; at least it was a break in the dull routine. Yet he hadn't been home for more than a day before he wished he was back in school. Reminded of the teasing, the cabbage, and Master Theobald, he wondered why he wasn't happy at home. And then he realized he wouldn't be happy anywhere. He felt restless, dissatisfied.

"You need a girl," Caramon advised.

"I hardly think so," Raistlin answered acerbically. He glanced over to a group of three sisters, pretending to be wholly absorbed in hanging the laundry over the vallenwood limbs to dry. But their attention was not on shirts and petticoats. Their eyes darted daring, smiling glances at Caramon. "Do you realize how silly you look, my brother? You and the others? Puffing up your chests and flexing your muscles, throwing axes at trees or flailing away at each other with your fists. All for what? To gain the attention of some giggling girl!"

"I get more than giggles, Raist," Caramon said, with a lewd

wink. "Come on over. I'll introduce you. Lucy said she thought you were cute."

"I have ears, Caramon," Raistlin returned coldly. "What she said was that your baby brother was cute."

Caramon flushed, uncomfortable. "She didn't mean it, Raist. She didn't know. I explained to her that we were the same age, and—"

Raistlin turned and walked away. The girl's heedless words had hurt him deeply, and his pain angered him, for he wanted to be above caring what anyone thought of him. It was this traitorous body of his, first sickly and frail, now teasing him with vague longings and half-understood desires. He considered it all disgusting anyway. Caramon was behaving like a stag during rutting season.

Girls, or the lack of them, were not his problem, at least not all of it. He wondered uneasily what was.

The heat broke suddenly that night in a violent thunderstorm. Raistlin lay awake to watch the bolts of light streak the roiling clouds with eerie pinks and oranges. He reveled in the booms of thunder that shook the vallenwoods and vibrated through the floorboards. A blinding flash, a deafening explosion, the smell of sulfur, and the sound of shattering wood told of a lightning strike nearby. Shouts of "Fire!" were partially lost in the crashing thunder. Caramon and Gilon braved the torrential rain to go out to help battle the blaze. Fire was their worst enemy. Though the vallenwood trees were more resistant to fire than most others, a blaze out of control could destroy their entire tree town. Raistlin stayed with his mother, who wept and trembled and wondered why her husband hadn't remained home to comfort her. Raistlin watched the progress of the flames, his spellbooks clasped fast in his hand in case he and his mother had to run for it.

The storm ended at dawn. Only one tree had been hit, three houses burned. No one had been injured; the families had escaped in time. The ground was littered with leaves and blasted limbs, the air was tainted with the sickening smell of smoke and wet wood. All around Solace, small streams and creeks were out of their banks. Fields that had been parched were now flooded.

Raistlin left his home to view the damage, along with almost every other person in Solace. He then walked to the edge of the tree line to see the rising water. He stared at the churning waters of the creek. Normally placid, it was now foam-flecked, swirling angrily, gnawing away at the banks that had long held it confined.

Raistlin felt complete sympathy.

* * * * *

Autumn came, bringing cool, crisp days and fat, swollen moons; brilliant colors, reds and golds. The rustle and swirl of the falling leaves did not cheer Raistlin's mood. The change of the season, the bittersweet melancholy that belongs to autumn, which brings both the harvest and the withering frost, served only to exacerbate his ill humor.

This day, he would return to school, resume boarding with Master Theobald. Raistlin looked forward to going back to school as he had looked forward to leaving—it was a change, at least. And at least his brain would have something to do besides torment him with images of golden curls, sweet smiles, swelling breasts, and fluttering eyelashes.

The late autumn morning was chill; frost glistened on the red and golden leaves of the vallenwood and rimed the wooden walkways, making them slippery and treacherous before the sun came out to dry them. Clouds hung gray and lowering over the Sentinel Peaks. The smell of snow was in the air. There would be snow on the mountaintop by the end of the week.

Raistlin thrust his clothes into a bag: two homespun shirts, underclothes, an extra pair of slops, woolen stockings. Most of his clothes were new, made by his mother. He needed the new clothes. He had gained in height that summer, keeping up with Caramon, though he lacked the bulk of his sturdy brother. The added height only served to emphasize Raistlin's excessive thinness.

Rosamun came out of her bedroom. Pausing, she stared at him with her faded blue eyes. "Whatever are you doing, child?"

Raistlin glanced up warily from his work. His mother's soft brown hair was brushed and combed and neatly arranged beneath a cap. She was wearing a clean skirt and bodice over a new blouse, a blouse she had sewn herself under the Widow Judith's tutelage.

Raistlin had tensed instinctively at the sound of her voice. Now, seeing her, he relaxed. His mother was having another good day. She had not had a bad day during his stay at home that summer, and Raistlin supposed they had the Widow Judith to thank for it.

He did not know what to make of the Widow Judith. He had been prepared to distrust her, prepared to discover something nefarious about her, some hidden motive for her selflessness. Thus far his suspicions had proven unfounded. She was what she appeared—a widow in her forties, with a pleasant face, smooth hands with long, graceful fingers, a melodious voice, a way with words, and an engaging laugh that always brought a smile to Rosamun's pale, thin face.

The Majere house was now clean and well organized, something it had never been before the Widow Judith's arrival. Rosamun ate meals at regular hours. She slept through the night, went to market, went visiting—always accompanied by the Widow Judith.

The Widow Judith was friendly to Raistlin, though she was not as free and easy with him as she was with Caramon. She was more reserved around Raistlin, and, he realized, she always seemed to be watching him. He could not do anything around the house without feeling her eyes on him.

"She knows you don't like her, Raist," Caramon said to him accusingly.

Raistlin shrugged. That was true, though he couldn't quite explain why. He did not like her and was quite certain she didn't like him.

One of the reasons may have been that Rosamun, Gilon, Caramon, and the Widow Judith were a family, and Raistlin was not part of it. This was not because he hadn't been invited, but because he willfully chose to remain on the outside. During the evenings when Gilon was home, the four would sit outdoors, joking and telling stories. Raistlin would remain indoors, poring over his school notes.

Gilon was a changed man now that his wife had been rescued from her storm-tossed mind, and was apparently resting comfortably in safer waters. The worry lines smoothed from his brow, he laughed more often. He and his wife could actually carry on a relatively normal conversation.

Summer work was closer to home; Gilon was able to be with his family more often. Everyone was pleased about this except Raistlin, who had grown accustomed to his father being gone, felt constrained when the big man was around. He didn't particularly like the change in his mother, either. He rather missed her odd fancies and flights, missed the times she had been his alone. He didn't like the new warmth between her and Gilon; their closeness made him feel further isolated.

Caramon was obviously Gilon's favorite, and Caramon adored his father. Gilon tried to take an interest in the other twin, but the big woodsman was very like the trees he cut— slow growing, slow moving, slow thinking. Gilon could not understand Raistlin's love of magic and though he had approved sending his son to the mage school, Gilon had secretly hoped the child would find it tedious and leave. He continued to nurture the same hope and always looked disappointed on the day when school recommenced and Raistlin began packing. But amidst the disappointment, there was now a relief. Raistlin this summer had been like a stranger boarding with the family, an irritable, unfriendly stranger. Gilon would never admit this, even to himself, but he was going to be glad to see one of his sons depart.

The feeling was mutual. Raistlin sometimes felt sorry he couldn't love his father more, and he was vaguely aware that Gilon was sorry he couldn't love his strange, unchancy son.

No matter, Raistlin thought, rolling up his stockings into a ball. Tomorrow I will be gone. He found it difficult to believe, but he was actually looking forward to the smell of cooked cabbage.

"What are you doing with your clothes, Raistlin?" Rosamun asked.

"I am packing, Mother. I return to Master Theobald's tomorrow to board there over the winter." He tried a smile at her. "Had you forgotten?"

"No," Rosamun said in tones colder than the frost. "I was hoping that you would not be going back there."

Raistlin halted his packing to regard his mother with astonishment. He had expected such words from his father.

"What? Not go back to my studies? Why would you think such a thing, Mother?"

"It is wicked, Raistlin!" Rosamun cried vehemently, with a passion frightening in its intensity. "Wicked, I tell you!" She stomped her foot, drew herself up. "I forbid you to go back there. Ever!"

"Mother . . ." Raistlin was shocked, alarmed, perplexed. He had no idea what to say. She had never before protested his chosen field of study. He had wondered, at times, if she even knew he was studying magic, much less cared. "Mother, some people think ill of mages, but I assure you that they are wrong."

"Gods of evil!" she intoned in a hollow voice. "You worship gods of evil, and at their behest, you perform unnatural acts and unholy rites!"

"The most unnatural thing I've done so far, Mother, is to fall off my stool and nearly split my skull open," said Raistlin dryly. Her accusations were so ludicrous, he found it difficult to take this conversation seriously.

"Mother, I spend my days droning away after my master, learning to say 'ah' and 'oo' and 'uh.' I cover myself with ink and occasionally manage to write something that is almost legible on a bit of parchment or scroll. I tramp about in fields picking flowers. That is what I do, Mother. That is all I do," he said bitterly. "And I assure you that Caramon's job mucking out stables and picking corn is far more interesting and far more exciting than magic."

He stopped talking, astonished at himself, astonished at his own feelings. Now he understood. Now he knew what had been chafing at him all summer. He understood the anger and frustration that bubbled like molten steel inside him. Anger and frustration, tempered by fear and self-doubt.

Ink and flowers. Reciting meaningless words day after day. Where was the magic? When would it come to him?

Would it come to him?

He shook with a sudden chill.

Rosamun put her arm around his waist, rested her cheek against his. "You see? Your skin—it's hot to the touch. I think you must have a fever. Don't go back to that dreadful school! You only make yourself sick. Stay here with me. I will teach you all you need to know. We will read books together and work out sums like we used to do when you were little. You will keep me company."

Raistlin found the idea surprisingly tempting. No more of the inanities of Master Theobald. No more silent, lonely nights in the dormitory, nights made all the more lonely because he was not alone. No more of this inner torment, this constant questioning.

What had happened to the magic? Where had it gone? Why did his blood burn more at the sight of some silly giggling girl than it did when he copied down his *oa*s and *ai*s?

He had lost the magic. Either that, or the magic had never been there. He had been fooling himself. It was time to admit defeat. Admit that he had failed. Return home. Shut himself away in this cozy, snug room, warm, safe, surrounded by his mother's love. He would take care of her. He would send the Widow Judith packing.

Raistlin bowed his head, unwilling she should see his bitter unhappiness. Rosamun never noticed, however. She caressed his cheek and playfully turned his face to the looking glass. The mirror had come with her from Palanthas. It was her prized possession, one of the few relics of her girlhood.

"We will have such splendid times together, you and I. Look!" she said coaxingly, regarding the two faces in the reflection with complacent pride. "Look how alike we are!"

Raistlin was not superstitious. But her words, spoken in all innocence, were so very ill-omened that he couldn't help but shudder.

"You're shivering," Rosamun said, concerned. "There! I said you had a fever! Come and lie down!"

"No, Mother. I am fine. Mother, please . . ."

He tried to edge away. Her touch, which had seemed so comforting, was now something loathsome. Raistlin was ashamed and appalled that he felt this way about his mother, but he couldn't help himself.

She only clasped him more tightly, rested her cheek against his arm. He was taller than she was by at least a head.

"You are so thin," she said. "Far too thin. Food doesn't stick to your bones. You fret it away. And that school. I'm sure it's making you ill. Sickness is a punishment for those who do not walk the paths of righteousness, so the Widow Judith says."

Raistlin didn't hear his mother, he wasn't listening to her. He was suffocating, felt as if someone were pressing a pillow over his nose and mouth. He longed to break free of his mother's grasp and rush outside, where he could gulp down huge drafts of fresh air. He longed to run and to keep on running, run into the sweet-scented night, journey along a road that would take him anywhere but here.

At that moment, Raistlin knew a kinship with his half-sister, Kitiara. He understood then why she had left, knew how she must have felt. He envied her the freedom of her life, cursed the frail body that kept him chained to home's hearth, kept him fettered in his schoolroom.

He had always assumed the magic would free him, as Kitiara's sword had freed her.

But what if the magic did not free him? What if the magic would not come to him? What if he had indeed lost the gift?

He looked into the mirror, looked into his mother's dream-ravaged face, and closed his eyes against the fear.

3

now was falling. The boys were dismissed early, told to go play outdoors until dinner. Exercising in the cold was healthful, expanded the lungs. The boys knew the real reason they were being sent outside. Master Theobald wanted to get rid of them.

He had been strangely preoccupied all that day, his mind—what there was of it—somewhere else. He taught class absentmindedly, not seeming to care whether they learned anything or not. He had not had recourse to the willow branch once, although one of the boys had drifted off to sleep shortly after lunch and slept soundly and noisily through the remainder of the afternoon.

Most of the boys considered such inattention on their master's part a welcome change. Three found it extremely uncomfortable, however, due to the fact that he would occasionally lapse into long, vacant silences, his gaze roving among these three eldest in his class.

Raistlin was among the three.

Outside, the other boys took advantage of the heavy snowfall to build a fort, form armies, and pelt each other with snowballs. Raistlin wrapped himself in a warm, thick cloak—a parting gift, oddly enough, from the Widow Judith—and left the others to their stupid games. He went for a walk among a stand of pines on the north side of the school.

No wind blew. The snow brought a hush to the land, muffling all sound, even the shrill shouting of the boys. He was wrapped in silence. The trees stood unmoving. Animals were tucked away in nest or lair or den, sleeping their winter sleep. All color was obliterated, leaving in its absence the white of the falling snow, the black of the wet tree trunks, the slate gray of the lowering sky.

Raistlin stood on the edge of the forest. He had intended to walk among the trees, to follow a snow-choked path that led to a little clearing. In the clearing was a fallen log, which served well as a seat. This was Raistlin's refuge, his sanctuary. No one knew about it. Pines shielded the clearing from the school and the play yard. Here Raistlin came to brood, to think, to sort through his collection of herbs and plants, to mull over his notes, reciting to himself the letters of the alphabet of the language of the arcane.

He had been certain, when he'd first marked the clearing as his own, that the other boys would find it and try to spoil it—drag off the log, perhaps; dump their kitchen scraps here; empty their chamber pots in it. The boys had left the clearing alone. They knew he went off somewhere by himself, but they made no attempt to follow him. Raistlin had been pleased at first. They respected him at last.

The pleasure had soon faded. He came to realize that other boys left him alone because, after the nettle incident, they detested him. They had always disliked him, but now they distrusted him so much that they derived no pleasure from teasing him. They left him severely alone.

I should welcome this change, he said to himself.

But he didn't. He found that he had secretly enjoyed the attention of the others, even if such attention had annoyed, hurt, or angered him. At least by teasing him they had acknowledged him as one of them. Now he was an outcast.

He had meant to walk to the clearing this day, but, standing on the outskirts, looking at the trackless snow flowing in smooth, frozen ripples around the boles of the trees, he did not enter.

The snow was perfect, so perfect that he could not bring himself to walk through it, leaving a floundering trail behind, marring the perfection.

The school bell rang. He lowered his head against the icy flakes that a slight, rising breeze was blowing into his eyes. Turning, he slogged his way back through the silence and the white and the black and the gray, back to the heat and the torpor and loneliness of the schoolroom.

* * * * *

The boys changed their wet clothes and filed down to supper, which they ate under the watchful, if somewhat vacant, eye of Marm. Master Theobald entered the room only if necessary to prevent the floor from being awash in soup.

Marm reported any misdeeds to the master, and so the bread-tossing and soup-spitting had to be kept to a minimum. The boys were tired and hungry after their hard-fought snow battles, and there was less horseplay than usual. The large common room was relatively quiet except for a few smothered giggles here and there, and thus the boys were extremely surprised when Master Theobald entered.

Hastily the boys clamored to their feet, wiping grease from their chins with the backs of their hands. They regarded his arrival with indignation. Dinner was their own personal time, into which the master had no right or reason to intrude.

Theobald either didn't see or decided to ignore the restless feet shuffling, the frowns, the sullen looks. His gaze picked out the three eldest: Jon Farnish; Gordo, the hapless butcher; and Raistlin Majere.

Raistlin knew immediately why the master had come. He knew what the master was going to say, what was going to happen. He didn't know how he knew: premonition, some hereditary offshoot of his mother's talent, or simple logical deduction. He didn't know and he didn't care. He couldn't think clearly. He went cold, colder than the snow, fear and exultation vying within him. The bread he had been holding fell from his nerveless hand. The room seemed to tilt beneath him. He was forced to lean against the table to remain standing.

Master Theobald called off the names of the three, names that Raistlin heard only dimly through a roaring in his ears, the roaring as of flames shooting up a chimney.

"Walk forward," said the master.

Raistlin could not move. He was terrified that he would collapse. He was too weak. Was he falling sick? The sight of Jon Farnish, tromping across the floor of the common room with a hangdog air, certain that he was in trouble, brought a derisive smile to Raistlin's lips. His head cleared, the chimney fire had burnt itself out. He strode forward, conscious of his dignity.

He stood before Theobald, heard the master's words in his bones, had no conscious recollection of hearing them in his ears.

"I have, after long and careful consideration, decided that you three, by virtue of your age and your past performance, will be tested this night to determine your ability to put to use the skills you have learned. Now, don't be alarmed."

This to Gordo, whose eyes, white-rimmed and huge with

consternation, seemed likely to roll from their sockets.

"This test is not the least bit dangerous," the master continued soothingly. "If you fail it, nothing untoward will happen to you. The test will tell me if you have made the wrong choice in wanting to study magic. If so, I will inform your parents and anyone else interested in your welfare"—here he looked very sharply at Raistlin—"that, in my opinion, your remaining here is a waste of time and money."

"I never wanted to be here!" Gordo blurted out, sweating. "Never! I want to be a butcher!"

Somebody laughed. Frowning in anger, the master sought the culprit, who immediately hushed and ducked behind one of his fellows. The others were silent. Certain that peace was restored, Theobald looked back at his pupils.

"I trust you two do not feel the same way?"

Jon Farnish smiled. "I look forward to this test, Master."

Raistlin hated Jon Farnish, could have slain him in that instant. He wanted to have spoken those words! Spoken them with that casual tone and careless confidence. Instead, Raistlin could only fumble and stammer, "I . . . I am . . . am ready. . . ."

Master Theobald sniffed as if he very much doubted this statement. "We will see. Come along."

He shepherded them out of the common room, the wretched Gordo sniveling and protesting, Jon Farnish eager and grinning, as if this were playtime, and Raistlin so wobbly in the knees that he could barely walk.

He saw his life balanced on this moment, like the dagger Caramon stood on its point on the kitchen table. Raistlin imagined being turned out of the school tomorrow morning, sent home with his small bundle of clothes in disgrace. He pictured the boys lining the walkway, laughing and hooting, celebrating his downfall. Returning home to Caramon's bluff and bumbling attempts to be sympathetic, his mother's relief, his father's pity.

And what would be his future without the magic?

Again Raistlin went cold, cold all over, cold and ice-hard with the terrible knowledge of himself.

Without the magic, there could be no future.

Master Theobald led them through the library, down a hallway to a spell-locked door leading to the master's private quarters. All the boys knew where the door led, and it was postulated among them that the master's laboratory—of which he often spoke—could be reached through this door. One night a group of the boys, led by Jon Farnish, had made a futile attempt to dispel the magic of the lock. Jon had been forced to explain the next day how he had burned his fingers.

The three boys in tow behind him, the master came to a halt in front of the door. He mumbled in a low voice several words of magic, words which Raistlin, despite the turmoil in his soul, made an automatic, concentrated effort to overhear.

He was not successful. The words made no sense, he could not think or concentrate, and they left his brain almost the moment they entered. He had nothing in his brain, nothing at all. He could not call to mind how to spell his own name, must less the complicated language of magic.

The door swung open. Master Theobald caught hold of Gordo, who was taking advantage of the spell being cast to do a disappearing act of his own. Master Theobald dug his pudgy fingers into Gordo's shoulder, thrust him, blubbering and whimpering, into a sitting room. Jon Farnish and Raistlin followed after. The door swung shut behind them.

"I don't want to do it! Please don't make me! A demon'll grab me sure!" Gordo howled.

"A demon! What nonsense! Stop this sniveling at once, you stupid boy!" Master Theobald's hand, from force of habit, reached for the willow branch, but he'd left that in the schoolroom. His voice hardened. "I shall slap you if you don't control yourself this instant."

The master's hand, though empty, was broad and large. Gordo glanced at it and fell silent, except for a snivel now and then.

"Won't do no good, me going down there," he said sullenly. "I'm rotten at this here magic."

"Yes, you are," the master agreed. "But your parents have paid for this, and they have a right to expect you to at least make the attempt."

He moved a fancifully braided rug aside with his foot, revealing a trapdoor. This, too, was wizard-locked. Again the master mumbled arcane words. He passed his hand three times over the lock, reached down, clasped hold of an iron ring, and lifted.

The trapdoor opened silently. A set of stone stairs led down into warm, scented darkness.

"Gordo and I will go first," Master Theobald said, adding caustically, "to clear the place of demons."

Grasping the unfortunate Gordo by the scruff of his neck, Theobald dragged him down the stairs. Jon Farnish clattered eagerly after him. Raistlin started to follow. His foot was on the top stair when he froze.

He was about to set foot into an open grave.

He blinked his eyes, and the image vanished. Before him were nothing more sinister than cellar stairs. Still, Raistlin wavered there on the threshold. He had learned from his mother to be sensitive to dreams and portents. He had seen the grave quite clearly and he wondered what it meant, or if it meant anything at all. Probably it was nothing more than his cursed fancy, his overactive imagination. Yet, still, he hovered on the stairs.

Jon Farnish was down there, except it wasn't Jon Farnish. It was Caramon, standing over Raistlin's grave, gazing down at his twin in pitying sorrow.

Raistlin shut his eyes. He was far from this place, in his clearing, seated on the log, the snow falling on him, filling his world, leaving it cold, pure, trackless.

When he opened his eyes, Caramon was gone and so was the grave.

His step quick and firm, Raistlin walked down the stairs.

4

The laboratory was not as Raistlin—or any of the other boys in the class—had imagined. Much speculation had been given to this hidden chamber during clandestine midnight sessions in the dormitory room. The master's laboratory was generally conceded to be pitch dark, knee-deep in cobwebs and bats' eyeballs, with a captured demon imprisoned in a cage in a corner.

The elder boys would whisper to the new boys at the start of the year that the strange sounds they could hear at night were made by the demon rattling his chains, trying to break free. From then on, whenever there was a creak or a bump, the new boys would lie in bed and tremble in fear, believing that the demon had freed itself at last. The night the cat, mousing among the pots and kettles, knocked an iron skillet off the wall caused a general outbreak of panic, with the result that the master, having been wakened by the heartrending cries of terror, heard the story and banned all conversation after the candles had been removed.

Gordo had been one of the most inventive when it came to giving life to the demon in the laboratory, effectively frightening the wits out of the three six-year-olds currently boarding at the school. But it was now apparent that Gordo had scared no one quite as much as himself. When he turned around and actually beheld a cage in the corner, its bars shining in the soft white light cast by a globe suspended from the ceiling, the boy's knees gave way and he sank to the floor.

"Drat the boy, whatever is the matter with you? Stand on your own two feet!" Master Theobald gave Gordo a prod and a shake. "Good evening, my beauties," the master added, peering into the cage. "Here's dinner."

The wretched Gordo turned quite pale, evidently seeing himself as the next course. The master was not referring to the boys, however, but to a hunk of bread that he dredged up from his pocket. He deposited the bread in the cage, where it was immediately set upon by four lively field mice.

Gordo put his hand on his stomach and said he didn't feel so good.

Under other circumstances, Raistlin might have been amused by the discomfiture of one of his most inveterate tormentors. Tonight he was far too pent up, anxious, eager, and nervous to enjoy the whimperings of the chastened bully.

The master made Gordo sit down on the floor with his head between his legs, and then went to a distant part of the laboratory to putter about among papers and inkpots. Bored, Jon Farnish began teasing the mice.

Raistlin moved out of the glare of the light, moved back into the shadows, where he could see without being seen. He made a methodical sweep of the laboratory, committing every detail to his excellent memory. Long years after he left Master Theobald's school, Raistlin could still shut his eyes and see every item in that laboratory, and he was only in it once.

The lab was neat, orderly, and clean. No dust, no cobwebs; even the mice were sleek and well groomed. A few magical spellbooks, bound in noncommittal colors of gray and tan, stood upon a shelf. Six scroll cases reposed in a bin designed to hold many more. There was an assortment of jars intended for storing spell components, but only a few had anything in them. The stone table, on which the master was supposed to perform experiments in the arcane, was as clean as the table on which he ate his dinner.

Raistlin felt a sadness seep into him. Here was the workshop of a man with no ambition, of a man in whom the creative spark had flickered out, presuming that spark had ever once been kindled. Theobald came to his lab not to create, but because he wanted to be alone, to read a book, throw crumbs to the mice in their cage, crush some oregano leaves for the luncheon stew, perhaps draw up a scroll now and then—a scroll whose magic might or might not work. Whether it did or it didn't was all the same to him.

"Feeling better, Gordo?" Master Theobald bustled about importantly, doing very little with a great deal of fuss. "Fine, I knew you would. Too much excitement, that's all. Take your place at the far end of the table. Jon Farnish, you take your place there in the center. Raistlin? Where the devil—oh! There you are!" Master Theobald glared at him crossly. "What are you doing skulking about there in the darkness? Come stand in the light like a civilized human being. You will take your place at the far end. Yes, right there."

Raistlin moved to his assigned seat in silence. Gordo stood hunch-shouldered and glum. The laboratory was a sad disappointment, and this was starting to look far too much like schoolwork. Gordo was bitter over the lack of a demon.

Jon Farnish took his seat, smiling and confident, his hands folded calmly on the table in front of him. Raistlin had never hated anyone in his life as much as he hated Jon Farnish at that moment.

Every organ in Raistlin's body was tangled up with every other organ. His bowels squirmed and wrapped around his stomach, his heart lurched and pressed painfully against his lungs. His mouth was dry, so dry his throat closed and set him coughing. His palms were wet. He wiped his hands surreptitiously on his shirt.

Master Theobald sat at the head of the table. He was grave and solemn and appeared to take exception to the grinning Jon Farnish. He frowned and tapped his finger on the table. Jon Farnish, realizing his mistake, swallowed his grin and was immediately as grave and solemn as a cemetery owl.

"That's better," said the master. "This test you are about to take is quite a serious matter, as serious as the Test you will take when you are grown and prepared to advance through the various ranks of magical knowledge and power. I repeat, this test is every bit as serious, for if you do not pass the one, you will never have a chance to take the other."

Gordo gave a great, gaping yawn.

Master Theobald cast him a reproving glance, then continued. "It would be advisable if we could give this test to every child who enrolls in one of the mage schools prior to his or her entrance. Unfortunately, that is not possible. In order to take this test, you must possess a considerable amount of arcane knowledge. Thus the conclave has deemed that a student should have at least six years of study before taking the elementary test. Those who have completed six years will be given the elementary test even if they have previously shown neither talent nor inclination."

Theobald knew, but did not say, that the failed student would then be placed under surveillance, watched throughout the rest of his life. It was improbable, but such a failure might become a renegade wizard, one who refused to follow the laws of magic as handed down and adjudicated by the conclave. Renegade wizards were considered extremely dangerous—rightly so—and were hunted by the members of the conclave. The boys knew nothing about renegade wizards, and Master Theobald wisely refrained from mentioning it. Gordo would have been a nervous wreck the remainder of his existence.

"The test is simple for one who possesses the talent, extremely difficult for one who does not. Every person wanting to advance in the study of magic takes the same elementary test. You are not casting a spell, not even a cantrip. It will take many more years of study and hard work before you have the discipline and control necessary to cast the most rudimentary of magical spells. This test merely determines whether or not you have what was called in the old days 'the god's gift.' "

He was referring to the old gods of magic, three cousins: Solinari, Lunitari, Nuitari. Their names were all that was left of them, according to most people on Ansalon. Their names clung to their moons, to the silver moon, the red, and the supposed black moon.

Wary of public opinion, aware that they were not universally liked or trusted, the wizards took care not to become involved in religious arguments. They taught their pupils that the moons influenced magic much the way they influenced the tides. It was a physical phenomenon, nothing spiritual or mystical about it.

Yet Raistlin wondered. Had the gods truly gone from the world, leaving only their lights burning in night's window? Or were those lights glints from immortal, ever-watchful eyes? . . .

Master Theobald turned to the wooden shelves behind him, opened a drawer. He drew out three strips of lamb's skin, placed a strip in front of each boy. Jon Farnish was taking this quite seriously now, after the master's speech. Gordo was resigned, sullen, wanting to end this and return to his mates. He was probably already concocting the lies he would tell about the master's laboratory.

Raistlin examined the small strip of lamb's skin, no longer than his forearm. The skin was soft, it had never been used, was smooth to the touch.

The master placed a quill pen and an inkpot in front of each of the three boys. Standing back, he folded his hands over his stomach and said, in solemn, sonorous tones, "You will write down on this lamb's skin the words I, *Magus*."

"Nothing else, Master?" asked Jon Farnish.

"Nothing else."

Gordo squirmed and bit the end of his quill. "How do you spell *Magus*?"

Master Theobald fixed him with a reproving stare. "That is part of the test!"

"What . . . what will happen if we do it right, Master?" Raistlin asked in a voice that he could not recognize as his own.

"If you have the gift, something will happen. If not, nothing," replied Master Theobald. He did not look at Raistlin as he spoke.

He wants me to fail, Raistlin understood, without quite knowing why. The master did not like him, but that wasn't the reason. Raistlin guessed that it had something to do with jealousy of his sponsor, Antimodes. The knowledge strengthened his resolve.

He picked up the quill, which was black, had come from the wing of a crow. Various types of quills were used to write various scrolls: an eagle's feather was extremely powerful, as was that of the swan. A goose quill was for everyday, ordinary writing, only to be used for magical penning in an emergency. A crow quill was useful for almost any type of magic, though some of the more fanatic White Robes objected to its color.

Raistlin touched the feather with his finger. He was extraordinarily conscious of the feather's feel, its crispness contrasting oddly with its softness. Rainbows, cast by the globe light, shimmered on the feather's glistening black surface. The point was newly cut, sharp. No cracked and sputtering pen for this important event.

The smell of the ink reminded him of Antimodes and the time he had praised Raistlin's work. Raistlin had long ago discovered, through eavesdropping on a conversation between the master and Gilon, that Antimodes was paying the bill for this school, not the conclave, as the archmagus had intimated. This test would prove if his investment had been sound.

Raistlin prepared to dip the quill in the ink, then hesitated, feeling a qualm of near panic. Everything he had been taught seemed to slide from his mind, like butter melting in a hot skillet. He could not remember how to spell *Magus*! The quill shook in his sweaty fingers. He glanced sidelong, through lowered lashes, at the other two.

"I'm done," said Gordo.

Ink covered his fingers; he'd managed to splash it on his face, where the black splotches overlapped the brown freckles. He held up the scroll, on which he'd first printed the word *Magos*. Having sneaked a peak at Jon Farnish's scroll, Gordo had hastily crossed out *Magos* and written *Magus* in next to it.

"I'm done," Gordo repeated loudly. "What happens now?"

"For you, nothing," said Theobald with a severe look.

"But I wrote the word just as good as him," Gordo protested, sulking.

"Have you learned nothing, you stupid boy?" Theobald demanded angrily. "A word of magic must be written perfectly, spelled correctly, the first time. You are writing not only with the lamb's blood but with your own blood. The magic flows through you and into the pen and from thence onto the scroll."

"Oh, bugger it," said Gordo, and he shoved the scroll off the table.

Jon Farnish was writing with ease, seemingly, the pen gliding over the sheepskin, a spot of ink on his right forefinger. His handwriting was readable, but tended to be cramped and small.

Raistlin dipped the quill in the ink and began to write, in sharply angled, bold, large letters, the words *I, Magus*.

Jon Farnish sat back, a look of satisfaction on his face. Raistlin, just finishing, heard the boy catch his breath. Raistlin looked up.

The letters on the sheepskin in front of Jon Farnish had begun to glow. The glow was faint, a dim red-orange, a spark newly struck, struggling for life.

"Garn!" said Gordo, impressed. This almost made up for the demon.

"Well done, Jon," said Master Theobald expansively.

Flushed with pleasure, Jon Farnish gazed in awe at the parchment and then he laughed. "I have it!" he cried.

Master Theobald turned his gaze to Raistlin. Though the master attempted to appear concerned, one corner of his lip curled.

The black letters on the sheepskin in front of Raistlin remained black.

Raistlin clutched the quill so violently he snapped off the top. He looked away from the exultant Jon Farnish, he paid no attention to the scornful Gordo, he blotted from his mind the leering triumph of the master. He concentrated on the letters in *I, Magus* and he said a prayer.

"Gods of magic, if you are gods and not just moons, don't let me fail, don't let me falter."

Raistlin turned inward, to the very core of his being, and he vowed, I will do this. Nothing in my life matters except this. No moment of my life exists except this moment. I am born in this moment, and if I fail, I will die in this moment.

Gods of magic, help me! I will dedicate my life to you. I will serve you always. I will bring glory to your name. Help me, please, help me!

He wanted this so much. He had worked so hard for it, for so long. He focused on the magic, concentrated all his energy. His frail body began to wilt beneath the strain. He felt faint and giddy. The globe of light expanded in his dazed vision to three globes. The floor was unsteady beneath him. He lowered his head in despair to the stone table.

The stone was cool and firm beneath his fevered cheek. He shut his eyes, hot tears burned the lids. He could still see, imprinted on his eyelids, the three globes of magical light.

To his astonishment, he saw that inside each globe was a person.

One was a fine, handsome young man, dressed all in white robes that shimmered with a silver light. He was strong and well muscled, with the physique of a warrior. He carried in his hand a staff of wood, topped by a golden dragon's claw holding a diamond.

Another was also a young man, but he was not handsome. He was grotesque. His face was as round as a moon, his eyes were dry, dark and empty wells. He was dressed in black robes, and he held in his hands a crystal orb, inside which swirled the heads of five dragons: red, green, blue, white, and black.

Standing between the two was a beautiful young woman. Her hair was as black as the crow's wing, streaked with white. Her robes were as red as blood. She held, in her arms, a large leather-bound book.

The three were vastly different, strangely alike.

"Do you know who we are?" asked the man in white.

Raistlin nodded hesitantly. He knew them. He wasn't quite sure he understood why or how.

"You pray to us, yet many speak our names with their lips only, not their hearts. Do you truly believe in us?" asked the woman in red.

Raistlin considered this question. "You came to me, didn't you?" he answered.

The glib answer displeased the god of light and the god of darkness. The man with the moon face grew colder, and the man in white looked grim. The woman in red was pleased with him, however. She smiled.

Solinari spoke sternly. "You are very young. Do you understand the promise you have made to us? The promise to worship us and glorify our names? To do so will go against the beliefs of many, may put you into mortal danger."

"I understand," Raistlin answered without hesitation.

Nuitari spoke next, his voice like splinters of ice. "Are you prepared to make the sacrifices we will require of you?"

"I am prepared," Raistlin answered steadily, adding, but only to himself, after all, what more can you demand of me that I have not already given?

The three heard his unspoken response. Solinari shook his head. Nuitari wore a most sinister grin.

Lunitari's laughter danced through Raistlin, exhilarating, disturbing. "You do not understand. And if you could foresee what will be asked of you in the future, you would run from this place and never come back. Still, we have watched you and we have been impressed with you. We grant your request on one condition. Remember always that you have seen us and spoken to us. Never deny your faith in us, or we will deny you."

The three globes of light coalesced into one, looking very much like an eye, with a white rim, a red iris, a black pupil. The eye blinked once and then remained wide open, staring.

The words *I, Magus* were all he could see, black on white lamb's skin.

"Are you ill, Raistlin?" The master's voice, as through a dank fog.

"Shut up!" Raistlin breathed. Doesn't the fool know they are here? Doesn't he know they are watching, waiting?

"*I, Magus.*" Raistlin whispered the words aloud. Black on white, he imbued them with his heart's blood.

The black letters began to glow red, like the sword resting in the blacksmith's forge fire. The letters burned hotter and brighter until I, Magus was traced in letters of flame. The lamb's skin blackened, curled in upon itself, was consumed. The fire died.

Raistlin, exhausted, sagged on his stool. On the stone table before him was nothing but a charred spot and bits of greasy ash. Inside him burned a fire that would never be quenched, perhaps not even in death.

He heard a noise, a sort of strangled croak.

Master Theobald, Gordo, and Jon Farnish were all staring at him, wide-eyed and openmouthed.

Raistlin slid off his stool, made a polite bow to the master. "May I be excused now, sir?"

Theobald nodded silently, unable to speak. He would later tell the story at the conclave, tell of the remarkable test performed by one of his young pupils, relate how the lamb's skin had been devoured by the flames. Theobald added, with due modesty, that it was his skill as a teacher that had undoubtedly inspired his young pupil, wrought such a miracle.

Antimodes would make a special point to inform Par-Salian, who noted the incident with an asterisk next to Raistlin's name in the book where he kept a list of every student of magic in Ansalon.

That night, when the others were asleep, Raistlin wrapped himself in his thick cloak and slipped outside.

The snow had stopped falling. The stars and moons were scattered like a rich lady's jewels across the black sky. Solinari was a shining diamond. Lunitari a bright ruby. Nuitari, ebony and onyx, could not be seen, but he was there. He was there.

The snow glistened white and pure and untouched in the lambent light of stars and moons. The trees cast double shadows that streaked the white with black, black tinged with blood-red.

Raistlin looked up at the moons and he laughed, ringing laughter that echoed among the trees, laughter that could be heard all the way to heaven. He dashed headlong into the woods, trampling the white unbroken snowbanks, leaving his tracks, his mark.

BOOK 3

The magic is in the blood, it flows from the heart. Every time you use it, part of yourself goes with it. Only when you are prepared to give of yourself and receive nothing back will the magic work for you.

—Theobald Beckman, Master

I

Raistlin sat on his stool in the classroom, hunched over his desk, laboriously copying a spell. It was a sleep spell, simple for an experienced wizard, but still far beyond the reach of a sixteen-year-old, no matter how precocious. Raistlin knew this because, though he had been forbidden to do so, he had attempted to cast the spell.

Armed with his elementary spellbook, smuggled out of school beneath his shirt, and the requisite spell component, Raistlin had tried to cast the sleep spell on his uneasy but steadfastly loyal brother. He had spoken the words, flung the sand into Caramon's face, and waited.

"Stop that, Caramon! Put your hands down."

"But, Raist! I got sand in my eyes!"

"You're supposed to be asleep!"

"I'm sorry, Raist. I guess I'm just not tired. It's almost suppertime."

With a deep sigh, Raistlin had returned the spellbook to its place at his desk, the sand to its jar in the laboratory. He had been forced to acknowledge that perhaps Master Theobald knew what he was talking about—on this occasion, at least. Casting a magic spell required something more than words and sand. If that was all it took, Gordo would have been a mage and not slaughtering sheep, as he was now.

"The magic comes from within," Master Theobald had lectured. "It begins at the center of your being, flows outward. The words pick up the magic as it surges from your heart up into your brain and from thence into your mouth. Speaking the words, you give the magic form and substance, and thus you cast the spell. Words spoken from an empty mouth do nothing but move the lips."

And though Raistlin more than suspected Master Theobald of having copied this lecture from someone else (in fact, Raistlin was to find it several years later, in a book written by Par-Salian), the young student had been impressed by the words and had noted them down carefully in the front of his spellbook.

That speech was in his thoughts as he copied—for the hundredth time—the spell onto scrap paper, preparatory to copying the spell into his primer. A leather-bound book, the primer was given to each novice mage who had passed his initial test. The novitiate would copy into his primer every spell committed to memory. In addition, he must also know how to pronounce correctly the words of the spell and how to write it onto a scroll, and he must know and have collected any components that the spell required.

Every quarter Master Theobald tested the novitiates—there were two in his school, Raistlin and Jon Farnish—on the spells they had learned. If the students performed to the master's satisfaction, they were permitted to write the spell into their primers. Only yesterday, at the end of the spring quarter, Raistlin had taken the test on his new spell and had passed it easily. Jon Farnish, by contrast, had failed, having transposed two letters in the third word. Master Theobald had given Raistlin permission to copy down the spell—the very sleep spell he had attempted to cast—into his primer. The master had sent Jon Farnish to copy the spell out two hundred times, until he could write it correctly.

Raistlin knew the sleep spell backward and forward and inside out. He could have written it upside down while standing on his head. Yet he could not make it work. He had even prayed to the gods of magic, asking for their help, as they had given him help during his elementary test. The gods were not forthcoming.

He did not doubt the gods. He doubted himself. It was some fault within him, something he was doing wrong. And so, instead of copying the spell into his primer, Raistlin was doing much the same as Jon Farnish, going over and over the words, meticulously writing down every letter until he could convince himself that he had not made a single mistake.

A shadow—a broad shadow—fell across his page.

He looked up. "Yes, Master?" he said, trying to hide his irritation at the interruption and not quite succeeding.

Raistlin had long ago realized that he was smarter than

Master Theobald and more gifted in magic. He stayed in the school because there was nowhere else to go, and, as this proved, he still had much to learn. Master Theobald could cast a sleep spell.

"Do you know what time it is?" Master Theobald asked. "It is dinnertime. You should be in the common room with the other boys."

"Thank you, but I'm not hungry, Master," Raistlin said ungraciously and went back to his work.

Master Theobald frowned. A well-fed man himself, one who enjoyed his meat and ale, he could not understand someone like Raistlin, to whom food was fuel to keep his body going and nothing more.

"Nonsense, you have to eat. What are you doing that is so important it causes you to skip a meal?"

Master Theobald could see perfectly well what Raistlin was doing.

"I am working at copying this spell, Master," Raistlin said, gritting his teeth at the man's idiocy. "I do not feel ready yet to write in my primer."

Master Theobald looked down at the scraps of paper littering the desk. He picked up one, then another. "But these are adequate. Quite good, in fact."

"No, there must be something wrong!" Raistlin said impatiently. "Otherwise I could have been able to cast—"

He had not meant to say that. He bit his tongue and fell silent, glowering down at his ink-stained fingers.

"Ah," said Master Theobald, with the ghost of a smile, which, since Raistlin was not looking, he did not see. "So you have been attempting a little spellcasting, have you?"

Raistlin did not reply. If he could have cast a spell now, he would have summoned demons from the Abyss and ordered them to haul off Master Theobald.

The master leaned back and laced his fingers over his stomach, which meant that he was about to launch into one of his lectures.

"It didn't work, I take it. I'm not surprised. You are far too proud, young man. Far too self-absorbed and self-satisfied. You are a taker, not a giver. Everything flows into you. Nothing flows out. The magic is in the blood, it flows from the heart. Every time you use it, part of yourself goes with it. Only when you are prepared to give of yourself and receive nothing back will the magic work for you."

Raistlin lifted his head, shook his long, straight brown hair out of his face. He stared straight ahead. "Yes, Master," he said coldly, impassively. "Thank you, Master."

Master Theobald's tongue clicked against the roof of his mouth. "You are seated on a very high horse right now, young man. Someday you will fall off. If the fall doesn't kill you, you might learn something from it." The master grunted. "I'm going to dinner now. I'm hungry."

Raistlin returned to his work, a scornful smile curling his lips.

2

That summer, the summer of the twins' sixteenth year, life for the Majere family continued to improve. Gilon had been hired to help cut a stand of pines on the slopes of Prayer's Eye Peak. The property belonged to an absentee lord, who was having the wood hauled north to build a stockade. The job paid well and looked as if it would last a long time, for the stockade was going to be a large one.

Caramon worked full time for the prospering Farmer Sedge, who had extended his land holdings and was now shipping grain, fruits, and vegetables to the markets of Haven. Caramon worked long hours for a portion of the crops, some of which he sold, the rest he brought home.

The Widow Judith was considered a member of the family. She maintained her own small house, but for all practical purposes, she lived at the Majeres'. Rosamun could not manage without her. Rosamun herself was much improved. She had not fallen into one of her trancelike states in several years. She and the widow performed the chores around the house and spent much of their time visiting the neighbors.

Had Gilon known exactly what such visits entailed, he might have been worried about his wife. But he assumed Rosamun and the widow were doing nothing more than sharing the latest gossip. He could not know, nor would he have believed, the truth of the matter.

Gilon and Caramon both liked the Widow Judith. Raistlin grew to dislike her more than ever, perhaps because during the summer he was home with her, whereas the other two were not. He saw the influence the widow wielded over his mother, and he disliked and distrusted it. More than once, he came in on their whispered conversations, conversations that would end abruptly upon his arrival.

He tried to eavesdrop, hoping to hear what the two were saying. The Widow Judith had excellent hearing, however, and he was usually discovered. One day, however, the two women happened to be sitting at the kitchen table beneath a window where several pies were cooling. Walking up on them from outside, his footsteps lost among the rustling of the leaves of the vallenwood tree, Raistlin heard their voices. He halted in the shadows.

"The High Priest is not pleased with you, Rosamun Majere. I have had a letter from him this day. He wonders why you have not brought your husband and children into the arms of Belzor."

Rosamun's response was meek and defensive. She had tried. She had spoken to Gilon of Belzor several times, but her husband had only laughed at her. He did not need to have faith in any god. He had faith in himself and his good right arm and that was that. Caramon said he was quite willing to attend the meetings of the Belzorites, especially if they served food. As for Raistlin . . . Rosamun's voice trailed off.

As for Raistlin, he was eager to hear more, but at that moment the Widow Judith rose to see to the pies and saw him standing at the corner of the house. He and Judith looked intently at each other. Neither gave anything away to the other, however, except a shared enmity. The Widow Judith brought in the pies and closed the shutters. Raistlin continued on to his garden.

Who in the Abyss is this Belzor, he wondered, and why does he want to embrace us?

"It's some sort of thing of mother's," said Caramon, upon questioning. "You know. One of those woman things. They all meet together and talk about stuff. What kind of stuff? I don't know. I went once but I fell asleep."

Rosamun never said anything to Raistlin about Belzor, rather to Raistlin's disappointment. He considered bringing up the matter himself, but he feared this would involve talking to the Widow Judith, and he avoided contact with her as much as possible. The master was off on his visit to the conclave. School was out for the summer. Raistlin spent his days planting, cultivating, and adding to his collection of herbs. He was gaining some small reputation among the neighbors for his knowledge of herbs, sold what he himself did not need and thus was able to contribute to the family's income. He forgot about Belzor.

The Majere family was happy and prosperous that summer, a summer that would stand out in the twins' minds as golden, a gold that shone all the more brightly in contrast to the coming darkness.

* * * * *

Raistlin and Caramon were walking along the road leading to Solace, returning from Farmer Sedge's. Caramon was coming back from work. Raistlin had gone to the farmer's to deliver a bundle of dried lavender. His clothes still smelled of the fragrant flower. From that time, he would never be able to abide the scent of lavender.

As they neared Solace, a small boy sighted them, began waving his arms, and broke into a run. He came pounding along the dusty track to meet them.

"Hullo, young Ned," said Caramon, who knew every child in town. "I can't play Goblin Ball with you right now, but maybe after dinner we—"

"Hush, Caramon," Raistlin ordered tersely. The child was wide-eyed and solemn as an owlet. "Can't you see? Something's wrong. What is it? What has happened?"

"There's been an accident," the boy managed to gasp, out of breath. "Your . . . your father."

He might have said more, but he'd lost his audience. The twins were racing for home. Raistlin ran as fast as he could for a short distance, but not even fear and adrenaline could keep his frail body going for long. His strength gave out and he was forced to slow down. Caramon kept going but, after a few moments, realized he was alone. He paused to look behind for his brother. Raistlin waved his brother on ahead.

Are you sure? Caramon's worried look asked.

I am sure, Raistlin's look answered.

Caramon nodded once, turned, and kept running. Raistlin made what haste he could, anxiety knotting his stomach and chilling him, causing him to shiver in the summer sunshine. Raistlin was surprised at his reaction. He had not supposed he cared this much for his father.

They had driven Gilon in a wagon from Prayer's Eye Peak back to Solace. Raistlin arrived to find his father still in the wagon with a crowd gathered around. At the news of the accident, almost everyone in town who could leave his work had come running, come to stare at the unfortunate man in mingled horror, concern, and curiosity.

Rosamun stood at the side of the wagon, holding fast to her husband's bloodstained hand and weeping. The Widow Judith was at her side.

"Have faith in Belzor," the widow was saying, "and he will be healed. Have faith."

"I do," Rosamun was saying over and over through pale lips. "I do have faith. Oh, my poor husband. You will be well. I have faith. . . ."

People standing nearby glanced at each other and shook their heads. Someone went to fetch the stable owner, who was supposed to know all about setting broken bones. Otik arrived from the inn, his chubby face drawn and grieved. He had brought along a jug of his finest brandy, his customary offering in any medical emergency.

"Tie Gilon to a stretcher," the Widow Judith said. "We'll carry him up the stairs. He will mend better in his own home."

A dwarf, a fellow townsman whom Raistlin knew by sight, glowered at her. "Are you daft, woman! Jouncing him around like that will kill him!"

"He shall not die!" said the Widow Judith loudly. "Belzor will save him!"

The townspeople standing around exchanged glances. Some rolled their eyes, but others looked interested and attentive.

"He better do it fast, then," muttered the dwarf, standing on tiptoe to peer into the wagon. Beside him, a kender was jumping up and down, clamoring, "Let me see, Flint! Let me see!"

Caramon had climbed into the wagon. Almost as pale as his father, Caramon crouched beside Gilon, anxious and helpless. At the sight of the terrible injuries—Gilon's cracked rib bones protruded through his flesh, and one leg was little more than a sodden mass of blood and bone—a low, animal-like moan escaped Caramon's lips.

Rosamun paid no attention to her stricken son. She stood at the side of the wagon, clutching Gilon's hand and whispering frantically about having faith.

"Raist!" Caramon cried in a hollow voice, looking around in panic.

"I am here, my brother," Raistlin said quietly. He climbed into the wagon beside Caramon.

Caramon grasped hold of his twin's hand thankfully, gave a shuddering sigh. "Raist! What can we do? We have to do something. Think of something to do, Raist!"

"There's nothing to do, son," said the dwarf kindly. "Nothing except wish your father well on his next journey."

Raistlin examined the injured man and knew immediately that the dwarf was right. How Gilon had managed to live this long was a mystery.

"Belzor is here!" the Widow Judith intoned shrilly. "Belzor will heal this man!"

Belzor, Raistlin thought bitterly, is taking his own sweet time.

"Father!" Caramon cried out.

At the sound of his son's voice, Gilon shifted his eyes—he could not move his head—and searched for his sons.

His gaze found them, rested on them. "Take care . . . your mother," he managed to whisper. A froth of blood coated his lips.

Caramon sobbed and covered his face with his hand.

"We will, Father," Raistlin promised.

Gilon's gaze encompassed both his sons. He managed a fleeting smile, then looked over at Rosamun. He started to say something, but a tremor of pain shook him. He closed his eyes in agony, gave a great groan, and lay still.

The dwarf removed his hat, held it to his chest. "Reorx walk with him," he said softly.

"The poor man's dead. Oh, how sad!" said the kender, and a tear trickled down his cheek.

It was the first time death had come so close to Raistlin. He felt it as a physical presence, passing among them, dark wings spreading over them. He felt small and insignificant, naked and vulnerable.

So sudden. An hour ago Gilon had walked among the trees, thinking of nothing more important than what he might enjoy for dinner that night.

So dark. Endless darkness, eternal. It was not the absence of light that was as frightening as the absence of thought, of knowledge, of comprehension. Our lives, the lives of the living, will go on. The sun shines, the moons rise, we will laugh and talk, and he will know nothing, feel nothing. Nothing.

So final. It will come to us all. It will come to me.

Raistlin thought he should be grieved or sorrowful for his father, but all he felt was sorrow for himself, grief for his own mortality. He turned away from the broken corpse, only to find his mother still clinging to the lifeless hand, stroking the cooling flesh, urging Gilon to speak to her.

"Caramon, we have to see to Mother," Raistlin said urgently.

"We must take her home."

But on turning, he found that Caramon was in need of assistance himself. He had collapsed near the body of his father. Painful, choking sobs wrenched him. Raistlin rested his hand comfortingly on Caramon's arm.

Caramon's big hand closed convulsively around his twin's. Raistlin could not free himself, nor did he want to. He found comfort in his brother's touch. But he didn't like the fey look on his mother's face.

"Come, Mother. Let the Widow Judith take you home."

"No, no!" cried Rosamun frantically. "I must not leave your father. He needs me."

"Mother," Raistlin said, now starting to be frightened. "Father is dead. There is nothing more—"

"Dead!" Rosamun looked bewildered. "Dead! No! He can't be! I have faith."

Rosamun flung herself on her husband. Her hands grasped his blood-soaked shirt. "Gilon! Wake up!"

Gilon's head lolled. A trickle of blood flowed from his mouth.

"I have faith," Rosamun repeated with a heartbroken whimper. Her hands were bloody, she clung to the blood-soaked shirt.

"Mother, please, go home!" Raistlin pleaded helplessly.

Otik took hold of Rosamun's hands and gently freed her grip. Another neighbor hurriedly covered the body with a blanket.

"So much for Belzor," said the dwarf in a grating undertone.

He had not meant his words to be overheard, but his voice was deep and had a good carrying quality to it. Everyone standing around heard him. A few looked shocked. Several shook their heads. One or two smiled grimly when they thought no one was watching.

The Widow Judith had done a good deal of proselytizing since her arrival in town, and she'd gained more than a few converts to her new faith. Some of those converts were regarding the dead man with dismay.

"Who's Belzor?" the kender asked eagerly in shrill tones. "Flint, do you know Belzor? Was he supposed to heal this poor man? Why didn't he, do you suppose?"

"Hush your mouth, Tas, you doorknob!" the dwarf said in a harsh whisper.

But this was a question many of the faithful newcomers were asking themselves. They looked to the Widow Judith for an answer.

The Widow Judith had not lost her faith. Her face hardened. She glared at the dwarf, glared even more fiercely at the kender, who was now lifting the corner of the blanket for a curious peep at the corpse.

"Perhaps he's been healed and we just haven't noticed," the kender offered helpfully.

"He has not been healed!" The Widow Judith cried out in dolorous tones. "Gilon Majere has not been healed, nor will he be healed. Why not, do you ask? Because of the sinfulness of this woman!" The Widow Judith pointed at Rosamun. "Her daughter is a whore! Her son is a witch! It is her fault and the fault of her children that Gilon Majere died!"

The pointing finger might have been a spear ripping through Rosamun's body. She stared at Judith in shock, then screamed and sank to her knees, moaning.

Raistlin was on his feet, climbing over the body of his father. "How dare you?" he said softly, menacingly to the widow. Reaching the side of the wagon, he vaulted out. "Get out of here!" He came face-to-face with the widow. "Leave us alone!"

"You see!" The Widow Judith backed up precipitously. The pointing finger shifted to Raistlin. "He is evil! He does the bidding of evil gods!"

A fire blazed up within Raistlin, blazed up white hot, consumed sense, consumed reason. He could see nothing in the glare of the blaze. He didn't care if the fire destroyed him, just so long as it destroyed Judith.

"Raist!" A hand grabbed him. A hand, strong and firm, reached into the midst of the blaze and grasped hold of him. "Raist! Stop!"

The hand, his brother's hand, dragged Raistlin out of the fire. The terrible white-hot glare that had blinded him died, the fire died, leaving him cold and shivering, with a taste of ashes in his mouth. Caramon's strong arms wrapped around Raistlin's thin shoulders.

"Don't harm her, Raist," Caramon was saying. His voice came out a croak, his throat was raw from weeping. "Don't prove her right!"

The widow, white-faced and blenching, had backed up against a tree. She glanced about at her neighbors. "You saw, good people of Solace! He tried to kill me. He's a fiend in human clothing, I tell you! Send this mother and her demon spawn away! Cast them out of Solace! Show Belzor that you will not tolerate such evil!"

The crowd was silent, their faces dark and impassive. Moving slowly, they came together to form a circle—a protective circle with the Majere family in the center. Rosamun crouched on the ground, her head bowed. Raistlin and Caramon stood close together, near their mother. Although Kitiara was not there—she had not been with the family in years—her spirit had been invoked, and she was also present, if only in the minds of her siblings. Gilon lay dead in the wagon, his body covered by a blanket. His blood was starting to seep through the wool. The Widow Judith stood outside the circle, and still no one spoke.

A man shoved his way through from the back of the crowd. Raistlin had only an indistinct impression of him; the still-smoldering fire within clouded his vision. But he would remember him as tall, clean-shaven, with long hair that covered his ears, fell to his shoulders. He was clad in leather, trimmed with fringe, and wore a bow over one shoulder.

He walked up to the widow.

"I think you are the one who had better leave Solace," he said. His voice was quiet, he wasn't threatening her, merely stating a fact.

The widow scowled at him and flashed a glance around at the people in the crowd behind him. "Are you going to let this half-breed talk to me like this?" she demanded.

"Tanis is right," said Otik, waddling forward to lend his support. He waved a pudgy hand, in which he still held his brandy jug. "You just go along back to Haven, my good woman. And take Belzor with you. He's not needed around here. We care for our own."

"Take your mother home, lads," said the dwarf. "Don't fret about your pa. We'll see to the burial. You'll want to be there, of course. We'll let you know when it's time."

Raistlin nodded, unable to speak. He bent down, grasped hold of his mother. She was limp in his hands, limp and shredded, like a rag doll that has been worried and torn by savage dogs. She gazed about her with a vacuous expression that Raistlin remembered well; his heart shriveled within him.

"Mother," he said in a choked voice. "We're going to go home now."

Rosamun did not respond. She did not seem to have heard him. She sagged, dead weight, in his arms.

"Caramon?" Raistlin looked to his brother.

Caramon nodded, his eyes filled with tears.

Between them, they carried their mother home.

3

The following morning, Gilon Majere was buried beneath the vallenwoods, a seedling planted on his grave as was customary among the inhabitants of Solace. His sons came to the ceremony. His wife did not.

"She's sleeping," said Caramon with a blush for his lie. "We didn't want to wake her."

The truth was, they couldn't wake her.

By afternoon, everyone in Solace knew that Rosamun Majere had fallen into one of her trances. She had fallen deep this time, so deep that she could hear no voice—however loved—that called to her.

The neighbors came, offering condolences and suggestions to aid in her recovery, some of which—the use of spirits of hartshorn, for instance, which she was to inhale—Raistlin tried. Others, such as jabbing her repeatedly with a pin, he did not.

At least not at first. Not before the terrible fear set in.

The neighbors brought food to tempt her appetite, for the word spread among their friends that Rosamun would not eat. Otik himself brought an immense basket of delicacies from the Inn of the Last Home, including a steaming pot of his famous spiced potatoes, Otik being firm in the belief that no living being and very few of the unliving could hold out long against that wonderful garlic-scented aroma.

Caramon took the food with a wan smile and a quiet thank-you. He did not let Otik into the house but stood blocking the door with his big body.

"Is she any better?" Otik asked, craning to see over Caramon's shoulder.

Otik was a good man, one of the best in Solace. He would have given away his beloved inn if he had thought that would have helped the sick woman. But he did enjoy gossip, and Gilon's tragic death and his wife's strange illness were the talk of the common room.

Caramon finally managed to close the door. He stood listening a moment to Otik's heavy footsteps tromping across the boardwalk, heard him stop to talk to several of the ladies of the town. Caramon heard his mother's name mentioned frequently. Sighing, he took the food into the kitchen and stacked it up with all the rest of the provisions.

He ladled spiced potatoes into a bowl, added a tempting slab of ham fresh baked in cider, and poured a glass of elven wine. He intended to take them to his mother, but he paused on the threshold of her bedroom.

Caramon loved his mother. A good son was supposed to love his mother, and Caramon had been as good a son as he knew how to be. He was not close to his mother. He felt closer to Kitiara, who had done more to raise both him and Raistlin than had Rosamun. Caramon pitied his mother with all his heart. He was extremely sad and worried for her, but he had to steel himself to enter that room as he imagined he would one day have to steel himself to enter battle.

The sickroom was dark and hot, the air fetid and unpleasant to breathe and to smell. Rosamun lay on her back on the bed, staring up at nothing. Yet she saw something, apparently, for her eyes moved and changed expression. Sometimes the eyes were wide, the pupils dilated, as if what she saw terrified her. At these times, her breathing grew rapid and shallow. At other times, she was calm. Sometimes she would even smile, a ghastly smile that was heartbreaking to see.

She never spoke, at least that they could understand. She made sounds, but these were guttural, incoherent. She never closed her eyes. She never slept. Nothing roused her or caused her to look away from whatever visions she saw, visions that held her enthralled.

Her bodily functions continued. Raistlin cleaned up after her, bathed her. It had been three days since Gilon's burial, and Raistlin had not left his mother's side. He slept on a pallet on the floor, waking at the least sound she made. He talked to her constantly, telling her funny stories about the pranks the boys played at school, telling her about his own hopes and dreams, telling her about his herb garden and the plants he grew there.

He forced her to take liquid by dipping a cloth in water, then holding it to her lips and squeezing it into her mouth, only a trickle at a time lest she choke on it. He had tried feeding her, too, but she had been unable to swallow the food, and he had been forced to give this up. He handled her gently, with infinite tenderness and unflagging patience.

Caramon stood in the doorway, watching the two of them. Raistlin sat beside his mother's bed, brushing out her long hair and reciting to her stories of her own girlhood in Palanthas.

You think you know my brother, Caramon said, talking silently to a line of faces. You, Master Theobald, and you, Jon Farnish, and you, Sturm Brightblade, and all the rest of you. You call him "Sly" and "Sneak." You say he's cold and calculating and unfeeling. You think you know him. I know him. Caramon's eyes filled with tears. I know him. I'm the only one.

He waited another moment until he could see again, wiping his eyes and his nose on the sleeve of his shirt, slopping the wine over himself in the process. This done, he drew in a last, deep breath of fresh air and then entered the dark and dismal sickroom.

"I brought some food, Raist," said Caramon.

Raistlin glanced at his brother, then turned back to Rosamun. "She won't eat it."

"I . . . uh . . . meant it for you, Raist. You got to eat something. You'll get sick if you don't," Caramon added, seeing his brother's head start to move in negation. "And if you get sick, what will I do? I'm not a very good nurse, Raist."

Raistlin looked up at his brother. "You don't give yourself enough credit, my brother. I remember times when I was ill. You would make shadow pictures on the wall for me. Rabbits . . ." His voice died away.

Caramon's throat closed, choked by tears. He blinked them away quickly and held out the plate. "C'mon, Raist. Eat. Just a little. It's Otik's potatoes."

"His panacea for all the ills of the world," Raistlin said, his mouth twisting. "Very well."

He replaced the brush on a small nightstand. Taking the plate, he ate some of the potatoes and nibbled a little on the ham. Caramon watched anxiously. His face fell in disappointment when Raistlin handed back the plate, still more than half filled with food.

"Is that all you want? Are you sure? Can I get you something else? We've got lots."

Raistlin shook his head.

Rosamun made a sound, a pitiful murmur. Raistlin moved

swiftly to attend her, bending over her, talking to her soothingly, helping her to lie more comfortably. He moistened her lips with water, chaffed the thin hands.

"Is . . . is she any better?" Caramon asked helplessly.

He could tell at a glance she wasn't. But he hoped he might be wrong. Besides, he felt the need to say something, to hear his own voice. He didn't like it when the house was so strangely quiet. He didn't like being cooped up in this dark, unhappy room. He wondered how his brother could stand it.

"No," Raistlin said. "If anything, she is worse." He paused a moment, and when he spoke next, his voice was hushed, awed. "It's as if she's running down a road, Caramon, running away from me. I follow after her, I call to her to stop, but she doesn't hear me. She doesn't pay any attention to me. She is running very fast, Caramon. . . ."

Raistlin stopped talking, turned away. He pretended to busy himself with the blankets.

"Take that plate back to the kitchen," he ordered, his voice harsh. "It will draw mice."

"I'll . . . I'll take the plate back to the kitchen," Caramon mumbled and hurried off.

Once in the kitchen, he flung the plate toward what he assumed was the table; he couldn't see very well for the blur in his eyes. Someone knocked on the door, but he ignored it, and after a while whoever it was went away. Caramon leaned against the fireplace, gulping in deep breaths, blinking very hard and fast, willing himself not to cry anymore.

Regaining his composure, he returned to the sickroom. He had news that would, he hoped, bring a small amount of cheer to his twin.

He found Raistlin seated once more by the bed. Rosamun lay in the same position, her staring eyes sunken in her head. Her wasted hands lay limp on the counterpane. Her wristbones seemed unnaturally large. Her flesh seemed to be slipping away with her spirit. She appeared to have deteriorated in just the few moments Caramon was gone. He shifted his gaze hurriedly away from her, kept it focused on his twin.

"Otik was here," Caramon said unnecessarily, for his brother had surely deduced this from the arrival of the potatoes. "He said that the Widow Judith left Solace this morning."

"Did she," Raistlin said, a statement, not a question. He looked around. A flicker of flame lit his red-rimmed eyes. "Where did she go?"

"Back to Haven." Caramon managed a grin. "She's gone to report us to Belzor. She left claiming he was going to come here and make us sorry we were ever born."

An unfortunate choice of phrase. Raistlin winced and looked quickly at their mother. Caramon took two swift steps, laid his hand on his brother's shoulder, gripped it hard.

"You can't think that, Raist!" he admonished. "You can't think that this is your fault!"

"Isn't it?" Raistlin returned bitterly. "If it hadn't been for me, Judith would have let mother alone. That woman came because of me, Caramon. I was the one she was after. Mother asked me to quit my magic once. I wondered why she should say such a thing. It was Judith, hounding her. If I had only known at the—"

"What would you have done, Raistlin?" Caramon interrupted. He crouched down beside his brother's chair, looked up at him earnestly. "What would you have done? Quit your school? Given up the magic? Would you have done that?"

Raistlin sat silent a moment, his hands absently plucking the folds of his worn shirt. "No," he said finally. "But I would have talked to mother. I would have explained to her."

He glanced at his mother. Reaching out, he took hold of the pitifully thin hand, squeezed it, not very gently, willing to see some response, even a grimace of pain.

He could have crushed that hand in his hand, crushed it like an empty eggshell, and Rosamun would have never so much as blinked. Sighing, he looked back at Caramon.

"It wouldn't have made any difference, would it, my brother?" Raistlin asked softly.

"None in the world," Caramon said. "None at all."

Raistlin released his mother's hand. The marks of his fingers were red on her pallid flesh. He took hold of his brother's hand and held it tightly. They sat together in silence for long moments, finding comfort in each other, then Raistlin looked quizzically at his brother.

"You are wise, Caramon. Did you know that?"

Caramon laughed, a great guffaw that broke like thunder in the dark room, alarmed him. He clapped his hand over his mouth, flushed red.

"No, I'm not, Raist," he said in a smothered whisper. "You know me. Stupid as a gully dwarf. Everyone says so. You got all the brains. But that's all right. You need them. I don't. Not so long as we're together."

Raistlin abruptly released his grip. He drew his hand away

and averted his face. "There is a difference between wisdom and intelligence, my brother." His voice was cold. "A person may have one without the other. Why don't you go for a walk? Or go back to work for your farmer?"

"But, Raist—"

"It's not necessary for both of us to remain here. I can manage."

Caramon rose slowly to his feet. "Raist, I don't—"

"Please, Caramon!" Raistlin said. "If you must know the truth, you fidget and fuss, and that drives me to distraction. You will feel better for the fresh air and exercise, and I will be better for the solitude."

"Sure, Raist," Caramon said. "If that's what you want. I'll . . . I guess I'll go see Sturm. His mother came to call and brought some fresh-baked bread. I'll just go and say thank you."

"You do that," Raistlin said dryly.

Caramon never knew what brought on these sudden dark and bitter moods, never knew what he'd said or done that quenched the light in his brother as surely as if he'd doused him with cold water. He waited a moment to see if his brother might relent, say something more, ask him to stay and keep him company. But Raistlin was dipping a bit of cloth into a pitcher of water. He held the cloth to Rosamun's lips.

"You must drink a little of this, Mother," he said softly.

Caramon sighed, turned, and left.

A day later, Rosamun was dead.

4

The twins buried their mother in the grave next to their father. Only a few people stood with them at the burial. The day was wet and chill, with a touch of early autumn in the air. Rain poured down steadily, soaking to the skin those who gathered around the grave. The rain drummed on the wooden coffin, formed a small pool in the grave. The vallenwood sprig they planted drooped, sad and forlorn, half-drowned.

Raistlin stood bareheaded in the rain, though Caramon had several times anxiously urged him to cover his head with the hood of his cloak. Raistlin did not hear his brother's pleas. He heard nothing but the fall of the drops on the wooden coffin, a small coffin, almost that of a child. Rosamun had shrunk to skin and bones in those last terrible days. It was as if whatever she was seeing held her fast in its claws, gnawed her flesh, fed off her, devoured her.

Raistlin knew he himself was going to fall ill. He recognized the symptoms. The fever already burned in his blood. He was alternately sweating and shivering. His muscles ached. He wanted so much to sleep, but every time he tried, he heard his mother's voice calling to him, and he would be instantly awake.

Awake to the silence, the dreadful silence.

He wanted to cry at the burial, but he did not. He forced the tears back down his throat. It wasn't that he was ashamed of them. He did not know for certain for whom he wept—for his dead mother or for himself.

He was not aware of the ceremony, was not aware of the passage of time. He might have been standing on the edge of that grave all his life. He knew it was over only when Caramon plucked at his sleeve. At that, it wasn't Caramon who convinced his twin to leave but the sound of the dirt clods striking the coffin, a hollow sound that sent a shudder through Raistlin.

He took a step, stumbled, and nearly fell into the grave. Caramon caught him, steadied him.

"Raist! You're burning up!" Caramon exclaimed in concern.

"Did you hear her, Caramon?" Raistlin asked anxiously, peering down at the coffin. "Did you hear her calling for me?"

Caramon put his arm around his twin. "We have to get you home," he said firmly.

"We must hurry!" Raistlin gasped, shoving aside his brother's hand. He seemed intent on leaping into the grave. "She's calling me."

But he couldn't walk properly. Something was wrong with the ground. It rolled like the back of a leviathan, rolled and pitched him off.

He was sinking, sinking into the grave. The dirt was falling on him, and still he could hear her voice. . . .

Raistlin collapsed, fell to the ground at the graveside. His eyes closed. He lay unmoving in the mud and fallen leaves.

Caramon bent over him. "Raist!" he called, giving him a little shake.

His twin did not respond. Caramon glanced around. He was alone with his brother, except for the gravedigger, who was shoveling as rapidly as he could to get in out of the wet. The other mourners had left as soon as decently possible, heading for the warmth of their homes or the crackling fire in the Inn of the Last Home. They had spoken their final condolences hurriedly, not really knowing what to say. No one had known Rosamun very well, no one had liked her.

There was no one to help Caramon, no one to advise him. He was on his own. He bent down, prepared to lift his brother in his arms and carry him home.

A pair of shining black boots and the hem of a brown cloak came into his view.

"Hello, Caramon."

He looked up, thrust back his hood to see better. The rain poured down, streamed from his hair into his eyes.

A woman stood in front of him. A woman around twenty years of age, maybe older. She was attractive, though not beautiful. Her hair, beneath her hood, was black and curled damply around her face. Her eyes were dark and bright, perhaps a little too bright, shining with a diamond's hardness. She wore brown leather armor, molded to fit over her curvaceous figure, a green loose-fitting blouse, green woolen hose, and the shining black boots that came to her knees. A sword hung from her hip.

She seemed familiar. Caramon knew he knew her, but he didn't have time to sort through the lumberyard that was his memory. He mumbled something about having to help his brother, but the woman was now down beside him, kneeling over Raistlin.

"He's my brother, too, you know," she said, and her mouth twisted in a crooked smile.

"Kit!" Caramon gasped, recognizing her at last. "What are you— Where did you— How did—"

"Here, we better get him somewhere warm and dry," Kitiara interrupted, taking charge of the situation, much to Caramon's relief.

She was strong, as strong as a man. Between the two of them, they lifted Raistlin to his feet. He roused briefly, stared around with unfocused eyes, muttered something. His eyes rolled back, his head lolled. He lost consciousness again.

"He's . . . he's never been this sick!" Caramon said, his fear something real and alive inside him, squeezing his heart. "I've never seen him this bad!"

"Bah! I've seen worse," said Kitiara confidently. "Lots worse. I've treated worse, too. Arrow wounds in the gut, legs cut off. Don't worry," she added, her smile softening in sympathy for Caramon's anguish. "I fought Death before over my baby brother and I won. I can do it again if need be."

They carried Raistlin up the long flight of stairs to the boardwalk, made their way beneath the dripping tree branches to the Majeres' small house. Once inside, Caramon built up the fire. Kit stripped off Raistlin's wet clothes with swift, unblushing efficiency. When Caramon ventured a mild, embarrassed protest, Kitiara laughed.

"What's the matter, baby brother? Afraid this will shock my delicate feminine sensibilities? Don't worry," she added with a grin and a wink, "I've seen men naked before."

His face extremely red, Caramon helped his sister lay Raistlin down in his bed. He was shivering so that it seemed he might fall out. He spoke, but he made no sense and would occasionally cry out and stare at them with wide, fever dilated eyes. Kit rummaged through the house, found every blanket, and piled them over him. She placed her hand on his neck to feel his pulse beat, pursed her lips in a thoughtful frown, and shook her head. Caramon stood by, watching anxiously.

"Is that crone still around?" Kit asked abruptly. "You know, the one who talked to trees and whistled like a bird and kept a wolf for a pet?"

"Weird Meggin? Yeah, she's still around. I guess." Caramon was doubtful. "I don't go to that part of town much. Father doesn't—" He paused, swallowed, and began over. "Father didn't want us to go there."

"Father isn't around anymore. You're on your own now, Caramon," Kitiara returned with brutal frankness. "Go to Weird Meggin's and tell her you need elixir of willow bark. And hurry up. We've got to bring down this fever."

"Elixir of willow bark," Caramon repeated to himself several times. He put on his cloak. "Anything else?"

"Not right now. Oh, and Caramon"—Kitiara halted him as he stood in the open doorway—"don't tell anyone I'm back in town, will you?"

"Sure, Kit," Caramon answered. "Why not?"

"I don't want to be bothered by a lot of tittle-tattlers snooping around and asking questions. Now, go along. Wait! Do you have any money?"

Caramon shook his head.

Kitiara reached into a leather purse she wore on her belt, fished out a couple of steel coins, and tossed them to him. "On your way back from the old crone's, stop by Otik's and buy a jug of brandy. Is there anything in the house to eat?"

Caramon nodded. "The neighbors brought lots of stuff."

"Ah, I forgot. The funeral meats. All right. Go on. Remember what I said: tell no one I'm here."

Caramon departed, a little curious about his sister's injunction. After several moments of long and considered thought, he at last decided that Kitiara knew what she was doing. If word got out that she was in town, every gossip from here to the Plains of Dust would be snooping around. Raistlin needed rest and he needed quiet, not a stream of visitors. Yes, Kit knew what she was doing. She would help Raistlin. She would.

Caramon generally took a positive view of things. He was not one to fret over what had happened in the past or worry about what might come in the future. He was honest and trusting, and like many honest, trusting people, he believed that everyone else was honest and trustworthy. He put his faith in his sister.

He hastened through the pouring rain to Weird Meggin's, who lived in a tumbledown shack that sat on the ground beneath the vallenwood trees, not far from the disreputable bar known as The Trough. Concentrating on his errand, muttering "willow bark, willow bark," to himself over and over, Caramon almost tripped over an ancient gray wolf lying across the threshold.

The wolf growled. Caramon backed up precipitously.

"Nice doggie," Caramon said to the wolf.

The wolf rose to its feet, the fur on its back bristling. Its lips parted in a snarl, showing extremely yellow but very sharp teeth.

The rain beat down on Caramon. His cloak was wet through. He stood ankle-deep in mud. He could see candlelight in the window and a figure moving around inside. He made another attempt to pass the wolf.

"There's a good dog," he said and started to pat the wolf on the head.

A snap of the yellow teeth nearly took off Caramon's hand.

Abandoning the door, Caramon thought he might tap on the windowpane. The wolf thought he wouldn't. The wolf was right.

Caramon couldn't leave. Not without the elixir. Shouting at the door wasn't very polite, but in these circumstances, it was all the desperate Caramon had left to try.

"Weird—I mean—"Caramon flushed, started over—"Mistress Meggin! Mistress Meggin!"

A face appeared in the window, the face of a middle-aged woman with gray hair pulled back tight. Her eyes were bright and clear. She didn't look crazy. She gazed intently at the sopping wet Caramon, then left the window. Caramon's heart sank into the mud, which seemed to be up around his knees now. Then he heard a grating sound, as of a bar being lifted. The door swung open. She spoke a word to the wolf, a word Caramon couldn't understand.

The wolf rolled over, all four paws in the air, and the crone scratched its belly.

"Well, boy," she said, looking up, "what do you want? The weather's a bit inclement for you to be throwing rocks at my house, isn't it?"

Caramon went red as a pickled beet. The rock-throwing incident had happened a long time ago, he'd been a small boy at the time, and he had assumed she wouldn't recognize him.

"Well, what do you want?" she repeated.

"Bark," he said in a low voice, ashamed, flustered, and embarrassed. "Some sort of bark. I . . . I forget what."

"What's it for?" Meggin asked sharply.

"Uh . . . Kit . . . No, I don't mean that. It's my brother. He has a fever."

"Willow bark elixir. I'll fetch it." The crone eyed him. "I'd ask you to come in out of the rain, but I'll wager you wouldn't."

Caramon peered past her into the shack. A warm fire looked inviting, but then he saw the skull on the table—a human skull, with various other bones lying about. He saw what looked like a rib cage, attached to a spine. If it had not been too horrible to even imagine, Caramon might have thought the woman was attempting to build a person, starting from the bones and working outward.

He took a step backward. "No, ma'am. Thank you, ma'am, but I'm quite comfortable where I am."

The crone grinned and chuckled. She shut the door. The wolf curled up on the threshold, keeping one yellow eye on Caramon.

He stood miserably in the rain, worried over his brother, hoping the crone wouldn't be long and wondering uneasily if he dared trust her. Perhaps she might need more bones for her collection. Perhaps she'd gone to get an ax. . . .

The door opened with a suddenness that made Caramon jump.

Meggin held out a small glass vial. "Here you go, boy. Tell your sister to have Raistlin swallow a large spoonful morning and night until the fever breaks. Understand?"

"Yes, ma'am. Thank you, ma'am." Caramon fumbled for the coins in his pocket. Realizing suddenly what she'd said, he stammered, "It's not . . . um . . . for my sister. She's not here . . . exactly. She's away. I don't—" Caramon shut his mouth. He was a hopeless liar.

Meggin chuckled again. "Of course she is. I won't say anything to anyone. Never fear. I hope your brother gets well. When he does, tell him to come visit me. I miss seeing him."

"My brother comes here?" Caramon asked, astonished.

"All the time. Who do you think taught him his herb lore? Not that dundering idiot Theobald. He wouldn't know a dandelion from a crab apple if it bit him on the ass. You remember the dose, or do you want me to write it down?"

"I . . . I remember," said Caramon. He held out a coin.

Meggin waved it away. "I don't charge my friends. I was sorry to hear about your parents. Come visit me yourself some time, Caramon Majere. I'd enjoy talking to you. I'll wager you're smarter than you think you are."

"Yes, ma'am," said Caramon politely, having no idea what she meant and no intention of ever taking her up on her offer.

He made an awkward bow and, holding the vial of willow bark elixir as tenderly as a mother holds her newborn child, he slogged through the mud to the staircase leading back up into the trees. His thoughts were extremely confused. Raistlin visiting that old crone. Learning things from her. Maybe he'd touched that skull! Caramon grimaced. It was all extremely baffling.

He was so flustered that he completely forgot he was supposed to stop at the inn for the brandy. He received a severe scolding from Kit when he reached home, and had to go back out in the rain after it.

5

aistlin was very ill for several days. The fever would sub-
side somewhat after a dose of the willow bark, but it
would always go back up again, and each time it seemed
to go higher. Kitiara made light of his twin's illness whenever
Caramon asked, but he could tell she was worried. Sometimes
in the night, when she thought he was asleep, he'd hear Kit give
a sharp sigh, see her drum her fingers on the arm of their
mother's rocking chair, which Kit had dragged into the small
room the twins shared.

Kitiara was not a gentle nurse. She had no patience with
weakness. She had determined that Raistlin would live. She was
doing everything in her power to force him to get better, and she
was irritated and even a little angry when he did not respond.
At that point, she decided to take the fight personally. The expression on her face was so grim and hard and determined that
Caramon wondered if even Death might not be a little daunted
to face her.

Death must have been, because that grim presence backed
down.

On the morning of the fourth day of his twin's illness, Caramon woke after a troubled night. He found Kit slumped over
the bed, her head resting on her arms, her eyes closed in slumber. Raistlin slept as well. Not the heavy, dream-tortured sleep
of his sickness, but a healing sleep, a restful sleep. Caramon
reached out his hand to feel his brother's pulse and, in doing so,
brushed against Kitiara's shoulder.

She bolted to her feet, caught hold of the collar of his shirt
with one hand, twisted the cloth tight around his neck. In her
other hand, a knife flashed in the morning sunlight.

"Kit! It's me!" Caramon croaked, half-strangled.

Kit stared at him without recognition. Then her mouth parted in a crooked grin. She let loose of him, smoothed the wrinkles from his shirt. The knife disappeared rapidly, so rapidly that Caramon could not see where it had gone.

"You startled me," she said.

"No kidding!" Caramon replied feelingly. His neck stung from where the fabric had cut into his flesh. He rubbed his neck, gazed warily at his sister.

She was shorter than he was, lighter in build, but he would have been a dead man if he hadn't spoken up when he did. He could still feel her hand tightening the fabric around his throat, cutting off his breathing.

An awkward silence fell between them. Caramon had seen something disquieting in his sister, something chilling. Not the attack itself. What he'd seen that bothered him was the fierce, eager joy in her eyes when she made the attack.

"I'm sorry, kid," she said at length. "I didn't mean to scare you." She gave him a playful little slap on his cheek. "But don't ever sneak up on me in my sleep like that. All right?"

"Sure, Kit," Caramon said, still uneasy but willing to admit that the incident had been his fault. "I'm sorry I woke you. I just wanted to see how Raistlin was doing."

"He's past the crisis," Kitiara said with a weary, triumphant smile. "He's going to be fine." She gazed down on him proudly, as she might have gazed down on a vanquished foe. "The fever broke last night and it's stayed down. We should leave him now and let him sleep."

She pushed the reluctant Caramon out the door. "Come along. Listen to big sister. By way of repaying me for that fright you gave me, you can fix my breakfast."

"Fright!" Caramon snorted. "You weren't frightened."

"A soldier's always frightened," Kit corrected him. Sitting down at the table, she hungrily devoured an apple, still green, one of this season's first fruits. "It's what you do with the fright that counts."

"Huh?" Caramon looked up from his bread slicing.

"Fear can turn you inside out," Kit said, tearing the apple with strong white teeth. "Or you can make fear work for you. Use it like another weapon. Fear's a funny thing. It can make you weak-kneed, make you pee your pants, make you whimper like a baby. Or fear can make you run faster, hit harder."

"Yeah? Really?" Caramon put a slice of bread on the toasting fork, held it over the kitchen fire.

"I was in a fight once," Kit related, leaning back in her chair and propping her booted feet on another nearby chair. "A bunch of goblins jumped us. One of my comrades—a guy we called Bart Blue-nose 'cause his nose had a kind of strange bluish tint to it—anyway, he was fighting a goblin and his sword snapped, right in two. The goblin howled with delight, figuring he had his kill. Bart was furious. He had to have a weapon; the goblin was attacking him from six directions at once, and Bart was dancing around like a fiend from the Abyss trying to keep clear. Bart takes it into his head that he needs a club, and he grabs the first thing he can lay his hand on, which was a tree. Not a branch, a whole god-damned tree. He dragged that tree right out of the ground—you could hear the roots pop and snap— and he bashed the goblin over the head, killed it on the spot."

"C'mon!" Caramon protested. "I don't believe it. He pulled a tree out of the ground?"

"It was a young tree," Kit said with a shrug. "But he couldn't do it again. He tried it on another, about the same size, after the fight was over, and he couldn't even make the tree's branches wiggle. That's what fear can do for you."

"I see," said Caramon, deeply thoughtful.

"You're burning the toast," Kit pointed out.

"Oh, yeah! Sorry. I'll eat that piece." Caramon snatched the blackened toast from the fork, put another in its place. A question had been nagging at him for the last day or so. He tried to think of some subtle way of asking, but he couldn't. Raistlin was good at subtleties; Caramon just blundered on ahead. He decided he may as well ask it and have done with it, especially since Kitiara appeared to be in a good mood.

"Why'd you come back?" he asked, not looking at her. Carefully he rotated the toast on the fork to brown the other side. "Was it because of Mother? You were at her burial, weren't you?"

He heard Kit's boots hit the floor and glanced up nervously, thinking he'd offended her. She stood with her back turned, staring out the small window. The rain had stopped finally. The vallenwood leaves, just starting to turn color, were tipped with gold in the morning sun.

"I heard about Gilon's death," Kitiara said. "From some woodsmen I met in a tavern up north. I also heard about Rosamun's . . . sickness." Her mouth twisted, she glanced sidelong at Caramon. "To be honest, I came back because of you, you and Raistlin. But I'll get to that in a moment. I arrived here the night Rosamun died. I . . . um . . . was staying with friends.

And, yes, I went to the burial. Like it or not, she was my mother. I guess her death was pretty awful for you and Raist, huh?"

Caramon nodded silently. He didn't like to think about it. Morosely he munched on the burnt toast.

"Do you want some eggs? I can fry 'em," he said.

"Yes, I'm starved. Put in some of Otik's potatoes, too, if you've got any left." Kit remained standing by the window. "It's not that Rosamun meant anything to me. She didn't." Her voice hardened. "But it would have been bad luck if I hadn't gone."

"What do you mean, 'bad luck'?"

"Oh, I know it's all superstitious nonsense," Kit said with a rueful grin. "But she was my mother and she's dead. I should show respect. Otherwise, well"—Kit looked uncomfortable—"I might be punished. Something bad might happen to me."

"That sounds like the Widow Judith," Caramon said, cracking eggshells, making a clumsy and ineffectual attempt at extricating the egg from the shell. His scrambled eggs were noted for their crunchy texture. "She talked about some god called Belzor punishing us. Is that what you mean?"

"Belzor! What a crock. There are gods, Caramon. Powerful gods. Gods who will punish you if you do something they don't like. But they'll reward you, too, if you serve them."

"Are you serious?" Caramon asked, staring at his sister. "No offense, but I've never heard you talk like that before."

Kitiara turned from the window. Walking over, her strides long and purposeful, she planted her hands on the table and looked into Caramon's face.

"Come with me!" she said, not answering his question. "There's a city up north called Sanction. Big things are happening there, Caramon. Important things. I plan to be part of them, and you can, too. I came back on purpose to get you."

Caramon was tempted. Traveling with Kitiara, seeing the vast world outside of Solace. No more backbreaking farm work, no more hoeing and plowing, no more forking hay until his arms ached. He'd use his arm for sword work, fighting goblins and ogres. Spending his nights with his comrades around a fire, or snug in a tavern with a girl on his knee.

"What about Raistlin?" he asked.

Kit shook her head. "I had hoped to find him stronger. Can he work magic yet?"

"I . . . I don't think so," said Caramon.

"Odds are he won't ever be able to use it, then. Why, the mages I've heard of are practicing their skills at the age of twelve! Still, I'm sure I could get a job for him. He's well schooled, isn't he? There's a temple I know about. They're looking for scribes. Easy work and fat living. What do you say? We could leave as soon as Raistlin is well enough to travel."

Caramon allowed himself one more glimpse of walking around this town called Sanction, armor clanking, sword rattling on his hip, the women admiring him. He put the vision away with a sigh.

"I can't, Kit. Raist would never leave that school of his. Not until he's ready to take some sort of test that they give in a big tower somewhere."

"Well, then, let him stay," Kitiara said, irritated. "You come alone."

She eyed Caramon, giving him almost the same look he'd imagined from the women in Sanction. But not quite. Kit was sizing him up as a warrior. Self-conscious, he stood straighter. He was taller than the boys his age, taller than most men in Solace. The heavy farm labor had built up his muscles.

"How old are you?" Kit asked.

"Sixteen."

"You'd pass for eighteen, sure. I could teach you what you'd need to know on our way north. Raistlin will be fine here on his own. He's got the house. Your father left it to you two, didn't he? Well, then! There's nothing stopping you."

Caramon might be gullible, he might be thickheaded—as his brother often told him he was—and slow of thought. But once he had made up his mind about something, he was as immovable as Prayer's Eye Peak.

"I can't leave Raistlin, Kit."

Kitiara frowned, angry, not accustomed to having her will thwarted. Folding her arms across her chest, she glared at Caramon. Her booted foot tapped irritably on the floor. Caramon, uncomfortable beneath her piercing gaze, ducked his head and whipped the eggs right out of the bowl.

"You could talk to Raistlin," Caramon said, his voice muffled by his shirt collar, into which he was speaking. "Maybe I spoke out of turn. Maybe he'll want to go."

"I'll do that," Kitiara said, her tone sharp. She was pacing the length of the small room.

Caramon said nothing more. He dumped what remained of the eggs into a skillet and placed it over the fire. He heard Kit's booted footfalls sound hollowly on the wood, winced at a particularly loud and angry stomp. When the eggs were cooked, the two sat down to breakfast in silence.

Caramon risked a glance at his sister, saw her regarding him with an affable air, a charming smile.

"These eggs are really good," said Kit, spitting out small bits of shell. "Did I ever tell you about the time the bandit tried to stab me in my sleep? What you did reminded me of the story. We'd had a hard fight that day, and I was dead tired. Well, this bandit . . ."

Caramon listened to this story and to many other exciting adventures during the day. He listened and enjoyed what he heard—Kit was an excellent storyteller. Every so often, Caramon would go to the bedroom to check on Raistlin and find him slumbering peacefully. When Caramon returned, he would hear yet another tale of valor, daring, battles fought, victory, and wealth won. He listened and laughed and gasped in all the right places. Caramon knew very well what his sister was trying to do. There could be only one answer. If Raistlin went, Caramon would go. If Raistlin stayed, so did Caramon.

That evening, Raistlin woke. He was weak, so weak that he couldn't lift his head from the pillow without help. But he was lucid and very much aware of his surroundings. He didn't appear all that surprised to see Kitiara.

"I had dreams about you," he said.

"Most men do," Kit returned with a grin and a wink. She sat down on the edge of the bed, and while Caramon fed his brother chicken broth, Kitiara made Raistlin the same proposition she'd made Caramon.

She wasn't quite as glib, talking to those keen blue, unblinking eyes that looked right through her and out the other side.

"Who is it you work for?" Raistlin asked when Kit had finished.

Kitiara shrugged. "People," she said.

"And what temple is this where you would have me work? Dedicated to what god?"

"It's not Belzor, that's for sure!" Kitiara said with a laugh.

When Caramon, spooning broth, tried to say something, Raistlin coldly shushed him.

"Thank you, Sister," Raistlin said at last, "but I am not ready."

"Ready?" Kit couldn't figure out what he was talking about. "What do you mean, 'ready'? Ready for what? You can read, can't you? You can write, can't you? So you don't have any talent for magic. You gave it a good try. It's not important. There are other ways to gain power. I know. I've found them."

"That's enough, Caramon!" Raistlin pushed away the spoon. Wearily he lay back down on the pillows. "I need to rest."

Kit stood up. Hands on her hips, she glared at him. "That addle-pated mother of ours had you wrapped in cotton, for fear you'd break. It's time you got out, saw something of the world."

"I am not ready," Raistlin said again and closed his eyes.

Kitiara left Solace that night.

"I'm only making a short trip," she told Caramon, drawing on her leather gloves. "To Qualinesti. Do you know anything about that place?" she asked offhandedly. "Its defenses? How many people live there? That sort of thing?"

"I know elves live there," Caramon offered after a moment's profound thought.

"Everyone knows that!" Kit scoffed.

Putting on her cloak, she drew her hood over her head.

"When will you be back?" Caramon asked.

Kit shrugged. "I can't say. Maybe a year. Maybe a month. Maybe never. It depends on how things go."

"You're not mad at me, are you, Kit?" Caramon asked wistfully. "I wouldn't want you to be mad."

"No, I'm not mad. Just disappointed. You'd have been a great warrior, Caramon. The people I know would have really made something of you. As for Raistlin, he's made a big mistake. He wants power, and I know where he could get it. If you both hang around here, you'll never be anything but a farmer, and he'll be—like that fellow Waylan—a coin-puking, rabbit-pulling conjurer who's the joke of half of Solace. It's such a waste."

She gave Caramon a slap on the cheek that was meant to be friendly but which left the red mark of her hand. Opening the door, Kit peered outside, looking in both directions. Caramon couldn't imagine what she was looking for. It was well past midnight. Most of Solace was in bed.

"Good-bye, Kit," he said.

"Good-bye, Baby Brother."

He massaged his stinging cheek and watched her walk off through the moonlit branches of the vallenwood, a black shadow against silver.

6

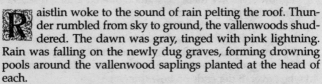

Raistlin woke to the sound of rain pelting the roof. Thunder rumbled from sky to ground, the vallenwoods shuddered. The dawn was gray, tinged with pink lightning. Rain was falling on the newly dug graves, forming drowning pools around the vallenwood saplings planted at the head of each.

He lay on his bed and watched the gray gradually lighten as the storm passed. All was quiet now, except for the incessant drip of water falling on sodden leaves. He lay without moving. Movement took an effort, and he was too tired. His grief had emptied him. If he moved, the dull, aching pain of his loss would flood in on him, and though the emptiness was bad, it wasn't as bad as the pain.

He could not feel the bedclothes under him. He could not feel the blanket that covered him. He had no weight or substance. Was this what it was like in that coffin? In that grave? To feel nothing, ever again? To know nothing? Life, the world, the people in the world go on, and you know nothing, forever surrounded by a cold and empty, silent darkness?

Pain burst the levee, surged in to fill the void. Pain and fear, hot, burning, welled up inside him. Tears stung his eyelids. He closed his eyes, squeezed them shut and wept, wept for himself and for his mother and father, for all those who are born of the darkness, who lift their wondering eyes to the light, feel its warmth on their skin, and who must return again to darkness.

He wept silently, so as not to wake Caramon. He did this not so much out of consideration for his brother's weariness as for his own shame at his weakness.

The tears ended, leaving him with a bad taste of salt and iron in his mouth, a clogged nose, and a tightness in his throat, which came from muffling his sobs. The bedclothes were damp; his fever must have broken during the night. He had only the vaguest recollection of being sick, a recollection tinged with horror—in his fevered dreams, he had become entwined with Rosamun. He was his mother, a shrunken corpse. People stood around the bed, staring down at him.

Antimodes, Master Theobald, the Widow Judith, Caramon, the dwarf and the kender, Kitiara. He begged and pleaded with them to give him food and water, but they said he was dead and he didn't need it. He was in constant terror that they would dump him in a coffin and lower him into the ground, into a grave that was Master Theobald's laboratory.

Remembering the terrible dreams robbed them of some of their power. The horror lingered, but it was not overwhelming. The wool blanket covering him was rough and chafed his skin; beneath it, he was wearing nothing.

He tossed the blanket aside. Weak and tottering from his illness, he stood up. The air was chill and he shivered, groped hastily for his shirt, which had been flung over the back of a chair. Dragging the shirt on over his head, he thrust his arms into the sleeves, then stood in the middle of the small room and wondered bleakly, What now?

There were two wooden beds in the room, each bed built into a wall. Raistlin crossed the room to look down on the slumbering form of his twin. Caramon was a late sleeper, a heavy sleeper. Usually he lay easily and comfortably on his back, his big body spread all akimbo, arms flung wide, one leg hanging off the bed, the other bent at the knee, leaning against the wall. Raistlin, by contrast, slept in a tight, huddled ball, his knees drawn up to his chin, his arms hugging his chest.

But Caramon's sleep this day was as restless and uneasy as his twin's. Fatigue kept him manacled to his bed, he was so exhausted that not even the most terrifying dreams could jolt his body from sleep. He rolled and tossed, his head jerked back and forth. His pillow lay on the floor, along with the blankets. He had twisted the sheet so that it straggled around him like a winding cloth.

He muttered and mumbled and panted, tugged at the collar of his nightshirt. His skin was clammy, his hair damp with sweat. He looked so ill that Raistlin, concerned, placed his hand on his brother's forehead to feel if he were running a fever.

Caramon's skin was cool. Whatever troubled him was of the mind, not the body. He shuddered at Raistlin's touch and begged, "Don't make me go there, Raist! Don't make me go there!"

Raistlin brushed aside a lock of the curly, tousled hair that was falling into his brother's eyes and wondered if he should wake him. His brother must have been awake many long nights and he needed his rest, but this was more like torture than sleep. Raistlin put his hand on his twin's broad shoulder, shook it.

"Caramon!" he called peremptorily.

Caramon's eyes flared wide. He stared at Raistlin and cringed. "Don't leave me! Don't! Don't leave me! Please!" He whimpered and flung himself about on the bed with such violence that he nearly fell on the floor.

This was not dreaming. It was vaguely familiar to Raistlin, then suddenly frighteningly familiar.

Rosamun. She had been much like this.

Perhaps this wasn't sleep. Perhaps this was a trance, similar to the trances into which Rosamun had stumbled, never to find her way back out.

Caramon had not previously evinced any signs that he had inherited his mother's fey talent. He was her son, however, and her blood—with all its strange fancies—ran in his veins. His body was weakened by nights of wakeful watching, tending his sick brother. His mind was upset by the tragic loss of his beloved father, then he had been forced to stand by helplessly and watch his mother dwindle away. With the body's defenses lowered, the mind's defenses confused and overwhelmed, his soul was laid bare and vulnerable. It might well retreat into dark regions never known to exist, there to find refuge from the battering armies of life.

What if I lose Caramon?

I would be alone. Alone without family or friend, for Raistlin could not count on Kitiara as family, nor did he want to. Her crudeness and her untamed animal nature disgusted him. That's what he told himself. In reality, he feared her. He foresaw that someday there would be a power struggle between them, and, alone, he was not certain that he was strong enough to withstand her. As for friends, on this point he could not delude himself. He had none. His friends were not his friends at all, they were Caramon's.

Caramon was often irritating, often annoying. His slow thought processes frustrated his quicker thinking twin, who was at times tempted to grab hold of Caramon and shake him on the faint hope that a sensible thought might accidentally tumble out. But now, faced with the possibility of losing his brother, Raistlin looked into the void where Caramon had been and realized how much he would miss him, and not for just companionship, or to have someone strong on which to lean. Mentally speaking, Caramon was not a brilliant swordsman, but he made a good fencing partner.

Besides, Caramon was the only person Raistlin had ever known who could come close to making him laugh. Shadow puppets on the wall, ridiculous rabbits . . .

"Caramon!" Raistlin shook his brother again.

Caramon only moaned and raised his hands, as if warding off some blow. "No, Raist! I don't have it! I swear I don't have it!"

Frightened, Raistlin wondered what to do. He left the bedroom, went in search of his sister, with some idea of sending Kit out to fetch Weird Meggin.

But Kitiara was gone. Her pack was gone; she must have left during the night.

Raistlin stood in the parlor of the silent house, the too-silent house. Kitiara had packed all Rosamun's clothes and possessions away in a wooden chest, stowed it under the bed. His mother's rocking chair remained, however, the only one of her possessions that Kit had not removed, mainly because there was a shortage of chairs in the house as it was. Rosamun's presence lingered like the fragrance of faded rose petals. The very emptiness, the lack of her, recalled his mother vividly to his mind.

Too vividly. Rosamun sat in the chair, rocking. She rocked leisurely back and forth, her dress rustling. The toes of her small feet, encased in soft leather shoes, lightly touched the floor and then slid beneath her dress when the chair rocked backward. Her head and her gaze remained level, her lips smiling at Raistlin.

He stared, willing with an aching heart for this to be true, even as a part of him knew it wasn't.

Rosamun ceased rocking, rose from the chair with grace and ease. He was conscious of sweet fragrance as she passed near him, a fragrance of roses. . . .

In the next room, his brother gave a fearful yell, a horrible scream, as though he were being burned alive.

The scent of roses in his nostrils, Raistlin searched the room, found what he sought. A dish of dried and withered rose petals had been placed on a table to sweeten the sickness-tainted air. He dipped his hand into the dish, and carried the rose petals into the bedroom.

Caramon clutched the sides of the bed, his hands white-knuckled. The bed shook beneath him. His eyes were wide open, staring at some horror visible only to himself.

Raistlin had no need to refer to his primer for the wording of the spell. The words were etched into his brain with fire, and like a wildfire racing across parched grass, so the magic raced from his brain down his spine, burned through every nerve, enflamed him.

He crushed the rose petals, strewed them over his brother's tormented form.

"Ast tasarak sinuralan kyrnawi."

Caramon's eyelids fluttered. He gave a great sigh, shuddered, then his eyes closed. He lay for a moment, flattened on the bed, not breathing, and Raistlin knew a fear unlike any he'd ever previously experienced. He thought his twin was dead.

"Caramon!" Raistlin whispered. "Don't leave me, Caramon! Don't!"

His hands gently brushed the rose petals from Caramon's still face.

Caramon drew a breath, long, deep, and easy. He let that breath go and then drew another, his chest rising and falling. His face smoothed, the dreams had not cut too deep, had not left their chisel mark upon him. The lines of weariness, grief, and sorrow would soon fade away, ripples on the surface of his customary genial tranquillity.

Weak with relief, Raistlin sank down beside his brother's bed, rested his head in his hands. It was only then, his eyes closed, seeing nothing but darkness, that Raistlin realized what he had done.

Caramon was asleep.

I cast the spell, Raistlin said inwardly. The magic worked for me.

The fire of the spellcasting flickered and died out, leaving him weak and shaking so that he could not stand, yet Raistlin knew such joy as he had never known in his life.

"Thank you!" Raistlin whispered, his fists clenched, his nails digging into his flesh. He saw again the eye, white, red, black, regarding him with satisfaction. "I won't fail you!" he repeated over and over. "I won't fail!"

The eye blinked.

A tiny pinprick of concern, of jealous doubt, jabbed him.

Had Caramon fallen into a trance? Was it possible that he had likewise inherited the magic?

Raistlin opened his eyes, stared hard and long at his slumbering brother. Caramon lay on his back, one arm flopped over the edge of the bed, the other across his forehead. His mouth was open, he gave a prodigious snore. He had never looked more foolish.

"I was mistaken," Raistlin said, and he pushed himself to his feet. "It was a bad dream, nothing more." He smiled scornfully at himself. "How could I have ever imagined that this great oaf would inherit the magic?"

Raistlin left the room on tiptoe, moving quietly so as not to disturb his brother, and shut the door to their room softly behind him. Entering the parlor, Raistlin sat down in his mother's rocking chair, and, rocking gently back and forth, he reveled fully in his triumph.

7

aramon slept that day through and on into the night. The next day he woke, recalled nothing of his dreams, was amused and even skeptical to hear his twin describe them.

"Pooh, Raist!" Caramon said. "You know I never dream."

Raistlin did not argue. He himself was gaining strength rapidly, was strong enough to sit at the kitchen table that morning with his brother. The day was warm; a soft breeze carried sounds of women's voices, calling and laughing. It was laundry day, and the women were hanging their wet clothes among the leaves to dry. The early autumn sunshine filtered through the changing leaves, casting shadows that flitted around the kitchen like birds. The twins ate breakfast in silence. There was much they had to talk about, much they needed to discuss and settle, but that could wait.

Raistlin touched each moment that passed, held each moment cupped in his mind until it slipped away through his fingers, to be replaced by another. The past and all its sorrow was behind him; he would never turn around to look back. The future, with its promise and its fears, lay ahead of him, shone warm on his face like the sunshine, darkened his face like the shadows. At this moment, he was suspended between past and future, floating free.

Outside, a bird whistled, another answered. Two young women let fall a wet sheet onto one of the town's guardsmen, who was walking his beat on the ground below. The sheet enveloped him, to judge by his muffled, good-natured cursing. The young women giggled and protested that it was an accident. They ran down the stairs to reclaim their linen and spend a few pleasant moments flirting with the handsome guard.

"Raistlin," said Caramon, speaking reluctantly, as if he, too, were under the spell of the sun, the breeze, the laughter, and loath to break it. "We have to decide what to do."

Raistlin couldn't see his brother's face for the sunshine. He was sensible of Caramon's presence, sitting in the chair opposite. Strong and solid and reassuring. Raistlin remembered the fear he'd experienced when he had thought Caramon was dead. Affection for his brother welled up inside him, stung his eyelids. Raistlin drew back out of the sun, blinking rapidly to clear his vision. The moments had begun to slide by faster and faster, no longer his to touch.

"What are our options?" Raistlin asked.

Caramon shifted his bulk in his chair. "Well, we turned down going with Kit. . . ." He let that hang a moment, silently asking if his twin might reconsider.

"Yes," Raistlin said, a note of finality.

Caramon cleared his throat, went on. "Lady Brightblade offered to take us in, give us a home."

"Lady Brightblade," said Raistlin with a snicker.

"She is the wife of a Solamnic knight," Caramon pointed out defensively.

"So she claims."

"C'mon, Raist!" Caramon was fond of Anna Brightblade, who had always been very kind to him. "She showed me a book with their family coat-of-arms. And she acts like a noble lady, Raist."

"How would you know how a noble lady acts, my brother?"

Caramon thought this over. "Well, she acts like what I imagine a noble lady would act like. Like the noble ladies in those stories . . ."

He fell silent, left his sentence unfinished, except in the minds of both twins. Like those stories Mother used to tell us. To speak of her aloud was to invoke her ghost, which remained inside the house.

Gilon, on the other hand, had departed. He had never been there much in the first place, and all he left behind was a vague, pleasant memory. Caramon missed his father, but already Raistlin was having to work to remember that Gilon was gone.

"I do care to have Sturm Brightblade as a brother," Raistlin commented. "Master My-Honor-Is-My-Life. He's so smug and arrogant, parading his virtue up and down the streets, making a show of righteousness. It's enough to make one puke."

"Ah, Sturm's not so bad," Caramon said. "He's had a rough

time of it. At least we know how our father died," he added somberly. "Sturm doesn't even know if his father's dead or alive."

"If he's that worried, why doesn't he go back and find out the truth?" Raistlin said impatiently. "He's certainly old enough."

"He can't leave his mother. He promised his father, the night they fled, that he'd take care of his mother, and he's bound by that promise."

"When the mob attacked their castle—"

"Castle!" Raistlin snorted.

"—they barely escaped with their lives. Sturm's father sent him and his mother out into the night with an escort of retainers. He told them to travel to Solace, where he would join them when he could. That was the last they heard of him."

"The knights must have done something to provoke the attack. People just don't suddenly take it into their heads to storm a well-fortified keep."

"Sturm says that there are strange people moving into the north, into Solamnia. Evil people, who want only to foment trouble for the knights, drive them out so that they can move in and seize control."

"And who are these unknown evil-doers?" Raistlin asked caustically.

"He doesn't know, but he thinks they have something to do with the old gods," Caramon replied, shrugging.

"Indeed?" Raistlin was suddenly thoughtful, recalling Kitiara's offer, her talk of powerful gods. He was also thinking back to his own experience with the gods, an experience he had wondered about since. Had it really happened? Or had it happened because he wanted it so much?

Caramon had spilled some water on the table, and now he was damming it up with his knife and fork, trying to divert the course of the tiny river so that it wouldn't drip onto the floor. He was busy with this as he spoke and did not look at his brother. "I said no. She wouldn't have let you go on with your schooling."

"What are you talking about?" Raistlin asked sharply, looking up. "Who wouldn't let me go on with my schooling?"

"Lady Brightblade."

"She said that, did she?"

"Yeah," Caramon answered. He added a spoon to the dam. "It's nothing against you, Raist," he added, looking up to see his brother's thin face grow hard and cold. "The Solamnic knights think that magic-users are outside the natural order of things. They never use wizards in battle, according to what Sturm says. Wizards lack discipline and they're too independent."

"We like to think for ourselves," said Raistlin, "and not blindly obey some fool commander who may or not have a brain in his head. Yet they say," he added, "that Magius fought at the side of Huma and that he was Huma's dearest friend."

"I know about Huma," Caramon said, glad to change the subject. "Sturm told me stories about him and how, long ago, he fought the Queen of Darkness and banished all the dragons. But I never heard of this Magius."

"No doubt the knights would like to forget that part of the tale. Just as Huma was one of the greatest warriors of all time, so Magius was one of the greatest wizards. During a battle fought against the forces of Takhisis, Magius was separated from Huma's side. The wizard fought on alone, surrounded by the enemy, until, wounded and exhausted, he could no longer summon the strength to cast his magic. That was in the days when wizards were not allowed to carry any weapon other than their magic. Magius was captured alive and dragged back to the Dark Queen's camp.

"They tortured him for three days and three nights, trying to force him to reveal the location of Huma's encampment so they could send assassins to kill the knight. Magius died, never revealing the truth. It was said that when Huma received the news of Magius's death and learned how he had died, he grieved so for his friend that his men thought they might lose him as well.

"Huma ordered that, from then on, wizards would be permitted to carry one small, bladed weapon, to be used as a last defense if their magic failed them. This we do in the name of Magius to this day."

"That's a great story," Caramon said, so impressed he let his river overflow. He went to fetch a cloth to wipe up the water. "I'll have to tell that to Sturm."

"You do that," Raistlin said wryly. "I'll be interested to hear what he has to say." He watched Caramon clean the floor, then said, "We have chosen not to join forces with our sister. We have decided that we do not want to be taken under the wing of a noble Solamnic lady. What do you suggest we do?"

"I say we live here, Raist," Caramon answered steadily. He stood up from his mopping. Hands on his hips, he surveyed the house as if he were a potential buyer. "The house is ours free and clear. Father built it himself. He didn't leave any debts. We don't owe anybody anything. Your school's paid for. We don't have to worry about that. I earn enough working for Farmer Sedge to keep us in food and clothes."

"It will be lonely for you when I am gone in the winter," Raistlin observed.

Caramon shrugged. "I can always stay with the Sedges. I do sometimes anyway if the snow blocks the road. Or I can stay with Sturm or some of our other friends."

Raistlin sat silent, brooding, frowning.

"What's the matter, Raist?" Caramon asked uneasily. "Don't you think it's a good plan"

"I think it's an excellent plan, my brother. I don't feel right about you supporting me, however."

Caramon's worried expression eased. "What does it matter? What's mine is yours, Raist, you know that."

"It does matter to me," Raistlin returned. "Very much. I must do something to pay my share."

Caramon gave the matter serious thought for about three minutes, but apparently that process hurt, for he began rubbing his head and said that he thought it must be about time for lunch.

He left to go rummage in the larder while Raistlin considered what he might do to add to their upkeep. He was not strong enough for farm labor, nor did he have the time for any other job, with his studies. His schooling now meant more than anything, was doubly important. Every spell he learned added to his knowledge . . . and to his power.

Power over others. He remembered Caramon, strong and muscular, falling into a deep slumber, lying comatose at the command of his weaker brother. Raistlin smiled.

Returning with a loaf of bread and a crock of honey, Caramon placed an empty vial down in front of his brother. "This belongs to that old crone, Weird Meggin. It had some sort of tree juice in it. Kit gave it to you to bring your fever down. I should probably return that to her," he said reluctantly, adding in an awed tone, "Do you know, Raist? She's got a wolf that sleeps on her door stoop and a human head sitting right smack on her kitchen table!"

Weird Meggin. An idea stirred in Raistlin's mind. He lifted the vial, opened it, sniffed. Elixir of willow bark. He could make that easily enough. Other herbs in his garden could be used for cures as well. He now had the power to cast minor magicks. People would pay good steel if he could ease a colicky baby into sleep, bring down a man's fever, or cause an itchy rash to disappear.

Raistlin fingered the vial. "I'll return this myself. You needn't come if you don't want to."

"I'm coming," Caramon said firmly. "Where did she get that skull, huh? Just ask yourself that. I wouldn't want to walk in and see your head in her dining room. You and me, Raist. From now on, we stick together. We're all each other's got."

"Not quite all, my dear brother," Raistlin said softly. His hand went to the small leather bag he wore at his waist, a bag containing his spell components. It held only dried rose petals now, but soon it would hold more. Much more.

"Not quite all."

Book 4

*Who wants or needs any gods at all? I certainly don't.
No divine force controls my life, and that's the way I like
it. I choose my own destiny. I am slave to no man. Why
should I be a slave to a god and let some priest or cleric
tell me how to live?*

—Kitiara uth Matar

I

wo years passed. Spring's gentle rains and summer's sunshine caused the vallenwood saplings on the grave site to straighten, sending forth green shoots. Raistlin spent winters at the school. He added another elementary spell—a spell he could use to determine if an object might be magical—to his spellbook. Caramon spent the winters working in the stables, the summers working at Farmer Sedge's. Caramon wasn't home much during the winter. The house was lonely without his brother and "gave him the creeps." When Raistlin returned, however, the two lived there almost contentedly.

That spring brought the customary May Day festival, one of Solace's largest celebrations. A huge fair was set up in a large area of cleared land on the town's southern borders.

Free at last to travel, now that the winter thaw had cleared the roads, merchants came from all parts of Ansalon, eager to sell the wares they had spent all winter making.

The taciturn, savage-looking Plainsmen traders were first to arrive, coming from villages with outlandish, barbaric names, such as Que-teh and Que-kiri. Clad in animal skins decorated with uncouth ornaments said to honor their ancestors, whom they worshiped, the Plainsmen held themselves aloof from the other inhabitants of the region, though they took their steel readily enough. Their clay pots were much prized; their hand-woven blankets were extraordinarily beautiful. Some of their other goods, such as the bead-decorated skulls of small animals, were coveted by the children, to the shock and dismay of their parents.

Dwarves, well dressed, wearing gold chains around their necks, traveled from their underground realm of Thorbardin, bringing with them the metalwork for which they were famous, displaying everything from pots and pans to axes, bracers, and daggers.

These Thorbardin dwarves sparked the first incident of the fair season. The Thorbardin dwarves were in the Inn of the Last Home, partaking of Otik's ale, when they began to make disparaging comments regarding that ale, which they maintained was far below their own high standards. A local hill dwarf took exception to these comments on Otik's behalf, added a few of his own relevant to the fact that a mountain dwarf wouldn't know a good glass of ale if it was poured over his head, which it subsequently was.

Several elves from Qualinesti, who had brought with them some exquisite gold and silver jewelry, maintained that the dwarves were all a pack of brutes, worse than humans, who were bad enough.

A brawl ensued. The guards were summoned.

The Solace residents took the side of the hill dwarf. The flustered Otik, not wanting to lose customers, was on both sides at the same time. He thought that perhaps the ale might not up to his usual high standards, was forced to admit that the Thorbardin gentlemen might be right on that point. On the other hand, Flint Fireforge was an exceptional judge of ale, having tasted a great deal of it in his time, and Otik felt called upon to bow to his expertise.

Eventually it was determined that if the hill dwarf would apologize to the mountain dwarves and the mountain dwarves would apologize to Otik, the entire incident would be forgotten. The leader of the Thorbardin dwarves, wiping blood from his nose, stated in surly tones that the ale was "drinkable." The hill dwarf, massaging a bruised jaw, mumbled that a mountain dwarf might indeed know something of ale, having spent enough nights on the barroom floor lying face first in it. The Thorbardin dwarf didn't like the sound of that, thought it might be another insult. At this juncture, Otik hastily offered a free round to everyone in the bar to celebrate their newfound friendship.

No dwarf alive has ever turned down free ale. Both sides went back to their seats, each group convinced that their side had won. Otik gathered up the broken chairs, the barmaids picked up the broken crockery, the guards drank a glass in honor of the innkeeper, the elves looked down their long noses at the lot of them, and the incident ended.

Raistlin and Caramon heard about the fight the next day as they shoved their way through the crowds milling among the booths and tents.

"I wished I'd been there." Caramon gave a gusty sigh and clenched his large fist.

Raistlin said nothing, he hadn't been paying attention. He was studying the flow of the crowds, trying to determine where would be the most advantageous place to establish himself. At length he settled on a spot located at the convergence of two aisles. A lace-maker from Haven was across from him on one side and a wine merchant from Pax Tharkas on the other.

Placing a large wooden bowl in front of a nearby stump, Raistlin gave Caramon his instructions.

"Walk to the end of this row, turn around, and stroll back. You're a farmer's son in town for the day, remember. When you come to me, stop and stare and point and create a commotion. Once the crowd begins to form around me, move to the outside of the circle and catch people as they walk past, urge them to take a look. Got that?"

"You bet!" said Caramon, grinning. He was enjoying himself immensely.

"And when I ask for a volunteer from the crowd, you know what you must do."

Caramon nodded. "Say I've never seen you before in my life and that there's nothing at all inside that box."

"Don't overact," Raistlin cautioned.

"No, no. I won't. You can count on me," Caramon promised.

Raistlin had his doubts, but there was nothing more he could do to alleviate them. He had rehearsed Caramon the night before, and he could only hope his twin would remember his lines.

Caramon departed, heading for the end of the row as he'd been directed. He was almost immediately waylaid by a stout little man in a garish red waistcoat, who drew Caramon toward a tent, promising that inside the tent Caramon could see the epitome of female beauty, a woman renowned from here to the Blood Sea, who was going to perform the ritual mating dance of the Northern Ergothians, a dance that was said to drive men into a frenzy. Caramon could witness this fabulous sight for only two steel pieces.

"Really?" Caramon craned his neck, trying to sneak a peek through the tent flap.

"Caramon!" His brother's voice snapped across the back of his neck.

Caramon jumped guiltily and veered off, much to the chagrin of the stout little man, who cast Raistlin a baleful look before catching hold of another yokel and resuming his spiel.

Raistlin positioned the wooden bowl so that it showed to best advantage, dropped a steel piece inside to "prime the pump," then laid out his equipment at his feet. He had balls for juggling, coins that would appear inside people's ears, a remarkable length of rope that could be cut and made perfectly whole again in an instant, silken scarves that would flow wondrously from his mouth, and a brightly painted box from which would emerge a peeved and disheveled rabbit.

He wore white robes, which he had laboriously sewn himself out of an old bed sheet. The worn spots were covered with stars and moon faces: red and black. No true wizard would have been caught dead wearing such an outlandish getup, but the general public didn't know any better and the bright colors attracted attention.

The juggling balls in his hands, Raistlin mounted the stump and began to perform. The multicolored balls—toys from his and Caramon's childhood—spun in his deft fingers, flashed through the air. Immediately several children ran over to watch, dragging their parents with them.

Caramon arrived, to loudly exclaim over the wonders he was witnessing. More people came to watch and to marvel. Coins clinked in the wooden bowl.

Raistlin began to enjoy himself. Although he was not performing real magic, he was casting a spell over these people. The enchantment was helped by the fact that they wanted to believe in him, were ready to believe in him. He liked the admiration of the children especially, perhaps because he remembered himself at that age, remembered his own awe and wonder, remembered where that awe and wonder had led.

"Wow! Would you look at that!" cried a shrill voice from the crowd. "Did you really swallow all those scarves? Doesn't it tickle when they come out?"

At first Raistlin thought the voice belonged to a child, then he noticed the kender. Dressed in bright green pants, a yellow shirt, and an orange vest, with an extremely long topknot of hair, the kender surged forward to the front of the crowd, which parted nervously at his coming, everyone clutching his purse. The kender stood in front of Raistlin, regarding him with open-mouthed admiration.

Raistlin cast an alarmed glance at Caramon, who hurried

over to stand protectively beside the wooden bowl that held their money.

The kender seemed familiar to Raistlin, but then kender are so appallingly different from normal people that they all look alike to the untrained eye.

Raistlin thought it wise to distract the kender from the wooden bowl. He did this by first extracting one of his juggling balls from the kender's pouch, then causing a shower of coins to fall from the kender's nose, much to the diminutive spectator's wild delight and mystification. The audience—quite a large audience now—applauded. Coins clinked into the bowl.

Raistlin was taking a bow when, "For shame!" a voice cried.

Raistlin rose from his bow to look directly into the face—the blotchy, vein-popping, infuriated face—of his schoolmaster.

"For shame!" Master Theobald cried again. He leveled a quivering, accusing finger at his pupil. "Making an exhibition of yourself before the masses!"

Conscious of the watching crowd, Raistlin tried to maintain his composure, though hot blood rushed to his face. "I know that you disapprove, Master, but I must earn my living the best way I know how."

"Excuse me, Master sir, but you're blocking my view," said the kender politely, and he reached up to tug at the sleeve of the man's white robe to gain his attention.

The kender was short and Master Theobald was shouting and waving his arms, which undoubtedly explains how the kender missed the sleeve and ended up tugging on the pouch of spell components hanging from the master's belt.

"I've heard how you've been earning your living!" Master Theobald countered. "Consorting with that witch woman! Using weeds to fool the gullible into thinking they've been healed. I came here on purpose to see for myself because I could not believe the stories were true!"

"Do you really know a witch?" asked the kender eagerly, looking up from the pouch of spell components.

"Would you have me starve, Master?" Raistlin demanded.

"You should beg in the streets before you prostitute your art and make a mockery of me and my school!" Master Theobald cried.

He reached out his hand to drag Raistlin down from the stump.

"Touch me, sir"—Raistlin spoke with quiet menace—"and you will regret it."

Theobald glowered. "Do you dare to threaten—"

"Hey, Little Fella!" Caramon cried, lumbering in between the two. "Toss that pouch over here!"

"Goblin Ball!" shouted the kender. "You're the goblin," he informed Master Theobald and sent the pouch whizzing over the mage's head.

"This yours, huh, wizard?" Caramon teased, capering and waving the pouch in front of Theobald's face. "Is it?"

Master Theobald recognized the pouch, clapped his hand to his belt where the pouch should be hanging. Blue veins popped out on his forehead, his face flushed a deeper red.

"Give that to me, you hooligan!" he cried.

"Down the middle!" yelled the kender, making an end sweep around the Master.

Caramon tossed the pouch. The kender caught it, amidst laughter and cheers from the crowd, who were finding the game even more entertaining than the magic. Raistlin stood on the stump, coolly watching the proceedings, a half-smile on his lips.

The kender reached up to throw a long pass back to Caramon when suddenly the pouch was plucked out of the kender's hand.

"What the—" The kender looked up in astonishment.

"I'll take that," said a stern voice.

A tall man in his early twenties, with eyes as blue as Solamnic skies, long hair worn in an old-fashioned single braid down his back, took hold of the pouch. His face was serious and stern, for he was raised to believe that life was serious and stern, bound with rules whose rigid iron bars could never be bent or dislodged. Sturm Brightblade closed the pouch's drawstrings, dusted off the pouch, and handed it, with a formal bow, to the furious mage.

"Thank you," said Master Theobald stiffly. Snatching back the pouch, he thrust it safely up his long, flowing sleeve. He cast a baleful gaze at the kender, and then, turning, he coldly regarded Raistlin.

"You will either leave this place or you will leave my school. Which is it to be, young man?"

Raistlin glanced at the wooden bowl. They had quite enough money for the time being, anyway. And in the future, what the master did not know would not hurt him. Raistlin would simply have to be circumspect.

With an appearance of humility, Raistlin stepped down from the stump.

"I am sorry, Master," said Raistlin contritely. "It won't happen again."

"I should hope not," said Master Theobald stiffly. He departed in a state of high dudgeon that would only increase upon his return home to find that most of his spell components, to say nothing of his steel pieces, had disappeared—and not by magic.

The crowd began to drift away, most of them quite satisfied, having seen a show well worth a steel coin or two. Soon the only people remaining around the stump were Sturm, Caramon, Raistlin, and the kender.

"Ah, Sturm!" Caramon sighed. "You spoiled the fun."

"Fun?" Sturm frowned. "That was Raistlin's schoolmaster you were tormenting, wasn't it?"

"Yes, but—"

"Excuse me," said the kender, shoving his way forward to talk to Raistlin. "Could you pull the rabbit out of the box again?"

"Raistlin should treat his master with more respect," Sturm was saying.

"Or make the coins come out of my nose?" the kender persisted. "I didn't know I had coins up my nose. You think I would have sneezed or something. Here, I'll shove this one up there, and—"

Raistlin removed the coin from the kender's hand. "Don't do that. You'll hurt yourself. Besides, this is our money."

"Is it? You must have dropped it." The kender held out his hand. "How do you do? My name is Tasslehoff Burrfoot. What's yours?"

Raistlin was prepared to coldly rebuff the kender—no human in full possession of his sanity, who wanted to keep firm hold on such sanity, would ever willingly associate with a kender. Raistlin recalled the stupefied look on Master Theobald's face when he had seen his precious spell components in the hands of a kender. Smiling at the memory, feeling that he was in the kender's debt, Raistlin gravely accepted the proffered hand. Not only that, but he introduced the kender to the others.

"This is my brother, Caramon, and his friend, Sturm Brightblade."

Sturm appeared extremely reluctant to shake hands with a kender, but they had been formally introduced and he could not avoid the handshake without appearing impolite.

"Hi, there, Little Fella," Caramon said, good-naturedly shaking hands, his own large hand completely engulfing the kender's and causing Tasslehoff to wince slightly.

"I don't like to mention this, Caramon," said the kender solemnly, "since we've only just been introduced, but it is very rude to keep commenting on a person's size. For instance, you wouldn't like it very much if I called you Beer Barrel Belly, would you?"

The name was so funny and the scene was so ludicrous—a mosquito scolding a bear—that Raistlin began to laugh. He laughed until he was weak from the exertion and was forced to sit down on the stump. Pleased and amazed to see his brother in such a good humor, Caramon burst out in a loud guffaw and clapped the kender on the back, kindly picked him up afterward.

"Come, my brother," said Raistlin, "we should gather our belongings and start for home. The fairgrounds will be closing soon. It was very good meeting you, Tasslehoff Burrfoot," he added with sincerity.

"I'll help," offered Tasslehoff, darting eager glances at the many colored balls, the brightly painted box.

"Thanks, but we can manage," Caramon said hurriedly, retrieving the rabbit just as it was disappearing into one of the kender's pouches. Sturm removed several of the silk scarves from the kender's pocket.

"You should be more careful of your possessions," Tasslehoff felt called upon to point out. "It's a good thing I was here to find them. I'm glad I was. You really are a wonderful magician, Raistlin. May I call you Raistlin? Thanks. And I'll call you Caramon, if you'll call me Tasslehoff, which is my name, only my friends call me Tas, which you can, too, if you like. And I'll call you Sturm. Are you a knight? I was in Solamnia once and saw lots of knights. They all had mustaches like yours, only more of it—the mustache, I mean. Yours is a bit scrawny right now, but I can see you're working on it."

"Thank you," Sturm said, stroking his new mustache self-consciously.

The brothers started moving through the crowd, heading toward the exit. Saying that he'd seen all he cared to see for the day, Tasslehoff accompanied them. Not caring to be seen in public in company with a kender, Sturm had been about to take his leave of them when the kender mentioned Solamnia.

"Have you truly been there?" he asked.

"I've been all over Ansalon," said Tas proudly. "Solamnia's a very nice place. I'll tell you about it if you'd like. Say, I have an idea. Why don't you come home with me for supper? All of you. Flint won't mind."

"Who's Flint? Your wife?" Caramon asked.

Tasslehoff hooted. "My wife! Wait till I tell him! No, Flint's a dwarf and my very best friend in all the world, and I'm his best friend, no matter what he says, except for maybe Tanis Half-Elven, who is another friend of mine, only he's not here right now, he's gone to Qualinesti where the elves live." Tas stopped talking at this juncture, but only because he'd run out of breath.

"I remember now!" exclaimed Raistlin, coming to a halt. "I knew you looked familiar. You were there when Gilon died. You and the dwarf and the half-elf." He paused a moment, eyeing the kender thoughtfully, then said, "Thank you, Tasslehoff. We accept your invitation to supper."

"We do?" Caramon looked startled.

"Yes, my brother," said Raistlin.

"You'll come, too, won't you?" Tasslehoff asked Sturm eagerly.

Sturm was stroking his mustache. "My mother's expecting me at home, but I don't believe she'll mind if I join my friends. I'll stop by and tell her where I'm going. What part of Solamnia did you visit?"

"I'll show you." Tasslehoff reached around to a pouch he wore on his back—the kender was festooned with pouches and bags. He pulled out a map. "I do love maps, don't you? Would you mind holding that corner? There's Tarsis by the Sea. I've never been there, but I hope to go someday, when Flint doesn't need my help so much, which he does dreadfully right now. You wouldn't believe the trouble he gets into if I'm not there to keep an eye on things. Yes, that's Solamnia. They have awfully fine jails there. . . ."

The two continued walking, the tall Sturm bent to study the map, Tasslehoff pointing out various places of interest.

"Sturm's taken leave of his senses," said Caramon. "That kender's probably never been anywhere near Solamnia. They all lie like . . . well, like kender. And now you've got us eating supper with one of them and a dwarf! It's . . . it's not proper. We should stick to our own kind. Father says—"

"Not anymore he doesn't," Raistlin interrupted.

Caramon paled and lapsed into an unhappy silence.

Raistlin laid his hand on his brother's arm in silent apology. "We cannot stay cooped up forever in our home, wrapped in a safe little cocoon," he said gently. "We finally have a chance to break free of our bindings, Caramon, and we should take it! We'll need a little time for our wings to dry in the sun, but soon we'll be strong enough to fly. Do you understand?"

"Yes, I think so. I'm not sure I want to fly, Raist. I get dizzy when I'm up too high." Caramon, added thoughtfully, "But if you're wet, you should definitely go home and dry off."

Raistlin sighed, patted his brother's arm. "Yes, Caramon. I'll change my clothes. And then we'll have dinner with the dwarf. And the kender."

2

The house of Flint Fireforge was considered an oddity and one of the wonders of Solace. Not only was it built on the ground, but it was also made entirely of stone, which the dwarf had hauled all the way from Prayer's Eye Peak. Flint didn't care what people said about him or his house. In the long and proud history of dwarfdom, no dwarf had ever lived in a tree.

Birds lived in trees. Squirrels lived in trees. Elves lived in trees. Flint was neither bird, nor squirrel, nor elf, thanks be to Reorx the Forger. Flint did not have wings, nor a bushy tail, nor pointed ears—all of which, as everyone knows, are indigenous to tree-dwelling species. He considered living in trees unnatural as well as dangerous.

"Fall out of bed and that'll be the last fall you ever take," the dwarf was wont to say in dire tones.

It was useless to point out to him, as did his friend and business partner, Tanis Half-Elven, that even in a tree house one fell out of bed and landed on the floor, likely suffering nothing worse than a bruised backside.

Tree house floors were made of wood, Flint maintained, and wood was known to be an untrustworthy building material, subject to rot, mice, and termites, likely to catch fire at any moment, leaky in the rain, drafty in the cold. A good, stiff puff of wind would carry it away.

Stone, now. Nothing could beat good, solid stone. Cool in the summer, warm in the winter. Not a drop of rain could penetrate stone walls. The wind might blow as hard as it liked, blow until it was red in the face, and your stone blocks would never so much as quiver. It was well known that stone houses were the only houses to have survived the Cataclysm.

"Except in Istar," Tanis Half-Elven would tease.

"Not even stone houses can be expected to survive having a great bloody mountain dropped down on top of them," Flint would return, always adding, "Besides, I have no doubt that way down in the Blood Sea, where all know the city of Istar was cast, certain lucky fish are living quite comfortably."

On this particular day, Flint was inside his stone house attempting to make some sense of the disorder in which he lived. Disorder was a constant state of affairs ever since the kender had moved in.

The two unlikely roommates had met on market day. Flint was showing his wares, and Tasslehoff, passing through town on his way to anywhere interesting, had stopped at the dwarf's stall to admire a very fine bracelet.

What happened next is subject to who tells the story. According to Tas, he picked up the bracelet to try it on, discovered it fit perfectly, and was going off in search of someone to ask the price.

According to Flint, he came out of the back of the booth, after a refreshing nip of ale, to find Tasslehoff and the bracelet both disappearing rapidly into the crowd. Flint nabbed the kender, who loudly and shrilly proclaimed his innocence. People stopped to watch. Not to buy. Just to watch.

Tanis Half-Elven, arriving on the scene, broke up the altercation, dispersed the crowd. Reminding the dwarf in low tones that such scenes were bad for business, Tanis persuaded Flint that he didn't really want to see the kender hung from the nearest vallenwood by his thumbs. Tasslehoff magnanimously accepted the dwarf's apology, which Flint couldn't recall ever having made.

That evening, the kender had showed up on Flint's doorstep, along with a jug of excellent brandy, which Tasslehoff claimed to have purchased at the Inn of the Last Home and which he had brought the dwarf by way of a peace offering. The next afternoon, Flint had awakened with a hammer-pounding headache to find the kender firmly ensconced in the guest bedroom.

Nothing Flint did or said could induce Tasslehoff to leave.

"I've heard tell that kender are afflicted with—what do they call it?—wanderlust. That's it. Wanderlust. I suppose you'll be coming down with that soon," the dwarf had hinted.

"Nope. Not me." Tas had been emphatic. "I've gone through that already. Outgrown it, you might say. I'm ready to settle down. Isn't that lucky? You really do need someone to look after you, Flint, and I'm here to fill the bill. We'll share this nice house all through the winter. I'll travel with you during the summer. I have the most excellent maps, by the way. And I know all the really fine jails. . . ."

Thoroughly alarmed at this prospect, more frightened than he'd ever been in his life, even when held captive by ogres, Flint had sought out his friend, Tanis Half-Elven, and had asked him to help him either evict the kender or murder him. To Flint's amazement, the half-elf had laughed heartily and refused. According to Tanis, life shared with Tasslehoff would be good for Flint, who was much too reclusive and set in his ways.

"The kender will keep you young," Tanis had said.

"Aye, and likely I'll die young," Flint had grumbled.

Living with the kender had introduced Flint to a great many people in Solace, most notably the town guardsmen, who now made the dwarf's house their first stop when searching for missing valuables. The sheriff soon grew tired of arresting Tas, who ate more than his share of prison food, walked off with their keys, and persisted in making helpful suggestions about how they could improve their jail. Finally, at the suggestion of Tanis Half-Elven, the sheriff had decided to quit incarcerating the kender, on the condition that Tas be remanded into Flint's custody. The dwarf had protested vehemently, but no one listened.

Now, every day after Flint's morning housecleaning, he would place any strange new objects he'd happened to find out on the door stoop. Either the town guard came to collect them or their neighbors would stop by and rummage through the pile, searching for items they had "dropped," items that the kender had thoughtfully "found."

Life with the kender also kept Flint active. He had spent half of this morning searching for his tools, which were never in their proper place. He'd discovered his most valuable and highly prized silver hammer lying in a pile of nutshells, having apparently been used as a nutcracker. His best tongs were nowhere to be found. (They would turn up three days later in the creek that ran behind the house, Tasslehoff having attempted to use them to catch fish.) Calling down a whole cartload of curses on the kender's topknotted head, Flint was searching for the tea kettle when Tasslehoff flung open the door with a heart-stopping bang.

"Hi, Flint! Guess what? I'm home. Oh, did you hit your head? What were you doing under there in the first place? I don't see why you should be looking for the tea kettle under the bed. What kind of doorknob would put a tea kettle under the—Oh, you did? Well, isn't that odd. I wonder how it got there. Perhaps it's magic! A magic tea kettle.

"Speaking of magic, Flint, these are some new friends of mine. Mind your head, Caramon. You're much too tall for our door. This is Raistlin and his brother Caramon. They're twins, Flint, isn't that interesting? They look sort of alike, especially if you turn them sideways. Turn sideways, Caramon, and you, too, Raistlin, so that Flint can see. And that's my new friend Sturm Brightblade. He's a knight of Solamnia! They're staying to dinner, Flint. I hope we've got enough to eat."

Tas concluded at this point, swelling with pride and the two lungfuls of air required for such a long speech.

Flint eyed the size of Caramon and hoped they had enough to eat as well. The dwarf was in a bit of a quandary. The moment they stepped across his threshold, the young men were guests in his house, and by dwarven custom that meant they were to be treated with the same hospitality he would have given the thanes of his clan, had those gentlemen ever happened to pay Flint a visit, an occurrence which was highly unlikely. Flint was not particularly fond of humans, however, especially young ones. Humans were changeable and impetuous, prone to acting rashly and impulsively and, in the dwarf's mind, dangerously. Some dwarven scholars attributed these characteristics to the human's short life span, but Flint held that was only an excuse. Humans, to his way of thinking, were simply addled.

The dwarf fell back on an old ploy, one that always worked well for him when confronted by human visitors.

"I would be very pleased if you could stay to dinner," said the dwarf, "but as you can see, we don't have a single chair that will fit you."

"I'll go borrow some," offered Tasslehoff, heading for the door, only to be stopped short by the tremendous cry of "No!" that burst simultaneously from four throats.

Flint mopped his face with his beard. A vision of the suddenly chairless people of Solace descending on him in droves caused him to break out in a cold sweat.

"Please do not trouble yourself," said Sturm, with that cursed formal politeness typical of Solamnic knights. "I do not mind sitting on the floor."

"I can sit here," Caramon offered, dragging over a wooden chest and plopping down on it. His weight caused the hand-carved chest to creak alarmingly.

"You have a chair that would fit Raistlin," Tasslehoff reminded him. "It's in your bedroom. You know, the one we always use whenever Tanis comes over to— Why are you making those faces at me? Do you have something in your eye? Let me look. . . ."

"Get away from me!" Flint roared.

His face flushed red, the dwarf fumbled in his pocket for the key to the bedroom. He always kept the door locked, changed the lock at least once a week. This didn't stop the kender from entering, but at least it slowed him down some. Stomping into the bedroom, Flint dragged out the chair that he saved for the use of his friend and kept hidden the rest of the time.

Positioning the chair, the dwarf took a good hard look at his visitors. The young man called Raistlin was thin, much too thin, as far as the dwarf was concerned, and the cloak he was wearing was threadbare and not at all suited to keep out the autumn chill. He was shivering, his lips were pale with the cold. The dwarf felt a bit ashamed for his lack of hospitality.

"Here you go," he said. Positioning the chair near the fire, he added gruffly, "You seem a bit cold, lad. Sit down and warm yourself. And you"—he glowered at the kender—"if you want to make yourself useful, go to Otik's and buy—buy, mind you!—a jug of his apple cider."

"I'll be back in two shakes of a lamb's tail," Tas promised. "But why two shakes? Why not three? And do lambs even have tails? I don't see how—"

Flint slammed the door on him.

Raistlin had taken his seat, edged the chair even closer to the fire. Blue eyes, of a startling clarity, regarded the dwarf with an intense gravity that made Flint feel extremely uncomfortable.

"It is not really necessary for you to give us dinner—" Raistlin began.

"It isn't?" exclaimed Caramon, dismayed. "What'd we come here for, then?"

His twin flashed him a look that caused the bigger youth to squirm uncomfortably and duck his head. Raistlin turned back to Flint.

"The reason we came is this: My brother and I wanted to thank you in person for speaking up for us against that woman"—he refused to dignify her with a name—"at our father's funeral."

Now Flint recalled how he knew these youngsters. Oh, he'd seen them around town since they were old enough to be underfoot, but he had forgotten this particular connection.

"It was nothing special," protested the dwarf, embarrassed at being thanked. "The woman was daft! Belzor!" Flint snorted. "What god worth his beard would go around calling himself by the name of Belzor? I was sorry to hear about your mother, lads," he added, more kindly.

Raistlin made no response to that, dismissed it with a flicker of his eyelids. "You mentioned the name 'Reorx.' I have been doing some studying, and I find that Reorx is the name for a god that your people once worshiped."

"Maybe it is," said Flint, smoothing his beard and eyeing the young man mistrustfully. "Though I don't know why a human book should be taking an interest in a god of the dwarves."

"It was an old book," Raistlin explained. "A very old book, and it spoke not only of Reorx, but of all the old gods. Do you and your people still worship Reorx, sir? I don't ask this idly," Raistlin added, a tinge of color staining his pale cheeks. "Nor do I ask to be impertinent. I am in earnest. I truly wish to know what you think."

"I do as well, sir," said Sturm Brightblade. Though he sat on the floor, his back was as straight as a pike staff.

Flint was astonished. No human had ever, in all the dwarf's hundred and thirty-some years, wanted to know anything at all about dwarven religious practices. He was suspicious. What were these young men after? Were they spies, trying to trick him, get him into trouble? Flint had heard rumors that some of the followers of Belzor were preaching that elves and dwarves were heretics and should be burned.

So be it, Flint decided. If these young men are out to get me, I'll teach them a thing or two. Even that big one there. Bash him in the kneecaps and he'll be cut down to about my size.

"We do," said Flint stoutly. "We believe in Reorx. I don't care who knows it."

"Are there dwarven clerics, then?" Sturm asked, leaning forward in his interest. "Clerics who perform miracles in the name of Reorx?"

"No, young man, there aren't," Flint said. "And there haven't been since the Cataclysm."

"If you've had no sign that Reorx still concerns himself over your fate, how can you still believe in him?" Raistlin argued.

"It is a poor faith that demands constant reassurance, young human," Flint countered. "Reorx is a god, and we're not supposed to understand the gods. That's where the Kingpriest of

Istar got into trouble. He thought he understood the minds of the gods, reckoned he was a god himself, or so I've heard. That's why they threw the fiery mountain down on top of him.

"Even when Reorx walked among us, he did a lot that we don't understand. He created kender, for one," Flint added in gloomy tones. "And gully dwarves, for another. To my mind, I think Reorx is like myself—a traveling man. He has other worlds he tends to, and off he goes. Like him, I leave my house during the summer, but I always come back in the fall. My house is still here, waiting for me. We dwarves just have to wait for Reorx to come back from his journeys."

"I never thought of that," said Sturm, struck with the notion. "Perhaps that is why Paladine left our people. He had other worlds to settle."

"I'm not sure." Raistlin was thoughtful. "I know this seems unlikely, but what if, instead of you leaving the house, you woke up one morning to find that the house had left you?"

"This house will be here long after I'm gone," Flint growled, thinking the young man was making a disparaging remark about his handiwork. "Why, look at the carving and joining of the stone! You'll not see the like between here and Pax Tharkas."

"That wasn't what I meant, sir," Raistlin said with a half-smile. "I was wondering . . . It seems to me . . . " He paused, making an effort to say exactly what he did mean. "What if the gods had never left? What if they are here, simply waiting for us to come back to them?"

"Bah! Reorx wouldn't hang about, lollygagging his time away, without giving us dwarves some sort of sign. We're his favorites, you know," Flint said proudly.

"How do you know he hasn't given the dwarves a sign, sir?" Raistlin asked coolly.

Flint was hard put to answer that one. He didn't know, not for sure. He hadn't been back to the hills, back to his homeland in years. And despite the fact that he traveled throughout this region, he hadn't really had that much contact with any other dwarves. Perhaps Reorx had come back and the Thorbardin dwarves were keeping the god a secret!

"It would be like them, damn their beards and bellies," Flint muttered.

"Speaking of bellies, isn't anybody else hungry?" Caramon asked plaintively. "I'm starved."

"Such a thing is not possible," said Sturm flatly.

"It is, too," Caramon protested. "I haven't had anything to eat since breakfast."

"I was referring to what your brother said," Sturm returned. "Paladine could not be in the world, witnessing the hardships my people have been forced to endure, and do nothing to intercede."

"From what I've heard, your people witnessed the hardships suffered by those under their rule calmly enough," Raistlin returned. "Perhaps because they were responsible for most of it."

"That's a lie!" Sturm cried, jumping to his feet, his fists clenched.

"Here, now, Sturm, Raist didn't mean that—" Caramon began.

"Are you telling me that the Solamnic knights did not actively persecute magic-users?" Raistlin feigned astonishment. "I suppose the mages simply grew weary of living in the Tower of High Sorcery in Palanthas, and that's why they fled from it in fear for their lives!"

"Raist, I'm sure Sturm didn't intend to—"

"Some call it persecution. Others call it rooting out evil!" Sturm said darkly.

"So you equate magic with evil?" Raistlin asked with dangerous calm.

"Don't most people with any sense?" Sturm returned.

Caramon rose to his feet, his own fists clenched. "I don't think you really meant that, did you, Sturm?"

"We have a saying in Solamnia. 'If the boot fits—' "

Caramon took a clumsy swing at Sturm, who ducked and lunged at his opponent, catching him in his broad midsection. Caramon went over backward with a "woof," Sturm on top of him, pummeling him. The two crashed into the wooden chest, breaking it into its component parts and smashing the crockery that was being stored inside. The two continued their scuffling on the floor, rolling and punching and flailing away at each other.

Raistlin remained sitting by the fire, watching calmly, a slight smile on his thin lips. Flint was disturbed by such coolness, so disturbed that he lost the moment when he might have stopped the fight. Raistlin did not appear worried, concerned, or shocked. Flint might have suspected him of having provoked this battle for his own amusement, except that he did not appear to be enjoying the show. His smile was not one of pleasure. It was faintly derisive, his look disdainful.

"Those eyes of his shivered my skin," Flint was later to tell Tanis. "There is something cold-blooded about him, if you take my meaning."

"I'm not sure I do. Are you saying that this young man deliberately provoked his brother and his friend into a fistfight?"

"Well, no, not exactly." Flint considered. "His question to me was sincere. I've no doubt of that. But then, he must have known how the talk of gods and all that hoo-hah about magic would affect a Solamnic knight. And if there was ever a Solamnic knight walking around without his armor, that is young Sturm for you. Born with a sword up his back, as we used to say.

"But that Raistlin." The dwarf shook his head. "I think he just liked knowing that he could make them fight, best friends and all."

"Hey, now!" Flint shouted, suddenly realizing that he wasn't going to have any furniture left if he didn't put an end to the brawl. "What do you think you're doing? You've broken my dishes! Stop that! Stop it, I say!"

The two paid no heed to the dwarf. Flint waded into the fray. A swift and expert kick to the outside of the kneecap sent Sturm rolling. He rocked in agony on top of the bits of broken crockery, clutching his knee and biting his lip to keep from crying out in pain.

Flint grabbed hold of a handful of Caramon's long, curly hair and gave it a swift, sharp tug. Caramon yelped and tried unsuccessfully to prize loose the dwarf's hold. Flint had a grip of iron.

"Look at you both!" the dwarf stated in disgust, giving Caramon's head a shake and Sturm another kick. "Acting like a couple of drunken goblins. And who taught you to fight? Your great-aunt Minnie? Both of you taller than me by a foot at least, maybe two feet for the young giant, and here you are. Flat on your back with the foot of a dwarf on your chest. Get up. Both of you."

Shamefaced and teary-eyed from the pain, the two young men slowly picked themselves up off the floor. Sturm stood balancing on one leg, not daring to trust his full weight to his injured knee. Caramon winced and massaged his stinging scalp, wondering if he had a bald spot.

"Sorry about the dishes," Caramon mumbled.

"Yes, sir, I am truly sorry," Sturm said earnestly. "I will make recompense for the damage, of course."

"I'll do better than that. I'll pay for it," Caramon offered.

Raistlin said nothing. He was already counting out money from their take at the fair.

"Darn right you'll pay for it," the dwarf said. "How old are you?"

"Twenty," answered Sturm.

"Eighteen," said Caramon. "Raist is eighteen, too."

"Since he knows we are twins, I'm certain Master Fireforge has figured that out," Raistlin said caustically.

Flint eyed Sturm. "And you plan to be a knight." The dwarf's shrewd gaze shifted to Caramon. "And you, big fellow. You figure on being a great warrior, I suppose? Sell your sword to some lord."

"That's right!" Caramon gaped. "How did you know?"

"I've seen you around town, carrying that great sword of yours—handling it all wrong, I might add. Well I'm here to tell both of you right now that the knights'll take one look at you and the way you fight, Sturm Brightblade, and they'll laugh themselves right out of their armor. And you, Caramon Majere, you couldn't sell your fighting skills to my old grannie."

"I know I have a lot to learn, sir," Sturm replied stiffly. "If I were living in Solamnia, I would be squire to a noble knight and learn my craft from him. But I am not. I am exiled here." His tone was bitter.

"There's no one in Solace to teach us," Caramon complained. "This town is way too quiet. Nothing ever happens here. You'd think we'd at least have a goblin raid or something to liven things up."

"Bite your tongue, lad. You don't know when you're well off. As for a teacher, you're looking at him." Flint tapped himself on the breast.

"You?" Both young men appeared dubious.

Flint stroked his beard complacently. "I had my foot on both of you, didn't I? Besides"—reaching out, he gave Raistlin a poke in the ribs that caused him to jump—"I want to talk to the book reader here about his views on a good many matters. No need to talk of money," the dwarf added, seeing the twins exchanging doubtful glances and guessing what they were thinking. "You can pay me in chores. And you can start by going to the inn and seeing what's become of that dratted kender."

As if the words had conjured him, the door was thrown open by the "dratted" kender.

"I've got the cider and a kidney pie that someone didn't want, and— Ah, there! I knew it!"

Tasslehoff gazed sadly at the remains of the chest and the broken dishes. "You see what happens, Flint, when I'm not around?" he said, solemnly shaking his topknot.

3

The unlikely friendship between the young humans, the dwarf, and the kender flourished like weeds in the rainy season, according to Tasslehoff. Flint took exception to being called a "weed," but he conceded that Tas was right. Flint had always had a soft spot in his gruff heart for young people, particularly those who were friendless and alone. He had first become acquainted with Tanis Half-Elven when he met that young man living in Qualinesti, an orphan that neither race would claim. Tanis was too human for the elves, too elven for humans.

Tanis had been raised in the household of the Speaker of the Sun and Stars, the leader of the Qualinesti, growing up with the Speaker's own children. One of those children, Porthios, hated Tanis for what he was. Another cousin, Laurana, loved Tanis too much. In that is another tale, however.

Suffice it to say that Tanis had left the elven kingdom some years ago. He'd gone for help to the first person—the only person—he knew outside of Qualinesti: Flint Fireforge. Tanis had no skill at all in working metal, but he did have a head for figures and a keen business sense. He soon discovered that Flint was selling his wares far below their true worth. He was cheating himself.

"People will be happy to pay more for quality workmanship," Tanis had pointed out to the dwarf, who was terrified that he would lose his clientele. "You'll see."

Tanis proved to be right, and Flint prospered, much to the dwarf's astonishment. The two became partners. Tanis began accompanying the dwarf on his summer travels. Tanis hired the wagon and the horses, put up the booths at the local fairs, made appointments to show Flint's wares privately to the well-to-do.

The two developed a friendship that was deep and abiding. Flint asked Tanis to move in with him, but Tanis pointed out that the dwarf's house was a bit cramped for the tall half-elf. Tanis's dwelling place was nearby, however, built up in the tree branches. The only quarrel the two ever had—and it wasn't really a quarrel, more of a grumbling argument—was over Tanis's trips back to Qualinesti.

"You're not fit for anything when you come back from that place," Flint said bluntly. "You're in a dark mood for a week. They don't want you around; they've made that plain enough. You upset their lives and they upset yours. The best thing for you to do is wash the mud of Qualinesti off your boots and never go back."

"You're right, of course," said Tanis reflectively. "And every time I leave, I swear I will never return. But something draws me back. When I hear the music of the aspen trees in my dreams, I know it is time for me to return home. And Qualinesti is my home. They can't deny it to me, no matter how they'd like to try."

"Bah! That's the elf in you!" Flint scoffed. " 'Music of the aspen trees!' Horse droppings! I haven't been home in one hundred years. You don't hear me carrying on about the music of the walnuts, do you?"

"No, but I have heard you express a longing for proper dwarf spirits," Tanis teased.

"That's completely different," Flint returned sagaciously. "We're talking life's blood here. I do wonder that Otik can't seem to get the recipe right. I've given it to him often enough. It's these local mushrooms, or what humans think pass for mushrooms."

Despite Flint's urgings, Tanis left that fall for Qualinesti. He was gone during Yule. The heavy snows set in, and it began to look as if he wouldn't be back before spring.

Flint had always been a bit lonely when Tanis was gone, though the dwarf would have cut off his beard before he admitted it. The inadvertent addition of Tasslehoff eased the dwarf's loneliness some, though Flint would have cut off his head before he admitted that. The kender's lively chatter filled in the silence, though the dwarf always irritably put a stop to it when he found himself becoming too interested.

Teaching the young humans how to handle themselves in a fight gave Flint a true feeling of accomplishment. He showed them the little tricks and skillful maneuvers he had learned from a lifetime of encounters with ogres and goblins, thieves and footpads, and other hazards faced by those who travel the unchancy roads of Abanasinia. He likened this feeling of satisfaction to that of turning out an exceptional piece of metalwork.

In essence, he was doing much the same: shaping and crafting young lives as he shaped and crafted his metal. One of them, however, was not particularly malleable.

Raistlin continued to "shiver" Flint's skin.

The twins were nineteen that winter, and they were spending the winter together.

Early in the fall, a fire had burned down Master Theobald's mage school, forcing him to relocate. By this time, Theobald was well known and trusted in Solace. The authorities—once assured that the fire had been from natural causes and not supernatural—gave him permission to open his new school within the town limits.

Raistlin no longer needed to board at the school. He could spend the winters at home with Caramon. But neither he nor Caramon were home much of the time.

Raistlin enjoyed the company of the dwarf and the kender. He required knowledge of the world beyond the vallenwoods, knowledge of a world in which he would soon be taking his place. Since acquiring the ability to cast his magic, he had dared to dream of his future.

Raistlin was now an assistant teacher at the school. Master Theobald hoped that by providing some honorable way for the young man to earn money, Raistlin would quit performing in public. Raistlin was not a particularly good teacher; he had no patience for ignorance and tended to be extremely sarcastic. But he kept the boys quiet during Master Theobald's afternoon nap, which was all the master required. Master Theobald had once mentioned that Raistlin might like to open a mage school himself. Raistlin had laughed in the master's face.

Raistlin wanted power. Not power over a bunch of mewling brats, dully reciting their *aa*s and *ai*s. He wanted the power he held over people when they watched him cast even minor cantrips. Their expressions of awe, their wide-eyed respect were deeply gratifying. He saw himself gaining increasing power over others.

Power for good, of course.

He would give money to the impoverished, health to the sickly, justice to evildoers. He would be loved, admired, feared, and envied. If he was going to hold sway over vast numbers of people (such are the ambitious dreams of youth!), he would need to know as much as possible about those people—all of them, not just humans. The dwarf and the kender proved to be excellent character studies.

The first thing Raistlin learned was that a kender's fingers are into everything, and a kender's hands will carry it off. He had been enraged the first time Tasslehoff appropriated the small bag in which the young mage proudly kept his one and only spell component.

"Look what I found!" Tasslehoff announced. "A leather pouch with the letter *R* on it. Let's see what's inside."

Raistlin recognized the pouch, which only moments earlier had been hanging from his belt. "No! Wait! Don't—"

Too late. Tas had opened the pouch. "There's a bunch of dried-up flowers in here. I'll just empty those out." He dumped the rose petals on the floor, looked back inside. "Nope, nothing else. That's odd. Why would anyone—"

"Give me that!" Raistlin snatched the pouch. He was literally trembling with rage.

"Oh, is that yours?" Tas looked up at him, eyes bright. "I cleaned it out for you. Someone had stuck a bunch of dead flowers inside it."

Raistlin opened his mouth, but words were not only inadequate, they were nonexistent. He could only glare, make incoherent sounds, and at least satisfy some of his anger by casting a furious glance at his laughing brother.

After losing the pouch and the rose petals twice more, Raistlin realized that outrage, threats of violence and/or legal action did not work with kender. He could never catch the deft fingers that could untie any knot, no matter how tight and slide the bag away with the lightness of touch of a spider. Coping with Tasslehoff required subtlety.

Raistlin conducted an experiment. He placed a rounded lump of brightly colored glass, acquired from leavings at the glassblowers, inside his pouch. The next time Tas "found" the pouch, he discovered the glass inside. Enchanted, he drew out the glass, dropped the pouch to the floor. Raistlin retrieved the pouch and his spell components intact. After that, he took to putting some trinket or interesting object (a bird's egg, a petrified beetle, a sparkling rock) in the pouch. Whenever he missed it, he knew where to look.

As Raistlin learned more about kender, Caramon was learning the fine and not-so-fine points of dwarven combat.

Due to the short stature of dwarves and the fact that they generally fight opponents much taller than themselves, dwarven fighting techniques are not elegant. Flint used a number of moves—groin kicks and rabbit punches, for example—that were not chivalrous, according to Sturm.

"I will not fight like a common street brawler," he protested.

The time of year was the deepest part of midwinter. Crystalmir Lake was frozen and snow-covered. Most people kept indoors where it was warm, toasting their feet and drinking hot punch. Flint had Sturm and Caramon outside, working them into a lather, "toughening them up."

"Is that so?" Flint walked over to stand beneath the tall young man. Drops of water from his panting breath coated Sturm's mustaches, making him look like walrus, according to Tasslehoff.

"And what will you do when you are attacked by a common street brawler, laddie?" Flint demanded. "Raise your sword to him in some fool salute while he kicks you in your privates?"

Caramon guffawed. Sturm frowned at the vulgarity, but conceded that the dwarf had a point. He should at least know how to counter such an attack.

"Goblins, now," Flint continued his lecture. "They're basically cowards, unless they're fired up with liquor, and then they're just plain crazed. A goblin will always try to jump you from behind, slit your throat before you know what's hit you. Like this . . . He'll use his hairy hand to muffle your scream, and with his other, draw the blade right across here. You'll bleed to death almost before your body hits the ground.

"Now, here's what you do. You use the goblin's own weight and forward movement against him. He comes at you, jumps on you like this. . . ."

"Let me be the goblin!" Tasslehoff begged, waving his hand. "Please, Flint! Let me!"

"All right. Now, the kender—"

"Goblin!" Tas corrected and leapt onto Flint's broad back.

"—jumps on you. What do you do? Just this."

Flint grabbed hold of the kender's two hands that were clutching for his throat and, bending double, flipped the kender over his head.

Tas landed hard on the frozen, snow-covered ground. He lay there a moment, gasping and gulping.

"Knocked the air clean out me!" he said when he could talk. He scrambled to his feet. "I've never not been able to breathe before, have you, Caramon? It's an interesting feeling. And I saw the stars and it's not even night. Do you want me to do it to you, Caramon?"

"Hah! You couldn't flip me!" Caramon scoffed.

"Maybe not," Tas admitted. "But I can do this."

Clenching his fist, he drove it right into Caramon's broad midriff.

Caramon groaned and doubled over, clutching his gut and sucking air.

"Well struck, kender," came an approving voice that rang out over the laughter of the others.

"Not bad, Tasslehoff. Not bad," said another.

Two people, heavily muffled in furs, were walking through the snow.

"Tanis!" Flint roared in welcome.

"Kitiara!" Caramon cried out in surprise.

"Tanis and Kitiara!" Tasslehoff yelled, though he'd never seen or met Kitiara before in his life.

"Here, now. Do you all know each other?" Tanis demanded. He looked from Caramon and Raistlin to Kitiara in astonishment.

"I should," answered Kitiara with her crooked grin. "These two are my brothers. The twins I was telling you about. And as for Brightblade, here, he and I used to play together." Her crooked smile gave the words a salacious meaning.

Caramon whistled and poked Sturm in the ribs. Sturm flushed in embarrassment and anger. Saying stiffly that he was needed at home, he bowed coldly to the newcomers, turned on his heel, and stalked off.

"What'd I say?" Kit asked. Then she laughed and, holding out her arms, invited her brothers to her embrace.

Caramon gave her a bear hug. Showing off his strength, he lifted her from the ground.

"Very good, little brother," she said, eyeing him approvingly when he set her down. "You've grown since I saw you last."

"Two whole inches," Caramon said proudly.

Raistlin turned his cheek to his sister, avoided her embrace. Kitiara, with a laugh and a shrug, kissed him, an obliging peck. He stood motionless beneath her scrutinizing gaze, his hands folded in front of him. He was wearing the robes of a mage now, white robes, a gift from his mentor, Antimodes.

"You've grown, too, baby brother," Kit observed.

"Raistlin's grown a whole inch," said Caramon. "It's my

cooking that's done it."

"That wasn't what I meant," said Kit.

"I know. Thank you, Sister," Raistlin replied. The two exchanged glances, in perfect accord.

"Well, well," said Kit, turning back to Tanis. "Who would have thought it? I leave my brothers babes in arms and come back to find them grown men. And this"—she turned to the dwarf—"this must be Flint Fireforge."

She held out her gloved hand. "Kitiara uth Matar."

"Your servant, ma'am," said Flint, accepting her hand.

The two shook hands with every mark of mutual pleasure in the meeting.

"And I'm Tasslehoff Burrfoot," said Tas, offering one hand to be shaken while the other was gliding toward the young woman's belt.

"How do you do, Tasslehoff," Kit said. "Touch that dagger and I'll use it to slice off your ears," she added good-naturedly.

Something in her voice convinced Tasslehoff that she meant what she said. Being rather fond of his ears, which served to prop up his topknot, Tasslehoff began to rummage through a pouch Tanis obviously didn't want.

Flint deemed that the lessons were over, invited his guests inside for a sip and a bite.

Tanis and Kit shed their cloaks. Kitiara was dressed in a long leather tunic that came to midthigh. She wore a man's shirt, open at the neck, and a finely tooled leather belt of elven make and design. She was unlike any woman the others had ever known, and none of them, including her brothers, seemed to know quite what to make of her.

Her gaze was that of a man, bold and straightforward, not the simpering, blushing modesty of a well-bred woman. Her movements were graceful—the grace of a trained swordsman—and she had the confidence and coolness of a blooded warrior. If she was a bit cocky, that only enhanced her exotic appeal.

"You've noticed my belt," she said, proudly exhibiting the hand-tooled leather girdle that encircled her slender waist. "It's a gift from an admirer."

None of those present had to look far to find the gift giver. Tanis Half-Elven watched Kit's every movement with open admiration.

"I've heard a lot about you, Flint," Kit added. "All good, of course."

"I haven't heard a thing about you," Flint returned, with his customary bluntness. "But I'll wager I will." He looked at Tanis, and mingled with his affection for his friend was a hint of concern. "Where did you two meet?"

"Outside of Qualinesti," said Tanis. "I was on my way back to Solace when I heard screams coming out of the woods. I went to investigate and found what I thought was this young woman being attacked by a goblin. I ran to her aid, only to discover that I'd been mistaken. The screams I'd heard were coming from the goblin."

"Qualinesti," Flint said, eyeing Kit. "What were you—a human—doing in Qualinesti?"

"I wasn't in Qualinesti," Kit said. "I was just near there. I've been in those parts several times. I pass through them on my way here."

"Way through from where?" Flint wondered.

Kit either didn't hear his question or she ignored it. He was about to repeat himself when she motioned her brothers to step forward for introductions.

"I'm Tanis Half-Elven," said Tanis, offering his hand.

Caramon, in his enthusiasm, almost shook the half-elf's hand off. Raistlin brushed his fingers across the half-elf's palm.

"I'm Caramon Majere, and this is my twin brother, Raistlin. We're Kit's half-brothers, really," Caramon explained.

Raistlin said nothing. He curiously examined the half-elf, about whom he'd heard much, for Flint talked about his friend daily. Tanis was dressed like a hunter, in a brown leather jerkin of elven make, green shirt and brown hose, brown traveling boots. He wore a sword at his waist, carried a bow and a quiver of arrows. His elven heritage was not readily apparent, except perhaps in the finely chiseled bones of his face. If his ears were pointed, it was impossible to tell, for they were covered over by his long, thick brown hair. He had the height of an elf, the broader girth of a human.

He was a handsome man, young looking, but possessing the gravity and maturity of a much older man. Small wonder he had attracted Kit's attention.

Tanis regarded the brothers in his turn, marveling at the coincidence. "Kit and I meet by chance on the road. We become friends, and then I arrive home to find her brothers and my best friends have become friends! This meeting was fated, that's all there is to it."

"For a meeting to be fated implies that something significant must come of it in the future. Do you foresee such an occurrence, sir?" Raistlin asked.

"I . . . I guess it could," Tanis stammered, taken aback. He wasn't quite certain how to respond. "In truth, I meant it as a joke. I didn't intend—"

"Don't mind Raistlin, Tanis," Kitiara interrupted. "He's a deep thinker. The only one in the family, by the way. Stop being so serious, will you?" she said to her younger brother in an undertone. "I like this man and I don't want you scaring him off."

She grinned at Tanis, who smiled back at her. Raistlin knew then that the half-elf and his sister were more than friends. They were lovers. The knowledge and the sudden image in his mind made him feel uncomfortable and embarrassed. He suddenly disliked the half-elf intensely.

"I'm glad to see you've been keeping my old friend Flint out of trouble, at least," Tanis continued. Embarrassed himself, he hoped to change to subject.

"Hah! Out of trouble!" Flint glowered. "Darn near drowned me, they did. It's lucky I survived."

The story of an ill-fated boat trip had to be told then and there, with everyone talking at once.

"I found the boat—" Tasslehoff began.

"Caramon, the big lummox, stood up in it—"

"I was only trying to catch a fish, Flint—"

"Upset the whole blasted boat. Gave us all a good soaking—"

"Caramon sank like a stone. I know, because I threw a whole lot of stones in the water, and they all went down just like Caramon, without even a bubble—"

"I was worried about Raist—"

"I was quite capable of taking care of myself, my brother. There was an air pocket underneath the overturned boat, and I was in no danger whatsoever, except of having an imbecile for a brother. Trying to catch a fish with your bare hands—"

"—jumped in after Caramon. I pulled him out of the water—"

"You did not, Flint! Caramon pulled himself out of the water. I pulled you out of the water. Don't you remember? You see what trouble you get into without me—"

"I do remember, and that wasn't the way it was at all, you dratted kender, and I'll tell you one thing," Flint stated emphatically, bringing the confused tale to a close. "I'm never setting foot in a boat again so long as I live. That was the first time, and it will be the last, so help me, Reorx."

"I trust Reorx will honor that vow," said Tanis. He clapped the dwarf affectionately on the shoulder and rose to leave. "I'm going to go see if my house is still standing. You want to come along?"

Tanis asked the question of Flint, but his eyes went to Kitiara.

"I'll go!" Tas signed on eagerly.

"No, you won't," Flint said, collaring the kender and hauling him backward.

"You're coming home with us, aren't you, Kit?" Caramon asked teasingly.

"Maybe later," said Kitiara. Reaching out, she took hold of Tanis's hand. "Much later."

"Oh, shut up," Raistlin said crossly when Caramon wanted to talk about it.

4

pring came to Solace, bringing with it budding flowers, baby lambs, nesting birds. Blood that had grown cold and sluggish in the winter warmed and thinned. Young men panted and girls giggled. Of all the seasons of the year, Raistlin detested springtime most.

"Kit didn't come home again last night," Caramon said with a wink over breakfast.

Raistlin ate bread and cheese, made no comment. He had no intention of encouraging this line of discussion.

Caramon needed no encouragement, however. "Her bed wasn't slept in. I'll bet I know whose bed was slept in, though. Not that they probably did much sleeping."

"Caramon," said Raistlin coldly, rising to his feet, leaving his breakfast mostly untouched. "You are a pig."

He carried the scraps of his meal to the two field mice he had captured and now kept in a cage, along with the tame rabbit. He had developed certain theories concerning the use of his herbs, and it seemed wiser to test out these theories on animals rather than his patients. Mice were easy to catch and cheap to maintain.

Raistlin's first experiment had not worked out, having fallen victim to the neighbor's cat. He had chastised Caramon quite severely for permitting the cat to enter the house. Caramon, who was fond of cats, promised to entertain the animal out-of-doors from then on. The mice were safe, and Raistlin was quite pleased with the results of his latest experiment. He poked the crumbs through the bars.

"It is bad enough our sister whoring herself, without you making dirty remarks about it," Raistlin continued, giving the rabbit fresh water.

"Aw, c'mon, Raist!" Caramon protested. "Kit isn't . . . what you said. She's in love with the guy. You can see that from the way she looks at him. And he's crazy about her. I like Tanis. Flint's told me a lot about him. Flint says that this summer Tanis'll teach me to use my sword and the bow and arrow. Flint says Tanis is the greatest archer who ever lived. Flint says—"

Raistlin ignored the rest of the conversation. Brushing the crumbs from his hands, he gathered up his books. "I must leave now," he said, rudely cutting his brother off in midsentence. "I am late for school. I will see you this evening, I suppose? Or perhaps you are going to move in with Tanis Half-Elven?"

"Well, no, Raist. Why should I move in with him?"

Sarcasm was lost on Caramon.

"You know, Raist, being with a girl is lots of fun," Caramon continued. "You never talk to any of them, and there's more than one who thinks you're pretty special. Because of the magic and so forth. And how you cured the Greenleaf baby of croup. They say that baby would have died if you hadn't helped her, Raist. Girls like that sort of thing."

Raistlin paused in the doorway, his cheeks faintly burning with pleasure. "It was only a mixture of tea and a root I read about called ipecacuanha. The baby had to throw up the phlegm, you see, and the root mixture caused the child to vomit. Do girls . . . do they truly talk about . . . about such things?"

Girls were, to Raistlin's mind, strange creatures, as unreadable as a magic spell from the tome of some high-ranking archmagus, and just as unattainable. Yet Caramon, who in some matters was as dense as a fallen log, talked to girls, danced the round dances popular at festivals with them, did other things with them, things that Raistlin dreamed about in the dark hours of the night, dreams that left him feeling ashamed and unclean. But then Caramon, with his brawny build, his curly hair, his big brown eyes and handsome features, was attractive to women. Raistlin was not.

The frequent illnesses that still afflicted him left him thin and bony, with no appetite for food. He had the same well-formed nose and chin as Caramon, but on Raistlin the features were more finely planed and pointed, giving him the sly, crafty appearance of a fox. He disliked round dancing, considered it a waste of time and energy, besides which it left him breathless, with a pain in his chest. He didn't know how to talk to girls, what to say. He had the feeling that, although they listened to him politely enough, behind those sparkling eyes, they were secretly laughing at him.

"I don't think they talk about ipe—ipe—ipecaca—whatever that long-tailed word was," Caramon admitted. "But one of them, Miranda, said it was wonderful the way you saved that baby's life. It was her little niece, you see. She wanted me to tell you."

"Did she?" Raistlin murmured.

"Yeah. Miranda's wonderful, isn't she?" Caramon gave a gusty sigh. "I've never seen anyone so beautiful. Oops"—he glanced outdoors, to see the sun starting to rise—"I've got to get going myself. We're planting today. I won't be home until after dark."

Whistling a merry tune, Caramon grabbed his pack and hastened off.

"Yes, my brother, you are right. She is very beautiful!" Raistlin said to the empty house.

Miranda was the daughter of a wealthy clothier, recently arrived to set up business in Solace. Her father's best advertisement, Miranda dressed in the finest clothes, cut and sewn in the very latest style. Long strawberry blond hair fell in lazy ringlets to her waist. Graceful and demure, fragile and winsome, innocent and good, she was utterly captivating, and Raistlin was not the only young man to admire her immensely.

Raistlin had sometimes fancied that Miranda would occasionally glance his way and that her look was inviting. But he always told himself that this was just wishful thinking. How could she possibly care about him? Whenever he saw her, his heart raced, nearly suffocating him. His blood burned, his skin grew cold and clammy. His tongue, normally so glib, could speak only inanities, his brain turned to oatmeal. He could not even look her in the face. Whenever he came close to her, he had difficulty keeping his hand from reaching out to caress one of those flame-colored curls.

There was another factor. Would I be as interested in this young woman if she had not won Caramon's admiration as well? Raistlin asked himself.

The top of Raistlin's mind answered immediately "Yes!" The depths pondered the question uneasily. What demon in Raistlin led to this constant competition with his own twin? A one-sided competition, at that, for Caramon was serenely unaware of it.

Raistlin recalled a story Tasslehoff had told them about a dwarf coming upon a slumbering red dragon. The dwarf attacked the sleeping dragon with ax and sword, hammered at it for hours until he was exhausted. The dragon never even woke up. Yawning, the dragon rolled over in its sleep and squashed the dwarf flat.

Raistlin empathized with that dwarf. He felt as if he were constantly battling his twin, only to have Caramon roll over on him and crush him. Caramon was the better-looking, the better liked, the better trusted. Raistlin was "deep," as Kit described him, or "subtle," as Tanis had once said of him, or "sly," as his classmates termed him. Most people tolerated his presence only because they liked his brother.

At least I am gaining some small reputation as a healer, Raistlin thought as he walked along the boardwalk, trying to avoid breathing in the fragrant spring air, which always made him sneeze.

But the glow of satisfaction no sooner was kindled in him, giving him some small share of warmth, when that infernal demon of his whispered bitterly, Yes, and perhaps that is all you will ever be—a minor mage, a weed-chopping healer—while your warrior brother does great deeds, wins great reward, and covers himself in glory.

"Oh, dear! Oh, my goodness!"

Startled, Raistlin came up short, with the realization that he'd just bumped into someone. He had been concentrating on his thoughts, hurrying along so that he wouldn't be late, and not watching where he was going.

Lifting his head, about to mutter some apology and push his way past, he saw Miranda.

"Oh, dear," she said again and peered over the edge of the railing. Several bolts of fabric lay scattered on the ground beneath them.

"I'm so terribly sorry!" Raistlin gasped. He must have plowed straight into her, causing her to drop the bolts of cloth. They had fallen off the boardwalk, tumbled in a spiral of bright color to the ground.

That was his first thought. His second—and one that caused him even more confusion—was that the boardwalk was wide enough for four people to walk on it abreast and there were only two of them on it at present. One of them, at least, must have been watching where she was going.

"Wait . . . wait here," Raistlin stammered. "I'll . . . I'll go pick them up."

"No, no, it was my fault," the girl returned. Her green eyes glowed like the new budding leaves of the trees that spread their limbs over them. "I was watching a pair of nesting sparrows. . . ." She blushed, which made her even prettier. "I wasn't looking. . . ."

"I insist," Raistlin said firmly.

"We'll go together, shall we?" Miranda forestalled him. "It's a lot to carry, for just one."

She shyly slid her hand into his.

Her touch sent flame through him, flame similar to that of his magic, only hotter. This flame consumed, the other refined.

The two walked side by side down the long stairs to the ground below. The area was still in shadow, the early morning sun was only just filtering through the shiny new leaves. Miranda and Raistlin gathered up the bolts of cloth slowly, taking their time. Raistlin said he hoped the dew would not harm the fabric. Miranda said that there had been no dew at all that morning, nothing to speak of, and that a good brushing would set them right.

He helped her fold up the long lengths of cloth, taking one end while she took the other. Every time they came together, their hands touched.

"I wanted to thank you personally," Miranda said, looking up at him during one of these moments as they stood there, the cloth held between them. Her eyes, glimmering through a veil of reddish blond eyelashes, were entrancing. "You saved my sister's baby. We're all so very grateful."

"It was nothing," Raistlin protested. "I'm sorry. I didn't mean that the way it sounded! The baby is everything, of course. What I meant was that what I did was nothing. Well, not that either. What I meant was—"

"I know what you meant," said Miranda and closed both of her hands over his.

They dropped the cloth. She lifted her lips, closed her eyes. He bent over her.

"Miranda! There you are! Stop dawdling, girl, and bring along that cloth. I need it for Mistress Wells's bodice."

"Yes, Mother." Miranda stooped, hastily gathered up the cloth in a bundle, not bothering to fold it. Holding the fabric in her arms, she whispered softly and breathlessly, "You will come to visit me some evening, won't you, Raistlin?"

"Miranda!"

"Coming, Mother!"

Miranda was gone, departing in a flutter of skirts and trailing fabric.

Raistlin remained standing where she'd left him, as if he'd

been struck by lightning and his feet had melted to the spot. Dazed and dazzled, he considered her invitation and what it meant. She liked him. Him! She had chosen him over Caramon, over all the other men in town who were vying for her affection.

Happiness, pure and untainted, happiness such as he had rarely experienced, poured over him. He basked in it, as in a hot summer sun, and felt himself grow like the newly planted seeds. He built castles in the air so rapidly that within seconds they were ready for him to take up residence.

He saw himself her acknowledged favorite. Caramon would envy him for a change. Not that what Caramon thought mattered, because Miranda loved him, and she was everything good and sweet and wonderful. She would bring out what was good in Raistlin, drive away those perverse demons—jealousy, ambition, pride—who were always plaguing him. He and Miranda would live above the clothier shop. He didn't know anything at all about running a business, but he would learn, for her sake.

For her sake, he would even give up his magic, if she asked him.

The laughter of children jolted Raistlin from his sweet reverie. He was now very late for school and would receive a severe scolding from Master Theobald.

A scolding which Raistlin accepted so meekly, gazing at Theobald with what might almost be termed an affectionate smile, that the master was more than half convinced his strangest and most difficult pupil had, at long last, gone quite mad.

* * * * *

That night—for the first time since he had started school, not counting those times when he was ill—Raistlin did not study his spellcasting. He forgot to water his herbs, left the mice and the rabbit to scrabble frantically in their cages, hungry for the food he neglected to give them. He tried to eat but couldn't swallow a mouthful. He dined on love, a dish far sweeter and more succulent than any served at the feast of an emperor.

Raistlin's one fear was that his brother would return before nightfall, for then he would have to waste time answering all sorts of stupid questions. Raistlin had his lie prepared, a lie brought to mind by Miranda herself. He had been called out to tend to a sick child. No, he did not need Caramon as an escort.

Fortunately Caramon did not return home. This was not unusual during planting season, when he and Farmer Sedge would stay out working in the fields by the light of the bright moon.

Raistlin left their house, walking the boardwalks. In his fancy, he walked on moonlit clouds.

He went to Miranda's house, but he was not going to visit her. Visiting a young unmarried woman after dark would not have been proper. He would speak to her father first, obtain his permission to court his daughter. Raistlin went only to gaze at the place where she lived, hoping perhaps to catch a glimpse of her through the window. He imagined her sitting before the fire, bent over her evening's sewing. She was dreaming of him, perhaps, as he was dreaming of her.

The clothier's business was on the lower level of his house, one of the largest in Solace. The lower level was dark, for the business was shut up for the night. Lights gleamed in the upper level, though, shining through gabled windows. Raistlin stood quietly on the boardwalk in the soft spring evening gazing up at the windows, waiting, hoping for nothing more than the sight of the light shining on her red-gold curls. He was standing thus when he heard a noise.

The sound came from down below, from a shed on the ground beneath the clothier's. Probably a storage shed. The thought came immediately to Raistlin's mind that some thief had broken into the shed. If he could catch the thief, or at least halt the robbery, he would, in his fevered, impossibly romantic condition, have a chance to prove himself worthy of Miranda's love.

Not stopping to think that what he was doing was extremely dangerous, that he had no means of protecting himself if he did come upon a thief, Raistlin ran down the stairs. He could see his way easily enough. Lunitari, the red moon, was full this night and cast a lurid glow along his path.

Reaching the ground, he glided forward silently, stealthily toward the shed. The lock on the door hung loose, the door was shut. The shed had no windows, but a soft light, just barely visible, gleamed out of a knothole on one side. Someone was definitely inside. Raistlin had been about to burst in the door, but common sense prevailed, even over love. He first would look through the knothole, see what was going on. He would be witness to the thief's activities. This done, he would raise the alarm, prevent the thief's escape.

Raistlin put his eye to the knothole.

Bundles of cloth had been stacked on one side of the shed, leaving a cleared place in the center. A blanket was spread on that cleared place. A candle stood on a box in a corner. On the blanket, indistinct in the shadows cast by the candle's wavering flame, two people writhed and panted and squirmed.

They rolled into the candle's light. Red curls fell across a bare white breast. A man's hand squeezed the breast and groaned. Miranda giggled and gasped. Her white hand raked across the man's naked back.

A broad, muscular back. Brown hair, brown curly hair, shone in the candlelight. Caramon's naked back, Caramon's sweat-damp hair.

Caramon nuzzled Miranda's neck and straddled her. The two rolled out of the light. Pants and heaves and smothered giggles whispered in the darkness, giggles that dissolved into moans and gasps of pleasure.

Raistlin thrust his hands into the sleeves of his robe. Shivering uncontrollably in the warm spring air, he walked silently and rapidly back to the stairs that were blood red in Lunitari's smugly smiling light.

5

Raistlin fled along the boardwalks, with no idea where he was or where he was going. He knew only that he could not go home. Caramon would be returning later, when his pleasure was sated, and Raistlin could not bear to see his brother, to see that self-satisfied grin and smell her scent and his lust still clinging to him. Jealousy and revulsion clenched Raistlin's stomach, sent bitter bile surging up his throat. Half blind, weak, and nauseous, he walked and walked, blind and uncaring, until he walked straight into a tree limb in the darkness.

The blow to his forehead stunned him. Dazed, he clung to the railing. Alone on the moonlit stairs, his hands dappled with the blood-red light, shaking and trembling with the fury of his emotions, he wished Caramon and Miranda both dead. If he had known a magical spell in that moment that would have seared the lovers' flesh, burned them to ashes, Raistlin would have cast it.

He could see quite clearly in his mind the fire engulfing the clothier's shed, see the flames—crackling red and orange and white-hot—consuming the wood and the flesh inside, burning, purifying . . .

A dull aching pain in his hands and wrists jolted him back to conscious awareness. He looked down to see his hands white-knuckled in the moonlight. He had been sick, he realized from the stench and a puddle of puke at his feet. He had no recollection of vomiting. The purging had done him some good apparently. He was no longer dizzy or nauseated. The rage and jealousy no longer surged inside him, no longer poisoned him.

He could look around now, take his bearings. At first, he recognized nothing. Then slowly he found a familiar landmark, then another. He knew where he was. He had traversed nearly the length of Solace, yet he had no memory of having done so. Looking back, it was as if he looked into the heart of a conflagration. All was red fire and black smoke and drifting white ash. He gave a deep sigh, a shuddering sigh, and slowly let go his stranglehold on the railing.

A public water barrel stood nearby. He dared not yet put anything into his shriveled stomach, but he moistened his lips and splashed water on the boards where he'd been sick. He was thankful no one had seen him, thankful no one else was around. He could not have borne with pity.

As Raistlin came to figure out where he was, he came to the realization that he shouldn't be here. This part of Solace was not considered safe. One of the first to be built, its dwellings were little more than tumbledown shacks, long since abandoned, the early residents having either prospered and moved up in Solace society or foundered and moved out of town altogether. Weird Meggin lived not far from here, and this was also the location of The Trough, which must have been very close by.

Drunken laughter drifted up through the leaves, but it was sporadic and muffled. Most people, even drunkards, were long abed. The night had crossed its midpoint, was in the small hours.

Caramon would be home by now, home and probably frantic with worry at the absence of his twin.

Good, Raistlin said sourly to himself. Let him worry. He would have to think up some excuse for his absence, which shouldn't be too difficult. Caramon would swallow anything.

Raistlin was chilled, exhausted, and shivering; he'd come out without a cloak, and he would have a long walk home. But still he lingered by the railing, looked back with uneasiness on the moment when he'd wished his brother and Miranda dead. He was relieved to be able to tell himself that he had not meant it, and he was suddenly able to appreciate the strict rules and laws that governed the use of magic. Impatient to gain power, he had never understood so clearly the importance of the Test, which stood like a steel gate across his future, barring his entry to the higher ranks of wizardry.

Only those with the discipline to handle such vast power were granted the right to use it. Looking back on the savagery of his emotions, his desire, his lust, his jealousy, his rage, Raistlin was appalled. The fact that his body—the yearnings and desires of his body—could have so completely overthrown the discipline of his mind disgusted him. He resolved to guard against such destructive emotions in the future.

Pondering this, he was just about to set out for home when he heard booted footsteps approaching. Probably the town guard, walking their nightly patrol. He foresaw annoying questions, stern lectures, perhaps even an enforced escort home. He sidled near the bole of the tree, crept into its shadow, out of Lunitari's light. He wanted to be alone, he wanted to talk to no one.

The person continued walking, moved out of the shadows cast by the tree leaves, and entered a red pool of moonlight. The person was cloaked and hooded, but Raistlin knew Kitiara immediately, knew her by her walk—her long, quick, impatient stride that never seemed to carry her to her destination fast enough.

She passed close by Raistlin. He could have reached out to brush her dark cloak, but he only shrank still deeper into the shadows. Of all the people he did not want to see this night, Kitiara was foremost. He hoped she would remove herself from his vicinity quickly, so that he could return home, and he was extremely frustrated to see her halt at the water barrel.

He waited for her to take her drink and go on, but, though she did drink from the gourd cup attached to the barrel by a rope, she didn't move on. She dumped the gourd back into the water; it fell with a splash. Crossing her arms, Kit leaned back against the barrel and took up a position of waiting.

Raistlin was stranded. He could not leave his tree. He could not step out into the moonlight without her noticing him. But by now he would not have left if he could have. He was intrigued and curious. What was Kitiara doing? Why was she out walking the streets of Solace at this time of night, walking alone, her half-elf lover nowhere to be seen?

She was meeting someone; that much was obvious. Kit was never good at waiting for anything, and this was no exception. She had not been standing two minutes before she stirred restlessly. She crossed her feet, uncrossed her feet, rattled the sword at her waist, slapped her leather gloved hands together, took another drink of water, and more than once leaned forward to peer impatiently down the walkway.

"I will give him five more minutes," she muttered. The night air was still, and Raistlin could hear her words quite clearly.

Footsteps sounded, coming from the direction in which Kit had been looking. She straightened, her hand going reflexively to the hilt of her sword.

The other figure was that of a man, also cloaked and hooded and reeking of ale. Even from where he stood, no more than ten paces from them, Raistlin could smell the liquor on the man. Kit wrinkled her nose in disgust.

"You sot!" Kit sneered. "Keep me waiting in the cold for hours while you suck down rotgut, will you! I've half a mind to slit your ale-swilling belly!"

"I am not past our meeting time," said the man, and his voice was cold and, surprisingly, sober. "If anything, I am early. And one cannot sit in a tavern, even in a tavern as wretched as The Trough, without drinking. Though I am thankful to say that more of that foul liquid the barkeep has the temerity to call ale is on me than is inside me. The barmaid helps herself to her own wares apparently. She managed to spill nearly a full flagon on me. . . . Did you hear that?"

Raistlin had shifted his position ever so slightly in order to relieve a sudden painful cramp in his left leg. He had made hardly any noise at all, yet the man had heard him, for the hooded face turned in Raistlin's direction. Steel flashed in the moonlight.

Raistlin held perfectly still, not even breathing. He did not want to be caught spying on his sister. Kit would be furious, and she had never had any qualms about relieving her anger with the flat of her hand. She might do worse now. And even if she didn't, even if she were inclined to be at all tenderhearted with her baby brother, then the man with the voice like frost-rimed iron would not.

Yet even as fear clenched his already shriveled belly, Raistlin realized that he did not dread being caught because he feared punishment, but because he would miss a chance to discover one of Kit's secrets. Kit had already tried to draw him into her world, place him under her influence. Raistlin was certain she would try again, and he had no intention of playing a subservient role to anyone. Someday he would have to oppose the wishes of his willful sister. He would need every weapon at his disposal for the combat.

"Your ears are playing tricks on you," Kit said after a moment's pause, during which both had listened intently.

"I heard something, I tell you," the man insisted.

"It must have been a cat, then. No one comes here this time of night. Let's get down to business."

Raistlin could see the flash of moonlight off the hilt of Kit's sword; she had drawn aside her cloak to remove a leather scroll case she carried tucked into her belt.

"Maps?" the man asked, looking down at the case.

"See for yourself," she said.

The man unscrewed the end and drew out several sheaves of paper. He spread these out, partially unrolled, on the lid of the water barrel, studied them in the moonlight.

"It's all there," Kit said complacently, pointing with a gloved finger. "Plus more than your lord asked for. The defenses of Qualinesti are delineated on the main map: number of guard posts, number of guards posted, how often the guards are changed, what type of weapons they carry, and so forth. I walked the entire border of Qualinesti myself twice. I've marked on a different map weak spots in their defense, possible areas of penetration, and I've indicated the easiest access routes from the north."

"This is excellent," the man said. He rolled up the sheaves of paper, slid them carefully back into the scroll case, and tucked the scroll case into the top of his boot. "My lord will be pleased. What else have you learned about Qualinesti? I hear you've taken a half-elf lover who was born in—ulp!"

Kit had grabbed hold of the ties of the drawstring on the man's hood. Giving them an expert twist, she jerked him, half strangled, toward her.

"You leave him out of this!" she told him, her voice soft and lethal. "If you think I would demean myself by sleeping with any man in order to gain information, you're wrong, my friend. And you could be dead wrong if you say or do anything to make him the least suspicious."

Steel glinted in the moonlight; Kit held a knife in her other hand. The man glanced down at it, glanced again at Kit's eyes, flashing brighter than the steel, and he raised his hands in deprecating agreement.

"Sorry, Kit. I didn't mean anything by it."

Kitiara released him. He rubbed his neck where the drawstring had cut into it. "How did you get away tonight?"

"I told him I was spending the evening with my brothers. I'll have my money now."

The man reached beneath his cloak, brought out a purse, and handed it over.

Kitiara opened the bag, held it to the light, and estimated the amount of the money quickly by eye. She held up a large coin, studied it, then tucked the coin into the palm of her glove. Pleased, she tied the purse to her belt.

"There's more where that came from if you happen to pick

up any additional information about Qualinesti and the elves. Information that you just happen to find 'lying around.' "

Kitiara chuckled. The money had put her in a good mood. "How do I contact you?"

"Leave a message at The Trough. I'll stop by whenever I'm passing this way. But won't you be traveling north soon?" he asked.

Kit shrugged. "I don't think so. I'm happy enough where I am for the time being. There's my little brothers to think of."

"Uh-huh," the man grunted.

"They're getting to the age where they could be of some use to us," Kit continued, ignoring him.

"I've seen them around town. The big one we could use as a soldier maybe, though he's clumsy as a kobold and looks about as bright. The other, though—the magic-user. Rumor has it that he's quite talented. My lord would be pleased to have him join his ranks."

"Rumor has it wrong! Raistlin can pull a coin out of his nose. That's about it. But I'll see what I can do." Kit held out her hand.

The man took hold of her hand, shook it, but didn't immediately let go. "Lord Ariakas would be pleased to have you join us as well, Kit. On a permanent basis. You'd make a fine commander. He said so."

Kit removed her hand from the man's grasp, placed it on the hilt of her sword. "I didn't know His Lordship and I were on such familiar terms," she said archly. "I've never met the man."

"He knows you, Kit. By sight and by reputation. He's impressed, and this"—the man indicated the map case—"will impress him further. He's prepared to offer you a place in his new army. It's a great opportunity. One day he will rule all of Ansalon, and after that all of Krynn."

"Indeed?" Kit lifted her eyebrow. She appeared impressed. "He doesn't think small, does he?"

"Why should he? He has powerful allies. Which reminds me. How do you feel about dragons?"

"Dragons!" Kit was amused. "I think they are fine for scaring the wits out of little children, but that's about all. What do you mean?"

"Nothing in particular. You wouldn't be fearful of them, would you?"

"I fear nothing in this world or the next," Kit said, a dangerous edge to her voice. "Does any man say different?"

"No one says different, Kit," the man responded. "My lord

has heard us all speak of your courage. That's why he wants you to join us."

"I'm happy here," Kit said, shrugging off the offer. "For the time being, at least."

"Suit yourself. The offer— By Takhisis, I heard that!"

Uncomfortable prickling sensations had been shooting up the backs of Raistlin's legs. He had tried to shift his foot, wiggle his toes, and he'd tried to do it silently. Unfortunately the board on which he stood was loose and creaked loudly when his foot moved.

"Spy!" the man said in his cold voice.

A flutter of black cloak, a leap, and a bound, and he was standing in front of Raistlin, his strong hand gripping Raistlin's cloak. Words of magic flew out of the young mage's head on wings of terror.

The man dragged Raistlin out from behind the tree. Forcing him to his knees, the man yanked off the hood of Raistlin's cloak. He grabbed a handful of Raistlin's hair, jerked his head back. Steel flashed red in the moonlight.

"This is what we do to spies in Neraka."

"You fool! Stop!" Kitiara's arm slammed into the man's hand, knocking the arm backward and the knife to the boardwalk.

The man turned on her in fury, his lust for blood hot. The point of her sword at his throat cooled him.

"Why did you stop me? I wasn't going to kill him. Not yet, anyhow. He'll talk first. I need to know who's paying him to spy on me."

"No one's paying him to spy on you," said Kitiara scornfully. "If he's spying on anyone, he's spying on me."

"You?" The man was skeptical.

"He's my brother," said Kitiara.

Raistlin crouched on his knees, his head bowed. Shame and embarrassment overwhelmed him. He could have wished to die rather than face his sister's wrath and, worse, her disdain.

"He's always been a little snoop," said Kitiara. "We call him the Sly One. Get up!"

She cuffed Raistlin across the face hard. He tasted blood.

To his astonishment, after she'd struck him, Kitiara put her arm around his neck, hugged him close.

"There, that was for being bad," she said to him playfully. "Now that you're here, Raist, let me introduce you to a friend of mine. Balif is his name. He's sorry he scared you like that. He thought you were a thief. Aren't you, sorry, Balif?"

"Yeah, I'm sorry," said the man, eyeing Raistlin.

"And you were acting like a thief, skulking around in the night. What are you doing out this late, anyway? Where were you?"

"I was with Weird Meggin," said Raistlin, wiping blood from his split lip. "She had found a dead fox. We were dissecting it."

Kit wrinkled her nose and frowned. "That woman's a witch. You should stay away from her. So, little brother," Kit said offhandedly, "what did you think about what Balif and I were discussing?"

Raistlin looked stupid, copying his twin's blank stare and dumbfounded expression. "Nothing." He shrugged. "I didn't hear that much of it. I was just walking by, and—"

"Liar," growled the man. "I heard a noise when we first started talking, Kit. He's been there the whole time."

"No, I haven't, sir." Raistlin spoke in conciliatory tones. "I was going to walk past, but I heard you mention dragons. I stopped to listen. I couldn't help myself. I have always been interested in stories of the old days. Particularly dragons."

"That's true," said Kitiara. "He's always got his nose in a book. He's harmless, Balif. Quit worrying. Run along home, Raist. I won't mention the fact that you've been with that witch woman to anyone."

His gaze met hers.

And I won't mention to Tanis the fact that you've been out in the night with another man, Raistlin promised her silently.

She smiled. They understood each other perfectly sometimes.

"Go along!" She gave him a shove.

Muscles stiff and aching, fear and blood leaving a bitter taste in his mouth, a taste that sickened him, he made his way across the boardwalk. Hearing sounds of footsteps and afraid that Balif was coming after him, Raistlin glanced back.

Balif was leaving by the stairs, his cloak swirling around him.

Kitiara had fished the coin out of her glove. She flipped it into the air, caught it. Leaning over the rail, she called after him, "I'll keep in touch!"

Raistlin heard the man's brief, cold laughter. Footsteps continued on the stairs and then died away as the man reached ground level.

Kitiara remained standing by the water barrel, her head lowered, her arms crossed over her chest. She was deep in thought. After a moment, she shook herself all over, as if shaking off all doubt and questions. Drawing her hood close to conceal her face, she set off at a brisk pace.

Raistlin took a circuitous route home, one that was longer but would insure he did not cross his sister's path. He mulled over Kit's conversation, trying to ferret out a meaning, but he was too stupid with fatigue to make any sense of it. His body was drained. It was all he could do to force himself to place one foot in front of the other, trudge the weary way back home.

Caramon would be awake, worried sick, asking questions.

Raistlin smiled grimly. He wouldn't have to lie. He would simply say that he'd spent the evening with their sister.

6

he twins turned twenty that summer.

Their Day of Life Gift was supposed to have been a joyous celebration. Kitiara gave them a party, inviting their friends to the Inn of the Last Home, treating them to supper and all the ale they could drink, which, in the dwarf's case, was an alarming amount. Everyone was having a good time, with the exception of the guests of honor.

Raistlin had been in a foul mood since spring, more than usually sarcastic and bitter, especially with his brother. Their mutual birthday, with its necessary reminders of their dead parents, only appeared to sharpen the edge of his bad humor.

Caramon was glum, having just heard the news that Miranda, the girl he currently adored, had suddenly up and married the miller's son. The unseemly haste with which the wedding was held gave rise to speculations of the most scandalous nature. Caramon's disappointment in the matter was lightened somewhat when he noticed that news of Miranda's nuptials actually brought a smile to Raistlin's face. The smile was dark and unpleasant, not the sort of smile that warms the heart, but it was a smile. Caramon took this as a good sign and hoped fervently that his currently unhappy home life would improve.

The Day of Life Gift party lasted well into the night, and the warmth and good spirits of everyone else soon thawed Raistlin's chill. This was the first celebration Kitiara had attended for her brothers since they were small, almost too small to remember. These past months were the longest period of time she had spent in Solace since her girlhood.

"For a backwater town, it isn't nearly as boring as I remember," she replied in answer to Raistlin's caustic query. "I don't have to be anywhere, not for a while, at least. I'm having fun, baby brother."

She was in wonderful spirits that night, and so was Tanis Half-Elven. The two sat next to each other and their mutual admiration was obvious. Each watched the other with warm, bright eyes. Each urged the other to tell favorite stories. With secret smiles and sidelong glances, each reminded the other of some joke known only to the two of them.

"Tonight's celebration is on me," said Kit, when it came time to settle the reckoning. "I'm paying for everything."

She tossed three large coins onto the table. Otik, his broad face beaming, reached out for them. Raistlin deftly slid his hand under Otik's, snatched up one of the coins, and held it to the light.

"Steel. Minted in Sanction," Raistlin observed, studying them. "Newly minted, I would say."

"Sanction," Tanis repeated, frowning. "That city has the reputation of an evil place. How did you come by coins from Sanction, Kit?"

"Yes, where did you find such an interesting coin, Sister?" Raistlin asked. "Look at this—it has a five-headed dragon stamped on it."

"An evil image," said Tanis, looking grave. "The ancient sign of the Dark Queen."

"Don't be silly! It's a coin, not some evil artifact! I won it playing at bones with a sailor," Kit said, her crooked smile limpid. "Lucky at bones, unlucky at love, so they say. But I proved them wrong. The very next day, I met you, lover." She leaned over to Tanis, kissed him on the cheek.

Her tone was easy, casual, her smile genuine. Raistlin would never have had reason to doubt her if he had not seen that coin, or one like it, sparkle in Lunitari's light only a month ago.

The half-elf believed her; that much was certain. But then Tanis was so besotted with Kitiara that she could have told him she'd sailed to the moon and back on a gnome ship and he would have asked her for details of the voyage.

None of the others questioned her either. Flint regarded all his friends with a patronizing, grandfatherly air, which was degenerating rapidly with every ale the dwarf drank. Tasslehoff roamed happily around the inn, much to the dismay of the other customers. The members of the party took turns rescuing people from the kender, who, after two pints of ale, was wont to regale them with his favorite Uncle Trapspringer stories. Flint and Tanis returned the customers' belongings or made restitution if the "borrowed, strayed or otherwise abandoned" personal possessions were irretrievably lost in the kender's many pouches.

As for Caramon, he was watching his twin with almost pitiful anxiety, willing desperately that Raistlin should have a good time. Caramon was elated when his morose brother actually looked up from the single glass of wine he had not even touched to ask, "Speaking of dragons, I am currently pursuing a course of study on beasts from antiquity. Does anyone know any stories about dragons?"

"I know one," offered Sturm, who, having imbibed two mugs of mead in honor of the occasion, was unusually loquacious.

He told the company a story about the Solamnic knight Huma and how he had fallen in love with a silver dragon, who had taken the disguise of a human female. The tale was well received and raised speculation. Dragons, good and evil, had once lived on Krynn; the old tales were filled with stories of them. Were such tales true? Did dragons really exist, and if so, what had happened to them?

"I've lived in this world a long time," said Tanis, "and I've never seen any sign of dragons. It's my belief that they exist only in the lays of the minstrels."

"If you deny the existence of dragons, you deny the existence of Huma Dragonbane," said Sturm. "He was the one who drove the dragons from the world, the good dragons agreeing to leave with the evil in order not to upset the balance. That is why you see no dragons."

"Uncle Trapspringer met a dragon once—" Tasslehoff began excitedly, but the party was slated to hear no more. Flint kicked the stool out from under Tas, depositing the kender and his ale on the floor.

"Dragons are kender tales," said Flint with a disgusted snort. "Nothing more."

"Dwarves tell dragon stories, too," Tas said, not at all disconcerted. He picked himself up, looked sadly into his empty ale mug, and traipsed off to ask Otik for a refill.

"Dwarves tell the best dragon stories," Flint stated. "Which is only natural, considering that we once competed with the great beasts for living space. Dragons, being quite sensible creatures, preferred to live underground. Oftentimes a dwarven thane would pick out a snug, dry mountain for his people, only to find that a dragon had entertained the same idea."

Tanis laughed. "You can't have it both ways, old friend. Dragons can't be false in kender tales and true in dwarf tales."

"And why not?" Flint demanded angrily. "Have you ever known a kender to speak a true word? And have you ever known a dwarf to lie?"

He was quite pleased with his argument, which made sense when viewed through the bottom of an ale mug.

"What do you say, Raist?" Caramon asked. His brother appeared to be taking an interest in this subject, unlike many subjects previous.

"As I said, I have read of dragons in my books," Raistlin replied. "They mention magical spells and artifacts related to dragons. The books are old, admittedly, but why would such spells and artifacts have been created if the beasts were only mythological?"

"Exactly!" cried Sturm, tapping his mug on the table and bestowing a rare look of approbation on Raistlin. "What you say is quite logical."

"Raist knows a story about Huma." Caramon was pleased to see the two almost friendly. "Tell it, Raist."

When he heard that the story dealt with magic-users, Sturm frowned again and pulled at his mustaches, but the frown gradually lessened as the story went along. He gave it grudging approval at the end, stating with a brusque nod, "The wizard showed great courage—for a magic-user."

Caramon flinched, fearing his brother would take offense at this remark and launch an attack. But Raistlin, his tale concluded, was watching Kitiara, did not even appear to have heard Sturm's comment. Relaxing, Caramon gulped down his ale, called for another, and yelped in pain as a small girl with fiery red curls leapt on him from behind, crawled like a squirrel up his back.

"Ouch! Confound it, Tika!" Caramon endeavored to rid himself of the child. "Aren't you supposed to be in bed?" he demanded, glaring around at the little girl with a mock ferocity that made her giggle. "Where's Waylan, your good-for-nothing father?"

"I don't know," the youngster replied with equanimity. "He went off somewhere. He's always going off somewhere. I'm staying with Otik until he comes back."

Otik bustled over, apologizing and scolding in the same breath. "I'm sorry, Caramon. Here, you young imp, what are you doing bothering the customers?" He grasped the child firmly, led her off. "You know better than that!"

"'Bye, Caramon!" Tika called, waving her hand delightedly.

"What an ugly little kid," Caramon muttered, turning back to his drink. "Did you ever see so many freckles?"

Raistlin had taken advantage of the distraction to lean over to his sister. "What do you think, Kit?" he asked with a slight smile.

"About what?" she asked nonchalantly. Her gaze was fixed on Tanis, who had gone to the bar for two more ales.

"Dragons," he said.

Kit cast him a sharp glance.

Raistlin met her scrutinizing gaze with bland innocence.

Kit shrugged, gave an affected laugh. "I don't think about dragons at all. Why should I?"

"It's just that I saw your expression change when I first brought up the subject. As if you were going to say something, then didn't. You've traveled so much. I'd be interested to hear what you had to say," he concluded respectfully.

"Pah!" Kit was brusque, appeared displeased. "The expression on my face was pain. My stomach's churning. I think that venison Otik fed us tonight was tainted. You were wise not to eat it. I've heard enough about Solamnic knights and about dragons," she added when Tanis returned. "It's silly arguing about something no one can prove. Let's change the subject."

"Very well," said Raistlin. "Let's talk about the gods, then."

"Gods! That's even worse!" Kit said, groaning. "I suppose you've become a convert of Belzor now, little brother, and that you're going to proselytize. Let's leave, Tanis, before he starts his harangue."

"I am not speaking of Belzor," Raistlin returned with a touch of asperity. "I am speaking of the old gods, those who were worshiped before the Cataclysm. The old gods were equated with dragons, and it is said that some of them existed in dragon form. Queen Takhisis, for example. Like her image on the coin. It seems to me that a belief in dragons must of necessity argue a belief in these gods. Or the other way round."

Everyone—with the exception of Kit, who rolled her eyes and kicked Tanis underneath the table—had an opinion. Sturm stated that he'd done some thinking about this since their last conversation, had spoken to his mother about Paladine. His mother stated that the knights still believed in the god of light. They were waiting for Paladine to return home with an apology for being gone so long. If so, the knights might be willing to forgive and forget the god's past misdeeds.

The elves, according to Tanis, were convinced that the gods—all the gods—had left the world due to the wickedness of humans. When humans were finally eradicated from the world—which must surely happen, since they were notoriously combative—then the true gods would return.

After giving the matter considerable thought, Flint was inclined to believe that Reorx, having been fed lies by the mountain dwarves, was holed up inside Thorbardin, with no knowledge that the hill dwarves were in need of his divine help.

"Trust a mountain dwarf to pretend that we don't exist. They wish we'd fall off the face of Krynn, that's what. We're a shame and an embarrassment to them," Flint concluded.

"Could you fall off the face of Krynn?" Tas asked eagerly. "How would you do it? My feet seem to be pretty firmly planted on the ground. I don't think I could drop off. What if I stood on my head?"

"If there was a true god in this world, the kender would have all dropped off it by now," Flint grumbled. "Would you look at that doorknob? Standing on his head!"

It might be more accurate to say that Tasslehoff was attempting to stand on his head. He had his head planted on the floor and was kicking his legs, trying to get his feet into the air, but not having much success. Finally he did manage to stand on his head, with the result that he almost immediately toppled over. Nothing daunted, he tried again, this time taking the precaution of placing himself next to a wall. Fortunately for the party and the rest of the customers, this endeavor absorbed the kender's attention and energies for a considerable length of time.

"If the ancient gods are still around somewhere," said Tanis, resting his hand on Kit's, urging her to be patient, to stay awhile longer, "then there should be some sign of their presence. In the old days, it was said that the clerics of the gods had the power to heal sickness and injuries, that they could even restore life to the dead. The clerics disappeared right before the Cataclysm and have not been seen since, at least that the elves have heard."

"Clerics of Reorx live," Flint maintained, his tone bitter. "I'm convinced of it. They're inside Thorbardin. All sorts of miracles are performed in the halls of our ancestors, halls where by rights we hill dwarves should be now!" He thumped the table with his fist.

"Come, old friend," Tanis admonished mildly. "You remember that time we met the mountain dwarf at the fair in Haven last fall. He claimed that it was the hill dwarves who had clerical powers and refused to share them with their cousins in the mountain."

"Of course he would say that!" Flint bellowed. "To ease his guilty conscience!"

"Tell us a story about Reorx," suggested Caramon, the peacemaker, but the dwarf was angry and wouldn't talk.

"Some of these followers of the new gods claim to have that power," Tanis stated, giving Flint time to cool off. "The clerics of Belzor, for one. The last time I was in Haven, they made a big show of it. Caused cripples to get up and walk and dumb people to speak. What do you say, Kit?"

He'd caught her in a prodigious yawn, which she didn't bother to hide. Raking back her curly hair, she laughed carelessly. "Who wants or needs any gods at all? I certainly don't. No divine force controls my life, and that's the way I like it. I choose my own destiny. I am slave to no man. Why should I be a slave to a god and let some priest or cleric tell me how to live?"

Tanis applauded her when she finished and saluted her with a raised glass. Flint was frowning and thoughtful. When his glance fell on Tanis, the frown deepened into concern. Sturm stared raptly into the fire, his dark eyes unusually bright, as if he saw Paladine's knights once more riding into battle in the name of their god. Caramon had long since dozed off. He lay with his head on the table, his hand still wrapped around his ale mug, softly snoring. Tasslehoff, to the wonder and amazement of all, had managed to stand on his head and was shrilly demanding that everyone look at him—quickly, before he fell off the face of Krynn.

"We've stayed long enough," Kit whispered to Tanis. "I can think of lots more interesting things to do than hang around here." Taking hold of his hand, she brought it to her lips, kissed his knuckles.

Tanis's heart was in his eyes, as the saying goes. His love and longing for her was apparent to everyone watching him. Everyone except Kit, who was now playfully nibbling on the knuckles she had previously been kissing.

"I'm going to have to leave Solace soon, Kit," he said to her softly. "Flint will be taking to the road any day now."

Kitiara rose to her feet. "All the more reason not to waste what time we have left. Good-bye, little brothers," she said, not looking at them. "Happy Day of Life Gift."

"Yes, best wishes," Tanis said, turning to Raistlin with a

warm smile. He patted the snoring Caramon on the shoulder.

Kitiara put her arm around the half-elf's waist, leaned into him. He placed his arm affectionately on her shoulder. Walking side by side, so closely that they almost tripped over each other's feet, the two left the inn.

Flint sighed and shook his head. "More ale," he called gruffly.

"Did you see me, Flint? Did you see me?" Tasslehoff, his face bright red, skipped back to the table. "I stood on my head! And I didn't fall off the face of Krynn. My head stuck to the floor just like my feet do. I guess you'd have to not have any part of you touching. Do you suppose if I jumped off the roof of the inn? . . ."

"Yes, yes, go ahead," Flint muttered, preoccupied.

The kender dashed away.

"I'll go stop him," Sturm offered and left in hasty pursuit.

Raistlin poked his brother, prodded him awake.

"Uh? What?" Caramon grunted, sitting up and peering around, bleary-eyed. He'd been dreaming of Miranda.

Raistlin raised his half-empty wineglass. "A toast, my brother. To love."

"To love," Caramon mumbled, sloshing ale on the table.

7

As it turned out, Tanis and Flint did not leave Solace that summer.

Caramon had already departed for work in the early morning dawn and Raistlin was putting his books together, preparatory to going to his school, when there was a knock on the door. Simultaneous with the knock, the door flew open and Tasslehoff Burrfoot jumped in.

Flint had been trying to teach the kender that a knock on the door was generally conceded among civilized peoples as an announcement of one's presence and a request to be admitted. One waited patiently at the door until the knock was answered and the door was opened by the person residing in the household.

Tasslehoff simply could not grasp the concept. Knocking on doors was not much practiced in the kender homelands. It wasn't necessary. Kender doors usually stood wide open. The only reason to shut them was during inclement weather.

If a visiting kender walked in on his hosts and found that they were engaged in some pursuit in which he was not particularly welcome, the visitor could either sit in the parlor and wait until his hosts showed themselves or he was free to leave—after ransacking the dwelling for anything interesting, of course.

Some uninformed people on Ansalon maintained that this custom was followed because kender had no locks on their doors. This was not true. All doors to kender dwellings had locks, generally a great many locks of differing types. The locks were only used when a party was in progress. There was no door knocking at these times. The guests were expected to pick the locks to obtain entry, this being the major form of entertainment for the evening.

Thus far, Flint had trained Tasslehoff to at least knock on the door, which he did, generally knocking on the door as he opened it, or else opening it and then knocking on it, as a way to loudly announce his presence in case no one noticed him.

Raistlin was prepared for Tasslehoff's arrival, having heard the kender shouting his name breathlessly six doors down and having heard the neighbors shout back to ask if he knew what time of the morning it was. He also heard Tas stop to inform them of the correct time.

"Well, they were the ones who asked," Tasslehoff said indignantly, swinging inside with the door. "If they didn't want to know, why were they shouting like that? I tell you" —he fetched a sigh as he settled himself down at the kitchen table— "I don't understand humans sometime."

"Good morning," said Raistlin, removing the teapot from the kender's hand. "I will be late for my classes. Was there something you wanted?" he asked severely as Tasslehoff was reaching for the bread and the toasting fork.

"Oh, yes!" The kender dropped the fork with a clatter and jumped to his feet. "I almost forgot! It's a good thing you reminded me, Raistlin. I'm extremely worried. No, thank you, I couldn't eat a thing. I'm too upset. Well, maybe a biscuit. Do you have any jam? I—"

"What do you want?" Raistlin demanded.

"It's Flint," said the kender, eating the jam out of the crock with a spoon. "He can't stand up. He can't lie down either, or sit down for that matter. He's in extremely bad shape, and I'm really worried about him. Truly worried."

The kender was obviously upset, because he shoved the jam pot away even though it still had some jam inside. He did put the spoon in his pocket, but that was only to be expected.

Raistlin retrieved the spoon and asked more about the dwarf's symptoms.

"It happened this morning. Flint got out of bed. and I heard him give a yell, which sometimes he does in the morning, but that's usually after I've gone into his room to say good morning when he wasn't exactly ready for it to be morning yet. But I wasn't in his room at all, and he still yelled. So I went into his room to see what was the matter, and there he was, bent double like an elf in a high wind. I thought he was looking at something on the floor, so I went over to look at whatever he was looking at, but then I found out he wasn't, or if he was he wasn't meaning to. He was looking at the floor because he couldn't do anything else.

" 'I'm stuck this way, you miserable kender!' That's what he said. I was miserable for him, so that was pretty accurate. I asked him what happened.

" 'I bent down to lace my boots and my back gave out.' I said I'd help him straighten up, but he threatened to hit me with the poker if I came near him, so—while it might have been interesting, being hit with a poker, something that's never happened to me before—I decided that hitting wasn't going to help Flint much, so I better come to you and see if you could suggest anything."

Tasslehoff regarded Raistlin with anxious expectancy. The young man had put his books down and was searching among jars containing unguents and potions that he'd concocted from his herb garden.

"Do you know what's wrong?" Tas asked.

"Has he been troubled with back pain before?"

"Oh, yes," said Tas cheerfully. "He said that his back has been hurting him ever since Caramon tried to drown him in the boat. His back and his left leg."

"I see. That's what I thought. It sounds to me as if Flint is suffering from a defluxion of rheum," Raistlin replied.

"A defluxion of rheum," Tas repeated the words slowly, savoring them. He was awed. "How wonderful! Is it catching?" he asked hopefully.

"No, it is not catching. It is an inflammation of the joints. It can also be known as lumbago. Although," Raistlin said, frowning, "the pain in the left leg might mean something more serious. I was going to send some oil of wintergreen home with you to rub into the afflicted area, but now I think I had better come take a look myself."

* * * * *

"Flint, you have an influx of runes!" Tasslehoff cried excitedly, racing through the door, which he had neglected to shut on his way out and which the dwarf, in his misery, could not manage to reach.

Flint had scarcely moved from the place where the kender had left him. He was bent almost double, his beard brushing the floor. Any attempt to straighten brought beads of sweat to his forehead and gasps of agony to his lips. His boots remained unlaced. He stood hunched over, alternately swearing and groaning.

"Runes?" the dwarf yelled. "What has this got to do with runes?"

"Rheum," Raistlin clarified. "An inflammation of the joints caused by prolonged exposure to cold or dampness."

"I knew it! That damn boat!" Flint said with bitter triumph. "I say it again: I'll never set foot in one of those foul contraptions again so long as I live, I swear it, Reorx." He would have stamped his foot upon the vow, this being considered proper among dwarves, but the movement caused him to cry out in pain and clutch the back of his left leg.

"I've got my wares to sell this summer. How am I supposed to travel like this?" he demanded irritably.

"You're not traveling," said Raistlin. "You are going back to bed, and you're going to stay there until the muscles relax. You're all knotted up. This oil will ease the pain. I'll need your help, Tas. Lift his shirt."

"No! Stay away from me! Don't touch me!"

"We're only trying to help you to—"

"What's that smell? Oil of what? Pine tree! You're not going to feed me any tree juice!"

"I'm going to rub it on you."

"I won't have it, I tell you! Ouch! Ouch! Get away! I have the poker!"

"Tas, go fetch Tanis," Raistlin ordered, seeing that his patient was going to be difficult.

Although he was extremely sorry to leave in the midst of such excitement, the kender ran off to deliver his message. Tanis returned in haste, alarmed by Tasslehoff's somewhat confused account that Flint had been attacked by runes, which Raistlin was trying to cure by making him swallow pine needles.

Raistlin explained the situation in more detailed and coherent terms. Tanis concurred in both the diagnosis and the treatment. Overriding the dwarf's vehement protests (first forcibly removing the poker from his hand), they rubbed the oil into his skin, massaged the muscles of his legs and arms until he was finally able to straighten his back enough to lie down.

Flint maintained the entire time that he was not going to bed. He was setting out on his summer travels to sell his wares. There was nothing any of them could do to stop him. He kept this up as Tanis helped him hobble to the bed, kept it up though he had to compress his lips against the pain that he said was like a goblin's poison dagger stuck in the back of his leg. He kept it up until Raistlin told Tas to run to the inn and ask Otik for a jug of brandy.

"What's that for?" Flint asked suspiciously. "You going to rub that on me now?"

"You're to swallow a dram every hour," Raistlin replied. "For the pain. So long as you stay in bed."

"Every hour?" The dwarf brightened. He settled himself more comfortably among the pillows. "Well, perhaps I'll just take today off. We can always start tomorrow. Make certain Otik sends the good stuff!" he bellowed after Tas.

"He won't be going anywhere tomorrow," Raistlin told Tanis. "Or the day after, or any time in the near future. He must stay in bed until the pain goes away and he can walk freely. If he doesn't, he could be crippled for life."

"Are you sure?" Tanis looked skeptical. "Flint's complained of aches and pains as long as I've known him."

"This is different. This is quite serious. It has something to do with the spine and the nerves that run up the leg. Weird Meggin treated a person who was suffering symptoms similar to this once, and I helped her. She explained it to me using a human skeleton she had dissected. If you would accompany me to her house, I could show you."

"No, no! That won't be necessary," Tanis said hurriedly. "I'll take your word for it." He rubbed his chin and shook his head. "But how in the name of the Forger of the World we're going to keep that ornery old dwarf in bed, short of tying him to the bedposts, is beyond me."

The brandy aided them in this endeavor, rendering the patient calm, though not quiet, and in a relatively good humor. He actually did what he was told and remained in bed voluntarily. They were all pleasantly surprised. Tanis praised Flint highly for being such a model patient.

What none of them knew was that Flint had actually made an attempt to get out of bed the first night he was incapacitated. The pain was excruciating, his leg had collapsed under him. This incident scared the dwarf badly. He began to think that perhaps Raistlin knew what he was talking about. Crawling back into bed, Flint determined secretly to stay there as long as it took to heal. Meanwhile, he had a good time ordering everyone about and making Caramon feel wretchedly guilty for having been the cause of it all.

Tanis certainly did not mind staying in Solace instead of traveling around Abanasinia. Kitiara remained in Solace as well, much to the astonishment of her brothers.

"I never thought I'd see Kit fall in love with any man,"

Caramon said to his twin one evening over supper. "She just doesn't seem the affectionate type."

Raistlin sneered. " 'Love' is not the word, my brother. Love involves caring, respect, fondness. I would term our sister's attachment for the half-elf as one of 'passion,' or perhaps 'lust' might be a better word. I would guess, from the stories our mother told us, that Kitiara is much like her father in that regard."

"I suppose," Caramon responded, looking uncomfortable. He never liked to talk about their mother if he could help it. His memories of her were not pleasant ones.

"Gregor's love for Rosamun was extremely passionate—while it lasted," Raistlin said, with ironic emphasis on the latter part of his sentence. "He found her different from other women, she amused him. I'm sure there is a certain amusement factor involved with Kitiara's relationship with the half-elf. He is undoubtedly very different from other men she has known."

"I like Tanis," Caramon said defensively, thinking that his brother's words disparaged his friend. "He's a great guy. He's giving me sword fighting lessons. I'm getting really good at it. He said so. I'll have to show you sometime."

"Of course you like Tanis. We all like Tanis," Raistlin said with a shrug. "He is honorable, honest, trustworthy, loyal. As I said, he is far different from any other man our sister has loved."

"You can't know that for sure," Caramon protested.

"Oh, I can, my brother. I can," Raistlin said.

Caramon wanted to know how, but Raistlin refused to elaborate. The twins were silent, finishing their meal. Caramon ate voraciously, devouring everything on his plate and then looking around for more. He had only to wait. Raistlin picked at his food, eating only the choicest morsels, shoving aside any bit of meat with the least amount of gristle or any piece that happened to be even slightly underdone. Caramon was always willing to finish the scraps.

He carried away the wooden bowls to be washed. Raistlin fed his mice and cleaned their cage, then went into the kitchen to help his brother.

"I wouldn't want anything bad to happen to Tanis, Raist," Caramon said, not looking up from his work.

"My dear brother, you have more water on the floor than you do in the bucket. No! Finish what you are doing. I will mop it up." Grabbing the rag, Raistlin bent down, wiped it over the stone flagon floor. "As for Tanis, he is quite old enough to take care of himself, Caramon. He is, I believe, well over one hundred."

"Maybe he's old in years, Raist, but he's not as old as you and I in some ways," Caramon said. He stacked up the wet bowls and utensils, wrung out the cloth, and shook the water from his hands, which he then wiped on his shirtfront.

Raistlin snorted, clearly disbelieving.

Caramon tried to make himself clear. "Because he's honest, he thinks everyone else is honest, too. And loyal and honorable. But you and I—we know that's not true. Especially it's not true with Kit."

Raistlin looked up swiftly. "What do you mean?"

Caramon flushed, ashamed for his sister. "She lied to Tanis about that money, Raist. The steel coins from Sanction. She told Tanis that she won the money playing at bones with a sailor. Well, I was with her a few days earlier when she came over here to see if I wanted to practice my sword fighting with her. When she was ready to leave, she sent me to fetch her cloak from the chest in the bedroom. When I picked up the cloak, the purse with the coins fell out and the coins spilled. I looked at one, because I'd never seen a coin like it. I asked her where they came from."

"What did she say?"

"She said that it was pay she'd earned for work she'd done up north. She said that there was lots more money where that came from and that I could earn my share and so could you, if you'd give up this foolery about magic and come with us. She said she wasn't ready to go north yet, that she was having too much fun here, and anyway I needed more training and you had to be convinced that you were . . ." Caramon hesitated.

"I was what?" Raistlin prodded him.

"A failure in magic. That's what she said, Raist. Not me, so don't get mad."

"I'm not mad. Why would she say such a thing?"

"It's because she's never seen you do any magic, Raist. I told her that you were real good, but she only laughed and said I was so gullible I'd swallow any bit of hocus-pocus. I'm not. You've taught me better than that," Caramon stated emphatically.

"I believe that I have taught you better than even I realized," Raistlin said, regarding his brother with a certain amount of admiration. "You knew all this and still kept quiet about it?"

"She told me not to say anything, not even to you, and I

wasn't going to, but I don't like it that she lied about the money, Raist. Who knows where it came from? And I didn't like that money either." Caramon shivered. "It had a strange feel to it."

"She didn't lie to you," Raistlin said, thoughtful.

"Huh?" Caramon was amazed. "How do you know that?"

"Just a hunch," Raistlin said evasively. "She's talked about working for people in the north before now."

"I don't want to go up there, Raist," Caramon said. "I've made up my mind. I'd rather be a knight, like Sturm. Maybe they'd let you be a war wizard, like Magius."

"I would like to train as a warrior mage," Raistlin said. "The knights would not have me, nor do I think they would take you either. But we could work together, perhaps in the mercenary line, combining sorcery and steel. Warrior mages are not common, and people would pay well for such skills."

Caramon was radiant with pleasure. "That's a great idea, Raist! When do you think we should start?" He looked prepared to rush out the door at that very moment.

"Not for some time yet," Raistlin returned, controlling his brother's impatience. "I would have to leave the school. Master Theobald would have apoplexy if I even mentioned such a thing. In his mind, magic is to be used only in such dire situations as starting campfires if the wood is wet. But we must not rush into this, Brother," he admonished, seeing Caramon already starting to polish his sword. "We need money. You need experience. And I need more spells in my spellbook."

"Sure, Raist. I think it's a great idea, and I plan to be ready." Caramon ceased his work, looked up, his expression solemn and troubled. "What do we say to Kit?"

"Nothing. Not until the time comes," Raistlin said. He paused a moment, then added with a grim smile, "And let her keep thinking I have no talent for magic."

"Sure, Raist, if that's what you want." Caramon couldn't quite figure that one out, but, figuring that Raistlin knew best, he always obeyed his brother's wishes. "What do we do about Tanis?"

"Nothing," Raistlin said quietly. "There is nothing we can do. He wouldn't believe us if we said anything bad about Kit because he doesn't want to believe us. You would not have believed me if I had said anything bad about Miranda, would you?" Raistlin asked with a tinge of bitterness.

"No, I guess not." Caramon sighed massively. He still

maintained his heart was broken, although he was now involved with three girls, at last count. "Isn't there anything we can do about Kit?"

"We watch her, my brother. We watch her very carefully."

8

Summer days drifted by in a haze of smoke from cooking fires, dust kicked up by travelers along the Solace road, and the morning mists that wound like wraiths among the boles of the vallenwood trees.

Flint kept to his bed, a surprisingly docile patient, though he grumbled enough for thirty dwarves, as Tasslehoff said, and complained that he was missing out on all the fun. He had, in fact, a very easy life of it. The kender waited on him hand and foot. Caramon and Sturm took turns visiting him every afternoon after their sword practice to demonstrate their newfound skills. Raistlin came by daily to rub oil of wintergreen into the dwarf's tight muscles, and even Kit dropped by occasionally to entertain Flint with accounts of fighting goblins and ogres.

Flint was so comfortable that Tanis was beginning to worry that the dwarf was enjoying his leisure too much. The pain in his back and leg had nearly subsided, but it was beginning to look as if Flint might never walk again.

Tanis called his friends together, hatched a plot to cause the dwarf to leave his bed, "without the use of gnome powder," as the half-elf put it.

"I hear there's a new metalsmith moving to Solace," Tasslehoff Burrfoot announced one morning as he fluffed up the dwarf's pillows.

"What's that?" Flint looked startled.

"A new metalsmith," the kender repeated. "Well, it's only to be expected. Word has gone out that you've retired."

"I have not!" Flint said indignantly. "I'm only taking a bit of a rest. For my health."

"I hear it's a dwarf. From Thorbardin."

Leaving this poisoned shaft inside the wound, guaranteed to

rankle, Tasslehoff left on his daily tour of Solace to see who was new in town and, more important, what interesting objects might find their way into his pouches.

Sturm was next to arrive, with a pot of hot soup sent by his mother. In regard to the dwarf's anxious questions, Sturm replied that he had "heard something about a new metalsmith coming to town" but added that he rarely paid attention to gossip and couldn't provide any more details.

Raistlin was a good deal more forthcoming, providing a great many details about the Thorbardin metalsmith, down to his clan and the length and color of his beard, also adding that the main reason the Thorbardin dwarf had chosen Solace as a place to locate his business was that "he'd heard they'd had no good metalwork done here in a long, long while."

By the time Tanis arrived late that afternoon, he was pleased but not terribly surprised to find Flint in his workshop, firing up the forge that been cold all summer long. The dwarf still walked with a limp (when he remembered) and still complained of pain in his back (particularly when he had to go rescue Tasslehoff from any number of minor disasters). But he never took to his bed again.

As for the Thorbardin metalsmith, he found that the air of Solace didn't agree with him. At least that's what Tanis said.

The summer had been a long one and a prosperous one for the people of Solace. Large numbers of travelers, the most travelers anyone could remember, passed through the town. The roads were relatively safe. There were thieves and footpads, certainly, but that was a fact of life on the road and not considered to be more than a nuisance. War was the great disrupter of travel, and no wars were being fought anywhere on Ansalon at this time, nor were any expected. Ansalon had been at peace for three hundred years, and everyone in Solace assumed complacently that the peace would last for another three hundred.

Almost everyone, that is. Raistlin believed differently, and it was for this reason that he had decided to concentrate his area of study in the realm of magic on war wizardry. It was not a decision based on a young boy's idealized picture of battle as something glorious and exciting. Raistlin had never played the games of war, as had the other children. He was not enamored of a martial life, nor was he at all excited at the thought of entering into battle. His was a calculated decision, made after long deliberation, and it had to do with one object: money.

The overheard conversation of Kitiara and the stranger had

a great deal to do with Raistlin's planning. He could repeat the conversation verbatim, and he went over the words in his mind almost nightly.

Up north—Sanction, presumably—a great lord with vast sums of money was interested in gaining information about Qualinesti. He was also interested in recruiting skilled warriors; he had loyal and intelligent agents working for him. A gully dwarf child could have taken this evidence and worked it to its logical conclusion.

Someday, somewhere, sometime soon, someone was going to need to put together an army to defend against this lord, and they would need to put it together fast. This unknown someone would pay highly for soldiers and even more highly for mages skilled in the art of combining sword and sorcery.

Raistlin assumed, and rightly so, that dealing death would pay him far better than mixing herbs to heal sick babies.

Having made this decision, he pondered on the best way to act upon it. He needed to acquire magical spells that were combative in nature, that much was certain. He would also need spells to defend himself, else his first fight would be his last. But what would he be defending against? What did a commander expect of a warrior mage? What would be his place in the ranks? What attack spells would be required? Raistlin knew little about soldiering, and he realized then that he needed to know more if he was going to make an effective war wizard.

The one person who might know the answers to these questions was the one person he dared not ask: Kitiara. He did not want to put ideas into her head. Asking Tanis Half-Elven was the same these days as asking his sister, for Tanis would surely discuss anything Raistlin said with Kit. Neither Sturm nor Flint would be of any help; knights and dwarves distrusted magic intensely and would never rely on a mage in a battle situation. Tasslehoff wasn't even a consideration. Anyone who asks a question of a kender deserves the answer.

Raistlin had secretly searched Master Theobald's library and found nothing useful.

"This age on Krynn will be called the Age of Peace," Master Theobald was wont to predict. "We are a changed people. War is an institution of unenlightened generations past. Nations have learned how to peacefully coexist. Humans, elves, and dwarves have learned to work together."

By pointedly ignoring each other, Raistlin thought. That is not coexistence. It is blindness.

When he looked into the future, he saw it ablaze with flame, awash in blood. He could see the coming wars so clearly, in fact, that he sometimes wondered if he hadn't inherited some of his mother's talent as a seer.

Convinced that his scheme was the right one, the one that would win him fame and fortune, Raistlin required only knowledge to put it into action. Such knowledge could come from only one source: books. Books his master did not have. How to acquire them?

The Tower of High Sorcery at Wayreth had the most extensive library of magic anywhere on Krynn. But as a novice mage, an initiate, not even yet an apprentice, Raistlin would not be permitted inside the Tower. His first entry into that fabled and dread edifice would be if and when he was invited to take the Test. The Tower of Wayreth was out of the question.

There were other sources for books of magic and books on magic: mageware shops.

Mageware shops were not numerous in this day and age, but they did exist. There was a mageware shop in Haven; Raistlin had heard Master Theobald speak of it. He knew the location, having made surreptitious inquiries.

One night, shortly after Flint's marvelous recovery, Raistlin knelt down beside a small wooden chest he kept in his room. The chest was guarded by a simple locking cantrip, one of the first magicks every mage learns, a spell that is absolutely essential in a world populated by kender.

Removing the cantrip with a single spoken command, a command that could be personalized to suit each wizard who utilized it, Raistlin opened the lid to the chest and took out of it a small leather purse. He counted the coins—completely unnecessary. He knew to the halfpence how much he had acquired. He deemed he had enough.

The next morning he broached the subject with his brother.

"Tell Farmer Sedge that you must take some time off, Caramon. We are traveling to Haven."

Caramon's eyelids opened so wide it seemed probable he might never be able to close them. He stared at his twin in wordless astonishment. The distance from Solace to Master Theobald's former school, about five miles, had been the farthest Caramon had ever traveled from his home in his life. The distance to the Lordcity of Haven was perhaps some ninety miles and seemed liked the end of the known world to Caramon.

"Flint is journeying to the Harvest Home Festival in Haven

next week. I heard him tell Tanis so last night. Tanis and Kit will undoubtedly travel along. I propose that we go with them."

"You bet we will!" cried Caramon. In his joy, he performed an impromptu dance upon the door stoop, causing the entire house to shake on its tree-limb foundations.

"Calm down, Caramon," Raistlin ordered irritably. "You'll crash through the floorboards again, and we can't spare the money for repairs."

"Sorry, Raist." Caramon quieted his elation, especially as he had a sobering thought. "Speaking of money, do we have enough? Going to Haven will cost plenty. Tanis will offer to pay for it, but we shouldn't let him."

"We have enough if we are frugal. I will handle that detail. You need not worry about it."

"I'll ask Sturm if he wants to go," Caramon said, his happiness returning. He rubbed his hands together. "It will be a real adventure!"

"I trust not," Raistlin said caustically. "It is a three-day journey by wagon on well-traveled roads. I see no adventuring involved."

Which only proved that he had not inherited his mother's gift of foresight after all.

9

he journey began as uneventfully as anyone could have wished, with the possible exception of two young and aspiring warriors eager to display their newfound skills. The weather was clear and cool, the sunshine warmed them pleasantly in the afternoons. Recent rains kept the dust down. The road to Haven was filled with travelers, for Harvest Home was the city's largest festival.

Tanis drove the wagon, which was filled to capacity with the dwarf's wares. Flint hoped to make money enough at the festival to help offset the amount he had lost over the summer. Raistlin rode up front with Tanis, to keep the half-elf company. Kitiara sometimes rode, sometimes walked. She was far too restless to ever do any one thing for long. Flint had a place in the back of the wagon, where he was comfortably ensconced among the rattling pots and pans, keeping a close eye upon his more valued wares: silver bracers and bracelets, necklaces set with precious stones. Sturm and Caramon walked alongside, ready for trouble.

The two young men peopled the road with bands of robbers, legions of hobgoblins (despite Tanis's amused assurances that a goblin had not been seen in Solace since the time of the Cataclysm), and hordes of ravening beasts from wolves to basilisks.

Their hopes for combat (nothing serious, a minor altercation would do) were aided and abetted by Tasslehoff, who took great delight in relating every tale he'd ever heard and quite a few he made up on the spot. Tales about unwary travelers having their hearts ripped out and eaten by ogres, travelers who were dragged off by bears, travelers who were changed into undead by wraiths.

The result was that Sturm kept his hand on the hilt of his

sword, coldly scrutinizing every person he met with such intensity that most of them figured Sturm himself for a thief and hurried to get out of his way. Caramon wore a perpetual scowl on his usually cheerful face, thinking that this made him look mean, though in reality, as Raistlin said, it only made him look bilious.

By the end of the first day, Sturm's hand was cramped from gripping his sword hilt, and Caramon had developed a splitting headache from keeping his jaw thrust forward at an unnatural angle. Kitiara's ribs ached from suppressed laughter, for Tanis would not allow her to openly ridicule the young men.

"They have to learn," he said. It was shortly after lunch, and Kit was riding on the wagon's seat between Tanis and Raistlin. "It doesn't hurt them to develop habits of watchfulness and caution on the road, even if they are overdoing it a bit. I remember when I was young. I was the exact opposite. I set off from Qualinesti without a care in the world or a brain in my head. I took everyone I met for a friend. It was a wonder I didn't end up in a ditch with my silly skull bashed in."

"When you were young," Kit scoffed. She squeezed his hand. "You talk like an old man. You are still young, my friend."

"In elven terms, perhaps," Tanis said. "Not in human. Don't you ever think about that, Kit?"

"Think about what?" she asked carelessly. In truth, she was not really paying attention. Having recently purchased a knife from Flint, a fine steel blade, she was engrossed in wrapping the handle with braided strips of leather.

Tanis persisted. "About the fact that I have lived well over a hundred of your human years. And that I will live hundreds more."

"Bah!" Kit bent over her work, her fingers quick at their task but not particularly efficient. The braided leather provided a better grip, but it wouldn't be much to look at. Kit didn't care how it looked. Finishing her task, she tucked the knife into the top of her boot. "You're only part elf."

"But I have an expanded life span compared to—"

"Hey, Caramon!" Kit yelled in mock alarm. "I think I saw something move over in that bush! Look at that great idiot. If anything did jump out at him, he'd pee in his pants. . . . What were you saying?"

"Nothing," Tanis said, smiling at her. "It wasn't important."

Shrugging, Kit jumped off the wagon to go tease Sturm by hinting that she was certain they were being followed by goblins.

Raistlin glanced at Tanis. The half-elf's smooth, unlined face—a face that would not be lined or wrinkled with age for perhaps another hundred years—was shadowed with unhappiness. He would be still a young man when Kitiara was an old, old woman. He would watch her age and die, while he remained relatively untouched by time.

The bards sang songs of the tragic love of elf for human. What would it be like? Raistlin pondered. To watch beauty and youth wither in those you love. To see them in their old age, in their dotage, while you are still young and vibrant. And yet, Raistlin considered, if the half-elf should fall in love with an elven woman, he would suffer a like fate, except that in this case he would be the one to age.

Raistlin regarded Tanis with new understanding and some compassion. He is doomed, the young mage reflected. He was doomed from birth. In neither world can he ever be truly happy. Talk of the gods playing a cruel joke on someone!

This brought to mind the three ancient gods of magic. Raistlin felt a twinge of conscience. He had not fulfilled his promise to them. If he truly believed in them, as he had professed to them so long ago, why was he constantly questioning and doubting his belief? He was reminded of the three gods yet again when, late in the day, the companions came upon a group of priests walking down the road.

The priests—twenty of them, men and women—walked down the center of the road in two files. They walked slowly, their expressions as solemn as if they were accompanying a body to the burial ground. They looked neither to the right nor the left, but kept their faces forward, their eyes lowered.

The slow-moving column traveling down the middle of the road had the effect—intentional or not—of seriously impeding the flow of traffic.

A great many people were on the Haven road this day. Flint was just one of several merchants traveling in that direction, transporting their stock in horse-driven carts or pushcarts or lugging bundles on their backs and heads. The wagons could not pass the priests, slowed to a funereal pace. Those traveling by foot were luckier, or so it seemed at first. They would start to circle around the double lines of the priests, walk about halfway, then suddenly stop in the road, fearful of moving, or fall hastily back.

Those on horseback who attempted to ride around the group failed when their animals shied nervously, dancing sideways into the brush, or balked completely, refusing to even come near the priests.

"What is it? What's going on?" Flint grumbled, waking from a refreshing nap in the warm autumn sun. He stood up inside the wagon, clumped his way forward. "What's the delay? At this rate, we'll arrive in Haven in time to do the May dance."

"Those priests up ahead," said Tanis. "They won't move off the road and no one can get around them."

"Maybe they don't know we're back here," Flint suggested. "Someone should tell them."

The driver of the lead wagon was attempting to do just that. He was shouting—politely shouting—for the priests to move to the side of the roadway. The priests paid no attention. They might have been deaf, every one of them. They continued walking down the center.

"This is ridiculous!" said Kit. "I'll go talk to them."

She strode forward, her cape whipping around her, her sword rattling. Tasslehoff dashed after her.

"No, Tas, Kit! Wait— Blast!" Tanis swore softly.

Tossing the reins to the startled Raistlin, the half-elf hastily climbed out of the wagon and hurried after the two. Raistlin grappled uncertainly with the reins; he'd never driven a wagon before in his life. Fortunately Caramon jumped up on the wagon. He brought the cart to a halt, watching.

Few creatures on Krynn can move as fast as an excited kender. By the time Tanis caught up with Kitiara, Tasslehoff was far ahead of them both. Tanis shouted for Tas to stop, but few creatures on Krynn are as deaf as an excited kender. Before Tanis could reach him, Tas was alongside one of the priests, a bald man, the tallest in line, who was bringing up the rear of the file on the right-hand side.

Tas reached out his hand in order to introduce himself, and then the kender performed an extremely remarkable feat, jumping two feet in the air straight up and three feet back simultaneously, to land in a confusion of bags and pouches in the middle of a hedgerow.

Tanis and Kit reached the kender as he was extricating himself and his pouches from the clinging branches of the hedge.

"He has a snake, Tanis!" Tasslehoff cried, brushing leaves and twigs from his best orange-and-green plaid trousers. "Each one of the priests is carrying a snake wrapped around his arm!"

"Snakes?" Kit wrinkled her nose, gazed after the priests in disgust. "What are they doing with snakes?"

"It was very exciting," Tas reported. "I went up to the first priest, and I was going to introduce myself, which is only polite, you know, except that he wouldn't look at me or talk to me. I reached out my hand to pluck at his sleeve, figuring he hadn't seen me, and the snake reared up its head and hissed at me," Tasslehoff said, thrilled almost past the ability to speak. Almost.

"I was just about to ask him if I could pet it—snakes have such wonderful dry skin—when it darted out its head at me, and that's when I jumped backward. I was bitten by a snake once when I was a little kender, and while being snake-bit is certainly an interesting experience, it's not one that should be repeated too often. As you say, Tanis, it's not conducive to one's health. Especially because I think this snake was of the poisonous sort. It had a hood over its head and a forked tongue and little beady eyes. Could one of you help me get this pouch loose? It's stuck on that branch."

Tanis untangled the straps of the pouch. By this time, Flint and Raistlin and Sturm had joined them, leaving a disgruntled Caramon to guard the wagon.

"From your description, the snake would appear to be a viper," Raistlin observed. "But I've never heard of vipers being found anywhere outside the Plains of Dust."

"If so, the viper must have had its fangs drawn," said Sturm. "I cannot imagine any sane person would walk along the road carrying a poisonous snake!"

"Then you have very limited imagination, brother," said a peddler, coming up level with them. "Though I'm not saying you're right when it comes to sanity. Their god takes the form of a viper. The snake is their symbol and a test of their faith. Their god gives them power over the viper so that it won't harm them."

"In other words, they're snake charmers," said Raistlin, his lip curling.

"Don't let them hear you call them that, brother," the peddler advised, casting the line of priests an uneasy sidelong glance. He kept his voice low. "They don't tolerate any disrespect. They don't tolerate much of anything, if it comes to that. This could be a real poor Harvest Home if they have their way."

"Why? What have they done?" Kit asked, grinning. "Shut down the alehouses?"

"What was that you said?" Flint could only hear part of the conversation, which was being carried on above his head. He crowded close to hear better. "What did she say? Shut down the alehouses?"

"No, nothing like that, though the priests don't touch the stuff themselves," the peddler returned. "They know they'd never get away with anything so drastic. But they might as well. I'm sorry to see them here. I'll be surprised now if anyone even shows up at the fair. They'll all be going to temple to see the 'miracles.' I've a mind to turn around and go back home."

"What is the name of their god?" Raistlin asked.

"Belzor, or some such thing. Well, good day to all of you, if that's possible anymore." The peddler trudged gloomily off, heading back down the road the way he'd come.

"Hey! What's going on?" Caramon bellowed from the wagon.

"Belzor," Raistlin repeated grimly.

"That was the name of that god the widow woman talked about, wasn't it?" Flint said, tugging at his beard.

"The Widow Judith. Yes, Belzor was the god. She was from Haven as well. I had forgotten that." Raistlin was thoughtful. He would not have imagined he could have ever forgotten the Widow Judith, but other events in his life had crowded her out. Now the memory returned, returned in force. "I wonder if we will find her here."

"We won't," said Tanis firmly, "because we're not going anywhere near those priests. We're going to the fair, concentrate on the business at hand. I don't want any trouble." Reaching out his hand, he caught hold of the kender's shirt collar.

"Oh, please, Tanis! I just want to go have another look at the snakes."

"Caramon!" Tanis shouted, hanging onto the wriggling kender with difficulty. "Drive the wagon off the road. We're stopping for the night."

Flint seemed inclined to argue, but when Tanis spoke in that tone, even Kitiara held her tongue. She shook her head, but she said nothing aloud.

Coming level with Raistlin, Kit said offhandedly, "Judith. Was that the woman who was responsible for our mother's death?"

"Our mother?" Raistlin repeated, regarding Kit in astonishment. When Kitiara mentioned Rosamun at all, which was seldom, she was referred to as "your" mother—spoken to the twins in a scathing tone. This was the first time Raistlin had ever heard Kit acknowledge a relationship.

"Yes, Judith is the woman," he said when he had recovered from his shock sufficiently to reply.

Kit nodded. With a glance at Tanis, she leaned near to Raistlin to whisper, "If you know how to hold your tongue, we might have some fun on this trip after all, little brother."

Sturm and Caramon insisted on setting a watch on their camp that night, though Kit asked, laughing, "Where do you think we are? Sanction?"

They built a fire, spread their blanket rolls near it. Other fires flared not far away. More than one traveler had decided to let Belzor's priests get a long head start.

Flint was in charge of cooking and prepared his famous traveler's stew, a dwarven recipe made from dried venison and berries, simmered in ale. Raistlin added some herbs he had found along the road, herbs which the dwarf regarded with suspicion but was eventually persuaded to add. He would not admit that they added to the flavor; dwarven recipes needed no alteration. But he consumed four helpings, just to make certain.

They kept the fire burning to ward off the night's chill. Seated around it, they passed the ale jug and told stories until the fire burned low.

Flint took a last swallow, called it a night. He planned to sleep in the wagon, to guard his wares from thieves. Kit and Tanis moved off into the shadows, where they could be heard laughing softly and whispering together. Caramon and Sturm argued over who should keep watch first and tossed a coin. Caramon won. Raistlin wrapped himself in his blanket, prepared to spend his first night outdoors, lying on the ground beneath the stars.

Sleeping on the ground was every bit as uncomfortable as he'd imagined it would be.

Silhouetted against the dying embers of the fire, Caramon whistled softly to himself, whittling a stick as he kept watch. Raistlin's last glimpse, before he drifted off into an uneasy slumber, was of Caramon's large body blotting out the starlight.

10

he kender kept an eager lookout the next day for the priests of Belzor, but they must have walked all night—either that or they turned off the road—because the companions did not run into them that day or the next.

The peddler may have held a pessimistic view as to the probable success of the Harvest Home Fair, but this was not the view of the general populace of Abanasinia. The road became more and more crowded, providing enough interesting subjects that Tasslehoff soon forgot all about the snakes, much to Tanis's relief.

Wealthy merchants, whose servants had been sent ahead with their wares, traveled along the road in ornate litters, borne on the shoulders of stout bearers. A noble family passed, accompanied by their retainers, the lord riding at the head on a large war-horse, the wife and daughter and the daughter's duenna following on smaller ponies. The horses were decorated in bright colored trappings, while that of the daughter was adorned with small silver bells on the bridle and silk ribbons braided into the mane.

The daughter was a lovely girl of about sixteen, who charitably bestowed a smile on Caramon and Sturm as she might have bestowed coins upon the poor. Sturm doffed his hat and made a courtly bow. Caramon winked at her and ran after the horse, hoping to speak to her. The noble lord frowned. The retainers closed ranks around the family. The duenna clucked in disapproval and, plucking a scarf over the young girl's head, admonished her in loud tones not to take notice of the riffraff one saw along the road.

Her harsh words wounded Sturm. "You behaved boorishly," he said to Caramon. "You have made us look ridiculous."

Caramon thought the episode was funny, however, and for

the next mile he minced along the side of the wagon on his tip-toes, his handkerchief covering his face, feigning to be disgusted by them all and shouting "riffraff" in falsetto tones.

The trip continued uneventfully until midafternoon.

Springing up from his place in the back of the wagon, Flint shouted, "Look out!" and pummeled Tanis on the shoulder by way of emphasizing the danger. "Drive faster! Hurry! They're coming closer!"

Expecting to see no less than an army of minotaurs in hot pursuit, Tanis looked behind him in alarm.

"Too late!" Flint groaned, as the wagon was immediately surrounded by a party of about fifteen laughing kender.

Fortunately for the dwarf, the kender were far more inter-ested in Tasslehoff than they were in the dwarf's wares. Always delighted to meet more of his kind, Tas jumped off the wagon into a thicket of small, outstretched arms.

There is a proscribed ritual involved in the meeting of kender who are strangers to one another. This ritual takes place whether the meeting is between two kender or twenty.

First come handshaking all around and formal introductions by name. Since it is considered extremely rude for one kender to forget or mistake the name of another, the introductions take some time.

"How do you do? My name is Tasslehoff Burrfoot."

"Clayfoot?"

"No, Burrfoot. Burr—as in the little sharp pointy things that stick to your clothes."

"Ah, Burrfoot! Nice to meet you. I am Eider Thistledown."

"Eiderdown?"

"Thistledown. Eider comes first. And this is Hefty Warblethroat."

"Glad to meet you, Tuftedhair Hotfoot."

"Tasslehoff Burrfoot," corrected Tasslehoff. "It is an honor to meet you, Flabby Cutthroat." And so on down the line.

Once all kender have been properly introduced and everyone knows the name of everyone else, they then move into the sec-ond phase of the ritual, which is determining if they are related. It is a known fact among kender that every kender born can trace his or her ancestry back to, around, up, or over the famous Uncle Trapspringer. Kinships are therefore easily established.

"Uncle Trapspringer was my mother's aunt's third cousin on her father's side by marriage," said Eider Thistledown.

"Isn't that amazing!" cried Tasslehoff. "Uncle Trapspringer

was my father's uncle's wife's second cousin once removed."

"Brother!" cried Eider, spreading his arms.

"Brother!" Tasslehoff rushed into them.

This also continued down the line of kender, ending with the determination that Tasslehoff was closely related to every single one of the fifteen, none of whom he had ever seen before in his life.

After this came the third phase. Tasslehoff inquired politely if any of his fellows had come across any interesting or unusual objects on his or her journeys. The other kender just as politely insisted that Tasslehoff should be the one to show off his acquisitions, with the result that all the kender plunked themselves down in the middle of the road. Emptying their pouches, they began to rummage through each other's belongings while traffic backed up behind them.

"Drive on, Tanis!" Flint urged in a hoarse whisper. "Faster! Faster! Maybe we'll lose him."

Well knowing that Tas could be involved with this entertaining project for a day at least, Tanis did as the dwarf recommended, though not with any hope of losing the kender no matter how fast they traveled.

That night as they were making camp Tasslehoff turned up, tired and hungry, not even wearing the same clothes anymore, but completely happy.

"Did you miss me, Flint?" he asked, plopping down beside the dwarf.

Ignoring Flint's resounding "No!" Tas proceeded to show the companions his newfound treasures. "Look, Flint. I have a whole lot of new maps. Truly fine maps. I've never seen maps nearly as good as these. My cousin says they came all the way from Istar, which isn't there anymore. It was smashed flat in the Cataclysm. These maps have little mountains drawn on them and little roads, and here's a tiny little lake. And they have the names all written in. I've never heard of any of these places, and I don't know where they are, but if I ever want to go there, I've got this map to show me what's there when I get there."

"If you don't know where something is, what good is the map, you doorknob?" Flint demanded.

Tas thought this over, then pointed out the flaw in the dwarf's logic. "Well, I can't get there without it, now, can I?"

"But you just said you didn't know where it was, so that means you can't get there with it!" Flint fumed.

"Ah, but if I ever do get there, I'll know where I am!"

Tasslehoff stated triumphantly, at which point Tanis changed the subject before the dwarf, now extremely red in the face, burst some important blood vessel.

The next day, around midday, they arrived at the gates of the Lordcity of Haven.

* * * * *

The residents of Haven were the ones who termed Haven, grandiosely, a Lordcity. In their minds, Haven rivaled the fabled northern metropolis of Palanthas. None of the inhabitants of Haven had ever traveled to Palanthas, which might account for this misnomer. Haven was, in reality, nothing grander than a large farming community located on extremely fertile land, whose rich soil was nourished on a semiyearly basis by the flooding of the White-rage river.

In these days of relative peace among the diverse races inhabiting Abanasinia, Haven's crops helped feed both the dwarves of Thorbardin and the humans of Pax Tharkas. The elves of Qualinesti did not relish human-grown food, but they had discovered that the vineyards on the sunny slopes of the Kharolis Mountains produced grapes of remarkable sweetness. These grapes were imported to Qualinesti to make wine that was famous throughout Ansalon. Haven hemp was much prized by the Plainspeople, who twisted it into strong, sturdy rope. Haven wood was used by the inhabitants of Solace to build their houses and businesses.

The Harvest Home Festival was therefore not only a celebration of another excellent year in the fields, but it was also a celebration of Haven itself, a tribute to its agrarian prosperity.

A wooden stockade surrounded the city, intended to keep out marauding bands of wolves more than armies. Haven had never been attacked and had no expectations of being attacked. This was the Age of Peace, after all. The gates of the wooden stockade were closed only at night, stood wide open during the day. Those manning the gates acted more as greeters than guards, exchanging friendly salutations with visitors they knew from years past and giving a hearty welcome to newcomers.

Flint and Tanis were well known and well liked. The sergeant-at-arms walked over to personally shake hands with the dwarf and the half-elf and to stare admiringly at Kitiara. The sergeant said they had missed Flint's customary visit, asked where they had been all summer. He listened with deep commiseration to Flint's tale of woe and assured the dwarf that his usual booth on the fairgrounds was waiting for him.

Tasslehoff was well known, too, apparently. The sergeant frowned at seeing the kender and suggested that Tas go lock himself up in jail right now, thereby saving everyone considerable time and trouble.

Tas said that he viewed it as extremely kind of the sergeant to make such a thoughtful offer, but the kender was forced to refuse it.

"Flint depends on me, you know," Tas said, fortunately out of the dwarf's hearing.

The sergeant welcomed the other young men, and when he heard it was their first visit to Haven, he said that he hoped they would not spend all their time working but would have a chance to see some of the sights. He shook hands once more with Flint, advised Tanis in an undertone that he was responsible for the kender, bowed to Kitiara, and then walked on to greet the next wagonload rolling through the wooden gates.

Once inside the stockade, they were accosted by a young man wearing sky-blue robes, who motioned their wagon to stop.

"What's this?" asked Tanis.

"One of those Belzor priests," Flint said, glowering.

"Does he have a snake? I want to see it!" Tasslehoff was prepared to jump off the wagon.

"Not now, Tas," Tanis said in a tone that Tas had, on occasion, actually obeyed. Just to make certain, Caramon caught the kender by the back of his green-and-purple striped vest and held on tightly.

"What can we do for you, sir?" Tanis called out over the hubbub of rolling carts, neighing horses, and jostling crowds.

"I would speak to the young man in the white robes," the priest answered, directing his attention to Raistlin. "Are you a wielder of magic, brother?"

"A novice mage, sir," Raistlin said humbly. "I have yet to take my Test."

The priest walked to the side of the wagon near where Raistlin sat, gazed up at him earnestly, intently.

"You are very young, brother. Are you aware of the evil in which you dabble—probably all unknowingly, I am sure?"

"Evil?" Raistlin leaned over the side of the wagon. "No, sir. I have no intention of doing evil. What do you mean?"

The priest clasped his hand over Raistlin's. "Come hear us outside the Temple of Belzor, brother. All will be explained.

Once you understand that you are worshiping false gods, you will renounce them and their evil arts. You will strip off those foul robes and walk once more in the sunlight. Will you come, brother?"

"Gladly!" Raistlin cried. "What you say terrifies me, sir."

"Huh? But, Raist—" Caramon started to protest.

"Hush, you big ninny!" Kitiara dug her nails into Caramon's arm.

The priest gave Raistlin instructions on how to find the temple, which, he said, was the largest building in Haven, located at the very center of the city.

"Tell me, sir," Raistlin said after noting down the directions, "is there a person connected with the temple whose name is Judith?"

"Why, yes, brother! She is our most holy priestess. It is she who imparts to us the will of Belzor. Do you know her?"

"Only by reputation," said Raistlin respectfully.

"It is sad that you are a professed user of magic, brother. Otherwise I could invite you inside the temple to witness the ceremony of the Miracle. Priestess Judith will be summoning Belzor to appear among us this very night. And she will be speaking to the Blessed of Belzor who have already passed over."

"I would like to see this," said Raistlin.

"Alas, brother. Mages are not permitted to witness the Miracle. Forgive me for saying this, brother, but Belzor finds your evil ways offensive."

"I'm not a mage," said Kit, with a charming smile for the young priest. "Could I come to the temple?"

"Certainly! All the rest of you are welcome. You will see wonderful miracles performed, miracles that will astound you, erase your doubts, and make you believe in Belzor with all your heart and soul."

"Thanks," said Kit. "I'll be there."

The priest solemnly pronounced the blessing of Belzor on them all, then took his leave, moving off to question the occupants of another arriving wagon.

Flint snorted in disdain, dusted the blessing off his clothes. "I don't need the good opinion of any god who thinks well of snakes. And you, lad. I admit that I don't much take to magic— no true dwarf does—but it seems to me that you're a damn sight better off being a wizard than a follower of Belzor."

"I agree with you, Flint," Raistlin said gravely. This was not the time to remind the dwarf of his many harangues against magic in all its shapes and forms. "But it will not hurt me to talk to this priest and find out what this worship of Belzor entails. Perhaps Belzor is one of the true gods for which we have all been searching. I would like very much to see these miracles of which they speak."

"Yes, I'm interested in this Belzor myself," said Kitiara. "I think I'll go to the temple tonight. You could come, too, little brother. All you'd have to do is change clothes and likely they'd never recognize you."

"You're not going to make me go with you, are you?" Caramon asked uneasily. "No disrespect to Belzor, but I've heard the taverns of Haven are real lively, particularly during fair time, and—"

"No, my brother," Raistlin said curtly. "You do not need to come."

"None of the rest of you need to come," Kit said. "Raist and I are the spiritual members of this family."

"Well, I think you're the crazy members of the family," Caramon stated. "Our first night in Haven, and you want to go visit a temple. And what was this business about some priestess named Judith?" He stopped, blinked. "Judith," he repeated, frowning. "Oh." He looked hard at his brother and at Kit. "I'm going."

"I'm going, too!" said Tas. "Maybe I'll get to see those snakes again, not to mention talking to those who have already passed over. What does that mean? What did they pass over? The roof?"

"I believe he means that they talk to the dead," Raistlin explained.

Tas's eyes widened. "I've never talked to dead people before. Do you suppose they'll let me speak to Uncle Trapspringer? Not that we're all that sure he's really dead, mind you. His funeral was sort of confused. The body was there one minute and gone the next. Uncle Trapspringer tended to be a bit absentminded when he got old, and some said maybe he just forgot that he was dead and wandered off. Or maybe he tried being dead and didn't like it, so he came back to life. Or it could be that the undertaker misplaced him. Anyhow, this would be one way to find out the truth."

"That settles it!" Flint grunted. "I'm not going anywhere near this Temple! It's bad enough talking to a live kender, let alone a dead one."

"I will go," said Sturm. "It is my duty to go. If they are

performing miracles in the name of Belzor, I should bring such news to the knighthood."

"I'll go," said Tanis, but that was understood, since Kitiara was going.

"You're all daft" was Flint's opinion as the wagon joined the rest of those headed for the fairgrounds.

"It looks like we're not going to have quite as much fun as we thought," Kit observed to Raistlin in an undertone, with a glance in Tanis's direction.

Raistlin paid small attention to her, however. He was keeping a watch for the Herbalists Street, where, according to Master Theobald, the mageware shop was located.

II

he streets of Haven were not named at this time, although this was one of the civic improvements currently under consideration, particularly after some adventurer had mentioned that the Palanthians not only named their streets but also erected signposts with the names written on them for the benefit of the confused traveler. Travelers to Haven were rarely confused; if you were tall enough, you could see from one end of the village to the other. However, the High Sheriff of Haven thought signposts an excellent idea and resolved to institute them.

Many of the roads in Haven already had names, logical names that had to do with the nature of the goods sold along that road, as in Market Street, Mill Street, Blade Street. Other names had to do with the nature of the road itself, such as Crooked Street or Three Forks, while still others were named after the families who lived on them. Herbalists Street was easy to find, more with the nose than the eyes.

Scents of rosemary, lavender, sage, and cinnamon drifted on the air, making a pleasant contrast to the strong smell of horse dung in the street. The merchant's stalls and shops of Herbalists Street were marked by bunches of dried plants hanging upside down in the sunshine. Baskets of seeds and dried leaves were arranged artfully along the roadside to tempt passersby into making purchases.

Raistlin asked Tanis to halt the wagon. "There are herbs here that I do not grow, some of which I am not familiar with. I would like to replenish my own supplies, as well as discuss their uses."

Tanis told Raistlin how to find Flint's place on the fairgrounds and bade him have fun. Raistlin jumped down from the wagon. Caramon followed, as a matter of course. Tasslehoff was in an agony of indecision, trying to decide whether to go with Raistlin or stay with Flint. Flint and the fairgrounds won out, mainly because, having peered up this street, the kender could see nothing except plants, and while plants were interesting, they just didn't compare to the wonders he knew awaited him at the fairgrounds.

Raistlin would have never permitted the kender to accompany him, but Tas's decision spared him an argument. He was not certain what to do with Caramon, however. Raistlin had planned to visit the mageware shop alone and in secret. He had told no one that he intended to go to the shop. He had told no one what he hoped to purchase. His instinct was to keep his secret, order his brother to go with Flint.

Raistlin rarely discussed his arcane art with his brother, never with his friends. He had not, since the days of his youth—days that he looked back upon and blushed over in shame—flaunted or openly displayed his magical skills.

He was well aware that his magic made some people nervous and uneasy. As well it should. Magic gave him a power over people, a power in which he reveled. He was wise enough to realize, however, that such power would be diminished if he used it repeatedly. Even magic becomes ordinary if used every day.

Raistlin's views toward people had changed over the years. Once he had sought to be loved and admired, much as his brother was loved and admired. Now, as Raistlin had come to understand himself, he faced the fact that he would never win the type of regard given his twin. In the house of Caramon's soul, the door stood always wide open, the window shutters were flung wide, the sun shone daily, anyone was welcome. There was not much furniture in Caramon's house. Visitors could see into every corner.

The house of Raistlin's soul was far different. The door was kept barred, opened only a crack to visitors, and then only a very few were permitted to cross the threshold. Once there, they were not allowed to come much farther. His windows were shut and shuttered. Here and there a candle gleamed, a warm spot in the darkness. His house was filled with furniture and objects strange and wonderful, but it was not messy or cluttered. He could instantly lay his hand on whatever was needed. Visitors could not find his corners, much less pry into them. Small wonder they never liked to stay long, were reluctant to return.

"Where are we going?" Caramon asked.

It was on the tip of Raistlin's tongue to order his brother back into the wagon. He rethought the matter, however. Without responding, he set off at a rapid walk down the street, leaving Caramon to stand flat-footed in the middle of the road.

"It is only common sense that he accompanies me," Raistlin said to himself. "I am a stranger in a strange town. I have no protection that I am willing to use, except under the most dire circumstances. I require Caramon's aid now as I will require it in the future. If I do become a war mage, as I intend, I will need to learn to fight at his side. I might as well get used to having him around."

The latter was said with something of a sigh, especially when Caramon came clomping up alongside, raising a great cloud of dust and demanding to know again where they were going, what they were looking for, and hinting that they could stop in a tavern along the way.

Raistlin halted. He turned to face his brother with a suddenness that caused Caramon to stumble backward in order not to step on his twin.

"Listen to me, Caramon. Listen to what I have to say and do not forget it." Raistlin's tone was hard, stern, and he had the satisfaction of seeing it hit Caramon like a slap in the face. "I am going to a certain place to meet a certain person and acquire certain merchandise. I am permitting you to accompany me because we are young and will consequently be taken for easy marks. But know this, my brother. What I do and what I say and what I buy are private, secret, known only to myself and to you. You will mention nothing of this to Tanis or Flint or Kitiara or Sturm or anyone else. You will say nothing of where we've been, who I've seen, what I've said or done. You must promise me this, Caramon."

"But they'll want to know. They'll ask questions. What do I say?" Caramon was clearly unhappy. "I don't like keeping secrets, Raist."

"Then you do not belong with me. Go back!" Raistlin said coldly and waved his hand. "Go back to your friends. I have no need of you."

"Yes, you do, Raist," Caramon said. "You know you do."

Raistlin paused. His steady gaze caught his brother's and held it. This was the decisive moment, the moment on which their future depended.

"Then you must make a choice, my brother. You must either pledge yourself to me or return to your friends." Raistlin held up his hand, halting his brother's quick answer. "Think about it, Caramon. If you remain with me, you must trust me completely, obey me implicitly, ask no questions, keep my secrets far better than you keep your own. Well, which will it be?"

Caramon didn't hesitate. "I'm with you, Raist," he said simply. "You're my twin brother. We belong together. It was meant to be this way."

"Perhaps," Raistlin said with a bitter smile. If that were true, he wondered very much who meant it and why. He'd like to have a talk with them someday.

"Come along then, my brother. Follow me."

* * * * *

According to Master Theobald, the mageware shop was located at the very end of Herbalists Street, on the left-hand side as you faced the north. Standing at some distance from the rest of the shops and dwellings, it was tucked back by itself amid a grove of oak trees.

Theobald had described it. "The shop is located on the lower floor of the house, living quarters above. It is difficult to see from the road. Oak trees surround it, as does a large walled-in garden. You will see the sign outside, however—a wooden board painted with an eye in colors of red, black, and white.

"I've never had any business there myself. I acquire everything I need from the Tower at Wayreth, you know," Master Theobald had added, with a sniff. "However, I'm sure Lemuel has some small items that mages of low rank might find valuable."

If Raistlin had learned nothing else from Theobald, he had learned to hold his tongue. He swallowed the caustic retort he would have once made, thanked the master politely, and was rewarded with the following bit of information, which might prove of inestimable value.

"I've heard that Lemuel has an interest in weeds the same as you," Theobald said. "You two should get along well."

Consequently Raistlin had brought with him a couple of rare species of plants he'd discovered, dug up, and carried home, and now had seedlings to share. He hoped in this way to curry Lemuel's favor, and if the books Raistlin wanted proved beyond his means, perhaps he might persuade their owner to lower the price.

The twins walked the length of Herbalists Street; Caramon taking his new duties and responsibilities with such extreme seriousness that he nearly tripped on his brother's heels in order to guard him, glared balefully at anyone who glanced twice at them, and rattled his sword constantly.

Raistlin sighed to himself over this, but he knew there was nothing he could do. Remonstrating with his brother, urging Caramon to relax and not be so conspicuous, would probably only confuse him. Eventually Caramon would fit comfortably into his role as bodyguard, but it would take time. Raistlin would just have to be patient.

Fortunately there were not that many people on the street to see them, since most of the herbalists were in the process of setting up stalls on the fairgrounds. On reaching the end of the street, they found it abandoned, no people in sight. Raistlin located the mageware shop easily enough. It was the only building on the left side of the road. Oak trees hid it from view, and there was the garden with its high stone wall. The sign of a mageware shop, the sign of the eye, was missing, however. The door was shut up tight, the windows were closed. The house might have been abandoned, but on peering over the wall, Raistlin saw that the garden was well tended.

"Are you sure this is the place?" Caramon asked.

"Yes, my brother. Perhaps the sign blew down in a storm."

"If you say so," Caramon muttered. He had his hand on the hilt of his sword. "Let me go to the door, then."

"Absolutely not!" Raistlin said, alarmed. "The sight of you, scowling and waving that sword around, would scare any wizard witless. He might turn you into a frog or something worse. Wait here in the road until I call for you. Don't worry. There's nothing wrong," Raistlin said with more assurance than he truly felt.

Caramon started to argue. Recalling his pledge, he kept silent. The threat about the frog might also have had something to do with his quick compliance.

"Sure, Raist. But you be careful. I don't trust these magic-users."

Raistlin walked to the door. His body tingled with both anticipation and dread, excitement at the idea of obtaining what he needed, dread to think that he might have come all this way only to find the mage gone. Raistlin was in such a state of nervous excitement by the time he reached the door that at first his strength failed him; he could not lift his trembling hand to knock, and when he did, his knock was so faint that he was forced to repeat it.

No one answered the door. No face came to peer curiously out the window.

Raistlin very nearly gave way to despair. His hopes and dreams of future success had been built around this one shop; he had never imagined that it might be closed. He had looked forward to gaining the books he needed for so long, he had come so far and he was so close, that he did not think he could bear the disappointment. He knocked again, this time much louder, and he raised his voice.

"Master Lemuel? Are you home, sir? I have come from Master Theobald of Solace. I am his pupil, and—"

A small window inside the door slid open. An eye in the window peered out at Raistlin, an eye filled with fear.

"I don't care whose pupil you are!" came a thin voice through the small opening. "What do you think you're doing, shouting that you're a mage at the top of your lungs? Go away!"

The window slid shut.

Raistlin knocked again, more peremptorily, said loudly, "He recommended your shop. I have come to purchase—"

The little window slid open. The eye appeared. "Shop's closed."

The window slid shut.

Raistlin brought in his reserves for the attack. "I have an unusual variety of plant with me. I thought that perhaps you might not be familiar with it. Black bryony—"

The window slid open. The eye was more interested. "Black bryony, you say? You have some?"

"Yes, sir." Raistlin reached into his pouch and carefully drew out a tiny bundle of leaves, stems, and fruits with the roots attached. "Perhaps you'd be interested . . ."

The window slid shut again, but this time Raistlin heard a bolt being thrown. The door opened.

The man inside the door was clad in faded red robes, covered with dirt at the knees where he was accustomed to kneeling in his garden. He must have been standing on tiptoe to put his eye to the small window in the door, because he was almost as short as a dwarf, compact and round, with a face that must once have been as ruddy and cheerful as the summer sun. Now he was like a sun that is eclipsed. His eyes were puckered with worry and his brow creased. He peered nervously out into the street, and at the sight of Caramon, his eyes widened in fear and he very nearly shut the door again.

Raistlin had his foot in it, however, and was quick to seize the handle with his hand. "May I present my brother, sir? Caramon, come here!"

Caramon obligingly came over, ducking his head and grinning self-consciously.

"Are you sure he's who he says he is?" the mage asked, regarding Caramon with intense suspicion.

"Yes, I'm certain he's my brother," Raistlin replied, wondering uneasily if he was having to deal with a lunatic. "If you look at us closely, you will note the resemblance. We are twins."

Caramon helpfully tried to make himself look as much like his brother as possible. Raistlin attempted to match Caramon's open, honest smile. Lemuel studied them for several long moments, during which Raistlin thought he would fly apart from the tension of this strange interview.

"I guess so." The mage didn't sound very convinced. "Did anyone follow you?"

"No, sir," said Raistlin. "Who would there be to follow us? Most people are at the fairgrounds."

"They're everywhere, you know," observed Lemuel gloomily. "Still, I suppose you're right." He looked long and hard down the street. "Would your brother mind very much going to check to make certain no one is hiding in the shadow of that building over there?"

Caramon looked considerably astonished but, at an impatient nod from his twin, did as he was told. He walked back down the street to a tumbledown shack, searched not only the shadow but took a look inside the building itself. He stepped back out into the street, lifting his hands and shrugging to indicate that he saw nothing.

"There, you see, sir," Raistlin said, motioning his brother back. "We are alone. The black bryony is very fine. I have used it successfully to heal scars and close wounds."

Raistlin held the plant in his palm.

Lemuel regarded it with interest. "Yes, I've read about it. I've never seen any. Where did you find it?"

"If I could come inside, sir . . ."

Lemuel eyed Raistlin narrowly, gazed at the plant longingly, made up his mind. "Very well. But I suggest that you post your brother outside to keep watch. You can't be too careful."

"Certainly," said Raistlin, weak with relief.

The mage pulled Raistlin inside, slammed shut the door so

rapidly that he shut it on the hem of Raistlin's white robes and was forced to open the door again to remove the cloth.

His twin gone, Caramon roamed about for a few moments, scratching his head and trying to figure out what to do. Eventually he found a seat on a crumbling stone wall and sat down to watch, wondering what it was he was supposed to watch for and what he was supposed to do if he saw it.

The interior of the mage's shop was dark. The shutters over the windows blocked out all the daylight. Lemuel lit two candles, one for himself and one for Raistlin. By the candle's light, he saw in dismay that everything was in disorder, with half-filled crates and barrels standing about. The shelves were bare, most of the merchandise had been packed away.

"A light spell would be less costly and more efficient than candles, I know," Lemuel confessed. "But their tormenting has me so upset that I haven't been able to practice my magic in a month. Not that I was all that good at it to begin with, mind you." He sighed deeply.

"Excuse me, sir," said Raistlin, "but who has been tormenting you?"

"Belzor," said the mage in a low tone, glancing about the darkened room as though he thought the god might jump out at him from the cupboard.

"Ah," said Raistlin.

"You know of Belzor, do you, young man?"

"I met one of his priests when I first came to town. He warned me that magic was evil and urged me to come to his temple."

"Don't do it!" Lemuel cried, shuddering. "Don't go anywhere near the place. You know about the snakes?"

"I saw that they carried vipers," Raistlin said. "The fangs are pulled, I suppose."

"Not so!" Lemuel shivered. "Those snakes are deadly poison. The priests trap them in the Plains of Dust. It is considered a test of faith to be able to hold the snakes without being bitten."

"What happens to those lacking in faith?"

"What do you suppose happens? They are punished. A friend told me. He was present during one of their meetings. I tried to go to one myself, but they refused to let me inside. They said I would pollute the sanctity of their temple. I was glad I didn't. That very day one of the snakes bit a young woman. She was dead within seconds."

"What did the priests do?" Raistlin asked, shocked.

"Nothing. The High Priestess said it was Belzor's will." Lemuel shook so that his candle flame wavered. "Now you know why I asked your brother to stand guard. I live in mortal fear of waking up one morning to find one of those vipers in my bed. But I won't live in fear long. They win. I'm giving up. As you see"—he waved his hand at the crates—"I'm moving out."

He held the candle near. "Might I take a closer look at that black bryony?"

Raistlin handed over the small parcel. "What have they done to you?" He had to ask the question several times and give Lemuel a gentle nudge before he could wrest the mage's attention away from examining the plant.

"The High Priestess herself came to me. She told me to close my shop or face the wrath of Belzor. At first I refused, but then they grew nasty. The priests would stand outside the shop. When anyone came, they'd shout out that I was a tool of evil."

"Me?" Lemuel sighed. "A tool of evil? Can you imagine? But the priests frightened people and they quit coming. And then one night I found a snakeskin hanging from the door. That was when I closed the shop and decided to move."

"Excuse me if I seem disrespectful, sir, but if you fear them, why did you try to go to their temple?"

"I thought it might placate them. I thought perhaps I could pretend to go along with them, just to keep them from hounding me. It didn't work." Lemuel shook his head sadly. "Moving wouldn't be so bad. The mageware shop itself never made a lot of money. It's my herbs and my plants that I'll miss. I'm trying to dig them up hoping to transplant them, but I'm afraid I'll lose most of them."

"The shop wasn't successful?" Raistlin asked, glancing around wistfully at the bare shelves.

"It might have been if I'd lived in a city like Palanthas. But here in Haven?" Lemuel shrugged. "Most of what I sold came from my father's collection. He was a remarkable wizard. An archmagus. He wanted me to follow in his footsteps, but his shoes were much too big. I couldn't hope to fill them. Just wasn't cut out for it. I wanted to be a farmer. I have a wonderful way with plants. Father wouldn't hear of it, however. He insisted that I study magic. I wasn't very good at it, but he kept hoping I'd improve with age.

"But then, when I was finally old enough to take the Test, the conclave wouldn't let me. Par-Salian told my father it would be tantamount to murder. Father was extremely disappointed. He left home that very day, some twenty years ago, and I haven't heard from him since."

Raistlin was barely listening. He was forced to admit that his trip had been in vain.

"I'm sorry," he said, but that was more for himself than the mage.

"Don't be," Lemuel said cheerfully. "I was relieved to see Father go, to tell you the truth. The day he left I plowed up the yard and put in my garden. Speaking of which, we should get this plant into water immediately."

Lemuel bustled off into the kitchen, which was located behind the shop in the back of the house. Here the shutters were open, letting in the sunlight. Lemuel blew out his candle.

"What type of wizard was your father?" Raistlin asked, blowing out his candle in turn.

"A war wizard," Lemuel replied, lovingly tending the black bryony. "This is really quite nice. You say you grew it? What sort of fertilizer do you use?"

Raistlin answered. He looked out the window onto Lemuel's garden, which, despite the fact that it was half dug up, was truly magnificent. At any other time, he would have been interested in Lemuel's herbs, but all he saw now was a blur of green.

A war wizard . . .

An idea was forming in Raistlin's mind. He was forced to discuss herbs for a few moments, but soon led the conversation back to the archmagus.

"He was considered one of the best," Lemuel said. He was obviously quite proud of his father, held no bitterness or grudges against the man. He brightened when he spoke of him. "The Silvanesti elves once invited him to come help them fight the minotaurs. The Silvanesti are very snooty. They almost never have anything to do with humans. My father said it was an honor. He was immensely pleased."

"Did your father take his spellbooks with him when he left?" Raistlin asked hesitantly, not daring to hope.

"He took some, I'm sure. The very powerful ones, no doubt. But he didn't bother with the rest. My guess is that he moved to the Tower of Wayreth, and in that case, you know, he wouldn't really need any of his elementary spellbooks. What type of soil would you recommend?"

"A bit on the sandy side. Do you still have them? The books, I mean. I would be interested in seeing them."

"Blessed Gilean, yes, they're still here. I have no idea how many there are or if they are of any importance. A lot of the mages I deal with . . . or rather used to deal with"—Lemuel sighed again—"aren't interested in war magic.

"Elves come here often, mostly from Qualinesti these days. Sometimes they have need of what they term 'human magic,' or sometimes they come for my herbs. You wouldn't think that, would you, young man? Elves being so good with plants themselves. But they tell me that I have several species that they have not been able to grow. One young man used to say that I must have elf blood in me somewhere. He's a mage, too. Perhaps you know him. Gilthanas is his name."

"No, sir, I'm sorry," Raistlin said.

"I suppose you wouldn't. And, of course, I don't have any elf blood at all. My mother was born and raised here in Haven, a farmer's daughter. She had the misfortune to be extremely beautiful, and that's how she attracted my father. Otherwise I would have been the son of some honest farmer, I'm sure. She wasn't very happy with my father. She said she lived in fear that he'd burn the house down. You say you use black bryony to close wounds? What part? The juice of the berry? Or do you grind the leaves?"

"About those books . . ." Raistlin hinted, when he had finally satisfied Lemuel as to the care, feeding, and uses of the black bryony.

"Oh, yes. In the library. Up the stairs and down the hall, second door on your left. I'll just go pot this. Make yourself at home. Do you suppose your brother would like something to eat while he keeps watch?"

Raistlin hastened up the stairs, pretending not to hear Lemuel call after him, wanting to know if the black bryony would prefer to be in direct sunlight or partial shade. He went straight to the library, drawn to it by the whispered song of magic, a teasing, tantalizing melody. The door was shut, but not locked. The hinges creaked as Raistlin opened it.

The room smelled of mold and mildew; it had obviously not been aired out in years. Dried mouse dung crunched under Raistlin's boot, dark shapes flitted into corners at his entrance. He wondered what mice found in this room to eat and hoped fervently that it wasn't the pages of the spellbooks.

The library was small, contained a desk, bookshelves, and scroll racks. The scroll racks were empty, to Raistlin's disappointment, but not his surprise. Magical spells inscribed on scrolls could be read aloud by those with the knowledge of the language of magic. They did not require nearly so much energy or the level of skill needed to produce a spell "by hand," as the saying went. Even a novice such as Raistlin could use a magical scroll written by an archmagus, provided the novice knew how to pronounce the words correctly.

Thus scrolls were quite valuable and charily guarded. They could be sold to other magi, if the owner did not have a use for them. The archmagus would have taken his scrolls with him.

But he had left behind many of his books.

Scattered and upended, some of the spellbooks lay on the floor, as if they had been considered, then discarded. Raistlin could see gaps on the shelves where the archmagus had presumably removed some valuable volume, leaving the unwanted to lie moldering on the shelf.

These remaining books, their white bindings now turned a dirty and dismal gray, their pages yellowed, had been considered valueless by their original owner. But in Raistlin's eyes, the books glittered with a radiance brighter than that of a dragon's hoard. His excitement overwhelmed him. His heart beat so rapidly that he became light-headed, faint.

The sudden weakness frightened him. Sitting down on a rickety chair, he drew in several deep breaths. The cure almost proved his undoing. The air was dusty. He choked and coughed, and it was some time before he could catch his breath.

A book lay on the floor almost at his feet. Raistlin picked it up, opened it.

The archmagus's handwriting was compact, with sharp, jutting angles. The distinctive leftward slant of the letters indicated to Raistlin that the man was a loner, preferred his own company to that of others. Raistlin was somewhat disappointed to find that this volume wasn't a spellbook at all. It was written in Common, with a smattering of what Raistlin thought might be the mercenary tongue, a cant used by professional soldiers. He read the first page and his disappointment faded.

The book gave detailed instructions on how to cast magical spells on ordinary weapons, such as swords and battle-axes. Raistlin marked the book as one of immense value—to him, at least. He set the book to one side and took up another. This was a spellbook, probably of very elementary spells, for it had no magical locks or prohibitions placed upon it. Raistlin could puzzle out a few of the words, but most were foreign to him. The book served to remind him of how much more he had yet to learn.

He regarded the book in bitterness and frustration. It had been cast aside by the great archmagus, the spells it contained beneath his notice. Yet Raistlin could not even decipher them!

"You are being foolish," Raistlin reprimanded himself. "When this archmagus was my age, he didn't know nearly as much as I do. Someday I will read this book. Someday I will cast it aside."

He laid the book down on top of the first and proceeded with his investigations.

Raistlin became so absorbed that he completely lost track of time. He was aware that twilight was coming on only when he found that he was having to hold the books to his nose to be able to read them. He was about to set off in search of candles when Lemuel tapped at the door.

"What do you want?" Raistlin demanded irritably.

"Excuse me for disturbing you," Lemuel said meekly, poking his head inside. "But your brother says that it will be dark soon and that you should be going."

Raistlin remembered where he was, remembered that he was a guest in this man's house. He jumped to his feet in shame and confusion. One of the precious volumes slid from his lap and tumbled to the floor.

"Sir, please forgive my rudeness! I was so interested, this is so fascinating, I forgot that I was not in my own home—"

"That's quite all right!" Lemuel interrupted, smiling pleasantly. "Think nothing of it. You sounded just like my father. Took me back in time. I was a boy again for a moment. Did you find anything of use?"

Raistlin gestured at the three large stacks of books near the chair.

"All these. Did you know that there is an account of the minotaur battle for Silvanesti in here? And this is a description of how to use battle spells effectively, without endangering your own troops. These three are books of spells. I have yet to look through the others. I would offer to buy them, but I know I do not have the means." He gazed sadly at the pile, wondering despairingly how he would ever manage to save up enough money.

"Oh, take them," Lemuel said, waving his hand casually around the room.

"What? Really, sir? Are you serious?" Raistlin caught hold of the back of the chair to steady himself. "No, sir," he said recovering. "That would be too much. I could never repay you."

"Pooh! If you don't take them, I'll have to move them, and I'm running out of crates." Lemuel spoke very glibly about leaving his home, but even as he tried to make this small joke, he was gazing sadly around him. "They'll only go into an attic, to be eaten by mice. I would much rather they were put to good use. And I think it would please my father. You are the son he wanted."

Tears stung Raistlin's eyes. His fatigue from the three days of travel, which included not only time on the road but also time spent climbing the mountains of hope and plummeting into the valleys of disappointment, had left him weak. Lemuel's kindness and generosity disarmed Raistlin completely. He had no words to thank the man and could only stand in humble, joyous silence, blinking back the tears that burned his eyelids and closed his throat.

"Raist?" Caramon's anxious voice came floating up the staircase. "It's getting dark and I'm starved. Are you all right?"

"You'll need a wagon to cart these home in," observed Lemuel.

"I have . . . my friend . . . wagon . . . at the fair . . ." Raistlin didn't seem to be able to manage a coherent sentence.

"Excellent. When the fair is ended, drive over here. I'll have these books all packed for you and ready to go."

Raistlin drew out his purse, pressed it into Lemuel's hand. "Please, take this. It isn't much, it doesn't nearly begin to cover what I owe, but I would like you to have it."

"Would you?" Lemuel smiled. "Very well, then. Although it's not necessary, mind you. Still, I recall my father saying once that magical objects should be purchased, never given as gifts. The exchange of money breaks whatever hold the previous owner may have had on them, frees them up for the next user."

"And if by chance you should ever come to Solace," Raistlin said, casting one more lingering look into the library as Lemuel shut the door, "I will give you slips and cuttings of every plant I have in my garden."

"If they are all as excellent as the black bryony," said Lemuel earnestly, "then that is more than payment enough."

12

Night had fallen by the time the brothers reached the fairgrounds, which were located about a mile outside the town's stockade. They had no difficulty finding their way. Campfires as numerous as fireflies marked the campsites of the vendors, their light warm and inviting. The fair itself was filled with people, though none of the stalls were open and would not be until the next day. Vendors continued to arrive, their wagons rolling down the rutted road. They called out greetings to friends and exchanged pleasant banter with rivals as they unloaded their wares.

Many of the buildings on the site were permanent. They had been built by those vendors who attended the fair frequently, were boarded up during the rest of the year. Flint's was one of these—a small stall with a sheltering roof. Hinged doors swung wide to permit customers a good view of the merchandise, displayed to best advantage on tables and shelves. A small room in back provided sleeping quarters.

Flint had an ideal location, about halfway into the fairgrounds, near the brightly colored tent of an elven flute maker. Flint complained a lot about the constant flute music that resonated from the tent, but Tanis pointed out that it drew customers their direction, so the dwarf kept his grumbling to himself. Whenever Tanis caught Flint tapping his toe to the music, the dwarf would maintain that his foot had gone to sleep and he was only attempting to revive it.

There were some forty or fifty vendors at the fair, plus various venues for entertainment: beer tents and food vendors, dancing bears, games of chance designed to part the gullible from their steel, rope walkers, jugglers, and minstrels.

Inside the grounds, those merchants who had already

arrived had unpacked and set up their merchandise, ready for tomorrow's busy day. Taking their leisure, they rested near their fires, eating and drinking, or ventured around the grounds to see who was here and who wasn't, exchanging gossip and wineskins.

Tanis had provided the twins with directions to Flint's booth; a few additional questions asked of fellow vendors led the two straight to the location. Here they found Kitiara pacing back and forth in front of the stall, which was closed up for the night, its doors bolted and padlocked.

"Where have you been?" Kitiara demanded irritably, her hands on her hips. "I've been waiting here for hours! You're still planning to go to the temple, right? What have you been up to?"

"We were—" Caramon began.

Raistlin poked his brother in the small of the back.

"Uh . . . just looking around town," Caramon concluded with a guilty blush that must have betrayed his lie if Kit hadn't been too preoccupied to notice.

"We didn't realize how late it was," Raistlin added, which was true enough.

"Well, you're here now, and that's what matters," Kit said. "There's a change of clothing for you, little brother, inside that tent. Hurry up."

Raistlin found a shirt and a pair of leather breeches belonging to Tanis. Both were far too big for the slender young man, but they would do in an emergency. He secured the breeches around his waist with the rope belt from his robe or they would have been down around his knees. Tying back his long hair and tucking it up beneath a slouch hat belonging to Flint, Raistlin emerged from the tent to chortles of raucous laughter from Caramon and Kitiara.

The breeches chafed Raistlin's legs, after the freedom of the comfortable robes; the shirt's sleeves kept falling down his thin arms, and the hat slid over his eyes. All in all, Raistlin was pleased with his disguise. He doubted if even the Widow Judith would recognize him.

"Come along, then," said Kit impatiently, starting off toward town. "We're going to be late as it is."

"But I haven't eaten yet!" Caramon protested.

"There's no time. You better get used to missing a few meals, young man, if you're going to be a soldier. Do you think armies lay down their arms to pick up frying pans?"

Caramon looked horrified. He had known that soldiering

was dangerous, the life of a mercenary a rough one, but it had not occurred to him that he might not be fed. The career he had been looking forward to ever since he was six suddenly lost a good deal of its luster. He stopped at a water well, drank two gourdfuls, hoping to quiet the rumblings of his stomach.

"Don't blame me," he said in an undertone to his twin, "if these growls scare the snakes."

"Where are Tanis and Flint and the others?" Raistlin asked his sister as they retraced their steps back into Haven.

"Flint's gone to the Daft Gnome, his favorite alehouse. Sturm went on ahead to the temple, not knowing if you two were going to honor us with your presence or not. The kender vanished—good riddance, I say." Kit never made any pretense of the fact that she considered Tasslehoff a nuisance. "Thanks to the kender, I managed to get rid of Tanis. I didn't think we wanted him along."

Caramon shot an unhappy glance at his brother, who frowned and shook his head, but Caramon was upset and doggedly ignored his twin's subtle warning.

"What do you mean, you got rid of Tanis? How?"

Kit shrugged. "I told him that a messenger had come by with word that Tasslehoff had been thrown into prison. Tanis promised the town guard that he'd be responsible for the kender, so there wasn't much he could do but go see to the matter."

"There's the temple—where that bright light is shining." Raistlin pointed, hoping his brother would take the hint and drop the subject. "I suggest we turn down this road." He indicated the Hostlers Street.

Caramon persisted. "Is Tas in prison?"

"If he's not now, he soon will be," Kit answered with a grin and wink. "I didn't tell much of a lie."

"I thought you liked Tanis," Caramon said in a low voice.

"Oh, grow up, Caramon!" Kit returned, exasperated. "Of course I like Tanis. I like him better than any other man I've ever known. Just because I like a man doesn't mean I want him hanging around every minute of every hour of every day! And you have to admit that Tanis is a bit of a spoilsport. There was this time I captured a goblin alive. I wanted to have some fun, but Tanis said—"

"I believe that this is the temple," Raistlin stated.

The temple of Belzor was a large and imposing structure, built of granite wrested from the nearby Kharolis Mountains and dragged into Haven on ox-drawn skids. The building had been erected hastily and possessed neither grace nor beauty. It was square in shape, short, and squat, topped with a crude dome. The temple had no windows. Carvings—not very good carvings—of hooded vipers adorned the granite walls. The building had been designed to be functional, to house the various priests and priestesses who labored in Belzor's name, and to hold ceremonies honoring their god.

About twenty priests formed a double line outside the temple, funneling the faithful and the curious into the open door. The priests held blazing torches in their hands and were friendly and smiling, inviting all to come inside to witness the miracle of Belzor. Six huge wrought-iron braziers, their iron legs made in the image of twisted snakes, had been placed on either side of the doorway. The braziers were filled with coal that, by the smell, had been sprinkled with incense. Flames leapt high, sending sparks flying into the night sky, filling the air with smoke laced with a cloying scent.

Kit wrinkled her nose. Caramon coughed; the smoke seemed to seize him by the throat. Raistlin sniffed, choked. "Cover your nose and mouth! Quickly!" he warned his brother and sister. "Don't breathe the smoke!"

Kit clapped her gloved hand over her nose. Raistlin covered his face with his shirt sleeve. Caramon fumbled for a handkerchief, only to find it missing. (It would be discovered the next day, inside Tasslehoff's pocket, where the kender had put it for safekeeping.)

"Hold your breath!" Raistlin insisted, his voice muffled by his sleeve.

Caramon tried, but just as he was entering the temple, shuffling along with a crowd of people going the same way, an acolyte used a gigantic feather fan to waft the smoke directly into Caramon's face. He blinked, gasped, and sucked in a huge breath.

"Get that thing away from us!" And when the acolyte didn't move fast enough to please her, Kit gave the youth a shove, nearly knocking the youngster down.

Kit caught hold of Caramon, who had veered drunkenly off to the right. Dragging him along, she swiftly mingled with the crowd entering the temple. Raistlin slid through the press of bodies, keeping close to his brother and sister.

They entered a wide corridor, which opened into a large arena located directly beneath the dome. Granite benches formed a circle around a recessed center stage. Priests guided the people to their seats, urging them to move to the center in order to accommodate the crowd.

"There's Sturm!" said Kit.

Ignoring a priest's instructions, she barged down several stairs to reach the front of the arena.

Caramon stumbled after her. "I feel awful strange," he said to his twin. He put his hand to his head. "The room's going round and round."

"I told you not to breathe in the smoke," Raistlin muttered, and did what he could to guide his brother's fumbling steps.

"What was that stuff?" Kit asked over her shoulder.

"They are burning poppy seeds. The smoke brings about a feeling of pleasant euphoria. I find it interesting to note that Belzor apparently likes his worshipers in a state of befuddlement."

"Yes, isn't it," Kit agreed. "What about Caramon? Will he be all right?"

Caramon wore a foolish grin on his face. He was humming a little song to himself.

"The effects will wear off in time," said Raistlin. "But don't count on him for any action for a good hour or so. Sit down, my brother. This is neither the time nor the place for dancing."

"What's been going on in here?" Kit asked Sturm, who had saved front row seats, right next to the arena.

"Nothing of interest," he said.

There was no need to lower their voices, the noise in the chamber was deafening. Affected by the smoke, people were giddy, laughing and calling out to friends as the priests directed them to their seats.

"I arrived early. What's the matter with everyone?" Sturm gazed about in disapproval. "This looks more like an alehouse than a temple!" He cast Caramon a reproving glance.

"I'm not drunk!" Caramon insisted indignantly and slid off the bench onto the floor. Rubbing his buttocks, he stood up, giggling.

"Those braziers burning outside. They're giving off some sort of poisoned smoke," Kit explained. "You didn't get a whiff of it, did you?"

Sturm shook his head. "No, they were just preparing the fires when I entered. Where is Tanis? I thought he was coming."

"The kender got himself arrested," Kit replied with an easy shrug. "Tanis had to go rescue him from jail."

Sturm looked grave. Although he was fond of Tasslehoff, the kender's "borrowing" distressed him. Sturm was always

lecturing Tas on the evils of theft, citing passages from a Solamnic code of law known as the Measure. Tas would listen
with wide-eyed seriousness. The kender would agree that
stealing was a terrible sin, adding that he couldn't imagine
what sort of wicked person would walk off with another person's most prized possessions. At this point, Sturm would discover he was missing his dagger or his money belt or the bread
and cheese he was intending to eat for lunch. The missing objects would be found on the person of the kender, who had
taken advantage of the lecture to appropriate them.

In vain, Tanis advised Sturm that he was wasting his time.
Kender were kender and had been that way since the time of the
Graygem, and there was no changing them. The aspiring knight
felt it his duty to try to change at least one of them. So far he
wasn't having much luck.

"Perhaps Tanis will come later," Sturm said. "I will save him
a seat."

Kit caught Raistlin's eye, smiled her crooked smile.

Once they were settled, with the drugged Caramon seated
between Kit and himself, where his twin could keep a firm hand
on him, Raistlin was free to inspect his surroundings. The inside
of the arena was very dimly lit by four braziers which stood on
the floor of the arena itself. Raistlin sniffed carefully, trying to
detect the odor that had first warned him of the presence of an
opiate. He smelled nothing unusual. Apparently the priests
wanted their audience relaxed, not comatose.

The brazier's light illuminated a large statue of a hooded
snake, which loomed at the far end of the arena. The statue was
crudely carved and, in direct light, would have looked
grotesque, even humorous. Seen by the flickering firelight, the
statue was rather imposing, particularly the eyes, which were
made of mirrors and reflected the light of the fires. The gleaming eyes gave the giant viper a very lifelike and frightening aspect. Several children in the audience were whimpering, and
more than one woman screamed on first sighting it.

A rope stretched around the arena prohibited entry. Priests
stood guard at various points, preventing the crowd from venturing inside. The only other object in the center of the arena
was a high-backed wooden chair.

"That's some big snake, huh?" said Caramon in loud tones,
staring glassy-eyed at the statue.

"Hush, my brother!" Raistlin pinched the flesh of his
twin's arm.

"Shut up!" Kit muttered from the other side, digging her elbow into Caramon's ribs.

Caramon subsided, mumbling to himself, and that was all they heard out of him until his head lolled forward onto his broad chest and he began to snore. Kit propped him against the granite riser of the seat behind them and turned her attention to the arena.

The outer doors slammed shut with a resounding boom, startling the members of the audience. The priests called for silence. With much shuffling, coughing, and whispering, the crowd settled down to await the promised miracles.

Two flute players entered the arena and began to play a dolorous tune. Doors on either side of the statue opened, and a procession of priests and priestess clad in sky-blue robes entered. Each carried a viper coiled in a basket. Raistlin examined the priestess closely, searching for the Widow Judith.

He was disappointed not to find her. The flute music grew livelier. The vipers lifted their heads, swaying back and forth with the motion of their handlers. Raistlin had read an account in one of Master Theobald's books on snake charming, a practice developed among the elves, who killed no living thing if they could help it but used the charming to rid their gardens of deadly serpents.

According to the book, the charm was not magical in nature. Snakes could be put into trances by means of music, a fact Raistlin had found difficult to credit. Now, watching the vipers and their reactions to the changes in the flute music, he began to think there might be something to it.

The audience was impressed. People gasped in awe and thrilled horror. Women gathered their skirts around their ankles and pulled children onto their laps. Men muttered and grasped their knives. The priests were unconcerned, serene. When their dance in honor of the statue concluded, they set the baskets containing the snakes on the floor of the arena. The vipers remained inside the baskets, their heads moving back and forth in a sleepy rhythm. Those people seated in the front rows watched the snakes warily.

The priests and priestesses formed a semicircle around the statue and began to chant. The chanting was led by a middle-aged man with long, gray-streaked black hair. His robes were a darker color than the robes of the other priests, were made of a finer cloth. He wore a gold chain around his neck, a chain from which hung the image of a viper. Word whispered around the room that this was the High Priest of Belzor.

His expression was genial, serene, though Raistlin noted that the man's eyes were much like the eyes of the statue; they reflected the light, gave none of their own. He recited the chants in a somnambular monotone that was punctuated with an occasional shout at odd moments, shouts perhaps intended to jolt into wakefulness members of the audience who had dozed off.

The chanting droned on and on. From mildly annoying, it soon became quite irritating, rasping on the nerves.

"This is intolerable," Sturm muttered.

Raistlin agreed. Between the echoing noise, the smoke of the fires burning in the braziers, and the stench of several hundred people crowded into a single windowless room, he was finding it increasingly difficult to breathe. His head ached, his throat burned. He didn't know how much longer he could stand this and hoped it would end soon. He feared he might fall ill and have to leave, and he had yet to find Judith. He had yet to witness these purported miracles.

The chanting ceased abruptly. An audible sigh whispered among the audience, whether of reverence or relief, Raistlin couldn't tell. A hidden door located inside the statue opened up, and a woman entered the arena.

Raistlin leaned forward, regarded her intently. There was no mistaking her, though it had been many years since he had last seen her. He had to make absolutely certain. Grabbing hold of Caramon's arm, Raistlin shook his twin into wakefulness.

"Huh?" Caramon gazed around dazedly. His eyes focused, he sat upright. His gaze was fixed on the priestess who had just entered, and Raistlin could tell from the sudden rigidity of his brother's body that Caramon had also recognized her.

"The Widow Judith!" Caramon said hoarsely.

"Is it?" Kit asked. "I only saw her once. Are you sure?"

"I'm not likely to ever forget her," Caramon said grimly.

"I recognize her as well," Sturm stated. "That is the woman we knew as the Widow Judith."

Kit smiled, pleased. Crossing her arms over her chest, she settled back comfortably, her bent leg propped over one knee, and stared at the priestess to the exclusion of anyone else in the temple.

Raistlin also watched Judith attentively, though the sight of her brought back intensely painful memories. He waited to see her perform a miracle.

The High Priestess was clad in sky-blue robes similar to

those the others wore, with two exceptions: Hers were trimmed in golden thread, and whereas the sleeves on the robes of the others fit tightly over their arms, her sleeves were voluminous. When she spread her arms wide, the sleeves made a rippling motion, providing her with an eerie, not-of-this-world aspect. This was further enhanced by her extremely pale complexion, a pallor that Raistlin suspected was probably enhanced by the skillful use of chalk. She had darkened her eyelids with kohl, rubbed coral powder on her lips to make them stand out in the flickering light.

Her hair was drawn back from her head, pulled back so tightly that it stretched the skin over her cheekbones, erasing many of her wrinkles, making her look younger. She was an impressive sight, one that the audience, in their opiated state, appreciated to the fullest. Murmurs of admiration and awe swept through the arena.

Judith raised her hands for silence. The audience obeyed. All was hushed, no one coughed, no baby whimpered.

"Those supplicants who have been deemed acceptable may now come forward to speak to those who have passed beyond," the High Priest called out. He had an oddly high-pitched voice for a man his size.

Eight people, who had been herded into a sort of pen on one side of the arena, now shuffled down the stairs in single file, guided by the priests. The supplicants were not permitted to step onto the floor of the arena itself, but were kept back by ropes.

Six were middle-aged women, dressed in black mourning clothes. They looked pleased and self-important as they entered behind the priests. The seventh was a young woman not much older than Raistlin, who looked pale and worn and sometimes put her hand to her eyes. She was also wearing mourning clothes, her grief was obviously fresh. The eighth was a stolid farmer in his forties. He stood rock still, stared straight ahead, his face carefully arranged so as to betray no emotion. He was not dressed in mourning and looked extremely out of place.

"Step forward and make your requests. What is it you would ask Belzor?" the High Priest called out.

The first woman was escorted to the fore by a priest. Standing in front of the High Priestess, she made her request.

She wanted to speak to her deceased husband, Arginon. "I want to make sure he's fine and wearing his flannel weskit to keep off the chill," she said. "This being what kilt him."

High Priestess Judith listened, and when the woman

finished, the High Priestess made a gracious bow. "Belzor will consider your request," she said.

The next woman came forward with much the same desire, to speak to a dead husband, as did the four who came after.

The High Priestess was gracious to each, promising that Belzor was listening.

Then the priests led forward the young woman. She pressed her hands together, gazed earnestly at the High Priestess.

"My little girl died of . . . of the fever. She was only five. And she was so afraid of the dark! I want to make sure . . . it's not dark . . . where she is. . . ." The bereaved mother broke down and sobbed.

"Poor girl," said Caramon softly.

Raistlin said nothing. He had seen Judith frown slightly, her lips compress in a tight, forbidding smile that he remembered very well.

The High Priestess promised, in a tone somewhat colder than that she had used with the others, that Belzor would look into the matter. The young woman was helped back to her place in line, and the priests led forth the farmer.

He appeared nervous but determined. Clasping his hands, he cleared his throat. In a loud and booming voice, speaking very rapidly, without a pause for breath or punctuation, he stated, "My father died six months ago we know he had money when he died 'cause he spoke of it when the fit was on him he must have hid it but we can't none of us find it what we want to know is where the money is hid thank you."

The farmer gave a curt nod and stepped back in line, nearly trampling the priest who had come up to escort him.

The audience murmured at this; someone laughed and was immediately stifled.

"I am surprised he was permitted to come forward with such an ignoble request," Sturm said in a low voice.

"On the contrary," Raistlin whispered, "I imagine that Belzor will look upon his request with favor."

Sturm looked shocked and tugged on his long mustache. He shook his head.

"Wait and see," Raistlin advised.

The High Priestess once more raised her hands, commanding silence. The audience held its breath, an air of excited expectation electrified the crowd. Most had been in attendance many times previous. This was what they had come to see.

Judith lowered her arms with a sudden dramatic gesture,

which caused the voluminous sleeves to fall and cover her hands, hiding them from sight. The High Priest began to chant, calling upon Belzor. Judith tilted her head. Her eyes closed, her lips moved in silent prayer.

The statue moved.

Raistlin's attention had been focused on Judith; he caught sight of the movement out of the corner of his eye. He shifted his gaze to the statue, at the same time drawing his brother's attention to it with a nudge.

"Huh?" Caramon gave a violent start.

The crude stone statue of the viper had come to life. It twisted and writhed, yet as Raistlin narrowed his gaze to focus on the statue, he was not convinced that the stone itself was moving.

"It's like a shadow," he said to himself. "It is as if the shadow of the snake has come to life . . . I wonder . . ."

"Do you see that?" Caramon gasped, awe-struck and breathless. "It's alive! Kit, do you see that? Sturm? The statue is alive!"

The shadowy form of the snake, its hood spread wide, slithered forward across the arena. The viper was enormous, the swaying head brushed the high domed ceiling. The viper, tongue flickering, crawled toward the High Priestess. Women cried out, children shrieked, men called hoarse warnings.

"Do not be afraid!" cried the High Priest, raising his hands, palm outward, to quiet the worshipers. "What you see is the spirit of Belzor. He will not harm the righteous. He comes to bring us word from beyond."

The snake slithered to a halt behind Judith. Its hooded head swayed benignly over her, its gleaming eyes stared out into the crowd. Raistlin glanced at the priests and priestesses in the arena. Some, especially the young, gazed up at the snake with wonder, utterly believing. The audience shared that belief, reveled in the miracle.

A subdued Kit was grudgingly impressed. Caramon was a firm believer. Only Sturm remained doubtful, it seemed. It would take more than a stone statue come to life to displace Paladine.

Judith's head lifted. She wore an expression of ecstasy, her eyes rolled back until only the whites showed, her lips parted. A sheen of sweat glistened on her forehead.

"Belzor calls forth Obadiah Miller."

The widow of the late Miller stepped nervously forward, her hands clasped. Judith shut her eyes, stood slightly swaying on her feet, in rhythm with the snake.

"You may speak to your husband," said the High Priest.

"Obadiah, are you happy?" asked the widow.

"Most happy, Lark!" Judith replied in an altered voice, deep and gravely.

"Lark!" The widow pressed her hands to her bosom. "That was his pet name for me! It is Obadiah!"

"And it would please me very much, my dear," the late Obadiah continued, "if you would give a portion of the money I left you to the Temple of Belzor."

"I will, Obadiah. I will!"

The widow would have spoken with her husband further, but the priest gently urged her to step back, permitting the next widow to take her place.

This one greeted her late husband, wanted to know if they should plant cabbages next year or turn the parcel of land on the sunny slope over to turnips. Speaking through Judith, the late husband insisted on cabbages, adding that it would please him very much if a certain portion of all their produce should be given to the Temple of Belzor.

At this, Kit sat up straight. She cast a sharp, questioning look at Raistlin.

He glanced at her sidelong, nodded his head once very slightly.

Kit lifted her brows, silently interrogating him.

Raistlin shook his head. Now was not the time.

Kit sat back, satisfied, the pleased smile again on her face.

The other widows spoke to their dead. Each time the deceased husband came forth, he managed to say something that only a wife would know. The husbands all concluded by requesting money for Belzor, which the widows promised, wiping away happy tears, to grant.

Judith asked that the farmer searching for his lost heritage come forward.

After a brief exchange between father and son concerning the ravages of the potato grub, an exchange which Belzor—speaking through Judith—appeared to find somewhat tedious, Judith brought the subject back to the hidden wealth.

"I have told Belzor where to find the money," said Judith, speaking for the late farmer. "I will not reveal this aloud, lest some dishonest person take advantage of the knowledge while you are away from home. Return tomorrow with an offering for the temple and the information will be imparted to you."

The farmer ducked his head several times, as grateful as if

Belzor had handed him a chest of steel coins on the spot. Then it was the turn of the bereaved young mother.

Recalling the forbidding expression on Judith's face, Raistlin tensed. He could not imagine that Belzor would extract much of an offering from this poor woman. Her clothes were worn. Her shoes were clearly castoffs from someone else, for they did not fit. A ragged shawl covered her thin shoulders. But she was clean, her hair was neatly combed. She had once been pretty and would be pretty again, when time rounded off the sharp corners of her bitter loss.

Judith's head rolled and lolled. When she spoke, it was in the high-pitched voice of a little child, a terrified child.

"Mama! Mama! Where are you? Mama! I'm afraid! Help me, Mama! Why don't you come to me?"

The young woman shuddered and reached out her hands. "Mother is here, Mia, my pet! Mother is here! Don't be frightened!"

"Mama! Mama! I can't see you! Mama, there are terrible creatures coming to get me! Spiders, Mama, and rats! Mama! Help me!"

"Oh, my baby!" The young woman gave a heartrending cry and tried to rush forward into the arena. The priest restrained her.

"Let me go to her! What is happening to her? Where is she?" the mother cried.

"Mama! Why don't you help me?"

"I will!" The mother wrung her hands, then clasped them together. "Tell me how!"

"The child's father is an elf, is he not?" Judith asked, speaking in her own voice, no longer that of a child.

"He—he is only part elven," the young woman faltered, startled and wary. "His great-grandfather was an elf. Why? What does that matter?"

"Belzor does not look with favor upon the marriage of humans with persons of lesser races. Such marriages are contrived, a plot of the elves, intended to weaken humanity so that we will eventually fall to elven domination."

The audience murmured in approval. Many nodded their heads.

"Because of her elven blood," Judith continued remorselessly, "your child is cursed, and so she must live in eternal darkness and torment!"

The wretched mother moaned and seemed near to collapsing.

"What folly is this?" Sturm demanded in a low, angry voice.

Several of his neighbors, overhearing, cast him baleful glances.

"Dangerous folly," said Raistlin and clasped his thin fingers around his friend's wrist. "Hush, Sturm! Say nothing. Now is not the time."

"You and your husband are not wanted in Haven," Judith stated. "Leave at once, lest more harm befall you."

"But where will we go? What will we do? The land is all we have, and that is not much! And my child! What will become of my poor child?"

Judith's voice softened. "Belzor takes pity on you, sister. Make a gift of your land to the temple, and Belzor might be prevailed upon to bring your child from darkness into light."

Judith's head lowered to her chest. Her arms fell limp to her sides. Her eyes closed.

The shadowy form of the viper retreated until it blended in with the statue, then vanished.

Judith raised her head, looked around as if she had no idea where she was or what had happened. The High Priest took hold of her arm, supported her. She gazed out upon the audience with a beatific smile.

The High Priest stepped forward. "The audience with Belzor is concluded."

The priests and priestesses picked up the baskets containing the charmed vipers. Forming into a procession, they circled the arena three times, chanting the name of Belzor, then they left through the door in the statue. Acolytes circulated among the crowd, graciously accepting all offerings made in Belzor's name, with Belzor's blessing.

The High Priest led Judith to the door leading out of the temple. Here she greeted worshipers, who begged for her blessing. A large basket stood at the floor at Judith's feet. Blessings were granted as the steel coins clinked.

The young mother stood bereft and alone. Catching hold of one of the acolytes, she begged, "Take pity on my poor child! Her heritage is not her fault."

The acolyte coldly removed her hand from his sleeve. "You heard the will of Belzor, woman. You are fortunate our god is so merciful. What he asks is a very small price to pay to free your child from eternal torment."

The young mother covered her face with her hands.

"Where'd the snake go?" asked Caramon, weaving unsteadily on his feet.

Raistlin kept firm hold on his brother, dissuaded him from making a foray into the arena in search of the giant viper. "Kitiara, you and Sturm take Caramon back to the fairgrounds and put him to bed. I will meet you there."

"I do not want to believe in this miracle," Sturm said, gazing at the statue, "but neither can I explain it."

"I can, but I'm not going to," Raistlin said. "Not now."

"What will you do?" Kit asked, catching hold of the reeling Caramon by the shirttail.

"I'll join you later," Raistlin said and left them before Kit could insist on coming with him.

He pushed his way through the roving acolytes with their offering baskets to the arena, where the mother of the dead child stood alone. One man, passing her, gave her a shove, called out, "Elven whore." A woman came up to her to say loudly, "It is well your child died. She would have been nothing but a pointy-eared freak!" The mother shrank away from these cruel words as from a blow.

Anger burned in Raistlin, anger kindled from words shouted long ago, words the weak use against those weaker than themselves. An idea formed in hot forge-fire of his rage. It emerged from the flames as steel, heated and ready for slagging. In the space of three steps, he had forged the plan in his mind, the plan he would use to bring High Priestess Judith to ruin, discredit all the false priests of Belzor, bring about the downfall of the false god.

Drawing near the unfortunate mother, Raistlin put out a hand to detain her. His touch was gentle, he could be very gentle when he wanted, yet the woman still shivered beneath his grasp in fright. She turned fearful eyes upon him.

"Leave me alone!" she pleaded. "I beg of you. I have suffered enough."

"I am not one of your tormentors, madam," Raistlin said in the quiet, calming tones he used to soothe the sick. His hand clasped over the mother's, and he could feel her shaking. Stroking her hand reassuringly, he leaned near and whispered, "Belzor is a fraud, a sham. Your child is at peace. She sleeps soundly, as though you had rocked her to sleep yourself."

The woman's eyes filled with tears. "I did rock her. I held her, and at the end, she was at peace, as you have said. 'I feel better now, Mama,' she told me, and she closed her eyes." The woman clutched frantically at Raistlin. "I want to believe you! But how can I? What proof can you give me?"

"Come to the temple tomorrow night."

"Come back here?" The mother shook her head.

"You must," said Raistlin firmly. "I will prove to you then that what I've told you is the truth."

"I believe you," she said and gave him a wan smile. "I trust you. I will come."

Raistlin looked back into the arena, at the long line of worshipers fawning over Judith. The coins in the basket gleamed in the light of the braziers, and more money continued to flow in. Belzor had done well for himself tonight.

One of the acolytes came up, rattled the collection basket in front of Raistlin hopefully.

"I trust we will see you at tomorrow night's ceremony, brother."

"You can count on it," said Raistlin.

13

aistlin returned to the fairgrounds, mulling over his plan in his mind. The forge-fire in his soul had burned very hot but the flames died quickly when exposed to the cool night air. Plagued with self-doubt, he regretted having made his promise to the bereaved mother. If he failed, he would be laughed out of Haven.

Shame and derision were far more difficult for Raistlin to contemplate than any physical punishment. He pictured the crowd hooting with mirth, the High Priest hiding his smugly pitying smile, the High Priestess Judith regarding his downfall in triumph, and he writhed at the thought. He began to think of excuses. He would not go to the temple tomorrow. He wasn't feeling well. The young mother would be disappointed, left bitterly unhappy, but she would be no worse off than she was now.

The right and proper thing to do would be to make a report to the Conclave of Wizards. They were the people most capable of dealing with the matter. He was too young, too inexperienced. . . .

Yet, he said to himself, think of the triumph if I succeed!

Not only would he ease the suffering of the mother, but he would also distinguish himself. How fine it would be to report not only the problem to the conclave, but to add modestly that he had solved it. The great Par-Salian, who had undoubtedly never heard of Raistlin Majere before, would take notice. A thrill came over Raistlin. Perhaps he would be invited to attend a meeting of the conclave! By this act, he would prove to others and to himself that he was capable of using powerful magicks in a crisis situation. Surely they would reward him. Surely the prize was worth the risk.

"In addition, I will be fulfilling my promise to the three gods who once took an interest in me. If I cannot prove their existence to others, at least I can shatter the image of this false god who is attempting to usurp them. In that way, I will draw their favorable attention as well."

He went over his plan in his mind again, this time eagerly, excitedly, searching for flaws. The only flaw that he could see lay within himself. Was he strong enough, skilled enough, brave enough? Unfortunately none of those questions would be answered until the time came.

Would his friends back him up? Would Tanis, who was nominally their leader, permit Raistlin to even try his scheme?

"Yes, if I approach them the right way."

He found the others gathered around a campfire they had built in back of Flint's stall.

Tanis and Kit sat side by side. Evidently the half-elf had not yet discovered Kit's deception. Caramon sat on a log, his head in his hands. Flint had returned from the tavern a bit tipsy, having fallen in with some hill dwarves from the Kharolis Mountains, who, though not of his clan, had traveled near his old homeland and were happy to share gossip and ale. Tasslehoff squatted by the campfire, roasting chestnuts in a skillet.

"You're back," said Kit as Raistlin appeared. "We were getting worried. I was just about to send Tanis to find you. He's already been out rescuing the kender."

Kit winked when Tanis wasn't looking. Raistlin understood. Caramon did, too, apparently. Lifting his head, his brow puckered, he looked at his twin, sighed, and lowered his head to his hands again.

"My head aches," he mumbled.

Tanis explained that he had found Tasslehoff, along with twenty other kender, incarcerated in the Haven jail. Tanis paid the fine levied on those who "knowingly and willingly associate with kender," extricated Tas from prison, and brought him forcibly back to the fairgrounds. Tanis trusted that tomorrow the distractions of the fair would keep the kender occupied and out of the town proper.

Tasslehoff was sorry to have missed the evening's adventure, especially the giant snake and the intoxicating smoke. The Haven jail had been a disappointment.

"It was dirty, Raistlin, and it had rats! Can you believe it? Rats! For rats I missed a giant snake and intoxicating smoke. Life is so unfair!"

Tas could never stay unhappy for long, however. Upon reflecting that he couldn't possibly be two places at the same time (except Uncle Trapspringer, who had done it once), the kender cheered up. Forgetting the chestnuts (which soon burned past eating), Tas sorted through all his newfound possessions, then, worn out by the day's excitement, he fell asleep, his head pillowed on one of his own pouches.

Flint shook his head at the story of Belzor. He stroked his long beard and said it didn't surprise him in the least. He expected nothing better of humans, present company excepted.

Kit considered it a fine joke.

"You should have seen Caramon," she told them, laughing. "Staggering about like a great drunken bear."

Caramon groaned and rose unsteadily to his feet. Mumbling something about feeling sick, he staggered off in the direction of the men's privies.

Sturm frowned. He did not approve of Kit's levity on serious subjects. "I do not like these followers of Belzor, but you must admit that we did see a miracle performed in that arena. What other explanation can there be, except that Belzor is a god and his priests have miraculous powers?"

"I'll give you an explanation," Raistlin said. "Magic."

"Magic?"

Kit laughed again. Sturm was disapproving. Flint said, "I knew it," though no one could figure out how.

"Are you certain, Raistlin?" Tanis asked.

"I am," Raistlin answered. "I am familiar with the spell she cast."

Tanis appeared dubious. "Forgive me, Raistlin. I'm not casting doubt on your knowledge, but you are only a novice."

"And as such I am fit for nothing except washing out my master's chamber pot. Is that what you are saying, Tanis?"

"I didn't mean—"

Raistlin dismissed the apology with an irritated wave of his hand. "I know what you meant. And what you think of me or my abilities makes no difference to me. I have further evidence that what I say is true, but it is obvious that Tanis does not care to hear it."

"I want to hear it," said Caramon stoutly. He had returned from his short jaunt, seemed to be feeling better.

"Tell us," said Kit, her dark eyes glinting in the firelight.

"Yes, lad, let us hear your evidence," said Flint. "Mind you, I knew it was magic all along."

"Bring me a blanket, my brother," Raistlin ordered. "I will

catch my death, sitting on this damp ground." When he was comfortable, seated on a blanket near the fire and sipping at a glass of mulled cider, which Kit brought him, he explained his reasoning.

"My first indication that something might be wrong was when I heard that the priests were forbidding users of magic to enter the temple. Not only that, but they are actively persecuting the one wizard who lives in Haven, a Red Robe named Lemuel. Caramon and I met him this afternoon. The priests forced him to close his mageware shop. They have frightened him into fleeing his home, the house where he was born. In addition to this, the priests have prohibited all mages from entering their temple when the 'miracle' is performed. Why? Because any magic-user, even a novice such as myself," Raistlin added in acid tones, "would recognize the spell Judith casts."

"Why did they force that friend of yours, that Lemuel, to close down his mageware shop?" Caramon asked. "How could a shop hurt them?"

"Shutting down Lemuel's mageware shop insures that the wizards who frequented that shop—wizards who might expose Judith—will no longer have a reason to come to Haven. When Lemuel leaves town, the priests will consider themselves safe."

"But then why did that priest invite you to the temple, little brother?" Kit asked.

"In order to make certain I would not be a nuisance," Raistlin replied. "Remember, he said that I would not be allowed inside to witness the 'miracle.' Undoubtedly, had I gone, they would have urged me to renounce magic and embrace Belzor."

"I'd like to embrace him," Caramon growled, flexing his big hands. "I've got the worst hangover I've ever had in my life, and I never touched a drop. Life's not fair, as the kender says."

"But those people who spoke to Belzor." Sturm was arguing in favor of the miracle. "How did the Widow Judith know all those things about them? A husband's pet name for his wife, where that farmer hid his money?"

"Remember, those people who appeared before Belzor were handpicked," Raistlin replied. "Judith probably interviewed them in advance. Through skillful questioning, she could elicit information from them, information about their husbands and family, information they don't realize they are providing. As for the farmer and the hidden money, they did not tell him publicly where to find it. When he comes to the temple, they'll tell him to search under the mattress. If that fails, they'll tell him he lacked faith in Belzor, and if he contributes more money, they'll offer him another place to search."

"There's something I don't understand," said Flint, thinking things over. "If this widow woman is a wizardess, why did she attach herself to your mother, then denounce her at your father's funeral?"

"That puzzled me, too, at first," Raistlin admitted. "But then it made sense. Judith was trying to introduce the worship of Belzor into Solace. Her first act when she arrived in town would be to seek out any magi who might prove to be a threat. My mother, who had some reputation as a seer, was an obvious choice. All the while Judith lived in Solace, she endeavored to build up her following. She was not performing any 'miracles' then. Perhaps she had not yet mastered the technique, or perhaps she was waiting until she had a suitable location and audience. Before she could proceed, however, you and Tanis thwarted her plan. Judith realized at my father's funeral that the people of Solace were not likely to fall in with her schemes.

"As we saw tonight, Judith and the High Priest of Belzor, who is probably her partner in this scheme, feed on people's worst qualities: fear, prejudice, and greed. The residents of Solace tend to be less fearful of strangers, more accepting of others simply because the town is a crossroads."

"It is an ugly game that widow woman's playing, bilking people out of what little they have," Flint stated grimly. He looked quite fierce, his brows bristled. "Not to mention tormenting that poor lass who lost her babe."

"It is an ugly game," Raistlin concurred. "And one I believe that we can end."

"I'm in," said Kit immediately.

"Me, too," Caramon said promptly, but that was a foregone conclusion. If his twin had proposed setting off on an expedition to find the Graygem of Gargath, Caramon would have started packing.

"If these 'miracles' are in reality nothing more than the deceitful tricks of a mage, then it is my duty to expose her," Sturm said.

Raistlin smiled grimly, and bit back a sharp retort. He had need of the erstwhile knight.

"I wouldn't mind giving that widow a black eye," said Flint reflectively. "What do you say, Tanis?"

"I want to hear Raistlin's plan first," Tanis stated with his customary caution. "Attacking people's faith is dangerous, more dangerous than attacking them physically."

"Count me in," said Tasslehoff, sitting up and rubbing his eyes. "What are we doing?

"Whatever it is, we don't need a kender," Flint said grumpily. "Go to sleep. Or, better yet, why don't you go back and tell 'em how to run their jail."

"Oh, I already did that," Tas said, sensing the excitement and waking up quickly. "They were extremely rude, even when I offered my most helpful suggestions. Can I come, too, Raistlin? Please? Where are we going?"

"No kender," said Flint emphatically.

"The kender may come," Raistlin said. "As a matter of fact, Tasslehoff is the key to my plans."

"There! You see, Flint!" Tas jumped to his feet, tapped himself proudly on the chest. "Me! I'm the key to the plan!"

"Reorx help us!" Flint groaned.

"I hope he will," Raistlin replied gravely.

14

Raistlin was up early the next day; he had been awake much of the night, finally falling into an uneasy sleep in the early hours of the morning. He woke from a dream he could not recall, but which left a feeling of disquiet in his mind. He had the impression he'd been dreaming about his mother.

Flint and Tanis were up early as well, arranging and rearranging the wares to best advantage. They had placed the bracers, with their beautiful engravings of griffins, dragons, and other mythical beasts, on a front shelf. Necklaces of silver braid, fine and delicate work, were laid out on red velvet. Silver and gold lover's rings, made to resemble clinging ivy, gleamed in wooden cases.

Flint was not happy with the way the wares were displayed, however. He was certain that the morning sun would cast a shadow over the stall, and that therefore the silver must go here, not there. Tanis listened patiently, reminded Flint that they'd been through this yesterday, and due to the shadow of an overhanging oak, the sun rays would fall on the silver and set the jewels sparkling only if it remained where it was.

They were still arguing when Raistlin went to the men's privies to perform his ablutions, splashing cold water from a communal bucket over his face and body. Shivering, he dressed quickly in his white robes. Caramon remained asleep inside their tent, snoring off the effects of the opiated smoke.

The air was chill and crisp, the sun was reddening the mountain peaks, already white from a smattering of snow. No clouds marred the sky. The day would warm pleasantly; the crowds at the fair would be brisk.

Flint called out for Raistlin to come settle the argument on the placement of the jewelry. Raistlin, who cared nothing about the matter and would have just as soon seen the jewelry on the roof as anyplace else, managed to escape by pretending he hadn't heard the dwarf's bellow.

He made his way through the fairgrounds, watched the activity with interest. Shutters were coming down, handcarts were being wheeled to the proper locations. The smells of bacon and fresh bread filled the air. The grounds were quiet, compared to the noise and confusion expected later in the day. Vendors called out to wish each other luck, or gathered together to share food and stories, or bartered for each other's work.

The vendors had only been here a day, and already they had formed their own community, complete with leaders, gossip, and scandals, bound together by the feeling of camaraderie, an "us against them" mentality. "Them" meant the customers, who were spoken of in the most disparaging terms and who would later be met with gracious smiles and servile attitudes.

Raistlin viewed this little world with amused cynicism until he came to the booth of one of the bakers. A young woman was arranging fresh, hot muffins in a basket. Their spicy cinnamon smell made a pleasant accompaniment to the smell of wood smoke from the brick ovens and tempted Raistlin to walk over and ask the price. He was fumbling for his few remaining pennies, wondering if he had enough, when the young woman smiled at him and shook her head.

"Put your money away, sir. You're one of us."

The muffin warmed his hands as he walked; the taste of apples and cinnamon burst on his tongue. It was undoubtedly the best muffin he had ever eaten, and he decided that being part of the small community was very pleasant, even if it all was a bit odd.

The streets of Haven were beginning to waken. Small children came bursting out of doors, squealing with excitement that they were going to go to the fair. Their harassed mothers darted out to retrieve them and wash their grimy faces. The town guard walked about with an important air, mindful of strangers visiting Haven and determined to impress.

Raistlin kept a watch out for any of the blue-robed priests of Belzor. When he saw some in the distance, he ducked hastily into the next block to avoid them. It was unlikely that any would have recognized him as the shabbily clad peasant from the night before, but he dared not take the chance. He had considered putting on the same disguise today, but reflected that he would have to explain the reason for the disguise to Lemuel, something he did not want to do if it could be avoided. The meek little man would most certainly try to dissuade Raistlin from going through with his plan. Raistlin did not feel equal to hearing any more arguments. He'd heard them all already from himself.

The sun's rays were melting the frost on the leaves in the street when Raistlin reached Lemuel's house. The house was quiet, and though this was not unusual for the reclusive mage, Raistlin realized uneasily that it was still very early in the morning. Lemuel might still be asleep.

Raistlin prowled about outside the house for several moments, not liking to wake the mage, but not liking the idea of leaving, of wasting all this time and energy. He walked around to the back of the house, hoping he could see inside one of the near windows. He was pleased and relieved to hear noises coming from the garden.

Finding a protruding brick in the lower portion of the garden wall, Raistlin set his foot upon it and hoisted himself up.

"Excuse me, sir. Lemuel," he called out softly, trying not to startle the nervous man.

He failed. Lemuel dropped his trowel and stared about him in consternation. "Who . . . who said that?" he demanded in a quavering voice.

"It's me, sir . . . Raistlin." He was conscious of his undignified position, clinging precariously to the wall, holding on with both hands.

After a moment's search, Lemuel saw his guest and greeted Raistlin most cordially, greetings which were cut short by Raistlin's foot slipping from the brick, causing him to disappear from the mage's sight with a startling abruptness. Lemuel opened the garden gate and invited Raistlin to enter, asking him anxiously as he did so if he'd seen any snakes near the house.

"No, sir," Raistlin answered, smiling. He had grown to like the nervous, fussy little man. Part of his motivation for proceeding with his plan—the unselfish part of his motives—was the determination that Lemuel should stay with his beloved garden. "The priests are down at the fairgrounds, finding new converts. So long as the fair runs, I do not think they will bother you, sir."

"We should be grateful for small blessings, as the gnome said when he blew off his hand when it might have been his head. Have you had breakfast? Do you mind very much if we take our food into the garden? I have a great deal of work to do there."

Raistlin indicated that he had already eaten and that he would be perfectly happy to go into the garden. He found the plots about a fourth of the way dug up, with plants arranged in neat bundles, ready for transport.

"Half of them won't survive the trip, but some of them will make it, and in a few years, I daresay I will have my old garden back again," Lemuel said, trying to be cheerful.

But his gaze roved sadly to the blackberry bushes, the cherry and apple trees, the enormous lilac bush. The trees and plants he could not take with him could never be replaced.

"Perhaps you won't have to leave, sir." Raistlin said. "I have heard rumors that some people think Belzor is a fraud and that they intend to expose him as such."

"Really?" Lemuel's face brightened, then fell again into shadow. "They won't succeed. His followers are much too powerful. Still, it is kind of you to give me hope, even if only for a moment. Now, what is it you want, young man?" Lemuel regarded Raistlin shrewdly. "Is someone ill? Do you need some of my medicines?"

"No, sir." Raistlin flushed slightly, embarrassed that he was so transparent. "I would like to look over your father's books again, if you don't mind."

"Bless you, young man, they're your books now," Lemuel said warmly, with such kindness that Raistlin determined then and there to bring down Belzor no matter what the cost and without a thought to his own ambition. He left the mage roving unhappily about his garden, trying to decide what could be safely transplanted and what should be left behind, hoping that the next owner would properly water the hydrangea.

Inside the library, Raistlin spent a moment looking fondly and proudly on the books—his books, soon to be his library—and then he set to work. He found the spell he was seeking without difficulty; the war mage had been a man of precise habits and had noted down each spell and its location in a separate volume. Upon reading a description of the spell—which the war mage had also included, apparently for his own reference—Raistlin was convinced beyond doubt that this indeed was the spell the High Priestess was casting.

He was further confirmed in his belief on noting that the spell required no components—no sand sprinkled over the eyes or bat guano rolled in the fingers. Judith had only to speak the words and make the appropriate gestures in order to work the magic. This was the reason for the voluminous sleeves.

The question now was, could he cast this same spell?

The spell was not exceptionally difficult, it did not require the skills of an archmage to cast. The spell would be easily accessible to an apprentice mage, but Raistlin was not even that. He was a novice, would not be permitted to apprentice himself until after he had taken the Test. By the laws of the conclave, he was forbidden to cast this spell until that time. The law was quite specific on that point.

The laws of the conclave were also quite specific on another point: If ever a mage met a renegade wizard, one who was operating outside the law of the conclave, it was the duty of that mage to either reason with the renegade, bring the renegade to justice before the conclave, or—in extreme cases—end the renegade's life.

Was Judith a renegade? This was a question Raistlin had spent the night pondering. It was possible she might be a black-robed wizard, using her evil magic to fraudulently obtain wealth and poison people's minds. Practitioners of evil magic, the Order of the Black Robes, worshipers of Nuitari, were an accepted part of the conclave's ranks. Though few outsiders could understand or accept what they considered a pact with the forces of darkness.

Raistlin recalled an argument he had presented to Sturm over this very point.

"We mages recognize that there must be balance in the world," Raistlin had tried to explain. "Darkness follows the day, both are necessary for our continued existence. Thus the conclave respects both the dark and the light. They ask that, in turn, all wizards respect the conclave's laws, which have been laid down over the centuries in order to protect magic and those who practice it. The loyalty of any wizard must be to the magic first, to all other causes second."

Needless to say, Sturm had not been convinced.

By Raistlin's own argument, it was possible that a black-robed wizardess could practice evil magic in disguise and still be condoned by the conclave, with one important exception: The conclave would most certainly frown upon the use of magic to promote the worship of a false god. Nuitari, god of the dark moon and darker magicks, was known to be a jealous god, one who demanded absolute loyalty from those who sought his favor. Raistlin could not imagine Nuitari taking kindly to Belzor under any circumstances.

In addition, Judith was slandering magic, threatening magic-users and endeavoring to persuade others that the use of magic was wrong. That alone would condemn her in the eyes of the conclave. She was a renegade, of that Raistlin had little doubt. He might run afoul of the conclave's laws in casting a spell before he was an accepted member of their ranks, but he had a solid defense. He was exposing a fraud, punishing a renegade, and, by so doing, restoring the repute of magic in the world.

Doubts at rest, his decision made, he started to work. He searched the library until he found a piece of lamb's skin, rolled up with others in a basket. He stretched the skin out on the desk, holding it flat beneath books placed at the corners. Unfortunately the vials containing lamb's blood, which he would need to use for ink, had all dried up. Having foreseen that this might be the case, Raistlin drew out a knife he had borrowed from his brother and laid it on the table, ready for use.

This done, he prepared to laboriously transfer the spell in the book to the lamb's skin. He would have liked to be able to cast the spell from memory, but as complex as the spell was—far more complex than any he had yet learned—he dared not trust himself. He had never yet performed magic in a crisis situation, and he had no idea how he would react to the pressure. He liked to think he would not falter, but he must not fall prey to over-confidence.

He had the time and solitude necessary to his work. He could concentrate his energy and skill into the transference of the spell to the scroll. He could study the words beforehand, make certain he knew the correct pronunciation, for he would have to speak the words—and speak them correctly—both when he copied the spell and when he cast it.

Settling down with the book, Raistlin pored over the spell. He spoke each letter aloud, then spoke each word aloud, repeating them until they sounded right in his ear, as a minstrel with perfect pitch tunes his lute. He was doing very well, and was feeling rather proud of himself, until he came to the seventh word. The seventh word in the spell was one he had never heard spoken. It might be pronounced any of several different ways, each with its own variant meaning. Which way was the right way?

He considered going to ask Lemuel about it, but that would mean having to tell Lemuel what he planned to do, and Raistlin had already ruled out that option.

"I can do this," he said to himself. "The word is made up of syllables, and all I have to do is to understand what each syllable does, then I will be able to pronounce each syllable correctly. After that, I will simply combine the syllables to form the word."

This sounded easy, but it proved far more difficult than he had imagined. As soon as he had the first syllable settled in his mind, the second appeared to contradict it. The third had nothing to do with the previous two. Several times Raistlin very nearly gave up in despair. His task seemed impossible. Sweat chilled on his body. He lowered his head to his hands.

"This is too hard. I am not ready. I must drop the whole idea, report her to the conclave, let some archmage deal with her. I will tell Kitiara and the rest that I have failed. . . ."

Raistlin sat up. He looked down at the word again. He knew what the spell was supposed to do. Surely, using logical deduction as well as studying related texts, he could determine which meanings were the ones required. He went back to work.

Two hours later, two hours spent searching through texts for every example of the use of the word or parts of the word in a magical spell that he could find, hours spent comparing those spells with each other, looking for patterns and relations, Raistlin sagged back in his chair. He was already weary, and the most difficult part—the actual copying—was before him. He felt a certain satisfaction, however. He had the spell. He knew how it was spoken, or at least he thought he did. The real test would come later.

He rested a few moments, reveling in his victory. His energy restored, he sliced open a cut about three inches long on his forearm, and, holding his arm over a dish he'd placed on the table for the purpose, he collected his own blood to use for ink. When he had enough, he pressed on the wound to stop the bleeding, wrapped his arm with a handkerchief.

He had just completed this when he heard footsteps advancing down the hall. Raistlin hurriedly drew his sleeve over his injured arm, flipped open the book to another page.

Lemuel peered in the door. "I hope I'm not disturbing you. I thought you might like some dinner. . . ." Seeing the dish of blood and the lamb's skin on the desk, the elder mage paused, looked quite startled.

"I'm copying a spell," Raistlin explained. "I hope you don't mind. It's a sleep spell. I've been having a bit of trouble with it, and I thought if I copied it, I could learn it better. And thank you for the offer, but I'm not really hungry."

Lemuel smiled, marveled. "What a very dedicated student you are. You would have never found me cooped up with my books on a sunny day during Harvest Home." He turned to leave, paused again. "Are you sure about dinner? The housekeeper has fixed rabbit stew. She's part elf, you know. Comes from Qualinesti. The stew is quite good, flavored with my own herbs—thyme, marjoram, sage . . ."

"That does sound good. Perhaps later," said Raistlin, who was not the least bit hungry but didn't want to hurt the mage's feelings.

Lemuel smiled again and hurried off, glad to return to his garden.

Raistlin went back to work. Flipping through the pages, he located the correct spell. He picked up the quill pen, made of the feather of a swan, the point tipped with silver. Such a writing instrument was rather extravagant, not necessary to the making of the scroll, but it showed that the archmage had been prosperous in his line of work. Raistlin dipped the pen's point in the blood. Whispering a silent prayer to the three gods of magic—not wanting to offend any one of them—he put the pen to the scroll.

The elegant quill wrote most smoothly, unlike other quills that would balk or sputter, causing the ruin of more than one scroll. The first letter seemed to glide effortlessly upon the lamb's skin.

Raistlin resolved to someday own such a pen. He guessed that Lemuel would have given it freely if Raistlin had asked, but Lemuel had already given his new friend a great deal. Pride forbade asking for more.

Raistlin copied out the spell, pronouncing each word as it was written. The work was painstaking and time-consuming. Sweat formed beneath his hair, trickled down his neck and breast. He had to stop writing after each word to rub the cramp from his hand, cramps that came from clutching the pen too tightly, and to wipe the sweat from his palm. He wrote the seventh word with fear in his heart and the thought as he completed the scroll that this might have been all for nought. If he had mispronounced that word, the entire scroll and all his careful work were worthless.

Reaching the end, he hesitated a moment before adding the final period. Closing his eyes, he again asked a prayer of the three gods.

"I am doing your work. I am doing this for you. Grant me the magic!"

He looked back on his work. It was perfect. No wobble in the *o*s. The curls on the *s* were graceful but not overdone. He cast an anxious glance at the seventh word. There was no help for it. He had done his best. He put the fine silver point of the quill to the lamb's wool and added the period that should start the magic.

Nothing happened. Raistlin had failed.

His eye caught a tiny flicker of light. He held his breath, wanting this as he had wanted his mother to live, willing this to happen as he had willed her to continue breathing. His mother had died. But the flicker of the first letter of the first word grew brighter.

It was not his imagination. The letter glowed, and the glow flowed to the second letter, and then to the second word, and so on. The seventh word seemed to Raistlin to absolutely blaze with triumph. The final dot sparked and then the glow died away. The letters were burned into the lamb's skin. The spell was ready for casting.

Raistlin bowed his head, whispered fervent, heartfelt thanks to the gods who had not failed him. Rising to his feet, he was overcome by dizziness, and nearly passed out. He sank back into the chair. He had no idea what time it was, was startled to see by the position of the sun that it was midafternoon. He was thirsty and hungry and had an urgent need for a chamber pot.

Rolling up the scroll, he tucked it carefully in a scroll case, tied the case securely to his belt. He pushed himself to his feet, made his way downstairs. After using the privies, he hungrily devoured two bowls of rabbit stew.

Raistlin could not recall having eaten so much in his entire life. Shoving aside his bowl, he leaned back in his chair, intending to rest for only a brief moment.

Lemuel found him sound asleep. The mage kindly covered the young man with a blanket, then left him sleeping.

15

Raistlin woke in late afternoon, groggy and stupid from a nap he had never intended to take. He had a stiff neck, and the back of his head ached where he had leaned against the chair. A sudden fear seized him that he had slept too long and missed the "miracle" slated for tonight at the temple. A glance at a pool of sunshine, meandering lazily through a screen of window-climbing ivy, reassured him. Rubbing the back of his neck, he threw off the blanket and went in search of his host. Fortunately he knew where to find him.

Lemuel was in his garden, working diligently, although he did not appear to have made much progress in his preparations for moving.

He confessed as much to Raistlin. "I start to do one thing, and then I think of another and I drop the first and move to the second, only to recall that I simply must do a third before either of them, so I leave to attend to that, only to recall that the first had to be done in advance. . . . " He sighed. "I'm not getting along very fast."

He gazed sadly at the upheaval that surrounded him—overturned pots, mounds of dirt, holes where plants had been uprooted. The plants themselves, looking forlorn and naked, lying on the ground with their roots shivering.

"I suppose it's because I've never been anywhere else but here. And I don't want to be anywhere else. To tell you the truth, I haven't even decided yet where I'm going. Do you think I would like Solace?"

"Perhaps you won't have to move after all," Raistlin said, unable to witness Lemuel's suffering without making some attempt to alleviate it. He couldn't tell his intent, but he could hint. "Perhaps something will happen that will cause Belzor's faithful to leave you alone."

"A second Cataclysm? Fiery mountains raining down on their heads?" Lemuel smiled wanly. "That's too much to hope for, but thank you for the thought. Did you find what you were looking for?"

"My studies went well," said Raistlin gravely.

"And will you stay for supper?"

"No thank you, sir. I must return to the fairgrounds. My friends will be concerned about me. And please, sir," Raistlin said by way of farewell, "do not give up hope. I have a feeling you will be here long after Belzor has gone."

Lemuel was considerably astonished at this and would have asked more questions had not Raistlin pointed out that the tulip bulbs were in danger of being carried away by a squirrel. Lemuel dashed off to the rescue. Raistlin checked for the twentieth time to make certain the scroll case hung from his belt, took his grateful leave, and departed.

"I wonder what he's up to . . ." Lemuel mused. Having chased off the thief, he watched Raistlin walk up the road in the direction of the fairgrounds. "He wasn't copying out any sleep spell, that's for certain. I may not be much of a mage, but even I could pull off a snooze without writing it down. No, he was copying something far more advanced, well beyond his novitiate rank. And all that about something happening to the Belzorites . . ."

Lemuel chewed worriedly on a sprig of mint. "I suppose I should try to stop him. . . ." He considered this option, shook his head. "No. It would be like trying to stop a gnomish juggernaut once it's in gear and rolling downhill. He would not listen to me, and of course there's no reason why he should. What do I know? And he might have a chance of succeeding. There's a lot going on behind those fox-fire eyes of his. A lot going on."

Muttering to himself, Lemuel started to return to his digging. He stood a moment, holding the trowel and staring down at his once tranquil garden, now in a state of chaos.

"Perhaps I should just wait and see what tomorrow brings," he said to himself, and after covering the roots of the plants he had already dug up, making certain that they were warm and damp, he went inside to eat his supper.

* * * * *

Raistlin arrived back at the fairgrounds just in time to prevent Caramon from turning out the town guard in search of him.

"I was busy," he replied testily, in response to his brother's persistent questioning. "Have you done as I ordered?"

"Kept hold of Tasslehoff?" Caramon heaved a long-suffering sigh. "Yes, between Sturm and me, we've managed, but I never want to have to go through anything like that again so long as I live. We had him occupied this morning, or at least we thought we did. Sturm said he wanted to look at Tas's maps. Tas dumped them all out, and he and Sturm spent an hour going over them. I guess I must have dozed off. Sturm got interested in looking at a map of Solamnia, and by the time I woke up and we realized what was what, the kender was gone."

Raistlin frowned.

"We went after him," Caramon said hurriedly. "And we caught up with him. Luckily he hadn't gone far—the fair is pretty interesting, you know. We found him, and after we took the monkey back to its owner, who'd been searching high and low for it . . . The monkey does tricks. You should see it, Raist. It's real cute. Anyway, the owner was hopping mad, although Tas said over and over that the monkey had accompanied him voluntarily, and the monkey did seem to like him—"

"Kindred spirits," observed Raistlin.

"—so by this time, the monkey's owner was yelling for the town guard. Tanis showed up about then, and we made off with Tas while Tanis explained it had all been a mistake and settled with the owner for a couple of steel for his trouble. Sturm decided then that a little military discipline was what was called for, so we took Tas to the parade ground and marched up and down for an hour. Tas thought that was great fun and would have kept it up, but due to the hot sun and the fact that we'd forgotten to bring any water, Sturm and I had to call it quits. We were about done in. The kender, of course, was feeling fine.

"We no more than got back to the fairgrounds when he sees some woman swallowing fire—she really did, Raist. I saw it, too. Tas runs off and we chase after him, and by the time we caught up, he'd lifted two pouches and a sugar bun and was just about to try putting hot coals into his mouth. We took the coals away and returned the pouches, but the sugar bun was gone except for some crumbs around Tas's lips. And then—"

Raistlin held up his hand. "Just answer me this: Where is Tasslehoff now?"

"Tied up," said Caramon wearily. "In the back of Flint's booth. Sturm's standing guard over him. It was the only way."

"Excellent, my brother," said Raistlin.

"Absolute hell," Caramon muttered.

Flint was doing quite well for himself at the fair. People crowded into his stall, kept the dwarf busy pulling rings from the cases and lacing on bracers. He had taken in a goodly quantity of steel, which he kept in a locked iron money box, as well as many items taken in trade. Bartering was an accepted practice at the fair, especially among the vendors. Flint had acquired a new butter churn (which he would trade to Otik for brandy), a washtub (his had sprung a leak), and a very fine tooled-leather belt. (His current belt was a tad too small. Flint claimed it had shrunk when he fell into Crystalmir Lake. Tanis said no, the belt was fine. It was the dwarf who had expanded.)

Raistlin avoided the crowd in the front of the booth, entered the back to find the kender tied securely to a chair, with Sturm seated in a chair opposite. If one were to judge by the expressions on the faces of the two, one might have guessed that Sturm was the prisoner. Tasslehoff, quite enjoying the novelty of being tied hand and foot, was passing the time by entertaining Sturm.

"—and then Uncle Trapspringer said, 'Are you sure that's your walrus?' And the barbarian said— Oh, hello, Raistlin! Look at me! I'm tied to a chair. Isn't this exciting? I'll bet Sturm would tie you up if you asked him politely. Would you, Sturm? Would you tie up Raistlin?"

"What happened to the gag?" Caramon asked.

"Tanis made me take it off. He said it was cruel. He doesn't know the meaning of the word," Sturm replied. He eyed Raistlin grimly, as though he would have liked to take the kender up on his offer. "I trust this will be worth it. I doubt now that anything short of the return of the entire pantheon of gods to denounce Belzor would be sufficient to recompense us for the day we've spent."

"Something less than that, perhaps, but just as effective," Raistlin replied. "Where is Kitiara?"

"She went off to look around the fairgrounds, but she promised she'd be back in time." Caramon quirked an eyebrow. "She said the atmosphere was too cold for comfort, if you take my meaning."

Raistlin nodded in understanding. She and Tanis had quarreled last night, a quarrel that had probably been overheard by most of the vendors and perhaps half the town of Haven. Tanis had kept his voice low; no one could hear what he was saying, but Kit had no such scruples.

"What do you take me for? One of your namby-pamby little elf maids who has to be clinging to you every second? I go where I please, when I please, and with whom I please. To tell you the truth, no, I didn't want you along. You can be such an old man sometimes, always trying to spoil my fun."

The quarrel had gone on long into the night.

"Did they make up this morning?" Raistlin asked his brother, glancing at Tanis's back. The half-elf stood behind the booth, counting money, answering questions, taking measurements, and noting down special orders.

"Silver and amethyst, if you please," a noble lady was dictating. "And a pair of earrings to match."

"No, not a chance," Caramon replied. "You know Kit. She was ready to kiss and make up, but Tanis . . ."

As if aware that they were talking of him, Tanis turned from dropping another three steel into the money box.

"Are you still planning to go through with this?" he asked.

"I am," Raistlin said.

Tanis shook his head. He had gray smudges beneath his eyes and looked tired. "I don't like it."

"No one asked you to," Raistlin returned.

An uncomfortable silence fell. Caramon flushed and bit his lip, embarrassed for his brother, yet too loyal to say anything. Sturm gave Raistlin a look of haughty disapproval, reminded Raistlin silently that he was not to be disrespectful to his elders. Tas was going to tell another Uncle Trapspringer story, but he couldn't think of one that seemed to fit, and so he kept quiet, wiggled unhappily in his chair. The kender would have run cheerfully into a dragon's open mouth and never turned a hair on his topknot, but anger among his friends always made him feel very uncomfortable.

"You are right, Raistlin. No one did ask me," Tanis said. He started to turn away, to go back to the front of the booth.

"Tanis," Raistlin called out. "I'm sorry. I had no right to speak to you—my elder—in that manner, as the knight here would remind me. I can offer as my excuse only that I have an extremely difficult task ahead of me tonight. And I remind you and everyone here"—his gaze swept them all—"that if I fail, I will be the one to pay the penalty. None of the rest of you will be implicated."

"And yet I wonder if you realize the enormous risk you're running," Tanis said earnestly. "This false religion is making Judith and her followers wealthy. By exposing her, you may be putting yourself into considerable danger. I think you should reconsider. Let others deal with her."

"Aye," said Flint, coming back behind the booth to bring more money for the iron box. He had overheard the latter part of the conversation. "If you'll take my advice, laddie, which you never do, I say we keep our noses out of this. I was thinking on this last night, and after what you told me about the people tormenting that poor lass who lost her babe, it is my opinion that the humans of Haven and Belzor deserve each other."

"You can't be serious, sir!" Sturm protested, shocked. "According to the Measure, if a person has knowledge of a law being broken and that person does nothing to halt it, then that person is as guilty as the lawbreaker. We should do everything in our power to stop this false priestess."

"We do that by reporting her to the proper authorities," Tanis argued.

"Who won't believe us," Caramon pointed out.

"I think—"

"Enough! I have made my decision!" Raistlin put an end to the arguments, which were making him doubt himself, undermining his carefully built fortifications. "I will go ahead with the plan. Those who want to help me can do so. Those who don't may go about their business."

"I will help," said Sturm.

"Me, too," Caramon replied loyally.

"And me! I'm the key!" Tas would have jumped up and down, except he found that jumping was difficult when it involved bringing along the chair to which he was tied. "Don't be mad, Tanis. It will be fun!"

"I'm not mad," Tanis said, his weary face relaxing into a smile. "I'm pleased that you young men are willing to risk danger for a cause you think is right. I trust that is why you're doing this," he said, with a pointed glance at Raistlin.

Never mind my motives, Raistlin advised the half-elf silently. You wouldn't understand them. So long as I achieve an outcome that pleases you and is beneficial to others, what do you care why I do what I do?

Annoyed, he was turning away when Kitiara strolled through the door of the stall. Elbowing aside several customers, who glared at her resentfully, she made her way behind the counter.

"I see we're all here. Ready to go feed Judith to the snakes?" she asked, grinning. "I'm among the chosen, by the way, baby brother. I've asked to speak to our dead mother, and the High Priestess has kindly granted my request."

This was not part of the plan. Raistlin had no idea what Kit was up to, but before he could question her, she draped her arm around Tanis, ran her hand caressingly over his shoulder. "Are you coming along to help us tonight, my love?"

Tanis pulled away from her touch.

"The fairgrounds don't shut down until dark," he said. "I have work to do here."

Kit drew close, nibbled at his ear. "Is Tanis still mad at Kitiara?" she asked in a playful tone.

He gently shoved Kit away. "Not here," he said, adding in a low voice, "We have a lot of things to talk over, Kit."

"Oh, for the love of— Talk! That's all you ever want to do!" Kit flared. "All last night, talk, talk, talk. So I told you a harmless little lie! It wasn't the first time, and it won't be the last. I'm sure you've lied to me plenty!"

Tanis paled. "You don't mean that," he said quietly.

"No, of course I don't. I say things I don't mean all the time. I'm a liar. Just ask anyone."

Kit strode angrily around the counter, giving Caramon a kick when he didn't move out of her way fast enough to suit her. "Are the rest of you coming?"

"Untie the kender," Raistlin ordered. "Sturm, you're in charge of Tas. And you, Tas"—he fixed the kender with a stern eye—"you must do exactly as I say. If you don't, you might be the one fed to the vipers."

"Ooh, how excit—" Tas saw by Raistlin's swiftly contracting brows that this was not the right response. The kender was suddenly extremely solemn. "I mean, yes, Raistlin. I'll do whatever you tell me to do. I won't even look at a snake unless you say to," he added with what he considered truly heroic self-sacrifice.

Raistlin suppressed a sigh. He could see great gaps opening in his plan, envision any number of things going wrong. For one, he was counting on a kender, which anyone in Krynn would tell him was sheer madness. Two, he was trusting in a would-be knight, who put honor and honesty over every other consideration, including common sense. Three, he had no idea what Kitiara was plotting on her own, and that was perhaps the most dangerous gap of all—a veritable chasm, into which they all might tumble.

"I'm ready, Raist," said Caramon stoutly. His loyalty was comforting to his brother, but then Caramon spoiled it by tugging proudly on his collar and adding, "I won't breathe the smoke. I wore this big shirt specially, so that I could pull it up over my head."

Presented with a vision of Caramon entering the temple with his shirt hiked up over his head, Raistlin shut his eyes and silently prayed to the gods—the gods of magic, and all true gods everywhere—to walk with him.

16

They arrived at the temple in time to mingle with the throng surging inside. The crowd was far larger tonight, word of Judith's "miracle" having circulated among the fairgoers, and included hill dwarves, several of the barbaric, feather-decorated Plainsmen, and a number of noble families, clad in fine clothes, accompanied by their servants.

Raistlin also saw, much to his dismay, several of their neighbors from Solace. He drew his shapeless felt hat low over his face, huddled into the thick black cloak he wore over his robes. He was actually glad to see that Caramon had his shirt pulled up to his ears, making him resemble a gigantic tortoise. Raistlin hoped none of their neighbors would recognize them and make some reference to their fellow villager's magic.

Raistlin was somewhat daunted by the turnout. People from all parts of Abanasinia would be witness to his performance. It had not occurred to him until now that he would be performing before a large audience. The thought was not a comfortable one. At that moment, if someone had appeared before him and offered him a bent penny to flee, he would have grabbed the coin and run.

Pride goaded him on. After his confrontation with Tanis, his fine talk before his siblings and friends, Raistlin could not back down now. Not without forfeiting their respect and losing any hold he might once again wield over them.

Crowding close behind Caramon, Raistlin used his brother's large body as a shield as they made their way through the crowd. Sturm kept near them, shepherding Tasslehoff with one hand on the kender's shoulder and the other plucking Tas's wandering fingers out of the worshipers' pouches and bags.

"I have to go down in front with the priests. It's a great seat!

Good luck," Kit called and waved her hand.

"Wait!" Raistlin struggled out from behind Caramon to try to reach his sister, but they were caught in a press of people and it was too late. Kitiara had seized hold of one of the priests and was now being led by him through the crowd.

What was she going to do?

Raistlin cursed his sister for her distrustful, secretive nature, but even as he muttered the words, he was forced to bite them off. Blood to blood, as the dwarves say. He might as well curse himself. He had said nothing of his plans to Kitiara.

"You can put your shirt down now!" he snapped at Caramon, nervousness making him irritable.

"Where do you want us?" Sturm asked.

"You and the kender go to the very back wall," Raistlin said, pointing to the upper tiers of seats in the arena. He gave them their final instructions. "Tas, when I shout 'Behold,' you start walking down the aisle. Walk slowly and keep your mind on what you're doing. Don't allow yourself to get distracted by anything, do you understand? If you obey me, you will see such wonderful magic as you've never seen in your entire life."

"I will, Raistlin," Tas promised. " 'Behold.' " He repeated the word several times, in order not to forget it. " 'Behold, behold, behold.' I saw a beholder once. Did I ever tell you—"

"No kender allowed," said a blue-robed priest, descending on them.

Unable and unwilling to lie, Sturm stood with his hand on the kender's shoulder. Raistlin's breath caught in his throat. He dared not intervene, dared not draw attention to himself. Fortunately for all of them, Tasslehoff was accustomed to being thrown out of places.

"Oh, he's just escorting me off now, sir," the kender said with a beaming smile.

"Is that true?"

Sturm, his mustaches bristling, inclined his head the merest fraction, the closest he had come in his entire life to telling a falsehood. Perhaps the Measure sanctioned lies in a good cause.

"Then I'm sorry for interfering with you, sir," said the priest in mollifying tones. "Please don't let me keep you from your task. The doors are in that direction." He waved his hand.

Sturm bowed coldly and dragged Tasslehoff away, shushing the kender's remarks with a stern "Silence!" and a shake of the small shoulder to emphasize the point.

Raistlin drew breath again.

"Where to?" Caramon asked, peering over the heads of the crowd.

"Somewhere near the front."

"Keep close behind me," Caramon advised.

Thrusting out with his elbows, he shouldered and jostled and eventually cleared a path through the throng. People scowled, but on noting his size, they kept any angry remarks they had been about to make to themselves.

The lower seats near the arena were filled. There was perhaps room for one person—and that a small person—at the end of the aisle. "Watch this," Caramon said to his brother with a wink.

Caramon plunked himself down on the empty seat, shifting and bumping his body against that of his neighbor, a wealthy woman, finely dressed, who glared at him. Coldly and pointedly, she moved away from his touch. Raistlin was wondering what this was going to accomplish, for there was still no room for him, when Caramon suddenly let out a great belch and then noisily passed gas.

People in the vicinity grimaced, regarded Caramon with disgust. The woman beside him clapped her hand over her nose and glared at Caramon, who gave a shamefaced grin.

"Beans for dinner," he said.

The woman rose to her feet. Sweeping her silk skirts, she favored him with a scathing glance and the comment, "Clod! I can't think why they permit your kind in here! I shall certainly protest!" She flounced off up the stairs, searching for one of the priests.

Caramon waved his brother to come sit down in the empty place beside him.

"I had not realized you could be so subtle, my brother," Raistlin murmured as he took his seat.

"Yeah, that's me! Subtle!" Caramon chuckled.

Raistlin searched the crowd and soon located Sturm, standing in the shadow of a pillar near an aisle. Tasslehoff was not visible, Sturm had probably stashed the kender in the shadows.

Sturm had been searching for Raistlin as well. Sighting him, Sturm gave a brief nod, jerked his thumb. A small hand shot out from behind Sturm's back, waved. Kender and knight were in position.

Raistlin turned to face the arena. He had no difficulty at all finding his sister. Kitiara stood in the pen in front of the arena, alongside the others who had been invited to speak to their dead kin.

As if aware of his gaze upon her, Kit grinned her crooked grin. Raistlin realized with some bitterness that she was calm, relaxed, even having fun.

He was not.

When the last stragglers had been hurried to their seats, the doors shut. The Temple grew dark. Fire sprang up from the braziers on the arena floor. The chanting began. The priests and priestess entered, bearing the charmed vipers in the baskets. Soon Judith would make her entrance. Raistlin's moment to act was fast approaching.

He was terrified. He knew very well what ailed him, recognized the symptoms—stage fright.

Raistlin had experienced stage fright before, but only very mildly, prior to his performances at the small fairs in Solace. The fear had always vanished the moment he began his act, and he had not worried about it.

He had never before performed to an audience of this size, an audience that must be considered hostile. He had never performed for stakes this large. His fear was a hundredfold greater than anything he'd previously experienced.

His hands were chilled to the bone, the fingers so stiff he did not think he could move them enough to draw the scroll from the case. His bowels gripped, and he thought for one horrible moment that he was going to be forced to leave to go find the privies. His mouth dried up. He could not speak a word. How was he to cast the spell if he couldn't talk? His body was drenched in sweat, he shivered with chills. His stomach heaved.

His performance was going to end in ignominy and shame, with him being sick all over himself.

The High Priest began his introduction. Raistlin didn't pay heed. He sat hunched over, miserable and deathly ill.

High Priestess Judith appeared in her blue robes. She was making her welcoming speech to the audience. Raistlin couldn't hear the words for the roaring in his ears. The time was fast approaching. Caramon was looking at him expectantly. Somewhere in the darkness, Kit was watching him. Sturm was waiting for his signal, so was Tasslehoff. They were waiting for him, counting on him, depending on him. They would understand his failure. They would be kind, never reproach him. They would pity him. . . .

Judith had lowered her arms. The sleeves cascaded down around her hands. She was preparing to cast the spell.

Raistlin fumbled at the scroll case, forcing his numb fingers to unfasten the lid. He drew forth the scroll, his hand shaking so he nearly dropped it. Panicked, afraid he would lose it in the darkness and not be able to recover it, he clenched his fist over it.

Slowly, trembling, Raistlin cast off his black cloak, rose to his feet. His neighbors glared at him in irritation. Someone behind him hissed loudly for him to sit down. When he didn't, more voices were raised. The commotion caused others to look in his direction, including one of the priests in the arena.

Raistlin searched his mind frantically for his carefully worded, oft-rehearsed speech. He couldn't recall any of it. Dazed by debilitating fear, he unrolled the scroll and looked at it, hoping it might give him some clue.

The letters of the magical words glowed faintly, pleasantly, as if they had been illuminated, the brush tipped with fire. The warmth of the magic spread from the scroll through his chilled fingers and brought with it reassurance. He possessed the ability to cast the spell, the skill to wield the magic. He would work his will on these people, hold them under his sway.

The knowledge enflamed him. An updraft of power consumed his fear.

His voice, when he spoke, was unfamiliar. Generally soft-spoken, he had not expected to sound so strong. He pitched his voice to where the acoustics would best amplify his words, and the result was dramatic. He startled even himself.

"Citizens of Haven," he called, "friends and neighbors. I stand before you to warn you that you are being duped!"

Mutterings and murmurs rumbled through the crowd. Some were angry, shouted for him to stop insulting the god. Others were annoyed, worried that he was going to disrupt the promised miracle. A few clapped, urged him on. They'd come to see a show, and this guaranteed that they'd get more than their money's worth. People craned their necks to see him, many stood up in their seats.

The priests and priestesses in the arena looked uncertainly at their leader, wondering what to do. At a signal from the High Priest, they raised their voices to try to drown out Raistlin's words with their chanting. Caramon was on his feet, standing protectively beside his brother, keeping a baleful eye upon the acolytes, who had grabbed torches and were hastening down the aisle toward them.

Raistlin paid no attention to the uproar. He was watching Judith. She had ceased her spell-casting. Locating him in the crowd, she stared at him. In the semidarkness, she did not recognize him. She saw his white robes, however, and immediately recognized her own danger. She was confounded, but only for a moment. Quickly she regained her composure.

"Beware the wizard!" she cried. "Seize him and take him away. His kind are forbidden in the temple. He comes to work his evil magic among us!"

"Let us hear more about evil magic, Widow Judith," Raistlin shouted.

She knew him then. Her face suffused with the blood of her rage. Her eyes widened, the white rims visible around the dilated pupils. Her pallid lips moved without speech. She stared at him, and he was appalled at the hatred he saw in her eyes, appalled and alarmed. His conviction wavered.

She sensed him faltering, and her lips parted in a terrible smile. She did what she should have done at first. Disdainfully she turned from him, ignored him.

The acolytes clattered down the steps toward him. Fortunately some of the audience had moved into the aisle, hoping to see better, and were blocking the way. Caramon, fists clenched, was ready to hold the acolytes off, but it would be only a matter of time before he was overwhelmed by sheer numbers.

"I can prove my accusations are true!" Raistlin cried. His voice cracked. People began to boo and hiss.

Embarrassed, feeling his audience slipping away, he struggled to retain his desperate hold. "The woman who calls herself a High Priestess performs what she calls a miracle. I say it is magic, and to prove it, I will cast the very same spell. Watch as I bring you another so-called god! Behold!"

Raistlin did not need the scroll. The words of the spell were in his blood. The magic formed a pool of fire around his fast-beating heart, his blood carried the magic into every part of his body. He recited the words of magic, pronouncing each correctly and precisely, reveling in the exhilarating sensation as the magic flowed like molten steel through his fingers, his hands, his arms.

Drawing on the energies of those watching him, utilizing even the hatred and fury of his enemies to his own advantage, Raistlin cast forth the magic. The spell streamed out of him, seemed to uplift him, carry him along on radiating waves of heat and fire.

A giant appeared before the audience. A fearful giant, a giant with a topknot, wearing green plaid pants and a purple silk shirt, a giant draped with pouches, a giant trying his very best to look as if he appreciated the enormity of the situation.

"Behold!" Raistlin called again. "The Giant Kender of Balifor!"

People gasped, then someone tittered. Someone else giggled, the nervous giggle of tense situations. The giant kender began moving down the aisle, his face so solemn and serious that his nose quivered with the effort.

"Summon Belzor!" cried one wit. "Sic Belzor on the kender!"

"My money's on the kender!" cried another.

Gales of merriment rippled through the crowd, most of whom had come to see a spectacle and were feeling well rewarded. A few of the faithful cried out in anger, demanded that the wizard cease his sacrilege, but the laughter, once started, was difficult to halt.

Laughter—a weapon as deadly as any spear.

"In this corner, Belzor . . ." cried out someone.

Roars of laughter. Four acolytes had made it down the stairs, were attempting to seize hold of Raistlin. Caramon pushed the acolytes back, knocking them aside with his bare hands.

Their neighbors, who were enjoying the show and didn't want it to end, joined in the shoving match. Some of the faithful sided with the acolytes. Three men who had come to the temple straight from the beer tent leapt eagerly into the fray, not caring whose side they took. A small riot erupted around Raistlin.

Shouts and screams and cries drew the attention of the Haven town guards who were in attendance. They had been glancing nervously at their captain, fearing that at any moment they might be ordered to arrest the giant kender. The captain himself was considerably baffled. He had sudden visions of the giant kender incarcerated in the Haven jail, with most of his torso and his topknotted head and shoulders sticking up through the hole they would have to cut in the roof.

Under these circumstances, a riot—plain and simple—was extremely welcome. Ignoring the giant kender, the captain ordered his men to quell the riot.

The giant kender continued to march down the aisle, but few were paying attention to him anymore. By this time, most of the people in the arena were on their feet.

The prudent, seeing that the situation was quickly getting dangerously out of hand, gathered up their families and headed for the exits.

Thrill-seekers stood on their seats, trying to obtain a better view. Young men in the audience charged gleefully across the arena to take part in the fight. Several children, escaping their frantic mothers, were in hot pursuit of the giant kender.

A group of visiting dwarves were taking on all comers and swearing that this was the best religious meeting they had attended since before the time of the Cataclysm.

Raistlin stood on the marble seat, where he had taken refuge. The knowledge that he had wrought this confusion, that he had fomented this chaos, appalled him. And then, it thrilled him.

He tasted the power and its taste was sweet, sweeter to him than love, sweeter than gain. Raistlin saw for himself the fatal flaws in his fellow mortals. He saw their greed and prejudice, their gullibility, their perfidy, their baseness. He despised them for it, and he knew, in that instant, that he could make use of such flaws for his own ends, whatever those ends might be. He could use his power for good, if he chose. He could use it for ill.

He turned, in his triumph, to the High Priestess.

She was gone. Kitiara was gone, too, Raistlin realized in consternation.

He caught hold of the back of Caramon's shirt—the only part of him he could reach—and gave it a jerk. Caramon was wrestling two of the acolytes. He held one at arm's length, his hand at the throat of another. All the while he was telling them over and over that they should just settle down and leave honest people alone. The jerk on his collar half-strangled Caramon, caused him to twist his head around.

"Let them go!" Raistlin shouted. "Come with me!"

Fists flailed around them, men heaved and shoved and shouted and swore. In their attempt to restore order, the guards increased the confusion. Raistlin took a moment to search the crowd for Sturm, but couldn't find him. The giant kender had disappeared, the spell faded as the audience's readiness to believe in the illusion subsided. Tasslehoff, returned to his normal size, was buried beneath an avalanche of small boys.

The magic was gone from Raistlin as well, leaving him drained, as if he had cut open an artery, spilled his life's blood. Every movement took an effort, every word spoken required concentrated thought. He longed desperately to curl up under a soft blanket and sleep, sleep for days. But he dared not. Yet when he took a step, he swayed and nearly fell.

Caramon took firm hold of his brother's arm. "Raist, you look terrible! What's the matter? Are you sick? Here, I'll carry you."

"You will not! Shut up and listen to me!" Raistlin had neither the time nor the energy to waste on Caramon's nonsense.

He started to thrust aside Caramon's supportive arm, then realized that he might well collapse without it. "Help me walk, then. Not that way, ninny! The door beneath the snake! We must find Judith!"

Caramon glowered. "Find that witch? What for? Good riddance. The Abyss take her!"

"You don't know what you're saying, Caramon," Raistlin gasped, foreboding sending a shudder through him. "Come with me or I will go myself."

"Sure, Raist," Caramon said, subdued, impressed by his brother's urgent tone. "Out of our way!" he cried, and punched a skinny town guardsman, who was trying ineffectually to get his hands around Caramon's thick neck.

Caramon helped Raistlin climb down from the seats, assisted him over the rope used to keep the faithful from entering the arena.

"Watch out for the vipers!" Raistlin warned, leaning on Caramon's strong arm. " The charm that held them is ended."

Caramon gave the snakes, swaying in their baskets, a wide berth. The High Priest and his followers had wisely fled the arena, leaving the vipers behind. Even as Raistlin spoke his warning, one of the snakes slid out of its basket and slithered across the floor.

People spilled into the arena, some trying to flee the melee, others seeking new opponents. A guard bumped into a brazier, spilling burning coals onto the straw which had been spread to deaden the noise. Gouts of flame shot up, wisps of smoke coiled into the air, further increasing the pandemonium as someone shouted hysterically that the building was on fire.

"This way!" Raistlin gestured toward the narrow doorway inside the stone statue of the snake.

The two entered a corridor of stone, lit by flickering torches. Several doors opened off the corridor on both sides. Raistlin looked into one of these, a large room, splendidly furnished, lit by hundreds of wax candles. In these rooms, Belzor's priests lived—lived well, by the looks of it—and worked. He had hoped to find Judith, but the room was empty, as was this part of the corridor. The followers of Belzor had deemed it wise to abandon the temple mob.

Glancing around in haste, Raistlin discovered that not all the faithful had fled. A lone figure crouched in a shadowed corner. He drew near to see it was one of the priestesses. Either she was injured or she had collapsed out of fear. Whatever the reason, the other servants of Belzor had abandoned her, left her huddled against the stone wall, weeping bitterly.

"Ask her where to find Judith!" Raistlin instructed. He deemed it wiser if he remained out of sight, hidden in the shadows behind his brother.

Caramon gently touched the priestess on the hand, to draw her attention. She started at his touch, lifted her tear-streaked face to stare at him fearfully.

"Where is the High Priestess?" Caramon asked.

"It wasn't my fault. She lied to us!" the girl said, gulping. "I believed her."

"Sure you did. Where—"

A scream, a scream of anger, rising shrilly to fear, was suddenly cut off, in a horrible gurgle. Raistlin was chilled to the bone with horror at the dreadful sound. The girl screamed herself, covered her ears with her hands.

"Where is Judith?" Caramon persisted. He had no idea what was going on, but he had his instructions. He wasn't going to let anything distract him. He shook the frightened girl.

"Her waiting room . . . is down there." The girl whimpered. She crouched on her knees. "You have to believe me! I didn't know . . ."

Caramon didn't wait to hear more. Raistlin was already moving down the corridor in the direction the girl had indicated. Caramon caught up with his twin at the end of the hall. Here the corridor branched off, ran in two different directions, forming a **Y**. The torches on the left side of the corridor, the side where Judith's room was located, had been doused. That portion of the temple was in darkness.

"We need light!" Raistlin commanded.

Caramon grabbed a torch from an iron sconce on the wall. He held it high.

Smoke from the burning straw in the arena had drifted through the doorway. The smoke slid in sinuous curls across the floor. The light shone on a single door which stood at the end of the dark corridor, gleamed off the symbol of the serpent made of gold which adorned the door.

"Did you hear that scream, Raist?" Caramon whispered uneasily, coming to a halt.

"Yes, and we weren't the only ones to hear it," Raistlin answered impatiently, casting his brother an annoyed glance. "What are you standing there for? Hurry up! People will be coming to investigate. We don't have much time."

Raistlin continued walking down the hall. After a moment's hesitation, Caramon hurried to his brother's side.

Raistlin rapped sharply on the door, only to find that it swung open at his touch.

"I don't like this, Raist," Caramon said, nervous and shaken. "Let's go."

Raistlin pushed on the door.

The room was brightly lit. Twenty or thirty thick candles stood on a ledge of stone inside the small chamber. Thick velvet curtains, hung from an interior door, closed off another room in the back, probably Judith's sleeping chamber. Wine in a pewter goblet and bread and meat, sustenance intended for the priestess's refreshment after her performance, had been placed on a small wooden table.

Judith no longer had need of food. Her performances were ended. The wizardess lay on the floor beneath the table. Blood covered the stone floor. Her throat had been slashed with such violence that the killer had almost severed the head from the neck.

At the horrible sight, Caramon retched, covered his eyes with his hands.

"Oh, Raist! I didn't mean it!" he mumbled, sickened. "About the Abyss! I didn't mean it!"

"Nevertheless, my brother," Raistlin said, regarding the corpse with terrible calm, "we may safely assume that the Abyss is where the Widow Judith is now residing. Come, we should leave immediately. No one must find us here."

As he started to turn away, he caught a flash out of the corner of his eye—torchlight glinting off metal. Looking closely, he saw a knife lying on the floor near the body. Raistlin knew that knife, he'd seen it before. He hesitated a split second, then, bending down, he snatched up the knife, slipped it into the sleeve of his robe.

"Quickly, my brother! Someone's coming!"

Outside, booted feet clattered; the girl was shrilly guiding the town guard to the High Priestess's chambers. Raistlin reached the door just as the captain of the guard entered, accompanied by several of his men. They stopped short at the sight of the body, alarmed and amazed. One guard turned away to be quietly sick in a corner.

The captain was an old soldier who'd seen death in many hideous aspects and was not unduly shocked by this one. He stared first at Judith, whom he had come to question about bilking money out of the good citizens of Haven, then he turned a stern gaze to the two young men. He recognized them both immediately as the two who had precipitated the evening's disastrous events.

Caramon, nearly as pale as the blood-drained corpse, said brokenly, "I—I didn't mean it."

Raistlin kept quiet, thinking quickly. The situation was desperate, circumstances were against them.

"What's this?" The captain pointed to a smear of blood on Raistlin's white robes.

"I have some small reputation as a healer. I bent down to examine her." Raistlin started to add, "to see if there were any signs of life." Glancing at the body, he realized how ludicrous that statement would sound. He clamped his mouth shut.

He was acutely aware of the knife clutched tightly in his hand. The blood on the hilt was sticky, was gumming his fingers. He was repulsed, would have given anything to have been able to wash it off.

Taking that knife had been an act of unbelievable stupidity. Raistlin cursed himself for his folly, couldn't imagine what had prompted him to do something so ill-judged. Some vague and instinctive desire to protect her, he supposed. She would have never done as much for him.

"The weapon's not here," said the captain after another glance at Raistlin's bloodstained robes and a cursory look around the room. "Search them both."

One of the guardsman seized hold of Raistlin, grabbed him roughly, pinned his arms. Another guard rolled up Raistlin's long sleeves, revealing the bloody knife, held fast in his blood-covered hand.

The captain smiled, grimly triumphant.

"First a giant kender, and now murder," he said. "You've had a busy night, young man."

17

The Haven jail was not a particularly nice jail, as Tasslehoff had complained. Located near the sheriff's house, the jail had once been a horse barn. It was drafty and cold, the dirt floors were strewn with refuse. The place stank of both horse and human piss and dung, mingled with vomit from those who had indulged too freely in dwarf spirits at the fair.

Raistlin didn't notice the smell, at least not after the first few seconds. He was too tired to notice. They could have hanged him—hanging being the penalty for murder in Haven—and he would not have protested. He sank down on a filthy straw mattress and fell into a sleep so deep that he didn't feel the rats skitter over his legs.

His dreamless, untroubled sleep provided much conversation among the jail's two guards. One held that such sleep was indicative of a mind innocent of murder, for all knew that a guilty conscience could never slumber peacefully. The other guard, older, scoffed at this notion. It proved the young man to be a hardened criminal, since he could sleep that soundly with the blood of his victim still on his hands.

Raistlin did not hear their arguments, nor did he hear the noisy voices of his fellow prisoners, mostly kender. The kender were filled with excitement, for this had been an eventful day, complete with a riot, a conflagration, a murder, and, most wonderfully, one of their own transformed into a giant. Not even Uncle Trapspringer had been known to accomplish such a magnificent feat. The giant kender was to become a celebrated figure in kender song and story ever after that, often seen striding across the oceans and hopping from mountaintop to mountaintop. If there was ever a night when the silver and red moons didn't rise, it was widely known that the giant kender had "borrowed" them.

Eager to discuss this momentous occasion, the kender were constantly in and out of each other's cells, picking the locks almost before the cell doors were shut. As soon as the guards had one kender locked up, two more were out roaming around.

"He's shivering," observed the young guard, glancing into Raistlin's cell during one of the few lulls given them by the kender, a lull that was quite ominous, if only they'd thought about it. "Should I get him a blanket?"

"Naw," said the jailkeep with a leer. "He'll be warm enough. Too warm, if you take my meaning. They say it's hotter'n the smithy's forge in the Abyss."

"I guess there'll be a trial first, before they hang him," said the young guard, who was new to the area.

"The sheriff will hold one, for form's sake." The jailer shrugged. "Myself, I don't see the need. He was caught with the knife in his hand standing over the body." He dredged up a filthy blanket. "Here, you can cover him up if you want. 'Twould be a shame if he caught cold and died before the hanging. Hand over the keys."

"I don't have the keys. I thought you had the keys."

As it turned out, the kender had the keys. They poured out of their cells and were soon having a picnic in the middle of the jail.

Intent on endeavoring to persuade the kender to return their keys, the jailer and the lone guard were too distracted to notice the flare of torchlight approaching the prison, nor could they hear over the shouts of the kender, the shouts of the approaching mob.

Raistlin, exhausted from the spellcasting and the sheriff's questioning, had fallen into a comatose-like sleep and heard nothing.

* * * * *

Caramon did not see the torchlight either. He was far from the jail, running as fast as he possibly could for the fairgrounds.

Caramon had narrowly escaped being made a prisoner himself. When questioned by Haven's sheriff, Caramon steadfastly denied all knowledge of the crime, denied it in the name of himself and his brother. Raistlin had wearily repeated his own story. He had knelt beside the body to examine the victim. He had no idea why he had picked up the knife or why he had tried to hide it. He had been in a state of shock, did not know what he was doing. He added, emphatically, that Caramon was not involved.

Fortunately a witness, the young priestess, came forward to claim that she had been speaking to Caramon in the hallway when they heard Judith scream. Caramon swore that his twin had been with him at the time, but the girl said she had seen only one of them.

Due to this alibi, the sheriff reluctantly released Caramon. He gave his brother one loving, anxious, worried look—a look that Raistlin ignored—and then hurried off to the fairgrounds.

On his way, Caramon mulled things over in his mind. People accused him of being dull-witted, slow. He was not dull-witted, but he was slow, though not in the popular use of the term, meaning stupid. He was a thinker, a slow and deliberate thinker, one who considered every aspect of a problem before finally arriving at the solution. The fact that he invariably arrived at the right solution often went unnoticed by most people.

Caramon had several miles to consider this terrible predicament. The sheriff had been quite candid. There would be a trial as a matter of form, though its outcome was a foregone conclusion. Raistlin would be found guilty of murder, he would pay for his crime by hanging. The hanging would likely take place that very day, as soon as they could assemble the gallows.

By the time he reached the fairgrounds, Caramon had come to a decision. He knew what he had to do.

The fairgrounds were quiet. Here and there a light shone from behind the shutters of a booth, although it was well into the morning hours. Some craftsmen were still hard at work replenishing their stock for tomorrow's opening. Tomorrow would be the last day of the fair, the last day to entice customers, the last day to urge the buyer to part with his steel.

Word of the excitement in Haven had either not yet reached the fairgrounds, or, if it had, the participants had listened to it as a good story, little thinking it would have any effect on them. They would feel differently in the morning. If there was a murder trial and a hanging tomorrow, attendance at the fair would fall to almost nothing, sales would be down.

Caramon found Flint's stall by tracing the lumpy outlines of the various buildings, silhouetted against the lambent light of stars and the red moon, which was full and exceedingly bright. Caramon took this as a good omen. Though Raistlin wore white robes, he had once remarked that he favored Lunitari.

Caramon looked for Sturm, but he was nowhere to be found, nor was Tasslehoff around. Caramon went to Tanis's tent, hesitated at the tent flap.

Desperate, Caramon had no compunction about interrupting any sort of pleasurable activity that might be taking place inside. Listening, he could hear nothing. He lifted the flap, peeked in. Tanis was alone, asleep, though not peacefully. He murmured something in an unknown language, probably elven, tossed restlessly. Evidently the quarrel remained unresolved. Caramon lowered the flap, backed away.

Entering the tent he shared with his twin, Caramon was not surprised to find Kitiara inside, rolled up in a blanket. By her even breathing, she was sleeping soundly and contentedly. Red moonlight flowed in after Caramon, as though Lunitari herself was intent on being present at this interview. Anger and awe vied for the uppermost position in Caramon's soul.

Squatting down, he touched Kit's shoulder. He had to shake her several times to rouse her, and by this and the poor job of acting she did on rolling over and feigning not to immediately recognize him, he concluded that she had been shamming, playing possum. Kit was not one to let anyone sneak up on her, as Caramon himself knew from past painful experience.

"Who is that? Caramon?" Kit affected a yawn, ran her hand through her tousled hair. "What do you want? What time is it?"

"They've arrested Raistlin," Caramon said.

"Yes, well, I'm not surprised. We'll pay his fine and get him out of jail in the morning." Kit drew the blanket over her shoulders, turned away.

"They've arrested him for murder." Caramon spoke to his sister's back. "For the murder of the Widow Judith. We found her dead in her chambers. Her throat had been cut. There was a knife beside the body. Raistlin and I both recognized that knife. We'd seen it before—on your knife belt."

He fell silent, waiting.

Kitiara held still a moment, then, throwing off the blanket, she sat up. She was dressed in her hose and long-sleeved shirt. She had removed her leather vest, but she was wearing her boots.

She was nonchalant, easy, even slightly amused. "So why did they arrest Raistlin?"

"They found him holding the knife."

Kit grimaced. "That was stupid. Baby brother usually doesn't make stupid mistakes like that. As for recognizing the knife"—she shrugged—"there are a lot of knives in this world."

"Not many with Flint's mark, or the way you wrap the hilt

with braided leather. It was your knife, Kit. Both Raistlin and I know it."

"You do, do you?" Kit quirked an eyebrow. "Did Raistlin say anything?"

"No, of course not. He wouldn't." Caramon was grim. "Not until I talked to you about it. But he's going to."

"They won't believe him."

"Then you're going to say something. You killed her, didn't you, Kit?"

Kitiara shrugged again, made no reply. The red moonlight, reflected in her dark eyes, never wavered.

Caramon stood up. "I'm going to tell them, Kit. I'm going to tell them the truth." He bent down, started to duck out the tent.

Kit twisted to her feet, seized hold of his sleeve. "Caramon, wait! There's something you have to consider. Something you haven't thought about." She tugged him back inside the tent, closed the flap, shutting out the moonlight.

"Well"—Caramon regarded her coldly—"what's that?"

Kit drew closer to Caramon. "Did you know Raistlin could do magic like that?"

"Like what?" Caramon was puzzled.

"Cast a spell like the one he cast tonight. It was a powerful spell, Caramon. I know. I've been around magic-users some, and I've seen . . . Well, never mind what I've seen, but trust me on this. What Raistlin did he shouldn't have been able to do. Not as young as he is."

"He's good at magic," Caramon said, still not comprehending what this was all about. He might have added, in the same tone, that Raistlin was good at gardening or at cooking fried eggs, for that was how Caramon viewed it.

Kit made an impatient gesture. "Are you part gully dwarf to be so thickheaded? Can't you understand?" She lowered her voice to a hissing whisper. "Listen to me, Caramon. You say Raistlin is good at magic. I say he's too good at magic. I hadn't realized it until tonight. I thought he was just playing at being a wizard. How could I know he was this powerful? I didn't expect—"

"What are you saying, Kit?" Caramon demanded, starting to lose patience.

"Let them have him, Caramon," Kitiara said, soft, quiet. "Let them hang him! Raistlin is dangerous. He's like one of those vipers. As long as he's charmed, he'll be nice. But if you cross him . . . Don't go back to the prison, Caramon. Just go to bed. In the morning, if anyone asks you about the knife, say it was his. That's all you have to do, Caramon. And everything will be over with quickly."

Caramon was struck dumb, her words hitting him like a blow that left him too dazed to think what to say.

Kit couldn't read the blank expression on his face in the darkness. Judging him by her own standards, she guessed that he was tempted.

"Then it's you and me, Caramon," she continued. "I've had an offer of a job up north. The pay is good, and it will keep getting better. It's mercenary work. What we always talked about doing, you and I. I'll put in a good word for you. The lord will take you on. He's looking for trained soldiers. You'll be free of Solace, free of entanglements"—she cast a narrow-eyed glance in the direction of Tanis's tent, then looked back to her half-brother— "free to do what you want. What do you say? Are you with me?"

"You want me . . . to let Raistlin . . . die?" Caramon asked hoarsely, the last word nearly choking him.

"Just let whatever's going to happen, happen," Kit said soothingly, spreading her hands. "It will be for the best."

"You can't mean that!" He stared, incredulous. "You're not serious."

"Don't be an idiot, Caramon!" Kit said sternly. "Raistlin's using you! He always has, he always will! He doesn't care a Flotsam penny for you. He'll use you to get what he wants, then when he's finished with you, he'll throw you away as if you were a bit of rag he'd use to wipe his ass. He'll make your life hell, Caramon! Hell! Let them hang him! It won't be your fault."

Caramon backed away from her, nearly taking down the tent post. "How can you . . . No, I won't do it!" He began fumbling with the tent flap, trying desperately to get out.

Kit lunged at him, dug her nails into his flesh. Her face loomed close to his, so close that he could feel her breath hot on his cheek. "I would have expected such an answer from Sturm or Tanis. But not you! You're not a sap, Caramon. Think about what I've said!"

Caramon shook his head violently. He felt nauseous, the same way he'd felt when he'd first seen the murdered corpse. He was still trying to get out of the tent, but he was so flustered and upset that he couldn't find his way.

Kit regarded him in silence, her hands on her hips. Then she gave a exasperated sigh.

"Quit it!" she ordered irritably. "Stop thrashing about! You're going to knock the tent over. Just calm down, will you? I didn't mean it. It was all a joke. I wouldn't let Raistlin hang."

"That's your idea of a joke?" Caramon wiped the chill sweat from his brow. "I'm not laughing. Are you going to tell them the truth?"

"What the hell good will that do?" Kit demanded, adding with a flash of anger, "You want to see me hang instead? Is that it?"

Caramon was silent, miserable.

"I didn't kill her," Kit said coldly.

"Your knife—"

"Someone stole it in the confusion in the temple. Took it from my belt. I would have told you if you had asked me, instead of accusing me like that. That's the truth. That's what happened, but do you think anyone will believe me?"

No, Caramon was quite certain no one would believe her.

"Come along," Kit ordered. "We'll wake Tanis. He'll know what to do."

She laced on her leather vest. Her sword lay on the floor, next to where she'd been sleeping. Grabbing hold of it, she buckled the belt around her waist.

"Not a word about my little joke to the half-elf," she said to Caramon, lightly stroking his arm. "He wouldn't understand."

Caramon nodded his head, unable to speak. He wouldn't tell anyone, ever. It was too shameful, too horrible. Perhaps it had been a joke—gallows humor. But Caramon didn't think so. He could still hear her words, the vehemence with which they were spoken. He could still see the eerie light in her eyes. He drew away from her. Her touch made his flesh crawl.

Kit patted him on the arm, as if he were a good child who had eaten all his porridge. Shoving past him, she strode out the tent, yelling Tanis's name as she walked.

Caramon was heading for the booth to wake up Flint when he heard a loud voice shouting, echoing through the fairgrounds.

"There's going to a wizard-burning! Come and see! They're going to burn the wizard!"

18

Raistlin started to wakefulness, a sense of danger bursting like lightning on his sleep, jolting him out of terrifying dreams. Instinctively he kept still, shivering beneath a thin blanket, until his mind was awake and active and he had located the source of the danger.

He smelled the smoke of burning torches, heard the voices outside the prison, and lay immobilized, listening fearfully.

"And I tell you men," the guard was saying, "the wizard's trial'll be held tomorrow. Today, that is. You'll have your say then before the High Sheriff."

"The High Sheriff has no jurisdiction in this case!" a deep voice responded. "The wizard murdered my wife, our priestess! He will burn this night, as all witches must burn for their heinous crimes! Stand aside, jailer. There's only two of you and more than thirty of us. We don't want innocent people to get hurt."

In the adjacent cells, the kender were chattering with excitement, shoving benches over to the windows in order to see and lamenting the fact that they were locked up in prison and would miss the wizard's roasting. At this, someone suggested they once again pick the lock. Unfortunately, following the theft of their keys, the guards had added a chain and padlock to the kenders' cell door, which considerably raised the level of difficulty. Nothing daunted, the kender set to work.

"Rankin! Go fetch the captain," the jailkeep ordered.

There came the sound of a scuffle outside, shouts, cursings, and a cry of pain.

"Here are the keys," said the same deep voice. "Two of you, enter the jail and bring him out."

"What about the captain of the guard and the sheriff?" a

voice asked. "Won't they try to interfere?"

"Some of our brethren have already dealt with them. They will not trouble us this night. Go fetch the wizard."

Raistlin jumped to his feet, trying desperately to quell his panic and think what to do. His few magic spells came to mind, but the jailer had taken away the pouches containing his spell components. Between his extreme weariness and his fright, he doubted if he had strength or wit enough to cast them anyway.

And what good would they do me? he reflected bitterly. I could not send thirty people to sleep. I might be able to cast a spell that would hold the cell door shut, but as weak as I am, I could not maintain it for long. I have no other weapons. I am helpless! Completely at their mercy!

The priests in their sky-blue robes appeared, holding their torches high, searching one cell after another. Raistlin fought the wild, panicked urge to hide in a shadowy corner. He pictured them finding him, dragging him out ignominiously. He forced himself to wait in stoic calm for them to reach him. Dignity and pride were all he had left. He would maintain them to the end.

He thought fleetingly, hopefully, of Caramon, but then dismissed the hope as being unrealistic. The fairgrounds were far from the prison. Caramon had no way of knowing what was going on. He would not return until morning, and by then it would be too late.

One of the priests stood in front of Raistlin's cell.

"Here he is! In here!"

Raistlin clasped his hands together tightly to keep from revealing how he trembled. He faced them defiantly, his face a cold, proud mask to conceal his fear.

The priests had keys to the cell; the jailer had not put up much of a fight. Ignoring the pleadings and wailings of the kender, who were having a difficult time removing the padlock, the priests opened Raistlin's cell. They seized hold of him, bound his hands with a length of rope.

"You'll not work any more of your foul magic on us," said one.

"It's not my magic you fear," Raistlin told them, speaking proudly, pleased that his voice did not crack. "It is my words. That is why you want to kill me before I can stand trial. You know that if I have a chance to speak, I will denounce you for the thieves and charlatans that you are."

One of the priests struck Raistlin across the face. The blow rocked him backward, knocked loose a tooth and split open his lip. He tasted blood. The cell and the priests wavered in his sight.

"Don't knock him unconscious!" scolded the other priest. "We want him wide awake to feel the flames licking him!"

They took hold of Raistlin by the arms, hustled him out of the cell, moving so rapidly that they nearly swept him off his feet. He stumbled after them, forced to almost run to keep from falling. Whenever he slowed, they jerked him forward, gripping his arms painfully.

The jailkeep stood huddled by the door, head down and eyes lowered. The young guard, who had apparently made some attempt to defend the prisoner, lay unconscious on the ground, blood forming a pool beneath his head.

The priests gave a cheer when Raistlin was brought forth. The cheer ceased immediately, at a sharp command from the High Priest. Quietly, with deadly intent, they surrounded Raistlin, looked to their leader for orders.

"We will take him back to the temple and execute him there. His death will serve as an example to others who may have it in mind to cross us.

"After the wizard's dead, we will claim that none of us saw the giant kender. We will send out our claque to make the same pronouncements. Soon those who did see it will begin to doubt their senses. We will maintain that the wizard, frightened of the power of Belzor, started a riot in order that he might slip away unnoticed and murder our priestess."

"Will that work?" asked someone dubiously. "People saw what they saw."

"They'll soon change their minds. Seeing the charred body of the wizard in front of the temple will help them reach the right decision. Those who don't will face the same fate."

"What about the wizard's friends? The dwarf and the half-elf and the rest of them?"

"Judith knew them, told me all about them. We have nothing to fear. The sister's a whore. The dwarf's a drunken sot who cares only for his ale mug. The half-elf's a mongrel, a sniveling coward like all elves. They won't cause any trouble. They'll be only too happy to slink out of town. Start chanting, someone," the High Priest snapped. "It will look better if we do this in the name of Belzor."

Raistlin managed a bleak smile, though it reopened the wound on his split lip. At the thought of his friends, his despair lessened and he grew hopeful. The priests didn't want him dead nearly as much as they needed the drama of his death, needed it to instill the fear of Belzor in the minds of the populace. This delay could work to his advantage. The noise and the light and the uproar in the town must be noticed, even as far away as the fairgrounds.

Taking up the chant, shouting praise to Belzor, the priests dragged Raistlin through the streets of Haven. The sound of loud chanting and the light of flaring torches brought people from their beds to the windows. Seeing the spectacle, they hastily donned their clothes, hurried out to watch. The ne'r-do-wells in the taverns left their drinking to see what all the commotion was about. They were quick to join the mob, and fell in behind the priests. Drunken shouts now punctuated the priests' chanting.

The pain of his swelling jaw made Raistlin's head ache unbearably. The ropes cut into his flesh, the priests pinched his arms. He struggled to remain on his feet, lest he fall and be trampled. It was all so unreal, he felt no fear.

Fear would come later. For now, he was in a nightmare existence, a dreamworld from which there would be no awakening.

The torchlight blinded him. He could see nothing but an occasional face—mouth leering, eyes gleefully staring—illuminated in the light, vanishing swiftly in the darkness, only to be replaced by another. He caught a glimpse of the young woman who had lost the child, saw her face, grieved, pitying, afraid. She reached out her hand to him as if she would have helped, but the priests shoved her brutally back.

The Temple of Belzor loomed in the distance. The stone structure had not been damaged in the fire, apparently, only portions of the interior. A crowd had gathered on the broad expanse of grass in front of the temple to watch a man in blue robes drive a large wooden pole into the ground. Other priests tossed faggots of wood around the stake.

Many of Haven's citizens were assisting the priests to build the pyre. Some of the very same citizens, who had only hours before jeered the priests, laughed at him and mocked him. Raistlin was not surprised. Here again was evidence of the ugliness of mankind. Let them be subjugated, robbed, and hoodwinked by Belzor. He and his followers deserved each other.

The priests and the mob hauled Raistlin down the street leading to the temple. They were very close to the stake now, and where was Caramon? Where were Kit and Tanis? Suppose the priests had managed to intercept them, waylay them? Suppose they were battling for their lives inside the fairgrounds, with no way to reach him? Suppose—chilling thought—they had seen that rescue was hopeless, had given up?

The mob picked up the chant, shouting, "Belzor! Belzor!" in an insane litany. Raistlin's hopes died, his fear sprang horribly to life. Then a voice rang out over the wild chanting and the shrieks and laughter.

"Halt! What is the meaning of this?"

Raistlin lifted his head.

Sturm Brightblade stood in the center of the street, blocking the priests' way, standing between the stake and its victim. Illuminated by the light of many torches, Sturm was an impressive sight. He stood tall and unafraid, his long mustaches bristling. His stern face was older than its years. He held naked steel in his hand; torchlight flared along the blade as if the metal had caught fire. He was proud and fierce, calm and dignified, a fixed point in the center of swirling turmoil.

The crowd hushed, from awe and respect. The priests in the vanguard halted, daunted by this young man who was not a knight but who was made knightly by his demeanor, his stance, and his courage. Sturm seemed an apparition, sprung from the legendary time of Huma. Uncertain and uneasy, the priests in front looked to the High Priest in the back for orders.

"You fools!" the High Priest shouted at them in fury. "He's one man and alone! Knock him aside and keep going!"

A rock sailed out from the midst of the watching mob, struck Sturm in the forehead. He clapped his hand over the wound, staggered where he stood. Yet he did not leave his place in the road, nor did he drop his sword. Blood poured from his face, obliterating his vision in one eye. Lifting his sword, he advanced grimly on the priests.

The mob had tasted blood, they were eager for more, so long as it wasn't their own. Several ruffians ran from the crowd, jumped on Sturm from from behind. Yelling and cursing, kicking and pummeling, the men bore him to the ground.

The priests hustled their captive to the stake. Raistlin cast a glance at his friend. Sturm lay groaning in the road, blood covered his torn clothing. And then the mob surged around Raistlin and he could see his friend no more.

He had quite given up hope. Caramon and the others were not coming. The knowledge came to Raistlin that he was going to die, die most horribly and painfully.

The wooden post thrust up from the center of the pile of wood, dry wood that snapped underfoot. The jutting branches caught on Raistlin's robes, tearing the cloth as the priests shoved him near the stake. Roughly they turned him around, so that he faced the crowd, which was all gleaming eyes and gaping, hungry mouths. The dry wood was being doused with liquid—dwarf spirits, by the smell of it. This was not the priests' doing, but some of the more drunken revelers.

The priests tied Raistlin's wrists together behind the stake, then they wound coils of rope around his chest and torso, binding him tightly. He was held fast, and though he struggled with all his remaining strength, he could not free himself. The High Priest had been going to make a speech, but some eager drunk flung a torch on the wood before the priests had finished tying up their prisoner, nearly setting the High Priest himself on fire. He and the others were forced to jump and skip with unseemly haste away from the pyre. The liquor-soaked wood caught quickly. Tongues of flame licked the tinder, began to devour it.

Smoke stung Raistlin's eyes, filled them with tears. He closed them against the flames and the smoke and cursed his feebleness and helplessness. He braced himself to endure the agonizing torment when the flames reached his skin.

"Hullo, Raistlin!" chimed a voice directly behind him. "Isn't this exciting? I've never seen anyone burned at the stake before. 'Course, I would much rather it wasn't you—"

All the while that Tasslehoff prattled, his knife cut rapidly through the knots on the rope that bound Raistlin's wrists.

"The kender!" came hoarse, angry shouts. "Stop him!"

"Here, I thought this might help!" Tas said hurriedly.

Raistlin felt the hilt of a knife shoved into his hand.

"It's from your friend, Lemuel. He says to—"

Raistlin was never to know what Lemuel said, because at that moment an enormous bellow broke over the crowd. People screamed and shouted in alarm. Steel flared in the torchlight. Caramon loomed suddenly in front of Raistlin, who could have broken down and wept with joy at the sight of his brother's face. Oblivious to the pain, Caramon snatched up whole bundles of burning wood and flung them aside.

Tanis had placed his back to Caramon's, swung the flat of his blade, knocking away torches and clubs. Kitiara fought at her lover's side. She was not using the flat of her blade. One priest lay bleeding at her feet. Kit fought with a smile on her lips, her dark eyes bright with the fun of it all.

Flint was there, wrestling with the priests who had hold of Tasslehoff and were trying to drag him into the temple. The dwarf attacked them with such roaring ferocity that they soon let loose of the kender and fled. Sturm appeared, wielding his sword with dispatch, the blood forming a mask on his face.

Haven's citizens, though sorry to see that the wizard wasn't going to go up in flames, were diverted and entertained by the daring rescue. The fickle mob turned against the priests, cheered the heroes. The High Priest fled for the safety of the temple. His cohorts—those who remained standing, at least—followed in haste. The mob hurled rocks and made plans to storm the temple.

Relief and the realization that he was safe, that he was not going to die in the fire, flooded through Raistlin in a tidal surge that left him faint and dazed. He sagged against his bonds.

Caramon snatched the ropes from around Raistlin's body and caught hold of his fainting brother. Lifting Raistlin in his arms, Caramon carried him away from the stake and laid him on the ground.

People crowded around, eager to help save the young man whom they had been just as eager to see burn to death only moments earlier.

"Clear off, you buggers!" Flint roared, waving his arms and glowering. "Give him air."

Someone handed the dwarf a bottle of fine brandy "to give to the brave young man."

"Thankee," Flint said and took a long pull to fortify himself, then handed over the bottle.

Caramon touched the brandy to Raistlin's lips. The sting of the liquor on his cut lip and the fiery liquid biting into his throat brought him to consciousness. He gagged, choked, and thrust the brandy bottle away.

"I have narrowly escaped being burned to death, Caramon! Would you now poison me?" Raistlin coughed and wretched.

He struggled to his feet, ignoring Caramon's protestations that he should rest. The mob had surrounded the temple, shouting that the priests of Belzor should all be burned.

"Was the young man hurt?" came a worried voice. "I have an ointment for burns."

"It's all right, Caramon," Raistlin said, halting his brother, who was attempting to shoo away the curious. "This is a friend of mine."

Lemuel gazed at Raistlin anxiously. "Did they hurt you?"

"No, sir. I have taken no hurt, thank you. I am only a little dazed by it all."

"This ointment"—Lemuel held up a small jar—"I made it myself. It comes from the aloe—"

"Thank you," said Raistlin, accepting the jar. "I don't need it, but I believe that my brother could use it."

He cast a glance at Caramon's hands, which were burned and blistered. Caramon flushed and grinned self-consciously, thrust his hands behind his back.

"Thank you for the knife," Raistlin added, offering to return it. "Fortunately I had no need to use it."

"Keep it! It's the least I can do. Thanks to you, young man, I won't have to leave my home."

"But you have given me your books," Raistlin argued, holding out the knife.

Lemuel waved the knife away. "It belonged to my father. He would have wanted a magus like you to have it. It certainly does me no good, although I did find it useful to aerate the soil around my gardenias. There's a quaint sort of leather thong that goes with it. He used to wear the knife concealed on his arm. A wizard's last defense, he called it."

The knife was a very fine one, made of sharp steel. By the slight tingle he experienced holding it, Raistlin guessed that it had been imbued with magic. He thrust the knife into his belt and shook hands most warmly with Lemuel.

"We'll be stopping by later for those books," Raistlin said.

"I should be very pleased if you and your friends would take tea with me," Lemuel replied, with a polite bow.

After more bows and further introductions and promises to drop by on their way out of town, Lemuel departed, eager to put his uprooted plants back in the ground.

This left the companions alone. The citizens who had surrounded the temple were dispersing. Rumor had it that the priests of Belzor had escaped by way of certain underground passages and were fleeing for their lives into the mountains. There was talk of forming a hunting party to go after them. It was now almost dawn. The morning was raw and chill. The drunks were dull-headed and sleepy. Men recalled that they had to work in the fields, women suddenly remembered their children left home alone. The citizens of Haven straggled off, left the priests to the goblins and ogres in the mountains.

The companions turned their steps back to the fairgrounds. The fair lasted for one more day, but Flint had already announced his intention of leaving.

"I'll not spend one minute longer than need be in this foul city. The people here are daft. Just plain daft. First snakes, then hangings, now burnings. Daft," he muttered into his beard.

"Just plain daft."

"You'll miss a day's sales," Tanis observed.

"I don't want their money," the dwarf said flatly. "Likely it's cursed. I'm seriously considering giving away what I've already taken."

He didn't, of course. The strongbox containing the money would be the first object the dwarf packed, stowing it securely and secretly underneath the wagon's seat.

"I want to thank you all," Raistlin said as they walked along the empty streets. "And I want to apologize for putting you at risk. You were right, Tanis. I underestimated these people. I didn't realize how truly dangerous they were. I will know better next time."

"Let's hope there isn't a next time," Tanis said, smiling.

"And I want to thank you, Kitiara," Raistlin said.

"For what?" Kit smiled her crooked smile. "For rescuing you?"

"Yes," said Raistlin dryly. "For rescuing me."

"Anytime!" Kit said, laughing and slapping him on the shoulder. "Anytime."

Caramon looked upset at this, and solemn. He turned his head away.

Battle suited Kitiara. Her cheeks were flushed, her eyes glittered, her lips were red, as if she had drunk the blood she spilled. Kit, still laughing, took hold of Tanis's arm, hugged him close. "You are a very fine swordsman, my friend. You could earn a good living with that blade of yours. I'm surprised you haven't considered something in the mercenary line."

"I earn a good living now. A safe living," he added, but he was smiling at her, pleased by her admiration.

"Bah!" Kit said scornfully. "Safety's for fat old men! We fight well together, side by side. I've been thinking . . ."

She drew Tanis away, lowered her voice. Apparently the quarrel between the two was forgotten.

"Aren't you going to thank me, too, Raistlin?" Tasslehoff cried, dancing around Raistlin. "Look at this." The kender sadly twitched his topknot over his shoulder. The smell of burnt hair was very strong. "I got a bit singed, but the fight was worth it, even if I didn't get to see you being burned at the stake. I'm pretty disappointed about that, but I know you couldn't help it." Tas gave Raistlin a conciliatory hug.

"Yes, Tas, I do thank you," Raistlin said and removed his new knife from the kender's hand. "And I want to thank you, Sturm.

What you did was extremely brave. Foolhardy, but brave."

"They had no right to try to execute you without first giving you a fair trial. They were wrong, and it was my duty to stop them. However . . ."

Sturm came to a halt in the road. Standing stiffly, his hand pressed against his injured ribs, he faced Raistlin. "I have given the matter serious thought as we've been walking, and I must insist that you turn yourself over to the High Sheriff of Haven."

"Why should I? I've done nothing wrong."

"For the murder of the priestess," Sturm said, frowning, thinking Raistlin was being flippant.

"He didn't kill the Widow Judith, Sturm," Caramon said quietly, calmly. "She was dead when we entered that room."

Troubled, Sturm looked from one twin to the other. "I have never known you to lie, Caramon. But I think you might if your brother's life depended on it."

"I might," Caramon agreed, "but I'm not lying now. I swear to you on the grave of my father that Raistlin is innocent of this murder."

Sturm gazed long at Caramon, then nodded once, convinced. They resumed walking.

"Do you know who did kill her?" Sturm asked.

The brothers exchanged glances.

"No," Caramon said and stared down at his boots, kicking up dust in the road.

* * * * *

It was daylight by the time they reached the fairgrounds. The vendors were opening their stalls, preparing for the morning's business. They received Raistlin as a hero, lauded his exploits, applauded as the companions walked to Flint's shop. But no one spoke to them directly.

Flint did not open his stall. Leaving the shutters closed, he began to move his wares to the wagon. When several of the other vendors, overcome by curiosity, did finally drop by to hear the tale, they were gruffly repulsed by the dwarf and went away, offended.

There was one more visitor, one more scare. The High Sheriff himself appeared, looking for Raistlin. Kit drew her sword, told her brother to make himself scarce, and it seemed as if there was going to be yet another fight. Raistlin told her to put away her weapon.

"I'm innocent," he said, with a significant look for his sister.

"You were nearly a crispy innocent," Kit returned angrily, sheathing her sword with an impatient thrust. "Go on, then. And don't expect me to save you this time."

But the sheriff had come to apologize. He did so, grudgingly and awkwardly. The young priestess had come forth to admit that she had seen Raistlin in company with his twin at the time the murder was committed. She had not told the truth before, she said, because she hated the wizard for what he had done to instigate Belzor's downfall. She was horrified by the High Priest's actions, wanted nothing more to do with any of them.

"What will happen to her?" Caramon asked worriedly.

"Nothing." The sheriff shrugged. "The young ones were like the rest of us—fooled completely by the murdered woman and her husband. They'll get over it. We all will, I suppose."

He fell silent, squinted into the sun that was just topping the trees, then said, not looking at them, "We don't take kindly to mages in Haven. Lemuel, now—he's different. He's harmless. We don't mind him. But we don't need any more."

"He should have thanked you," Caramon said, puzzled and hurt.

"For what?" Raistlin asked with a bitter smile. "Destroying his career? If the sheriff didn't know that Judith and the rest of Belzor's followers were frauds, then he's one of the biggest fools in Abanasinia. If he did know, then he was undoubtedly being paid well to leave them alone. Either way, he's finished. You had better let me put some ointment on those burns, my brother. You are obviously in pain."

Once he had treated Caramon, cleaning the burns and covering them with the healing salve, Raistlin left the others to finish the packing, went to lie down in the wagon. He was completely and utterly exhausted, so tired he was almost sick, He was just about to climb inside when a stranger clad in brown robes approached him.

Raistlin turned his back on him, hoping the man would take the hint and leave. The man had the look of a cleric, and Raistlin had seen clerics enough to last him a lifetime.

"I want just a moment, young man," the stranger said, plucking at Raistlin's sleeve. "I know you have had a trying day. I want to thank you for bringing down the false god Belzor. My followers and I are eternally in your debt."

Raistlin grunted, pulled his arm away, and climbed into the wagon. The man hung on to the wagon's sides, peered over them.

"I am Hederick, the High Theocrat," he announced with a self-important air. "I represent a new religious order. We hope to gain a foothold here in Haven now that the rogues of Belzor have been driven away. We are known as the Seekers, for we seek the true gods."

"Then I hope very much that you find them, sir," Raistlin said.

"We are certain of it!" The man had missed the sarcasm. "Perhaps you'd be interested—"

Raistlin wasn't. The tents and bedrolls had been stacked in one corner of the wagon. Unfolding a blanket, he spread it out over the pile of tenting, lay down.

The cleric hung about, yammering about his god. Raistlin covered his head with the hood of his robe and, eventually, the cleric departed. Raistlin thought no more of him, soon forgot the man entirely.

Lying in the wagon, Raistlin tried to sleep. Every time he closed his eyes, he saw the flames, felt the heat, smelled the smoke, and he was wide awake, awake and shivering.

He recalled with terrifying clarity his feeling of helplessness. Resting his hand on the hilt of his new knife, he wrapped his fingers around the weapon, felt the blade, cold, sharp, reassuring. From now on, he would never be without it. His last measure of defense, even if it meant his life was his to take and not his enemy's.

His thoughts went from this knife to the other knife, the bloody knife he'd found lying beside the murdered woman. The knife he had recognized as belonging to Kitiara.

Raistlin sighed deeply, and at last he was able to close his eyes, relax into slumber.

Rosamun's children had taken their revenge.

BOOK 5

The aspiring magus, Raistlin Majere, is hereby summoned to the Tower of High Sorcery at Wayreth to appear before the Conclave of Wizards on the seventh day of the seventh month at the seventh minute of the seventh hour. At this time, in this place, you will be tested by your superiors for inclusion into the ranks of those gifted by the three gods, Solinari, Lunitari, Nuitari.

—The Conclave of Wizards

I

That winter was one of the mildest Solace had known, with rain and fog in place of snow and frost. The residents packed away their Yule decorations for another year, took down the pine boughs and the mistletoe, and congratulated themselves on having escaped the inconveniences of a hard winter. People were already talking of an early spring when a terrifying and most unwelcome visitor came to Solace. The visitor was Plague, and accompanying him was his ghastly mate, Death.

No one was certain who invited this dread guest. The number of travelers had increased during the mild winter, any one of them might have been a carrier. Blame was also ascribed to the standing bogs around Crystalmir Lake, bogs that had not frozen as they should have during the winter. The symptoms were the same in all cases, beginning with a high fever and extreme lethargy, followed by headache, vomiting, and diarrhea. The disease ran its course in a week or two; the strong and healthy survived it. The very young, the very old, or those in weak health did not.

In the days before the Cataclysm, clerics had called upon the goddess Mishakal for aid. She had granted them healing powers, and the plague had been virtually unknown. Mishakal had left Krynn with the rest of the gods. Those who practiced the healing arts in these days had to rely on their own skill and knowledge. They could not cure the disease, but they could treat the symptoms, try to prevent the patient from becoming so weak that he or she developed pneumonia, which led inevitably to death.

Weird Meggin worked tirelessly among the sick, administering her willow bark to break the fever, dosing the victims with a bitter concoction the consistency of paste, which seemed to help those who could be persuaded to choke it down.

Many of Solace's residents derided the old crone, terming her "cracked" or a witch. These very same people were among the first to ask for her the moment they felt the fever grip them. She never failed them. She would come at any time, day or night, and though her manner was a little strange—she talked constantly to herself and insisted on the unusual practice of washing her hands continually and forced others in the sickroom to do so as well—she was always welcome.

Raistlin began by accompanying Weird Meggin on her rounds. He assisted her in sponging the feverish bodies, helped persuade sick children to swallow the bad-tasting medicine. He learned how to ease the pain of the dying. But as the plague spread and more and more of Solace's citizens were caught in its lethal grip, Raistlin was forced by sheer necessity to tend patients on his own.

Caramon was among the first to catch the disease, a shock to the big man, who had never been sick in his life. He was terrified, certain he was going to die, and nearly wrecked the bedroom in his delirium, fighting snakes carrying torches, who were trying to set him on fire.

His strong body threw off the contagion, however, and since he had already survived the disease, he was able to assist his brother in caring for others. Caramon worried constantly that Raistlin would catch the plague. Frail as he was, he would not survive it. Raistlin was deaf to his brother's pleas to remain safely at home. Raistlin had discovered to his surprise that he gained a deep and abiding satisfaction in helping those stricken with the illness.

He did not work among the sick out of compassion. In general, he cared nothing for his neighbors, considered them dull and boorish. He did not treat the sick for monetary gain; he would go to the poor as readily as the rich. He found that what he truly enjoyed was power—power he wielded over the living, who had come to regard the young mage with hope bordering on reverence. Power he was sometimes able to wield over his greatest, most dread foe, Death.

He did not catch the plague, and he wondered why. Weird Meggin said it was because he made certain to wash his hands after tending to the sick. Raistlin smiled derisively, but he was too fond of the crazy old woman to contradict her.

At length, Plague slowly opened his clenched skeletal fingers, released Solace from his deadly grip. Solace's residents, acting under Weird Meggin's instructions, burned the clothes and bedding of those who had been ill. The snow came at last, and when it did, it fell on many new graves in Solace's burial ground.

Among the dead was Anna Brightblade.

It is written in the Measure that the duty of the lady wife of a knight is to feed the poor and tend to the sick of the manor. Though she was far from the land where the Measure was written and obeyed, Lady Brightblade was faithful to the law. She went to the aid of her sick neighbors, caught the disease herself. Even when she felt its first effects, she continued to nurse until she collapsed.

Sturm carried his mother home and ran to fetch Raistlin, who treated the woman as best he could, all to no avail.

"I'm dying, aren't I, young man?" Anna Brightblade asked Raistlin one night. "Tell me the truth. I am the wife of a noble knight. I can bear it."

"Yes," said Raistlin, who could hear the popping and crackling sounds of fluid gathering in the woman's lungs. "Yes, you are dying."

"How long?" she asked calmly.

"Not long now."

Sturm knelt at his mother's bedside. He gave a sob and lowered his head to the blanket. Anna reached out her hand, a hand wasted from the fever, and stroked her son's long hair.

"Leave us," she said to Raistlin with her customary imperiousness. Then, looking up at him, she smiled wanly, her stern expression softened. "Thank you for all you have done. I may have misjudged you, young man. I give you my blessing."

"Thank you, Lady Brightblade," Raistlin said. "I honor your courage, madam. May Paladine receive you."

She looked at him darkly, frowned, thinking he blasphemed, and turned her face from him.

In the morning, as Caramon fixed his twin a bowl of hot gruel to sustain him through the rigors of the day, there came a knock on the door. Caramon opened it to admit Sturm. The young man was haggard and deathly pale, his eyes red and swollen. He was composed, however, had control of himself.

Caramon ushered his friend inside. Sturm sank into a chair, his legs collapsing beneath him. He had slept little since the first day of his mother's illness.

"Is Lady Brightblade . . ." Caramon began, but couldn't finish. Sturm nodded his head.

Caramon wiped his eyes. "I'm sorry, Sturm. She was a great lady."

"Yes," said Sturm in a husky voice. He slumped in the chair. A tremor of a dry sob shuddered through his body.

"How long has it been since you ate anything?" Raistlin demanded.

Sturm sighed, waved an uncaring hand.

"Caramon, bring another bowl," Raistlin ordered. "Eat, Sir Knight, or you will shortly follow your mother to the grave."

Sturm's dark eyes flashed in anger at Raistlin's flippant tone. He started to refuse the food, but when he saw that Caramon had picked up the spoon, was intending to feed him like a baby, Sturm muttered that perhaps he could manage a mouthful. He ate the entire bowl, drank a glass of wine, and the color returned to his wan cheeks.

Raistlin shoved aside his own bowl only half eaten. This was customary with him, however; Caramon knew better than to protest.

"My mother and I talked near the end," Sturm said in a low voice. "She spoke of Solamnia and my father. She told me that she had long ago ceased believing he was alive. She had kept up the pretense only for my sake."

He lowered his head, pressed his lips tightly together, but shed no tears. After a moment, his composure regained, he looked at Raistlin, who was gathering his medicines, preparing to set out.

"Something strange happened at . . . the end. I thought I would tell you, to see if you had ever heard the like. Perhaps it is nothing but a manifestation of the disease."

Raistlin looked up with interest. He was making notes on the illness, recording symptoms and treatments in a small book for future reference.

"My mother had fallen into a deep sleep, from which it seemed that nothing could rouse her."

"The sleep of death," Raistlin said. "I have seen it often with this illness. Sometimes it can last for several days, but whenever it comes, the patient never wakes."

"Well, my mother did wake," Sturm said abruptly.

"Indeed? Tell me precisely what occurred."

"She opened her eyes and looked, not at me, but beyond me, to the door to her room. 'I know you, sir, do I not?' she said hesitantly, adding querulously, 'Where have you been all this time? We've been expecting you for ages.' Then she said, 'Make haste,

Son, bring the old gentleman a chair.'

"I looked around, but there was no one there. 'Ah,' my mother said, 'you cannot stay? I must come with you? But that will mean leaving my boy all alone.' She seemed to listen, then she smiled. 'True, he is a boy no longer. You will watch over him when I am gone?' And then she smiled, as if reassured, and drew her last breath.

"And this is the strangest part. I had just risen to go to her when I thought I saw, standing beside her, the figure of an old man. He was a disreputable old man, wearing gray robes with a shabby sort of pointed hat." Sturm frowned. "He had the look of a magic-user. Well? What do you think?"

"I think that you had gone a long time without food or sleep," Raistlin replied.

"Perhaps," Sturm said, still frowning, puzzled. "But the vision seemed very real. Who could the old man have been? And why was my mother pleased to see him? She had no use for magic-users."

Raistlin headed for the door. He had been more than patient with the bereaved Sturm and he was tired of being insulted. Caramon cast him an apprehensive glance, fearing that his brother might lash out, make some sarcastic comment, but his twin departed without saying another word.

Sturm left soon after, to arrange for his mother's burial.

Caramon heaved a doleful sigh and sat down to finish off the remainder of his brother's uneaten breakfast.

2

Spring performed its usual miracle. Green leaves sprouted on the vallenwoods, wildflowers bloomed in the graveyard; the small vallenwoods planted on the graves grew at the rapid pace customary to the tree, bringing solace to the grief-stricken. The spirits of those who had died flourished, were renewed in the living tree.

This spring brought another disease into Solace—a disease known to be carried by kender, a disease that is often contagious, especially among the young, who had just come to realize that life was short and very sweet and should be experienced to the fullest. The disease is called wanderlust.

Sturm was the first to catch it, although his other friends had exhibited the same symptoms. His case had been coming on ever since the death of his mother. Bereft and alone, his thoughts and dreams looked northward, to his homeland.

"I cannot give up the hope that my father still lives," he confessed to Caramon one morning. It was now his custom to join the twins for breakfast. Eating alone, in his own empty house, was too much to bear. "Though I admit that my mother's argument has some merit. If my father is alive, why did he never once try to contact us?"

"There could be lots of reasons," said Caramon stoutly. "Maybe he's being held prisoner in a dungeon by a mad wizard. Oh, sorry, Raist. I didn't mean that the way it sounded."

Raistlin snorted. He was occupied in feeding his rabbits, paying scant attention to the conversation.

"Whatever the case," Sturm said, "I intend to find out the truth. When the roads are open, within the month, I plan to travel north to Solamnia."

"No! Name of the Abyss," exclaimed Caramon, startled.

Raistlin, too, was amazed. He turned from his work, cabbage leaves in his hand, to see if the young man was serious.

Sturm nodded his head. "I have wanted to make such a journey for the past three years, but I was loath to leave my mother for an extended period of time. Now there is nothing to hold me. I go, and I go with her blessing. If, in fact, my father is dead, then I have my inheritance to claim. If he lives—"

Sturm shook his head, unable to complete the expression of the dream, too wonderful to possibly come true.

"Are you going alone?" Caramon asked, awed.

Sturm smiled, a rare thing for the usually solemn and serious young man. "I had hoped that you would come with me, Caramon. I would ask you, too, Raistlin," he added more stiffly, "but the journey will be long and difficult, and I fear it might tax your health. And I know that you would not want to be so far from your studies."

Ever since their return from Haven, Raistlin had spent every moment he could spare studying the tomes of the war magus. He had added several new spells to his spellbook.

"On the contrary, I am feeling unusually strong this spring," Raistlin remarked. "I would be able to take my books with me. I thank you for the offer, Sturm, and I will consider it, as will my brother."

"I'm going," Caramon said. "So long as Raist comes, too. And as he says, he has been really strong. He hasn't been sick hardly at all."

"I am glad to hear it," Sturm said, though without much enthusiasm. He knew very well that the twins would not be separated, although he had hoped against all reason to be able to persuade Caramon to leave Raistlin behind. "I remind you, Raistlin, that magic-users are not venerated in my country. Although, of course, you would be accorded the hospitality due any guest."

Raistlin bowed. "For which I am deeply grateful. I will be a most accommodating guest, I assure you, Sturm. I will not set the bed linens on fire, nor will I poison the well. In fact, you might find certain of my skills useful on the road."

"He's a really good cook," stated Caramon.

Sturm rose to his feet. "Very well. I will make the arrangements. My mother left me some money, although not much. Not enough for horses, I fear. We will have to travel on foot."

The moment the door closed behind Sturm, Caramon began capering around the small house, upsetting the furniture and wreaking havoc in his delight. He even had the temerity to give his brother a hug.

"Have you gone mad?" Raistlin demanded. "There! Look what you've done. That was our only cream pitcher. No, don't try to help! You've caused enough damage. Why don't you go polish your sword or sharpen it or whatever you do to it?"

"I will! A great idea!" Caramon rushed off to his bedroom, only to run back a moment later. "I don't have a whetstone."

"Go borrow one from Flint. Or better still, take your sword to Flint's and work on it there," Raistlin said, mopping up spilled cream. "Anything to get you out from underfoot."

"I wonder if Flint would like to come along. And Kit and Tanis and Tasslehoff! I'll go see."

His brother gone and the house quiet, Raistlin picked up the pieces of the broken pitcher and threw them away. He was as excited over the prospect of a journey to new and distant lands as his brother, though he had more sense than to smash the crockery over it. He was considering which of his herbs to pack, which he might find along the roadside, when there came a knock at the door.

Thinking it might be Sturm, Raistlin called out, "Caramon has gone to Flint's."

The knock was repeated, this time with the sharp rapping of an impatient visitor.

Raistlin opened the door, regarded his guest in amazement and surprise and not a little concern.

"Master Theobald!"

The mage stood upon the boardwalk outside the house. He wore a cloak over his white robes and carried a stout staff, indications that he had been traveling.

"May I come in?" Theobald asked gruffly.

"Certainly. Of course. Forgive me, Master." Raistlin stood aside, ushered his guest across the threshold. "I was not expecting you."

That was quite true. In all the years that Raistlin had attended the master's school, Theobald had never once paid a visit to Raistlin's home, nor evinced the slightest inclination to do so.

Bemused and somewhat apprehensive—his exploits in Haven had been widely reported throughout Solace—Raistlin invited his master to be seated in the only good chair in the house, the chair that happened to be his mother's rocking chair. Theobald declined all offers of food and wine.

"I do not have time to linger. I have been gone for a week, and I have not yet been home. I came here immediately. I have just returned from the Tower at Wayreth, from a meeting of the conclave."

Raistlin's uneasiness increased. "Isn't a meeting of the conclave at this early time of year somewhat unusual, Master? I thought they were always held in the summer."

"It is indeed unusual. We wizards had matters of great import to discuss. I was specially sent for," Theobald added, stroking his beard.

Raistlin made suitable comments, all the while wishing impatiently and with increasing nervousness that the provoking old fart would come to the point.

"Your doings in Haven were among the topics of discussion, Majere," Theobald said, glowering at Raistlin, brows bristling. "You broke many rules, not the least of which was casting a spell far above your capability."

Raistlin would have pointed out that the spell was obviously not above his capability to cast, since he had cast it, but he knew that this would be lost on Theobald.

"I did what I thought was right under the circumstances, Master," Raistlin said, as meekly and contritely as he could.

"Rubbish!" Theobald snorted. "You know what was right under the circumstances. You should have reported the wizardess to us as a renegade. We would have dealt with the matter in time."

"In time, Master," Raistlin emphasized. "Meanwhile, innocent people were being bilked out of what little they had, others were being driven from their homes. The charlatan priestess and her followers were causing irreparable harm. I sought to end it."

"You ended it, all right," Theobald said with dark implications.

"I was exonerated from her murder, Master," Raistlin returned, his tone sharp. "I have a writ from the High Sheriff of Haven himself proclaiming my innocence."

"So who did kill her?" Theobald asked.

"I have no idea, Master," Raistlin replied.

"Hunh," Theobald grunted. "Well, you handled the matter badly, but, still, you handled it. Damn near got yourself killed in the process, I understand. As I said, the conclave discussed the matter."

Raistlin kept silent, waited to hear his punishment. He had

already determined that if they forbade him to practice magic, he would defy them, become a renegade himself.

Theobald withdrew a scroll case. He opened the lid, taking an unconscionable length of time about it, fussing and fumbling clumsily until Raistlin was tempted to leap across the room and wrest the case from the man's hand. Finally the lid came off. Theobald removed a scroll, handed it across to Raistlin.

"Here, pupil. You might as well see this for yourself."

Now that the scroll was in his hands, Raistlin wondered if he had the courage to read it. He hesitated a moment to insure that his hands did not tremble and betray him, then, with outward nonchalance masking inward apprehension, he unrolled the scroll.

He tried to read it, but his nervousness impaired his eyesight. The words would not come into focus. When they did, he did not comprehend them.

Then he could not believe them.

Amazed and aghast, he stared at his master. "This . . . this can't be right. I am too young."

"That is what I said," Theobald stated in nasty tones. "But I was overruled."

Raistlin read the words again, words that, though they were not in the least magical, began to glow with the radiance of a thousand suns.

The aspiring magus, Raistlin Majere, is hereby summoned to the Tower of High Sorcery at Wayreth to appear before the Conclave of Wizards on the seventh day of the seventh month at the seventh minute of the seventh hour. At this time, in this place, you will be tested by your superiors for inclusion into the ranks of those gifted by the three gods, Solinari, Lunitari, Nuitari.

To be invited to take the Test is a great honor, an honor accorded to few, and should be taken seriously. You may impart knowledge of this honor to members of your immediate family, but to no others. Failure to accede to this injunction could mean the forfeiture of the right to take the Test.

You will bring with you your spellbook and spell components. You will wear robes representing the alliance of your sponsor. The color of the robes you will wear, if and when you are apprenticed—i.e., your allegiance to one of the three gods—will be determined during the Test. You will carry no weapons, nor any magical artifacts. Magical artifacts will be provided during the Test itself in order to judge your skill in the handling of said artifacts.

In the unfortunate event of your demise during the Test, all personal effects will be returned to your family.

You may be provided with an escort to the Tower, but your escort should be aware that he or she will not be permitted to enter the Guardian Forest. Any attempt by the escort to force entry will result in most grievous harm to the escort. We will not be held responsible.

That last sentence had been written, then crossed out, as if the writer had experienced second thoughts. An addendum had been inserted.

An exception to this rule is made in regard to Caramon Majere, twin brother to the aforementioned contestant. Caramon Majere is expressly desired to attend his brother's testing. He will be admitted into the Guardian Forest. His safety will be guaranteed, at least during the time he is inside the forest.

Raistlin lowered the scroll, let it roll back upon itself. His hands lacked the strength to hold it up, keep it open. To be invited to take the Test so young, to be even considered capable of taking the Test at his novitiate stage, was an honor of incredible magnitude. He was overcome with joy, joy and pride.

Of course, there was that cautionary phrase, *In the event of your demise*. Later, in the small hours of the night, when he would lie awake, unable to sleep for his excitement, that sentence would rise up before him, a skeletal hand reaching out to grasp him, drag him down. But now, filled with confidence in himself, proud of his achievements and the fact that these achievements had evidently impressed the members of the conclave, Raistlin had no fear, no qualms.

"I thank you, Master," he began when he could control his voice sufficiently to speak.

"Don't thank me," Theobald said, standing. "It is likely that I am sending you to your doom. I won't have your death on my conscience. I told Par-Salian as much. I go on record as being opposed to this folly."

Raistlin accompanied his guest to the door. "I am sorry you have so little faith in me, Master."

Theobald made an impatient gesture with his hand. "Come to me if you have any questions on your spellbook."

"I will do so, Master," said Raistlin, privately resolving that he would see Theobald in the Abyss first. "Thank you."

After the master had gone and Raistlin had shut

the door behind him, it was now Raistlin's turn to
caper about the house. Transported with happiness,
he lifted the skirts of his robes and performed several of the round-dance steps Caramon had struggled for years to teach him.

Entering at that moment, Caramon stared openmouthed at
his brother. His astonishment increased tenfold when Raistlin
ran over to his twin, flung his arms around him, embraced him,
then burst into tears.

"What's wrong?"

Caramon misread his brother's emotions, his heart almost
stopped in terror. He dropped his sword, which fell to the floor
with a resounding clang, to clutch at his twin. "Raistlin! What's
wrong? What's the matter? Who died?"

"Nothing is the matter, my brother!" Raistlin cried, laughing
and drying his tears. "Nothing in the world is the matter! For
once, everything is right."

He waved the scroll, which he still held in his hand, pranced
about the small room until he collapsed, out of breath but still
laughing, in his mother's rocking chair.

"Shut the door, my brother. And come sit beside me. We have
a great deal to discuss."

3

wearing Caramon to secrecy regarding the Test proved a difficult task. In his exuberance, Raistlin showed Caramon the precious document summoning them both to the Tower at Wayreth. Caramon came across the unfortunate line *in the event of your demise* and was extremely upset. So upset that, at first, he vowed Raistlin should not go, that he would have Tanis and Sturm and Flint and Otik and half the population of Solace sit on Raistlin before he should take a Test where the penalty for failure was death.

Raistlin was at first touched by Caramon's very genuine concern. Exhibiting unusual patience, Raistlin tried to explain to his twin the reasoning behind such drastic measures.

"My dear brother, as you yourself have seen, magic wielded by the wrong hands can be extremely dangerous. The conclave wants only those among their ranks who have proven that they are disciplined, skillful, and—most important—dedicated body and soul to the art. Thus those who merely dabble in magic, who practice it for their own amusement, do not want to take the Test, because they are not prepared to risk their lives for the magic."

"It is murder," Caramon said in a low voice. "Murder, plain and simple."

"No, no, my brother." Raistlin was soothing. Thinking of Lemuel, Raistlin smiled as he added, "Those deemed not suitable for taking the Test are prohibited from doing so by the conclave. They permit only those magi who have an excellent chance of passing to take the Test. And, my dear brother, very, very few fail. The risk is extremely minor and, for me, no risk at all. You know how hard I have worked and studied. I can't possibly fail!"

"Is that true?" Caramon lifted his pale, haggard face, regarded his twin with a searching, unblinking gaze.

"I swear it." Raistlin sat back in the rocker, smiled again. He couldn't keep from smiling.

"Then why do they want me to come with you?" Caramon asked suspiciously.

Raistlin was forced to pause before answering. Truth to tell, he didn't know why Caramon should be invited to come along. The more Raistlin thought about it, the more he resented the fact. Certainly it was logical for his brother to escort him as far as the forest, but why should he come farther? It was extremely unusual for the conclave to permit entry to their Tower to any person outside their ranks.

"I'm not sure," Raistlin admitted at last. "Probably it has something to do with the fact that we are twins. There is nothing sinister about it, Caramon, if that's what you are thinking. You will merely accompany me to the Tower and wait until I have finished the Test. Then we will return home together."

Envisioning that triumphant journey back to Solace, Raistlin's spirits, which had been shadowed a moment before, were elevated to the heavens and sparkled bright as the stars.

Caramon was dolefully shaking his head. "I don't like it. I think you should discuss it with Tanis."

"I tell you again, I am not permitted to discuss it with anyone, Caramon!" Raistlin said angrily, losing patience at last. "Can't you get that through your gully-dwarf skull?"

Caramon looked unhappy and uneasy, but still defiant.

Raistlin left the rocking chair. Hands clenched to fists, he stood over his brother, stared down at him, spoke to him with passionate intensity.

"I am commanded to keep this secret, and I will do so. And so will you, my brother. You will not mention this to Tanis. You will not mention this to Kitiara. You will not mention this to Sturm or anyone else. Do you understand me, Caramon? No one must know!"

Raistlin paused, drew a breath, then said quietly, so that there could be no doubt of his sincerity, "If you do—if you ruin this chance for me—then I have no brother."

Caramon went white to the lips. "Raist, I—"

"I will disown you," Raistlin pressed on, knowing that the iron must strike to the heart. "I will leave this house, and I will never come back. Your name will never be spoken in my presence. If I see you coming down the road, I will turn and walk the opposite direction."

Caramon was hurt, deeply hurt. His big frame shuddered, as

if the point Raistlin had driven home was in truth steel.

"I guess . . . it means a lot . . . to you," Caramon said brokenly, lowering his head, staring at his clasped hands.

Raistlin was softened by his brother's anguish. But Caramon had to be made to understand. Kneeling beside his twin, Raistlin stroked his brother's curly hair.

"Of course this means a lot to me, Caramon. It means everything! I have worked and studied almost my entire life for this chance. What would you have me do—cast it aside because it is dangerous? Life is dangerous, Caramon. Just stepping out that door is dangerous! You cannot hide from danger. Death floats on the air, creeps through the window, comes with the handshake of a stranger. If we stop living because we fear death, then we have already died.

"You want to be a warrior, Caramon. You practice with a real sword. Isn't that dangerous? How many times have you and Sturm very nearly sliced off each other's ears? Sturm has told us of the young knights who die in the tourneys held to test their knighthood. Yet if you had the chance to fight in one of those, wouldn't you take it?"

Caramon nodded. A tear fell on the clasped hands.

"What I do is the same thing," Raistlin said gently. "The blade must be forged in the fire. Are you with me, my brother?" He pressed his hand over Caramon's. "You know that I would stand at your side, should you ever fight to prove your mettle."

Caramon lifted his head. In his eyes, there was new respect and admiration. "Yes, Raist. I'll stand with you. I understand, now that you've explained it. I won't say a word to anyone. I promise."

"Good." Raistlin sighed. The elation had drained away. The battle with his brother had sapped his energy, leaving him weak and exhausted. He wanted to lie down, to be quiet and alone in the comforting darkness.

"What do I tell the others?" Caramon asked.

"Whatever you choose," Raistlin returned, heading for his room. "I don't care, so long as you make no mention of the truth."

"Raist . . . " Caramon paused, then asked, "You wouldn't do what you said, would you? Disown me? Claim that you never had a brother?"

"Oh, don't be such an idiot, Caramon," Raistlin said and went to his bed.

4

Caramon informed Sturm the next day that neither he nor his brother could accompany him to Solamnia. Sturm tried arguing and persuading, but Caramon remained adamant, though he could give no clear reason for his change of heart. Sturm marked Caramon as being worried and preoccupied about something. Assuming that Raistlin had decided not to go and had forbidden his brother to go without him, Sturm—though offended and hurt—said no more about the matter.

"If you want a traveling companion, Brightblade, I'll go with you myself," Kitiara offered. "I know the fastest and best routes north. Plus, from what I've heard, there's dark doings happening up that way. We shouldn't either of us travel alone, and since we're heading the same direction, it makes sense that we travel together."

The three were in the Inn of the Last Home, drinking a glass of ale. Having stopped by her brother's home, Kit had recognized immediately that the twins were up to something and was angry when they maintained that nothing unusual was going on. Well aware that she would never be able to pry the secret from Raistlin, she hoped to be able to tease the truth out of the more pliable Caramon.

"You and Tanis would be most welcome, Kitiara," Sturm said, recovering from his initial astonishment at her offer. "I did not ask you at first because I knew Tanis planned to accompany Flint on his summer journeys, but—"

"Tanis won't be going with me," Kit said tonelessly, flatly. She drained her tankard of ale and loudly called out for Otik to bring her another.

Sturm looked over at Caramon, wondering what was going on. Tanis and Kitiara had been together all winter, closer and more affectionate than ever.

Caramon shook his head to indicate that he had no idea.

Sturm was troubled. "I'm not certain—"

"Fine. It's settled. I'm coming," Kit said, refusing to listen to any arguments. "Now, Caramon, tell me why you and that wizard brother of yours won't come with us. Four traveling the road is much safer. Besides, there's some people up north I want you to meet."

"Like I told Sturm, I can't go," Caramon said.

His usually cheerful face was shadowed, grave. He hadn't drunk even a sip of his ale, which had by now gone flat. Shoving it aside, he stood up, flung a coin on the table, and left.

He didn't feel comfortable around Kitiara anymore. He was glad she was leaving, relieved that Tanis wasn't going with her. He had often felt that he should tell Tanis the truth about that night. Tell Tanis that Kit had been the one to murder Judith. Tell Tanis that she had urged Caramon to let Raistlin take the blame, to let Raistlin die.

She had claimed that she was joking. Still . . .

Caramon gave a relieved sigh. She would leave, and if they were lucky, she would not return. Caramon was worried about Sturm, who would be traveling in Kit's company, but on reflection, Caramon decided that the young knight, bolstered by his reliance on the Oath and the Measure, could look after himself. Besides, as Kit said, traveling alone was dangerous.

Caramon's main concern was for Tanis, who would be terribly hurt by Kit's decision to leave. Caramon figured—logically—that Kitiara, the restless firebrand, was the one who had ended the relationship.

It was Raistlin who discovered the truth.

Although he had several months to wait before he and Caramon would undertake their journey to the Tower, Raistlin began immediately to make preparations. One of these involved the re-tooling of the leather thong that held the knife on Raistlin's wrist, concealed beneath his robes. A flick of that wrist was supposed to cause the knife to drop down, unseen, into the mage's hand.

At least that was how the thong was designed to work. Raistlin's wrist was far thinner than the wrist of the war mage who had originally worn it, however. When Raistlin tried wearing the contraption, the thong itself dropped into his hand. The knife fell to the floor. He took it to Flint, hoping the dwarf could fix it.

Flint, looking the thong over, was impressed with the workmanship, thought it might be dwarven.

According to Lemuel, the Qualinesti elves had made the knife and the thong as a gift to their friend, the war mage.

Raistlin made no mention of this, however. He agreed with the dwarf that the thong was undoubtedly constructed by some great dwarven leatherworker. Flint offered to adjust the size if Raistlin would leave the thong with him for a week or two.

Raistlin had his hand on the doorknocker, was about to knock, when he heard faint voices inside. The voices belonged to Tanis and Flint. Raistlin could distinguish only a few words, but one was "Kitiara."

Certain that any conversation about his sister would cease if he were introduced into it, Raistlin carefully and quietly lowered his hand from the knocker. He looked to see if anyone was in sight. Finding that he was alone, Raistlin slipped around the side of the house to Flint's workshop. The dwarf had opened the window to let in the soft spring breeze. Hidden from view by a fall of purple clematis, which grew up the side of the workshop, Raistlin stood to one side of the window.

Any qualms he might have had about eavesdropping on his friends were easily settled. He had often wondered how much Tanis knew about Kit's activities: midnight meetings with strangers, the murder of the priestess . . . Was Kit fleeing danger? Had Tanis threatened to denounce her? And where did that leave Raistlin if this were the case? Quite understandably, he had small faith in his sister's loyalty.

"We've been arguing for days," Tanis was saying. "She wants me to come north with her."

The conversation was interrupted by a moment's furious hammering. When that was finished, the talk resumed.

"She claims to have friends who will pay large sums to those skilled with bow and blade."

"Even half-elves?" Flint grunted.

"I pointed that out, but she says—rightly so—that I could hide my heritage if I wanted. I could grow a beard, wear my hair long to cover my ears."

"A fine sight you'd look with a beard!"

Flint plied the hammer again.

"Well? Are you going?" he asked when the hammering had stopped.

"No, I'm not," Tanis said, speaking reluctantly, loath to share his feelings even with his longtime friend. "I need time away from her. Time to think things through. I can't think when I'm around Kitiara. The truth is, Flint, I'm falling in love with her."

Raistlin snorted, almost laughed. He swallowed his mirth, fearing to give himself away. He would have expected something inane like this from Caramon, but not the half-elf, who had certainly lived long enough to know better.

Tanis spoke more rapidly, relieved to be able to talk about it. "The one time I ever even hinted at marriage, Kit laughed me to scorn. She scolded me about it for days after. Why did I want to ruin all our fun? We shared a bed, what more could I want? But I'm not happy just sharing my bed with her, Flint. I want to share my life with her, my dreams and hopes and plans. I want to settle down. She doesn't. She feels trapped, caged. She's restless and bored. We quarrel continually, over stupid things. If we stayed together, she would come to resent me, perhaps even hate me, and I couldn't bear that. I will miss her terribly, but it's better this way."

"Bah! Give her a year or two with those friends of hers up north and she'll be back. Maybe then she'll be receptive to your proposal, lad."

"She may come back." Tanis was silent a moment, then he added, "But I won't be here."

"Where are you going, then?"

"Home," Tanis replied quietly. "I haven't been home in a long time. I know this means I won't be with you on the first part of your travels, but we could meet in Qualinesti."

"We could, but . . . well . . . The truth of it is, I won't be going that way, Tanis," Flint said, clearing his throat. He sounded embarrassed. "I've been meaning to talk this over with you, but I never seemed to find the right time. I guess this is as good as any.

"That fair at Haven soured me, lad. I saw the ugly faces beneath the masks humans wear, and it left a bad taste in my mouth. Talking to those hill dwarves made me start thinking of my own home. I can never go back to my clan. You know the reason for that, but I've a mind to visit some of the other clans in the vicinity. It will be a comfort to me, being with my own kind. I've been thinking about what that young scamp Raistlin says about the gods. I'd like to find out if Reorx is around somewhere, maybe trapped inside Thorbardin."

"Searching for some sign of the true gods . . . It's an interesting idea," Tanis said. He added with a sigh, "Who knows? In looking for them, I might find myself along the way."

The pain and sadness in the half-elf's voice made Raistlin ashamed of having listened in on this private conversation. He was leaving his post, heading for the front door, prepared to announce himself by conventional means, when he heard the dwarf say dourly,

"Which of us has to take the kender?"

5

It was the last day of the month of Spring Blossom time. The roads were open. Travelers were abroad, once more filling the Inn of the Last Home to capacity. They ate Otik's potatoes, praised his ale, and told stories of gathering trouble in the world, stories of armies of hobgoblins on the march, of ogres moving down from their hidden holdings in the mountains, hints of creatures more fearsome than these.

Sturm and Kit were planning to leave the first of Summer Home. Tanis was leaving that day, too, explaining somewhat lamely that he wanted to be in Qualinesti in time for some sort of elven celebration involving the sun. Truth was, he knew very well that he could not go back to his empty house, the house that would always echo with her laughter. Flint was to accompany his friend part of the way, and so he, too, was setting off the next day.

It was known now among the companions that Raistlin and Caramon were making a journey themselves—a fact discovered by Kit, who was consumed with curiosity regarding Caramon's unusual circumspectness and who consequently bullied and teased him until he let fall that much.

Fearful that Kitiara would break his twin's resolve in the end, force him to reveal his secret, Raistlin hinted that they were going to seek out their father's relations, who had presumably come from Pax Tharkas. If their friends had looked at a map, they would have noted that Pax Tharkas was located in exactly the opposite direction from the Wayreth Forest.

No one did look at a map, because the only maps available were in the possession of Tasslehoff Burrfoot, who was not present. One of the reasons the companions had come together this last night, other than to bid each other farewell and safe roads, was to determine what to do about the kender.

Sturm began by stating in no uncertain terms that kender were not welcome in Solamnia. He added that any knight seen traveling in the company of a kender would be ruined, his reputation damned and blasted forever.

Kit said shortly that her friends in the north had no use for kender whatsoever, and she made it clear that if Tasslehoff valued his skin, he'd find some other route to travel. She fixed her gaze pointedly and haughtily upon Tanis. Relations between the two were strained. Kit had thought for certain that Tanis would beg her to stay, either that or travel with him. He had done neither, and she was angry.

"I cannot take Tas into Qualinesti," Tanis said, avoiding her gaze. "The elves would never permit it."

"Don't look at me!" Flint stated, alarmed to see them do just that. "If any of my clansmen were to so much as set eyes upon me in company with a kender, they'd lock me up for a crazy Theiwar, and I would be hard pressed to say they were wrong. Tasslehoff should go with Raistlin and Caramon to Pax Tharkas."

"No," said Raistlin with a finality in his tone that boded no argument. "Absolutely not."

"What do we do with him, then?" Tanis asked in perplexity.

"Bind him and gag him and stash him in the bottom of a well," Flint advised. "Then we sneak off in the middle of the night, and he might—I repeat, he might—not find us."

"Who are you stashing at the bottom of a well?" came a cheerful voice. Tasslehoff, having sighted his friends through the open window, decided to save himself the wearisome walk around to the front door. Hoisting himself up onto the window ledge, he climbed inside.

"Mind my ale mug! You nearly kicked it over! Get off the table, you doorknob!" Flint caught his ale mug, held it close to his chest. "If you must know, it's you we're talking of stashing in the well."

"Are you? How wonderful!" Tas said, his face lighting up. "I've never been at the bottom of a well before. Ah, but I just remembered. I can't."

Reaching out, Tas kindly patted Flint's hand. "I appreciate the thought. I truly do, and I'd almost stay behind to do it, but you see, I'm not going to be here."

"Where are you going?" Tanis asked the question with trepidation.

"Before I start, I want to say something. I know you've been arguing over who takes me along, haven't you?" Tas looked sternly around at the group.

Tanis was embarrassed. He had not meant to hurt the kender's feelings. "You can come with us, Tas," he began, only to be interrupted by a horrified "He cannot!" from Flint.

Tas raised his small hand for silence. "You see, if I go with one of you, then that will make the others feel bad, and I wouldn't like that to happen. And so I've decided to go off on my own. No! Don't try to make me change my mind. I'm going back to Kendermore, and, no offense"—Tas looked quite severe—"but the rest of you just wouldn't fit in there."

"You mean the kender wouldn't allow us to enter their land?" Caramon asked, insulted.

"No, I mean you wouldn't fit in. Especially you, Caramon. You'd take the roof off my house the moment you stood up. Not to mention squashing all my furniture. Now, I could make an exception for Flint. . . ."

"No you couldn't!" said the dwarf hurriedly.

Tasslehoff went on to describe the wonders of Kendermore, painting such an interesting picture of that carefree shire, where the concepts of private property and personal possessions are completely unknown, that every person at the table firmly resolved never to go anywhere near it.

The issue of the kender settled, there was nothing left but to say good-bye.

The companions sat for a long time at their table. The setting sun gleamed a fiery ball in the red portion of the stained-glass windows, shone orange in the yellow, and a strange sort of green in the blue. The sun seemed to linger as long as the companions, spreading its golden light throughout the sky, before slipping down past the horizon, leaving a warm afterglow behind.

Otik brought candles and lamps to drive away the shadows, along with an excellent supper of his famous spiced potatoes, lamb stew, trout from Crystalmir Lake, bread, and goat's cheese. The food was excellent; even Raistlin ate more than his usual two or three nibbling bites, actually devouring an entire trout. When every speck was eaten—nothing ever went to waste, with Caramon there to finish off the leftovers—Tanis called Otik over to settle the bill.

"The meal is on the house, my friends—my very dear friends," Otik said. He wished them all a safe journey and shook hands with every one of them, including Tasslehoff.

Tanis invited Otik to share a glass, which he did. Flint invited him to share another, and another after that. Otik shared so many glasses that eventually, when his services were required in the kitchen, young Tika had to help him stagger off.

Other Solace residents stopped by the inn, came to their table to say good-bye and offer their good wishes. Many were Flint's customers, sorry to hear of his leaving, for he had sold out all his stock and let it be known that he expected to be gone as long as a year. Many more came to say farewell to Raistlin, much to the secret astonishment of the rest of the company, who had no idea that the caustic, sharp-tongued, and secretive young man had so many friends.

These were not friends, however. They were his patients, come to express their gratitude for his care. Among these was Miranda. No longer the town beauty, she was wan and pale in her black mourning clothes. Her baby had been among the first to perish with the plague. She gave Raistlin a sweet kiss on his cheek and thanked him, in a choked voice, for being so gentle with her dying child. Her young husband also offered his thanks, then led away his grieving wife.

Raistlin watched her depart, thankful in his heart that he had been warned away from following down that pretty, rose-strewn path. He was uncommonly nice to his brother that night, much to the astonishment of Caramon, who couldn't imagine what he had done to earn Raistlin's gratitude.

Strangers at the inn noticed the odd assortment of friends, mainly due to the fact that either Tanis or Flint dropped by to return valuables that had been appropriated by the kender. The strangers shook their heads and raised their eyebrows.

"It takes all kinds to make this world," they said, and by the disparaging tones in which they spoke, it was obvious that they didn't believe the old homily in the slightest. In their view, it took their kind and no other.

The night deepened. Darkness gathered around the inn. The shadows crept into the inn itself, for the other customers were gone to their beds, taking their lamps or candles with them to light their way. A pleasantly soused Otik had long ago rolled into his bed, leaving the cleaning up to be done by Tika, the cook, and the barmaids.

They scrubbed the tabletops and swept the floor; the clatter of crockery could be heard coming from the kitchen. Still the companions sat at their table, loath to part, for each felt, in his or her own heart, that this parting would be a long one.

At length, Raistlin, who had been nodding where he sat for some time, said quietly, "It is time for us to go, my brother. I need my rest. I have much studying to do tomorrow."

Caramon made some unintelligible response. He had drunk more than his share of ale. His nose was red, and he was at that stage of drunkenness in which some men fight and others blubber. Caramon was blubbering.

"I, too, must take my leave," said Sturm. "We need to make an early start, put several miles behind us before the heat of the day sets in."

"I wish you would change your mind and come with us," Kitiara said softly, her eyes on Tanis.

Kit had been the loudest, brashest, liveliest person in the group, except when her gaze would fall on Tanis, and then her crooked smile would slip a little. Moments later, her smile would harden, and her laughter would blare out harshly, the noisiest person at the table. But as the jollity waned and the inn grew quieter, the shadows deepened around them, Kit's laughter died away, her stories began but never came to a close. She drew nearer and nearer to Tanis, and now she clasped his hand tightly beneath the table.

"Please, Tanis," she said. "Come north. You will find glory in battle, wealth, and power. I swear it!"

Tanis hesitated. Her dark eyes were warm and soft. Her smile trembled with the intensity of her passion. He had never seen her look more lovely. He was finding it more and more difficult to give her up.

"Yes, Tanis, come with us," Sturm urged warmly. "I cannot promise you wealth or power, but glory must surely be ours."

Tanis opened his mouth. It seemed he would say "yes." Everyone expected him to say "yes," including himself. When the "no" came out, he looked as startled as anyone at the table.

As Raistlin would say later to Caramon, on their way home that night, "The human side of Tanis would have gone with her. It was the elven side of him that held him back."

"Who wants you along anyway?" Kit flared, angry, her pride hurt. She had not anticipated failure. She slid away from him, stood up. "Traveling with you would be like traveling with my own grandfather. Sturm and I will have lots more fun without you."

Sturm appeared somewhat alarmed at this statement. The pilgrimage to his homeland was a sacred journey. He wasn't going north to "have fun." Frowning, he smoothed his mustaches and repeated that they needed to make an early start.

An uncomfortable silence fell. No one wanted to be the first to leave, especially now, when it seemed likely that their parting would end on a discordant note. Even Tasslehoff was affected. The kender sat quiet and subdued, so unhappy that he actually returned Sturm's money pouch. Tas returned the pouch to Caramon, but the thought was there.

"I have an idea," said Tanis at last. "Let us plan to meet again in the autumn, on the first night of Harvest Home."

"I might be back, I might not," said Kit, shrugging with a careless air. "Don't count on me."

"I trust I will not be back," Sturm said emphatically, and his friends knew what he meant. A return to Solace in the autumn would mean his quest to find his father and his heritage had failed.

"Then we will meet every year after, on the first night of Harvest Home in the fall, those of us who are here," Tanis suggested. "And let us take a vow that five years from now we will return here to the inn, no matter where we are or what we are doing."

"Those of us who are still alive," Raistlin said.

He had intended his words as a joke, but Caramon sat up straight, the shock of his brother's words penetrating his alcohol-induced befuddlement. He cast his twin a frightened glance, a glance that Raistlin deflected with narrowed eyes.

"It was only a small attempt at humor, my brother."

"Still, you shouldn't say things like that, Raist," Caramon entreated. "It's bad luck."

"Drink your ale and keep silent," Raistlin returned irritably.

Sturm's stern expression had eased. "That is a good idea. Five years. I pledge myself to return in five years."

"I'll be back, Tanis!" Tas said, hopping about in excitement. "I'll be here in five years."

"You'll likely be in some jail in five years," Flint muttered.

"Well, if I am, you'll bail me out, won't you, Flint?"

The dwarf swore it would be a cold day in the Abyss before he bailed the kender out of jail one more time.

"Are there cold days in the Abyss?" Tasslehoff wondered. "Are there any sort of days at all in the Abyss, or is it mostly dark and spooky like a giant hole in the ground, or is it filled with blazing fire? Don't you think the Abyss would be a great place to visit, Raistlin? I'd really like to go there someday. I'll bet not even Uncle Trapspringer has—"

Tanis called for silence, just in time to prevent Flint from up-ending his ale mug over the kender's head. Tanis placed his hand, palm down, in the center of the table.

"I vow on the love and friendship I feel for all of you"—his gaze touched each of his friends, gathered them together—"that I will return to the Inn of the Last Home on the first night of Harvest Home five years hence."

"I will be back in five years," said Kit, resting her hand over Tanis's. Her expression had softened. Her grip on him tightened. "If not sooner. Much sooner."

"I vow on my honor as the knight I hope to become that I will return in five years," Sturm Brightblade said solemnly. He placed his hand over Tanis's and Kit's.

"I'll be here," said Caramon. His large hand engulfed the other hands of his friends.

"And I," said Raistlin. He touched the back of his brother's hand with his fingertips.

"Don't forget me! I'll be here!" Tasslehoff crawled on top of the table to add his small hand to the pile.

"Well, Flint?" Tanis said, smiling at his old friend.

"Confound it, I may have more important things to do than come back to this place just to see your pasty faces," Flint grumbled.

He took hold of the hands of all his friends in his own gnarled and work-hardened hands. "Reorx walk with you until we meet again!" he said, then turned his head, stared very hard out the window at nothing.

The inn's door had long ago been locked for the night. A yawning barmaid was on hand to let them out. Raistlin said his good-byes quickly. He was eager to go home to his rest, and he waited impatiently at the door for his brother. Caramon embraced Sturm, the two longtime friends holding each other close. They parted in silence, both unable to speak. Caramon shook hands with Tanis, and he would have hugged Flint, but the dwarf, scandalized, told him to "get along home." Tasslehoff flung his arms as far as they would go around Caramon, who playfully tweaked the kender's topknot in return.

Kitiara stepped forward to embrace her brother, but Caramon seemed not to see her. Raistlin was now tapping his foot in irritation. Caramon hurried off, brushing past Kit without a word. She stared after him, then grinned, shrugged. Sturm's good-byes were brief and formal, accompanied by low and respectful bows for Tanis and Flint. Kit arranged a meeting place and then Sturm left.

"I think I'll stay a little longer," said Tas. He was just about to upend his pouches to look over his day's "findings" when there came a heavy knock on the door.

"Oh, hullo, Sheriff," Tas called cheerfully. "Looking for someone?"

Tasslehoff departed in the company of the sheriff. The kender's last words were for someone to remember to get him out of jail in the morning.

Kit stood in the doorway, waiting for Tanis.

"Flint, you coming?" Tanis asked.

The barmaid had taken the candles away. Flint sat in the darkness. He made no response.

"The girl's wanting to close up," Tanis urged.

Still no response.

"I'll take care of him, sir," the barmaid said softly.

Tanis nodded. Joining Kit, he put his arm around her, drew her close. The two walked side by side into the night.

The dwarf sat there, by himself, until dawn.

BOOK 6

The blade must pass through the fire, else it will break.

—Par-Salian

1

It was the sixth day of the seventh month. Antimodes stood in the window of his room in the Tower of Wayreth gazing out into the night. His room was one of many rooms in the tower open to mages arriving to study, to confer, or—as was Antimodes—to participate in giving the Test, which would be held on the morrow.

The tower's accommodations were of various sizes and designs, from small cell-like rooms for the apprentice mages to larger and more lavish rooms reserved for the archmagi. The room in which Antimodes was comfortably ensconced was his customary room, his favorite. Since the archmage was fond of travel, known to drop by at unexpected times, Par-Salian saw to it that the room was always kept ready for his friend's arrival.

Located near the top part of the tower, the suite consisted of a bedroom and a parlor, with a small balcony that sometimes overlooked the Forest of Wayreth and sometimes did not, depending on where the magical forest happened to be at the moment.

If the forest was not there, Antimodes would often conjure up a view himself. Vast fields of yellow wheat, or perhaps crashing surf, depending on what he felt in the mood for that day. The forest was not there this night, but since it was dark and Antimodes was tired from his day's travel, he did not bother with landscaping. He had been standing on the balcony, cooling himself in the evening breeze. Leaving the shutters open to keep the air circulating—it was unusually hot that night—he returned to a small desk, continued his frowning perusal of a scroll, a perusal which already had been interrupted by dinner.

A knock on the door again interrupted him.

"Enter," he called in an irritated tone.

The door opened silently. Par-Salian thrust his head inside.

"Am I disturbing you? I can come back. . . ."

"No, no. My dear friend." Antimodes rose hastily to his feet to greet his visitor. "Come in, come in. I am very glad to see you. I was hoping we might have a chance to talk before tomorrow. I would have gone to you, but I feared to disturb you at your work. I know how busy you are just prior to a testing."

"Yes, and this Test will prove more difficult than most. You are studying a new spell?" Par-Salian glanced at the scroll on the desk, which was partially unrolled.

"It is one I bought," said Antimodes with a grimace. "And as it turns out, I believe I was swindled. It is not what the man promised me."

"My dear Antimodes, didn't you read it first?" Par-Salian asked, shocked.

"I only glanced over it quickly. The fault is mine, a fact which merely increases my annoyance."

"I don't suppose you could return it."

"Afraid not. One of those deals in an inn. I should know better, of course, but I have been searching for this spell for a long time, and she was so very kind, not to mention pretty, and assured me that this would do precisely what I wanted." He shrugged. "Ah, well. Live and learn. Please, sit down. Will you have some wine?"

"Thank you." Par-Salian tasted the pale yellow liquid, rolled it on his tongue. "Conjured or purchased?"

"Purchased," Antimodes said. "Conjured lacks body, to my mind. Only the Silvanesti elves know how to do it right, and it's becoming harder and harder to acquire good Silvanesti wine these days."

"Too true," Par-Salian agreed. "King Lorac used to bring me several bottles whenever he visited, but it has been many years since he has been to see us."

"He's sulking," Antimodes observed. "He thought he should have been elected head of the conclave."

"I don't think that is it. Yes, he did feel he deserved the position, but he readily admitted that he was extremely busy with his duties as ruler of the Silvanesti. If anything, I think he wanted to be granted the honor so that he could have politely turned it down."

Par-Salian frowned thoughtfully. "Do you know, my friend, I have the strangest feeling that Lorac is hiding something from us. He doesn't come to see me anymore because he fears discovery."

"What do you think it is? Some powerful artifact? Is there one missing?"

"Not to my knowledge. I could be wrong. I hope I am."

"Lorac was always one to act on his own, the conclave be damned," Antimodes observed.

"Still, he abided by our rules as much as any elf ever abides by rules not of his own making." Par-Salian finished his wine, permitted himself another glass.

Antimodes was silent and thoughtful, then he said abruptly, "The gods grant Lorac good of it, then. He'll need it, I fear. Whatever it is. You received my last report?"

"I did." Par-Salian sighed. "I want to know this: Are you absolutely certain of your facts?"

"Certain? No, of course not! I will never be certain until I see with my own eyes!" Antimodes waved his hand. "It is rumor, hearsay, nothing more. Yet . . ." He paused, then said softly, "Yet I believe it."

"Dragons! Dragons returning to Krynn. Takhisis's dragons, no less! I hope, my friend," Par-Salian said earnestly, "I hope and pray that you are wrong."

"Still, it fits in with what facts we do know. Did you approach our black-robed brethren about this as I advised?"

"I discussed the matter with Ladonna," Par-Salian said. "Not mentioning where or how I had heard anything. She was evasive."

"Isn't she always?" Antimodes said dryly.

"Yes, but there are ways to read her if you know her," Par-Salian said.

Antimodes nodded. He was an old friend, a trusted friend. There was no need between them to mention that Par-Salian knew Ladonna better than most.

"She has been in fine spirits for the last year," Par-Salian continued. "Happy. Elated. She has also been extremely busy with something, for she has visited the tower only twice, and that to go through our collection of scrolls."

"I do have verification for my other news," Antimodes said. "As I had heard, a wealthy lord in the north is recruiting soldiers, and he is not being very particular about the type of soldiers he recruits. Ogres, hobgoblins, goblins. Even humans willing to trade their souls for loot. A friend of mine attended one of his rallies. Vast armies are being raised, armies of darkness. I even have a name for this lord—Ariakas. Do you know him?"

"I seem to remember something of him—a minor magus, if I'm not mistaken. Far more interested in gaining what he wanted quickly and brutally by the sword than by the more subtle and elegant means of sorcery."

"That sounds like the man." Antimodes sighed, shook his head morosely. "The sun is setting. Night is coming, my friend, and we cannot stop it."

"Yet we may be able to keep a few lights burning in the darkness," Par-Salian said quietly.

"Not without help!" Antimodes clenched his fist. "If only the gods would give us a sign!"

"I'd say Takhisis has already done just that," Par-Salian said wryly.

"The gods of good, I mean. Will they let her walk over them?" Antimodes demanded, impatient and exasperated. "When will Paladine and Mishakal finally make known their presence in the world?"

"Perhaps they are waiting for a sign from us," Par-Salian observed mildly.

"A sign of what?"

"Of faith. That we trust in them and believe in them, even though we do not understand their plan."

Antimodes regarded his friend narrowly. Then, leaning back in his chair, continuing to keep his gaze on Par-Salian, Antimodes scratched his raspy jaw. Par-Salian bore up under the intense scrutiny. He smiled to let his friend know that his thinking was traveling along the right road.

"So that is what this is all about," Antimodes said after a moment.

Par-Salian inclined his head.

"I wondered. He is so very young. Skilled, admittedly, but very young. And inexperienced."

"He will gain in experience," Par-Salian said. "We have some time before us, do we not?"

Antimodes considered the matter. "These ogres and goblins and humans must be trained, molded into a fighting force, which may prove extremely difficult. As it stands now, they would just as soon kill each other as the enemy. Ariakas has a monumental job on his hands. If rumor is true and the dragons have returned, they must also be controlled in some manner, although it will take those of strong will and courage to accomplish that! So, yes, in answer to your question, I say that we have time. Some time, but not much. The young man will never wear the white robes. You know that, don't you?"

"I know that," Par-Salian replied calmly. "I've been listening to Theobald rant and rave about Raistlin Majere for years, practically ever since he started school as a child. I know his faults: He is secretive and conniving, arrogant, ambitious, and hungry."

"He is also creative, intelligent, and courageous," Antimodes added. He was proud of his ward. "Witness his deft handling of that renegade witch, Judith. He cast a spell far above his level of ability, a spell he should not have even been able to read, let alone command. And he cast it by himself, without help."

"Which only goes to prove that he will bend rules, even break them if it suits his purpose," Par-Salian said. "No, no. Don't feel the need to defend him further. I am aware of his merits as I am aware of his weaknesses. That is why I invited him to take the Test, rather than bring him up before the Conclave on charges, as I should do by rights, I suppose. Do you think he murdered her?"

"I do not." Antimodes was firm. "If for no other reason than cutting someone's throat is not Raistlin's style. Far too messy. He is a skilled herbalist. If he had wanted her dead, he would have slipped a little nightshade into her tarbean tea."

"You believe him capable of murder, then?" Par-Salian asked, frowning.

"Who among us is not, given the right set of circumstances? There is a rival tailor in my town, an odious man who cheats his customers and spreads vicious lies about his competitors, including my brother. I myself have been tempted more than once to send Bigby's Crushing Hand knocking on his door." Antimodes looked quite fierce when he said this.

Par-Salian hid a smile in another glass of wine.

"You yourself used to say that those who walk the paths of night had better know how to see in the dark," Antimodes continued. "You don't want him bumbling about blindly, I suppose."

"That was part of my reasoning. The Test will teach him a few things about himself. Things he might not like to know, but which are necessary to his understanding of himself and the power he wields."

"The Test is a humbling experience," Antimodes said with something between a sigh and shudder.

Their faces lengthened, they cast surreptitious glances at each other to see if their thoughts were once more traveling in similar directions. It seemed that the thoughts were concurrent as evidenced by the fact that they had no need to name the personage about whom they now spoke.

"He will undoubtedly be there," said Antimodes in a low voice. He glanced around guardedly, as if he feared they might be overheard in the chamber, a chamber that stood alone in the topmost part of the tower, a chamber to which no one but the two of them had access.

"Yes, I fear so," said Par-Salian, looking grave. "He will take particular interest in this young man."

"We should finish him, once and for all."

"We've tried," Par-Salian said. "And you know the results as well as I do. We cannot touch him on his plane of existence. Not only that, but I suspect that Nuitari guards him."

"He should. He never had a more loyal servant. Talk of murders!" Leaning forward, Antimodes spoke in a conspiratorial undertone. "We could limit the young man's access to him."

"And what of freedom of will? That has always been the hallmark of our orders. A freedom many have sacrificed their lives to protect! Do we throw the right to choose our own destinies to the Abyss?"

Antimodes was chastened. "Forgive me, friend. I spoke in haste. I am fond of the young man, though. Fond and proud of him. He has done me great credit. I would hate to see harm befall him."

"Indeed he has done you credit. And he will continue to do so, I hope. His own choices will lead him on the path he is to walk, as our choices led us. I trust they may be wise ones."

"The Test will be hard on him. He is a frail youth."

"The blade must pass through the fire, else it will break."

"And if he dies? What of your plans then?"

"Then I will look for someone else. Ladonna spoke to me of a promising young elf magus. His name is Dalamar. . . ."

Their conversation turned to other matters, to Ladonna's pupil, dire events in the world, and eventually to the area that interested them most—magic.

Above the Tower, silver Solinari and red Lunitari shone brightly. Nuitari was there as well, a dark hole in the constellations. The three moons were full this night, as was necessary for the Test.

In the lands beyond the tower, far, far away from the room where the two archmagi sipped their elven wine and spoke of the fate of the world, the young mages who were traveling to the Tower to take the Test slept restlessly, if they slept at all. In the morning, the Forest of Wayreth would find them, lead them to their fate.

Tomorrow some might sleep, never to wake again.

2

The twins' journey to the tower took them over a month. They had expected it would take longer, for they had thought they would be traveling on foot. Shortly after their friends had left Solace, a messenger arrived to say that two horses had been delivered to the public stables in the name of Majere. The horses were gifts from Raistlin's sponsor, Antimodes.

The young men traveled southwest through Haven. Raistlin stopped to pay his respects to Lemuel, who reported that the temple of Belzor had been razed, its stone blocks used to build homes for the poor. This had been accomplished under the auspices of a new and apparently harmless religious order known as the Seekers. Lemuel had reopened his mageware shop. He showed Raistlin the black bryony, which was flourishing. He asked where they were bound. Raistlin replied that they were traveling for fun, taking a roundabout route to Pax Tharkas.

Lemuel looked very grave at this, wished them luck and a safe road many times, and sighed deeply when they left.

The two continued their journey, riding south along the western slopes of the Kharolis Mountains, skirting the borders of Qualinesti.

Although they kept close watch, they saw no elves. Yet the two were always aware of the elves watching them. Caramon suggested visiting Tanis, seeing the elven kingdom. Raistlin reminded him that their journey was secret, they were supposed to be in Pax Tharkas. Besides, he doubted if they would be able to convince the elves to admit them. The Qualinesti took more kindly to humans than did their cousins, the Silvanesti, but with evil rumors flying on dark wings from the north, the Qualinesti were wary of strangers.

On the last morning of their journey along the border, the two woke to find an elven arrow embedded at the foot of each of their bedrolls. The Qualinesti's message was clear: We have allowed you to pass, but don't come back.

The brothers breathed a little easier once they were out of elven lands, but they could not relax their vigilance, for now began their search for the wayward Forest of Wayreth. The lands in this part of Abanasinia were wild and desolate. Once the two were set upon by thieves, another time a band of goblins passed by so near that the twins could have reached out and smacked one on its scaly hide.

The bandits had thought to jump defenseless young travelers. Caramon's sword and Raistlin's fiery spells soon apprised them of their mistake. The bandits left one of their number dead on the road, the rest dashed off to bind their wounds. The goblins proved too numerous to fight, however. The brothers took refuge in a cave until the troop had marched past, heading northward at a rapid pace.

The twins spent four days searching for the forest. Caramon, frustrated and nervous, said more than once that they ought to turn back. He consulted three maps—one given him by Tasslehoff, one provided by an innkeeper in Haven, and another taken from the body of the thief. Not one of the maps showed the forest in the same location.

Raistlin soothed his brother's concerns with as much calm as he could muster, though he himself was starting to worry. Tomorrow was the seventh day, and they had seen no sign of the forest.

That night they spread their bedrolls in a clearing of scraggly pines. They awakened to find themselves lying beneath the huge, spreading bows of enormous oak trees.

Caramon almost fled then and there. The oak trees were not ordinary oak trees. He saw eyes in the knotholes, he heard spoken words in the rustling of the leaves. He heard words in the songs of the birds as well. Though he couldn't understand them clearly, the birds seemed to him to be warning him to leave.

The twins gathered their belongings, mounted their horses. The oak trees stood shoulder to shoulder, stalwart guards blocking their path. Raistlin regarded the trees in silence a moment, summoning his courage. He urged his horse forward. The oaks parted, forming a clear path that led straight to the tower.

Caramon tried to ride after his brother. The trees glared at him with hatred, the leaves rustled in anger. His courage failed him. Fear took hold of him, wrung him, left him weak and helpless, powerless to move.

"Raist!" he cried hoarsely.

Raistlin turned. Seeing his brother's predicament, he rode back. He reached out, took hold of his brother's hand.

"Do not be afraid, Caramon. I am with you."

The two entered the forest together.

*   *   *   *   *

On the seventh day of the seventh month, seven magi were ushered into a large courtyard at the base of the Tower of High Sorcery.

Four men and three women: Four were human, two elven, and one appeared to be half-human, half-dwarf, a rather unusual combination for a magic-user. The youngest by almost five years was Raistlin Majere, the only one to arrive with an escort. The others glanced askance at the young mage, observed his delicate features, his pallor, and the excessive thinness that made him appear younger than he was.

They wondered why he was here, and why he was permitted to have a family member with him. The elves were open in their disdain. The half-dwarf suspected the young man of having sneaked in uninvited, though he could not say how.

The garden courtyard in the Tower of High Sorcery was an eerie place, crisscrossed with corridors of magic. Magi passed through here regularly, traveling the magic pathways on errands to the tower or on business of their own. Those standing in the garden could not see the travelers on their hidden pathways, but it seemed to them that they could feel the breath of their passing.

The older, more experienced magi who frequented the tower grew accustomed to the sudden shifting eddies of magic that swirled about the courtyard. This being the first occasion any of the novices had visited the tower, they found the voices that spoke from nothingness, the sudden whiffs of air down the back of the neck, the half-seen flash of a hand or foot, most disturbing.

The initiates and the single lone warrior stood in the courtyard, waiting for what they hoped would be the beginning of their lives as one of this elite group of wizards. The initiates tried not to think about the fact that this might be the last day of their lives.

Caramon jumped, with a clatter of sword and leather armor, and whipped around to stare fearfully behind him.

"Hold still! You are making a fool of yourself, Caramon," Raistlin admonished as they stood waiting in the courtyard.

"I felt a hand touch my back," Caramon said, pale and sweating.

"Very probably," Raistlin murmured, unperturbed. "Pay it no mind."

"I don't like this place, Raist!" Caramon's voice sounded unnaturally loud in the whispering stillness. "Let's go back home. You're a good enough mage without having to put up with this!"

His words carried quite clearly. The other initiates turned to stare. The upper lip of one of the elves curled in a sneer.

Raistlin felt the hot blood flood his face. "Hush, Caramon!" he rebuked, his voice quivering with anger. "You are shaming us both!"

Caramon shut his mouth, bit his lip.

Raistlin deliberately turned his back on his twin. He could not fathom why the conclave had insisted on Caramon's being a part of his testing.

"Unless they plan on aggravating me to death," Raistlin muttered to himself.

He tried to ignore Caramon's presence, concentrating on banishing his own nervous fears. There was no reason he should be afraid. He had studied his spellbook, he knew it inside out, could have recited his spells backward while standing on his head, if that was what the judges might require. He had proven that he could work his magic under pressure. He would not fall apart, nor would his spell fall apart, in tense situations.

He need not be concerned about his abilities to perform magic during the Test. Nor was he particularly worried about the intangible portions of the Test, the part wherein the mage learns more about himself. Introspective from birth, Raistlin was confident that he knew all there was to know about his own inner workings.

For him, the Test would be a mere formality.

Raistlin relaxed, discovered that he was actually looking forward to the Test. His worries eased, he spent the time waiting for the judges to arrive in studying the fabled Tower of Wayreth.

"I will see it often in the future," he said to himself and envisioned traveling the unseen pathways, tending herbs in the garden, studying in the great library.

MargaRet Weis

The tower at Wayreth was in actuality two towers, constructed of polished black obsidian. The main towers were surrounded by a wall in the shape of an equilateral triangle, with three smaller towers located at each of the angles. The wall surrounded the garden, where grew many varieties of herbs used not only for spell components, but also for healing and cooking.

The tops of the walls had no battlements, for the tower was protected by strong magicks. The forest would not permit the entry of anyone unless he had been invited by the conclave. If an enemy did, by some mischance, manage to stumble into the forest, the magical creatures roaming within would deal with the foe.

There was need for such precautions. Long ago there had been five Towers of High Sorcery, centers for magic on Ansalon. During the rise of Istar, the Kingpriest, who secretly feared magic and the power of wizards, outlawed magic. He caused mobs to rise against the wizards, hoping to eradicate them.

The wizards might have fought back, and some advocated the use of force, but the conclave deemed such drastic action unwise. Defending themselves would result in tragic loss of life on both sides. The Kingpriest and his followers wanted bloody conflict. Then they could point an accusing finger at the wizards and say, "We were right! They are a menace and should be destroyed!"

The conclave made a bargain with the Kingpriest. The wizards would abandon their towers, retreat to a single tower located in Wayreth. Here they would continue to study unmolested. The Kingpriest, though disappointed that the wizards chose not to fight, agreed. He had already taken control of the Tower of High Sorcery at Istar, and now he looked forward to gaining the exquisitely lovely tower in Palanthas. He planned to make it a temple to his greatness.

As he entered the tower to claim it, a black-robed wizard, purportedly insane, leapt from one of the tower's upper windows. The wizard impaled himself upon the sharp barbs of the iron fence below. With his dying breath, he cast a curse upon the tower, saying that none should inhabit it except the Master of Past and Present.

Who was this mysterious master? No one could say. Certainly it was not the Kingpriest. As he watched, horrified, the tower altered in appearance, becoming so hideous in aspect that those looking at it were constrained to cover their eyes. Even then, those who saw it were forever haunted by the dreadful sight.

The Kingpriest sent for powerful clerics to try to lift the curse. Surrounded by the Shoikan Grove, a forest of fear, the tower was guarded by the dark god Nuitari, who paid no attention to prayers uttered to any god except himself. The clerics of Paladine came, but they ran whimpering from the site. The clerics of Mishakal tried to enter. They barely escaped with their lives.

When the gods cast down the fiery mountain on Ansalon, the Cataclysm sent Istar to the bottom of the Blood Sea. Quakes broke the continent of Ansalon, ripping it apart, forming new seas, creating new mountain ranges. The city of Palanthas shook on its foundations, houses and buildings toppled. Yet not a leaf in the Shoikan Grove so much as shivered.

Dark, silent, empty, the tower waited for its master, whoever that may be.

Raistlin pondered the history of the towers. In his mind, he was already walking the halls of the Tower of Wayreth, an accepted and revered wizard, when an unseen bell chimed seven times.

The seven initiates, who had been walking in the garden, visiting with each other, or standing apart, reciting their spells to themselves, came to a halt. All talking ceased.

Some faces paled in fear, others flushed in excitement. The elves, priding themselves on showing no emotion before humans, appeared nonchalant, bored.

"What's that?" Caramon asked, hoarse with nervousness.

"It is time, my brother," Raistlin said.

"Raist, please . . ." Caramon began.

Seeing the expression on his brother's face—the narrowed eyes, the frowning brows, the hard, firm set of the lips—Caramon swallowed his final plea.

A disembodied hand appeared, floating above the roses in the center of the garden.

"Oh, shit!" Caramon breathed. His hand closed convulsively over the hilt of his sword, but he did not need his brother's warning glance to understand that he should not draw any weapon on these grounds. He doubted if he could have found the strength to do so.

The hand beckoned. The initiates drew their hoods over their heads, placed their hands in the sleeves of their robes, and silently walked in the direction the hand indicated, heading for a small tower located between the two larger towers.

Raistlin and his brother, who had been the last to arrive,

brought up the rear of the line.

The hand pointed at the door in the foremost tower, a door whose knocker was the head of a dragon. No one was required to knock to gain entry. The door opened silently as they approached.

One by one, each of the initiates filed inside. Leaving the sunlit garden, they entered a darkness so thick that all were temporarily blinded. Those in front halted, uncertain where to go, afraid to go anywhere that they could not see. Those coming behind them bunched up inside the doorway. Caramon, entering last, blundered into all of them.

"Sorry. Excuse me. I didn't see—"

"Silence."

The darkness spoke. The initiates obeyed. Caramon was silent, too, or tried to be. His leather creaked, his sword rattled, his boots clattered. His stentorian breathing echoed throughout the chamber.

"Turn to your left and walk toward the light," ordered the voice that was as disembodied as the hand.

The initiates did as commanded. A light appeared, and they moved toward it with quiet, shuffling steps, Caramon tromping along loudly behind.

A small corridor of stone, lit by torches whose pale fire burned steadily, gave no warmth and made no smoke, opened into a vast hall.

"The Hall of Mages," Raistlin whispered, digging his nails into the flesh of his arms, using the pain to contain his excitement.

The others shared his awe, his elation. The elves dropped their stoic masks. Their eyes shone, their lips parted in wonder. Each one of the initiates had dreamed of this moment, dreamed of standing in the Hall of Mages, a place forbidden, a place most people on Krynn would never see.

"No matter what happens, this is worth it," Raistlin said silently.

Only Caramon remained unaffected, except by fear. He hung his head, refused to look to left or right, as if hoping that if he did not look, it would all go away.

The chamber walls were obsidian, shaped smooth by magic. The ceiling was lost in shadow. No pillars supported it.

Light shone, white light that illuminated twenty-one stone chairs, arranged in a semicircle. Seven of the chairs bore black cushions, seven of them red cushions, and seven white cushions.

Here was the meeting place of the Conclave of Wizards. A single chair stood in the center of the semicircle. This chair was slightly larger than the rest. Here sat the head of the conclave. The cushion on the chair was white.

At first glance, the chairs were empty.

At second glance, they were not. Wizards occupied them, men and women of different races, wearing the different colors suitable to their orders.

Caramon gasped and lurched unsteadily on his feet. Raistlin's hand closed viciously over his twin's arm, probably hurting his brother as much as it supported him.

Caramon was having a very bad time of it. He had never taken either magic or his brother's gift for magic seriously. To him, magic was coins dribbling from the nose, bunnies popping up unexpectedly, giant kender. Even that spell had impressed Caramon only moderately. When it came down to it, the kender had not really turned into a giant at all. It was only illusion, trickery. Trickery and magic had been all muddled up in Caramon's mind.

This was not trickery. What he witnessed was a raw display of power, intended to impress and intimidate. Caramon continued to fear for his brother. If he could have, he would have snatched Raistlin from that place and fled. But somewhere in the depths of Caramon's mind, he was finally beginning to understand the high stakes for which his brother gambled, stakes high enough that it might be worth betting his life.

The wizard in the center chair rose to his feet.

"That is Par-Salian, head of the conclave," Raistlin whispered to his brother, hoping to save Caramon from yet another gaffe. "Be polite!"

The initiates bowed respectfully, Caramon along with the rest.

"Greetings," said Par-Salian in a kind and welcoming tone.

The great archmage was in his early sixties at the time, though his long white hair, wispy white beard, and his stooped shoulders made him look older. He had never been robust, had always preferred study to action. He worked constantly to develop new spells, refine and enhance old ones. He was eager for magical artifacts as a child is eager for sugarplums. His apprentices spent much of their time traveling the continent in search of artifacts and scrolls or in tracking down rumors of such.

Par-Salian was also a keen observer and participant in the politics of Ansalon, unlike many wizards who held themselves above the trivial, everyday dealings of an ignorant populace. The head of the conclave had contacts in every single government of any importance on Ansalon. Antimodes was not Par-Salian's only source of information. He kept most of his knowledge secret and to himself, unless it benefited his plans to do otherwise.

Though few knew the full extent of his influence in Ansalon, an aura of wisdom and power surrounded Par-Salian with an almost visible halo of white light, shining so brightly that the two Silvanesti elves, who held most humans in the same regard as other races held kender, bowed low to him and then bowed again.

"Greetings, initiates," Par-Salian repeated, "and guest."

His gaze went to Caramon, seemed to strike right to the big man's heart and set him trembling.

"You have each come at the appointed time by invitation to undergo tests of your skills and your talent, your creativity, your thought processes, and, most importantly, the testing of yourself. What are your limits? How far can you push beyond those limits? What are your flaws? How might those flaws impede your abilities? Uncomfortable questions, but questions we each must answer, for only when we know ourselves—faults and strengths alike—will we have access to the full potential that is within us."

The initiates stood silent and circumspect, nervous and awed and anxious to begin.

Par-Salian smiled. "Don't worry. I know how eager you are, and therefore I will not indulge in long speeches. Again I want to bid you welcome and to extend my blessing. I ask that Solinari be with you this day."

He lifted his hands. The initiates bowed their heads. Par-Salian resumed his seat.

The head of the Order of Red Robes stood up, moved briskly on to the business at hand.

"When your name is called, step forward and accompany one of the judges, who will take you to the area where the testing will begin. I am certain you are all familiar with the criteria of the testing, but the conclave requires me to read it to you now, so that none can later claim he or she entered into this unknowingly. I remind you that these are guidelines only. Each Test is specially designed for the individual initiate and may include all or only a part of what the guidelines call for.

" 'There shall be at least three tests of the initiate's knowledge of magic and its use. The Test shall require the casting of all of the spells known to the initiate, at least three tests that cannot be solved by magic alone, and at least one combat against an opponent who is higher in rank than the initiate.' Do you have any questions?"

Not one of the initiates did; the questions were locked in each person's heart. Caramon had a great many questions, but he was too awed to be able to ask them.

"Then," said the Red Robe, "I ask that Lunitari walk with you."

He sat back down.

The head of the Order of Black Robes rose to her feet. "I ask that Nuitari walk with you." Unfurling a scroll, she began to read off names.

As each name was called, the initiate stepped forward, to be met by one of the members of the conclave. The initiate was led in silence and with the utmost solemnity into the shadows of the hall, then vanished.

One by one, each of the initiates departed until only one, Raistlin Majere, remained.

Raistlin stood stoically, with outward calm, as the numbers of his fellows dwindled around him. But his hands, inside his sleeves where they could not be seen, clenched to fists. The irrational fear came to him that perhaps there had been some mistake, that he was not supposed to be here. Perhaps they had changed their minds and would send him off. Or perhaps his loutish brother had done something to offend them, and Raistlin would be dismissed in shame and ignominy.

The Black Robe finished reading the names, shut the scroll with a snap, and still Raistlin stood in the Hall of Mages, except that now he stood alone. He maintained his rigid pose, waited to hear his fate.

Par-Salian rose to his feet, came forward to meet the young man. "Raistlin Majere, we have left you to the last because of the unusual circumstances. You have brought an escort."

"I was requested to do so, Great One," Raistlin said, the words coming in a whisper from his dry mouth. Clearing his throat, he said, more forcefully, "This is my twin brother, Caramon."

"Welcome, Caramon Majere," said Par-Salian. His blue eyes, in their maze of wrinkles, peered deep into Caramon's soul.

Caramon mumbled something that no one heard and subsided into unhappy silence.

"I wanted to explain to you why we requested the presence of your brother," Par-Salian continued, shifting his astute gaze back to Raistlin. "We want to assure you that you are not unique, nor have we singled you out. We do this in the case of all twins who come to the testing. We have discovered that twins have an extremely close bond, closer than most siblings, almost as if the two were in reality one being split in twain. Of course, in most cases, both twins take up the study of magic, both having a talent for it. You are unusual in this respect, Raistlin, in that you alone show a talent for the art. Have you ever had any interest in magic, Caramon?"

Called upon to speak, to answer such a startling question, one that he had in truth never even considered, Caramon opened his mouth, but it was Raistlin who answered.

"No, he has not."

Par-Salian looked at the two of them. "I see. Very well. Thank you for coming, Caramon. And now, Raistlin Majere, will you be so good as to accompany Justarius? He will take you the area where the Test begins."

Raistlin's relief was so great that he was momentarily faint and dizzy, obliged to close his eyes until he regained his balance. He paid scant attention to the Red Robe who stepped forward, aware only that it was an older man who walked with a pronounced limp.

Raistlin bowed to Par-Salian. Spellbook in hand, he turned to accompany the Red Robe.

Caramon took a step to follow his twin.

Par-Salian was quick to intervene. "I am sorry, Caramon, but you cannot accompany your brother."

"But you told me to come," Caramon protested, fear giving him the voice he had lacked.

"Yes, and it will be our pleasure to entertain you during your brother's absence," Par-Salian said, and though his tone was pleasant, there was no arguing with his words.

"Good . . . good luck, Raist," Caramon called out awkwardly.

Raistlin, embarrassed, ignored his brother, pretended he had not heard him. Justarius led the way into the shadows of the hall.

Raistlin was gone, walking where his brother could not follow.

"I have a question!" Caramon cried. "Is it true that sometimes the initiates die—"

He was talking to a door. He was inside a room, a very

comfortable room that might have been lifted from one of the finest inns in Ansalon. A fire burned on the hearth. A table, loaded with food, all of Caramon's favorite dishes, and a most excellent ale.

Caramon paid no attention to the food. Angry at what he considered high-handed treatment, he tried to open the door.

The handle came off in his hands.

Now extremely fearful for his brother, suspecting some sort of sinister intent on Raistlin's life, Caramon was determined to rescue his twin. He hurled himself at the door. It shook beneath his weight but did not budge. He beat at the door with his fists, shouting for someone to come and release him.

"Caramon Majere."

The voice came from behind him.

Startled and alarmed, Caramon turned around so fast that he tripped over his own feet. Stumbling, he clutched at the table and stared.

Par-Salian stood in the center of the room. He smiled reassuringly at Caramon.

"Forgive my dramatic arrival, but the door is wizard-locked, and it's such a bother removing the spell and then putting it on again. Is the room comfortable? Is there anything we might bring you?"

"Damn the room!" Caramon thundered. "They told me he might die."

"That is true, but he is aware of the risks."

"I want to be with him," said Caramon. "I'm his twin. I have that right."

"You are with him," said Par-Salian softly. "He takes you everywhere."

Caramon didn't understand. He wasn't with Raistlin, they were trying to trick him, that's all. He brushed the meaningless words aside.

"Let me go to him." He glowered and clenched his fists. "Either you let me go or I'll tear down this Tower stone by stone."

Par-Salian stroked his beard to hide his smile. "I'll make a bargain with you, Caramon. You permit our tower to remain standing, unharmed, and I'll permit you to watch your brother as he takes his Test. You will not be allowed to help or assist him in any way, but perhaps watching him may alleviate your fears."

Caramon thought it over. "Yeah. All right," he said. Once he knew where Raistlin was, Caramon figured he could go to him if he needed help.

"I'm ready. Take me to him. Oh, and thanks, but I'm not thirsty now."

Par-Salian was pouring water from a pitcher into a bowl.

"Sit down, Caramon," he said.

"We're going to go find Raist—"

"Sit down, Caramon," Par-Salian repeated. "You want to see your twin? Look into the bowl."

"But it's only water. . . ."

Par-Salian passed his hand over the water in the bowl, spoke a single magic word, scattered a few crumbled leaves of plants into the water.

Sitting down, planning to first humor the old man and then grab him by his scrawny throat, Caramon looked into the water.

Raistlin trudged down a lonely, little-traveled road on the outskirts of Haven. Night was falling, a stiffening breeze swayed the treetops, sent autumn leaves flying. There was a smell of lightning in the humid air. He had been traveling all day on foot, he was tired and hungry, and now a storm was approaching. All thought of spending the night sleeping on the ground vanished from his mind.

A tinker he had met earlier had told him, in response to a question, that there was an inn up ahead, an inn with the droll name of the Inn Between. The tinker added the warning that the inn had an evil reputation, was known to be frequented by the wrong sort of crowd. Raistlin didn't care what sort of crowd drank there, so long as the inn had a bed beneath a roof and they let him sleep in it. He had little fear of thieves. It must be obvious from his shabby robes that he carried nothing of value. The very sight of those robes—the robes of a magic-user—would make the ordinary footpad think twice before accosting him.

The Inn Between, so called because it was located equidistant between Haven and Qualinesti, did not look propitious. The paint on its hanging sign was faded past recognition—no great loss to the art community. The owner, having expended his wit on the name, had not been able think of any way to illustrate it beyond a huge red **X** in the middle of a squiggle that might have been a road.

The building itself had a sullen and defiant air, as if it were tired of being teased about its clever name and would, in a fit of ill temper, tumble down upon the head of the next person who mentioned it. The shutters were half closed, giving its windows a suspicious squint. Its eaves sagged like frowning brows.

The door opened with such reluctance that Raistlin, on the

first try, thought the inn might have closed down. He could hear voices and laughter inside, smell the scent of food. A second, more forceful push, caused the door to relinquish. It opened grudgingly, with a screech of rusted hinges, slammed shut quickly behind him, as much as to say, "Don't blame me. I did my best to warn you."

The laughter stopped at Raistlin's entrance. The inn's guests turned their heads to look at him, consider him, prepare to take whatever action they deemed appropriate. The bright light of a roaring fire partially dazzled him. He could see nothing for a moment until his eyes adjusted, and therefore he had no idea whether any of the guests had taken an unusual interest in him. By the time he could see, they had all gone back to doing whatever it was they were doing.

Most of them, that is. One group, consisting of three cloaked and hooded figures, seated on the far side of the room, paid him considerable attention. When they resumed their conversation, they put their heads together, talking excitedly, occasionally lifting their heads to cast glittering-eyed glances in his direction.

Raistlin found an empty booth near the fire, sat down thankfully to rest and warm himself. A glance at the plates of his fellow guests showed that the food was plain fare. It didn't look particularly tasty, but didn't appear likely to poison him either. Stew being the only dish offered, he ordered that, along with a glass of wine.

He ate a few bites of unnameable meat, then pushed the bits of potato and coagulated gravy around with his spoon. The wine was surprisingly good, with a taste of clover. He relished it and was regretting that his meager purse could not afford him a second glass when a cool pitcher appeared at his elbow.

Raistlin lifted his head.

One of the cloaked men who had been so interested in Raistlin stood at his table.

"Greetings, stranger," the man said, speaking Common with a slight accent, an accent that reminded Raistlin of Tanis.

Raistlin was not surprised to see an elf, though he was extremely surprised to hear the elf add, "My friends and I noticed how much you enjoyed the wine. It comes from Qualinesti, as do we. My friends and I would like to share this pitcher of our fine wine with you, sir."

No respectable elf would be found drinking in a human-owned tavern. No respectable elf would initiate a conversation with a human. No respectable elf would buy a human a pitcher of wine. This gave Raistlin a pretty good idea of the status of his new acquaintances.

They must be dark elves—those who have been "cast from the light" or exiled from the elven homelands, the worst possible fate that can befall an elf.

"What you drink and with whom you drink is your prerogative, sir," Raistlin said warily.

"It's not prerogative," the elf returned. "It's wine."

He smiled, thinking himself clever. "And it's yours, if you want it. Do you mind if I sit down?"

"Forgive me for seeming rude, sir. I am not in the mood for company."

"Thank you. I accept the invitation." The elf slid into the seat opposite.

Raistlin rose to his feet. This had gone far enough. "I bid you good evening, sir. I am in need of rest. If you will excuse me . . ."

"You're a magic-user, aren't you?" the elf asked. He had not removed the hood that covered his head, but his eyes were visible. Almond-shaped, they gleamed hard and clear, as if the liquid orbs had frozen.

Raistlin saw no need to answer such an impertinent and perhaps dangerous question. He turned away, intending to bargain with the innkeeper for a patch of floor near the fire in the common room.

"Pity," said the elf. "It would be your good fortune if you were—a magic-user, I mean. My friends and I"—he nodded his head in the direction of his two hooded companions—"have in mind a little job where a wizard might come in handy."

Raistlin said nothing. He did not leave the table, however, but remained standing, regarded the elf with more interest.

"There's money to be had," the elf said, smiling.

Raistlin shrugged.

The elf was puzzled at his reaction. "Odd. I thought humans were always interested in money. It seems I was wrong. What might tempt you? Ah, I know. Magic! Of course. Artifacts, enchanted rings. Spellbooks."

The elf rose gracefully to his feet. "Come meet my brethren. Hear what we've got in mind. Then if you happen to run across a mage"—the elf winked—"you could let him know he could make his fortune by joining up with us."

"Bring the wine," Raistlin said. Walking through the inn, he joined the other two elves at their table.

The elf, smiling, picked up the pitcher and brought it along.

Raistlin knew something about the Qualinesti from Tanis, probably knew more than most humans, for he had questioned the half-elf extensively on elven ways and practices. The three were tall and slender, as are all elves, and though most elves look alike to humans, Raistlin thought he detected a certain resemblance between them. All three had green eyes and peculiarly jutting, pointed chins. They were young, probably around two hundred. They wore short swords beneath their cloaks—he could hear the metal strike the chairs occasionally—and probably carried knives. He could hear the creak of leather armor.

He wondered what crime they had committed that was vile enough to be sent into exile, a punishment worse than death to elves. He had the feeling he was about to find out.

The elf who had spoken to Raistlin was the spokesman for the group. The other two rarely opened their mouths. Perhaps they didn't speak Common. Many elves did not, scorned to learn a human language.

"I am Liam." The elf made introductions. "This is Micah and Renet. And your name would be? . . ."

"Of little interest to you, sir," Raistlin replied.

"Oh, but I assure you, it is, sir," Liam returned. "I like to know the name of any man with whom I'm drinking."

"Majere," Raistlin said.

"Majere?" Liam frowned. "One of the ancient gods was called by that name, I believe."

"And so am I." Raistlin sipped at his wine. "Though I do not claim godhood. Please explain the nature of this job, sir. I don't find the company of dark elves so appealing that I want to prolong this interview."

An angry glint came into the eye of one of the other elves, the one called Renet. His fist clenched, he started to stand. Liam snapped words in elven, shoved his friend back down in his seat. Raistlin's question was answered, however. At least one of the other elves understood Common.

Raistlin himself spoke a smattering of Qualinesti, having learned the language from Tanis. He did not let on that he understood what was being said, however, thinking he might pick up useful information if the elves imagined they could speak freely among themselves in their own tongue.

"This is no time to be thin-skinned, Cousin. We need this human," Liam said in elven.

Shifting to Common, he added, "You must forgive my cousin, sir. He's a bit hot-tempered. I think you might be a little friendlier toward us, Majere. We're doing you a big favor."

"If you are looking for friends, I suggest you talk to the barmaid," Raistlin said. "She looks as if she could accommodate you. If you want to hire a mage, then you should explain the job."

"You are a mage, then," Liam asked with a sly grin.

Raistlin nodded.

Liam eyed him. "You look very young."

Raistlin was growing irritated. "You are the one who approached me, sir. You knew what I looked like when you invited me to join you." He started to rise. "It seems I have wasted my time."

"All right! All right! I don't suppose it matters how young you are, so long as you can do the work." Liam leaned forward, lowered his voice. "Here is the proposal. There's a mage living in Haven who owns a mageware shop. He's human, like yourself. His name is Lemuel. You know him?"

Raistlin did in fact know Lemuel, having had dealings with him in the past. He considered Lemuel a friend, hoped to find out what these unsavory elves wanted, with a view toward warning him.

Raistlin shrugged. "Whom I know is my own affair and none of yours."

Micah, jerking a thumb at Raistlin, muttered in elven, "I don't much like this mage of yours, Cousin."

"Nobody's asking you to like him," Liam returned in elven, scowling. "Drink your wine and keep your mouth shut. I do the talking."

Raistlin watched blandly, with the vacant expression of one who has no idea what is being said.

Liam shifted back to Common. "Now then, our plan is this: We enter the mage's house in the night, steal the valuables from his shop, turn them into good, hard steel. That's where you come in. You'll know what's worth the taking and what isn't, plus you'll know where to sell the goods and get us a fair price. You will receive your share, of course."

Raistlin was scornful. "As it happens, sir, I have frequented the shop of this Lemuel, and I can tell you right now that you are wasting your time. He has nothing of value. His entire collection is worth twenty steel at most, hardly fit payment for your trouble."

Raistlin assumed that this would end the conversation, that he had discouraged the thieves from pursuing their nefarious scheme. At all events, he would warn Lemuel to take suitable precautions.

"If you gentlemen will excuse me . . ."

Liam reached out, grabbed hold of Raistlin's wrist. Feeling the mage stiffen, Liam let go, though his strong, thin-fingered hand hovered near. He exchanged glances with his cousins, as if asking their agreement to proceed. Reluctantly both nodded.

"You are right about the shop, sir," Liam admitted. "But perhaps you are not familiar with what the mage has hidden in his cellar below the kitchen."

As far as Raistlin knew, Lemuel had nothing hidden in the cellar. "What does he have hidden?"

"Spellbooks," Liam answered.

"Lemuel once had a few spellbooks in his possession, but I know for a fact that he sold them."

"Not all of them!" Liam sunk his voice to beneath a whisper. "He has more. Many more. Ancient spellbooks from back before the Cataclysm! Spellbooks that many thought were lost to this world! That is the true prize!"

Lemuel had never mentioned such books to Raistlin. He had, in fact, pretended that Raistlin had acquired all the books in the older mage's possession. Raistlin felt betrayed.

"How do you know this?" he asked sharply.

Liam smiled unpleasantly. "You are not the only one with secrets, sir."

"Then, once more, I bid you good night."

"Oh, for the love of the Queen, tell him!" said one of the cousins in Qualinesti. "We are wasting time! Dracart wants those spellbooks delivered within the fortnight!"

"Dracart forbade us—"

"Tell him part of the truth, then,"

Liam turned back to Raistlin. "Micah visited the shop on the pretext of buying herbs. If you know this Lemuel, you know that he is stupid and naive, even by human standards. He left Micah alone in the shop while he went to his garden. Micah made a wax impression of the key to the front door."

"How do you know of the existence of the spellbooks?" Raistlin persisted.

"I tell you again, that must be our secret," Liam said, a hard and dangerous edge to his voice.

Guessing that this Dracart, whoever he was, had knowledge of the books, Raistlin tried another question, asking as innocently as he could, "And what do you intend to do with these spellbooks?"

"Sell them, of course. What possible use could they be to us?" Liam smiled. His cousins smiled. The elf's tone was persuasive, he did not blink an almond eye.

Raistlin considered. He was angered that Lemuel had lied about the existence of such valuable spellbooks. But he wanted no harm to come to the mage, for all that.

"I will not be party to murder," Raistlin said.

"Nor will we!" Liam stated emphatically. "This Lemuel has many friends in the elven lands, guest friends who would feel obligated to avenge his death. The mage is not at home. He has left to visit these friends of his in Qualinost. The house is empty. An hour's work and we will be rich men! As for you, you can either take your share in magic artifacts or we will pay you in hard steel."

Raistlin wasn't thinking of money. He wasn't thinking of the fact that the elves were lying to him, that they were undoubtedly intending to use him and then find a way to conveniently get rid of him. He was thinking of spellbooks—ancient spellbooks, perhaps spellbooks that had been stolen from the besieged Tower of High Sorcery in Daltigoth, or rescued from the drowned Tower of Istar. What wealth of magic lay within their covers? And why was Lemuel keeping them secret, hidden away?

Raistlin had the answer immediately. These must be books of black magic. That was the only logical explanation. Lemuel's father had been a war wizard of the White Robes. He could not destroy the books. By strictest law, no member of one order could willfully destroy any magical artifact or spellbook belonging to another. Magical knowledge, no matter from whence it came, who produced it, or whom it might benefit, was precious and deserved protection. But he might have been tempted to conceal those spellbooks he considered evil. By hiding such books away, he could both preserve them and keep them from falling into the hands of his enemies.

It is my duty to look into this matter, Raistlin convinced himself. Besides, if I do not go with these elves, they will only find someone else, someone who might harm the books.

Thus Raistlin rationalized, but in his heart was the undeniable longing to see these books, to hold them and feel their power. Perhaps unlock their secrets . . .

"When do you propose to do this?" Raistlin asked.

"Lemuel left town two days ago. We are pressed for time. Tonight? Are you with us?"

Raistlin nodded. "I am with you."

4

The red and silver moons shone brightly; the orbs were close this night, as if the two gods were leaning their heads together, to whisper and laugh over the follies they viewed from high above. The silver and red light shone down on the thieves. Raistlin cast two shadows as he walked along the road. The shadows stretched before him. One shadow, tinged with silver, went to his right; the other, haloed by red, to his left. He could have almost imagined diverging paths, except that, in essence, both shadows were black.

They took a roundabout way to Lemuel's house to avoid passing through town. Raistlin did not recognize the route. They were coming from a different angle, and he was startled— startled and ill at ease—to suddenly see the mage's house loom in front of him before he was expecting it. The house was the same as Raistlin remembered, held the same appearance of being abandoned that it had worn the first time he had visited Lemuel. No lights shone in the windows, nor was there a single sound of anything living within. Lemuel had been at home then. What if he were at home now?

These dark elves would have no compunction about killing him.

Micah produced the skeleton key he had made, fitted it into the lock. The other two elves kept watch. Their cloaks were cast aside, providing easy access to their weapons. They were well equipped with daggers and knives, the weapons of thieves, weapons of assassins.

Raistlin felt a deep loathing for these dark elves, a loathing that extended to himself, for he was standing in the moonlight in the dead of night alongside them, preparing to enter a man's house without his knowledge or his permission.

I should turn right now and walk away, he thought to himself.

The door opened soundlessly. Beyond, it was dark and still. Raistlin hesitated only a moment, then he slipped inside.

He could have rationalized the situation. He had come too far to back out, the dark elves would never let him escape alive. He might have continued to pretend that he was doing this for Lemuel's own good to relieve him of books which must be a burden on the mage's soul.

Now that he was here, now that he was committed, Raistlin scorned to do either. He already loathed himself for the crime that he was about to commit, he didn't intend to add to that loathing by lying about his motives. He hadn't come here out of fear or constraint, he wasn't here in the name of loyalty and friendship.

He was here for the magic.

Raistlin stood in the darkness in the mageware shop with the elves, his heart beating fast with excitement and anticipation.

"The human cannot see in the dark," Liam said in Qualinesti. "We don't want him falling over something and breaking his neck."

"At least not until we are finished with him," Micah said, with a trilling, musical laugh that accorded oddly with his dire words.

"Strike a light."

One of the elves produced quickmatch, put the match to a candle standing on the counter. The elves politely handed the candle to Raistlin, who just as politely took it.

"This way." Micah led them from the shop.

Raistlin could have supplied himself with light, magical light, but he did not mention this to the elves. He chose to save his energy. He was going to need it before this night was out.

The four left the shop, entered the kitchen, which Raistlin remembered from his first visit. They continued through the pantry, entered a door, and passed into a small storage room containing a veritable thicket of mops and brooms. Working swiftly and silently, the elves cleared these to one side.

"I see no spellbooks," Raistlin remarked.

"Of course you don't," Liam grunted, barely biting off the appellation "fool." "I told you. They are hidden in the cellar. The trapdoor is beneath that table."

The table in question was a butcher's block, used to cut meat. Made of oak, it was stained with the blood of countless animals.

Raistlin was amused to see that the sight and smell disgusted the dark elves, who were prepared to murder humans without compunction, but who looked queasy over the idea of steaks and lamb chops. Holding their breaths against what must have been to them a malodorous stench, Micah and Renet hauled the table to one side. Both hastily wiped their hands on a towel when they had finished.

"We will put back all as we have found it when we leave," Liam said. "This Lemuel is such a stupid, unobservant little man. He will likely go for years without noticing that the books have been discovered and removed."

Raistlin admitted the truth of this statement. Lemuel cared for nothing except his garden, took little interest in magic unless it pertained to his herbs. He had probably never even looked at these books, was merely obeying his father's injunction to keep them hidden.

When Raistlin took the books to the tower at Wayreth— which he fully intended to do, confessing his own sins at the time—the conclave could inform Lemuel that the books had been removed. As for what the conclave might do to Raistlin, he considered it likely that they would reprimand him for thievery, but probably nothing more severe. The conclave would not take kindly to the fact that these valuable spellbooks had been concealed all these years. Of the two crimes, they would consider concealment the greater.

Raistlin hoped their sanctions would fall on the father, if he still lived, not on the son.

Micah tugged at the handle of the trapdoor. It did not budge, and at first the elves thought it might be locked, either with bolts or magic. The elves checked for bolts, Raistlin cast a minor spell which would ascertain the presence of magic. No bolts were visible, neither was there a wizard-lock. The trapdoor was stuck tight, the wood having swelled with the damp. The elves wrenched and tugged and eventually the door popped open.

Cold air, cold and dank as the breath of a tomb, flowed up out of the darkness below. The air had a foul smell that caused the elves to wrinkle their noses and back off. Raistlin covered his mouth with the sleeve of his robe.

Micah and Renet cast furtive glances at Liam, fearful he was going to order them to walk down into that chancy darkness. Liam himself looked uneasy.

"What is that stench?" he wondered aloud. "It's like something died down there. Surely books on magic, even human books on magic, could not smell that bad."

"I am not afraid of a bad smell," Raistlin said scornfully. "I will go down to see what is amiss."

Micah was not happy at this; he took offense at Raistlin's suggestion of cowardice, though not offense enough to enter the cellar. The elves discussed the matter in their own language. Raistlin listened, diverted by their arrogance. They did not even consider the possibility that a human might be able to understand their language.

Renet concluded that Raistlin should go down alone. It was possible the spellbooks might have a guardian. Raistlin was a human and therefore expendable. Micah argued that since Raistlin was a mage, he might grab several of the spellbooks and abscond with them, traveling the corridors of magic, where the elves could not follow.

Liam had a solution to that problem. Giving gracious permission for Raistlin to enter the cellar first, the elf posted himself at the top of the stairs, armed with a bow and a nocked arrow.

"What is this?" Raistlin demanded, feigning ignorance.

"In order to protect you," Liam replied smoothly. "I am an excellent shot. And although I do not speak the language of magic, I understand a little of it. I would be able to tell, for example, if someone in that cellar were to try casting a spell that would make him disappear. I doubt if he would have time to complete the spell before my arrow struck him through the heart. But do not hesitate to call out if you find yourself in danger."

"I feel safe in your hands," Raistlin said, bowing to hide his sardonic smile.

Lifting the skirts of his robes—gray-colored robes, now that he looked at them—holding the candle high, he cautiously descended the steps that led into the darkness.

The staircase was a long one, longer than Raistlin had anticipated, leading deep under the ground. The stairs were carved of stone, a stone wall extended along on the right side, the stairs were open on his left. He shifted the candle as he walked, sending its pale light into as many portions of the cellar as it would reach, trying to catch a glimpse of something—anything. He could make out nothing. He continued his descent.

At last his foot touched dirt floor. He looked back up the stairs to see the elves small and diminished, a far distance away, almost as if they stood upon another plane of existence. He could hear their voices faintly; they were perturbed that he had passed beyond their sight. They decided that they would go down to find him.

Flashing the candle about, Raistlin tried to see as much as he could before the elves arrived. The candle's feeble light did not extend far. Expecting to hear the elves' soft footfalls, Raistlin was startled to hear a deep booming sound instead. A blast of air extinguished his candle, leaving him trapped in a darkness so deep and impenetrable that it might have been the darkness of Chaos, out of which the world was formed.

"Liam! Micah!" Raistlin called, and was alarmed when the names echoed back to him.

Nothing more than echoes. The elves did not answer.

Trying his best to hear over the rush of blood to his head, Raistlin distinguished faint sounds, as of someone pounding on a door. He gathered by this and the fact that the elves hadn't responded to his call that the trapdoor had inexplicably slammed shut, leaving him on one side and the elves on the other.

Raistlin's first panicked impulse was to use his magic for light. He stopped himself before casting the spell. He would not act on impulse. He would think the situation through calmly, as calmly as possible. He decided that it was best to remain in the darkness. Light would reveal to him whatever was down here. But light would also reveal him to whatever was down here.

Standing in the dark, he pondered the situation. The first notion that came to him was that the elves had lured him down here to leave him to his death. He abandoned this quickly. The elves had no reason to kill him. They had every reason to want to get into the cellar. They hadn't lied about the spellbooks, that much he had ascertained from their private conversations. The continued pounding on the trapdoor reassured him. The elves wanted to open that door as much as he wanted it open.

This decided, he took the precaution of moving, as quietly as he could, to put the stone wall at his back. His sight gone, he relied on his other senses, and almost immediately, now that he was calmer, he could hear breathing. Someone else's breathing. He was not alone down here.

It was not the breathing of a fearsome guardian, not the deep, harsh snufflings of an ogre, not the husky, whistling breaths of a hobgoblin. This breathing was thin and raspy, with a slight rattle. Raistlin had heard breathing like this before—in the rooms of the sick, the elderly.

Although somewhat reassuring, the sound shattered his

calculations as to what he might find down in the cellar. The first wild thought was that he was about to meet the owner of the books, Lemuel's father. Perhaps the old gentleman had chosen to retire to the cellar, to spend his life with his precious books. Either that or Lemuel had locked his father in the cellar, a feat which, considering the father was a respected archmagus, was highly unlikely.

Raistlin stood in the dark, his fear diminishing by the moment as nothing untoward happened to him, his curiosity increasing. The breathing continued, uneven, fractured, with a gasp now and again. Raistlin could hear no other sounds in the cellar, no jingle of chain mail, creak of leather, rattle of sword. Above, the elves were hard at work. By the sounds of it, they were attacking the trapdoor with an ax.

And then a voice spoke, very near him. "You're a sly one, aren't you?" A pause, then, "Clever, too, and bold. It is not every man who dares stand alone in the darkness. Come! Let's have a look at you."

A candle flared, revealing a plain wooden table, small and round. Two chairs stood opposite each other, the table in between. One of the chairs was occupied. An old man sat in the chair. One glance assured Raistlin that this old man was not Lemuel's father, the war magus who fought at the side of elves.

The old man wore black robes, against which his white hair and beard shone with an eerie aura. His face arrested attention; like a landscape, its crevices and seams gave clues to his past. Fine lines spreading from the nose to the brow might have represented wisdom in another. On him, the lines ran deep with cunning. Lines of intelligence around the hawk-black eyes tightened into cynical amusement. Contempt for his fellow beings cracked the thin lips. Ambition was in his outthrust jaw. His hooded eyes were cold and calculating and bright.

Raistlin did not stir. The old man's face was a desert of desolation, harsh and deadly and cruel. Raistlin's fear smote him full force. Far better that he should fight an ogre or hobgoblin. The words to the simple defensive spell that had been on Raistlin's lips slipped away in a sigh. He imagined himself casting it, could almost hear the old man's mocking, derisive laughter. Those old hands, large-knuckled, large-boned, and grasping, were empty now, but those hands had once wielded enormous power.

The old man understood Raistlin's thoughts as if he'd spoken them aloud. The eyes gazed in Raistlin's direction, though he stood shrouded in the darkness.

"Come, Sly One. You who have swallowed my bait. Come and sit and talk with an old man."

Still Raistlin did not move. The words about bait had shaken him.

"You really might as well come sit down." The old man smiled, a smile that twisted the lines in his face, sharpening mockery into cruelty. "You're not going anywhere until I say you may go." Lifting a knotted finger, he pointed it straight at Raistlin's heart. "You came to me. Remember that."

Raistlin considered his options: He could either remain standing in the darkness, which was obviously not offering him much protection, since the old man seemed to see him clearly. He could make a desperate attempt to escape back up the steps, which would probably be futile and make him look foolish, or he could grasp his courage and assert what dignity remained, confront the old man, and find out what he meant by his strange references to bait.

Raistlin walked forward. Emerging out of the darkness into the candle's yellow light, he took a seat opposite the old man.

The old man studied Raistlin in the light, did not appear particularly pleased with what he saw.

"You're a weakling! A sniveling weakling! I've more strength in my body than I see in yours, and my body is nothing but ashes and dust! What good will you do me? This is just my luck! Expecting an eagle, I am given a sparrow hawk. Still"—the old man's mutterings were only barely audible—"there is hunger in those eyes. If the body is frail, perhaps that is because it feeds the mind. The mind itself is desperate for nourishment, that much I can tell. Perhaps I judged hastily. We will see. What is your name?"

Raistlin had been clever and glib with the dark elves. In the company of this daunting old man, the young one answered meekly, "I am Raistlin Majere, Archmagus."

"Archmagus . . ." The old man lingered over the word, tasting it in his mouth. "I was once, you know. The greatest of them all. Even now they fear me. But they don't fear me enough. How old are you?"

"I have just turned twenty-one."

"Young, young to take the Test. I am surprised at Par-Salian. The man is desperate, that much is apparent. And how do you think you've done thus far, Raistlin Majere?" The old man's eyes crinkled, his smile was the ugliest thing Raistlin had ever seen.

"I'm sorry, sir, I don't know what you're talking about. What do you mean, how have I done? Done—"

Raistlin caught his breath. He had the sensation of rousing from a dream, one of those dreams that are more real than waking reality. Except that he had not dreamed this.

He was taking the Test. This was the Test. The elves, the inn, the events, the situations were all contrived. He stared at the candle flame and thought back frantically, wondering, as the old man had asked, how he had done.

The old man laughed, a chuckle that was like water gurgling beneath the ice. "I never tire of that reaction! It happens every time. One of the few pleasures I have left. Yes, you are taking the Test, young magus. You are right in the middle of it. And, no, I am not part of it. Or rather I am, but not an officially sanctioned part."

"You mentioned bait. 'I came to you,' that was what you said." Raistlin kept fast hold of his courage, clenching his hands so that no shiver or tremor should betray his fear.

The old man nodded. "By your own choices and decisions, yes, you came to me."

"I don't understand," Raistlin said.

The old man helpfully explained. "Some mages would have heeded the tinker's warning, never entered such a disreputable inn. Others, if they had entered, would have refused to have anything to do with dark elves. You went to the inn. You spoke to the elves. You fell in with their dishonest scheme quite readily." The old man again raised the knotted finger. "Even though you considered the man you were about to rob a friend."

"What you say is true." Raistlin saw no point in denying it. Nor was he particularly ashamed of his actions. In his mind, any mage, with the possible exception of the most bleached White Robe, would have done the same. "I wanted to save the spellbooks. I would have returned them to the conclave."

He was silent a moment, then said, "There are no spellbooks, are there?"

"No," replied the old man, "there is only me."

"And who are you?" Raistlin asked.

"My name is not important. Not yet."

"Well, then, what do you want of me?"

The old man made a deprecating gesture with the gnarled and knotted hand. "A little favor, nothing more."

Now it was Raistlin who smiled, and his smile was bitter. "Excuse me, sir, but you must be aware that since I am taking the Test, I am of very low ranking. You appear to be—or have been—a wizard of immense skill and power. I have nothing that you could possibly want."

"Ah, but you do!" The old man's eyes gleamed with a hungry, devouring light, a flame that made the candle's flame dim and feeble by contrast. "You live!"

"For the time being," Raistlin said dryly. "Perhaps not much longer. The dark elves will not believe me when I tell them there are no ancient spellbooks down here. They will think that I have magically spirited them away for my own use." He glanced around. "I don't suppose there is any way to escape from this cellar."

"There is a way—my way," said the old man. "My way is the only way. You are quite right, the dark elves will kill you. They're not thieves as they pretend, you know. They are high-ranking wizards. Their magic is exceptionally powerful."

Raistlin should have recognized that at once.

"Not giving up, are you?" the old man asked with a sneer.

"I am not." Raistlin lifted his head, gazed steadily at the old man. "I was thinking."

"Think away, young magus. You're going to have to think hard to overcome three-to-one odds. Make that twelve-to-one, since each dark elf is four times as powerful as yourself."

"This is the Test," Raistlin said. "It is all illusion. Admittedly some magi die taking the Test, but that is through their own failure or inadvertence. I have done nothing wrong. Why should the conclave kill me?"

"You have talked to me," the old man said softly. "They are aware of that, and that may well prove your downfall."

"Who are you, then," Raistlin asked impatiently, "that they fear you so?"

"My name is Fistandantilus. Perhaps you've heard of me."

"Yes," said Raistlin.

Long ago, in the turbulent and desperate years following the Cataclysm, an army of hill dwarves and humans laid siege to Thorbardin, the great underground city of the mountain dwarves. Leading this army, instrumental in its formation, intending to use the army to achieve his own driving ambition, was a wizard of the Black Robes, a wizard of immense power, a renegade wizard openly defying the conclave. His name was Fistandantilus.

He built a magical fortress known as Zhaman and from there launched his attack against the dwarven stronghold.

Fistandantilus fought the dwarves with his magic, his armies fought with ax and sword. Many thousands died on the plains or in the mountain passes, but the wizard's army faltered. And the dwarves of Thorbardin claimed victory.

According to the minstrels, Fistandantilus plotted one last spell, a spell of catastrophic power that would split the mountain, lay Thorbardin open to conquest. Unfortunately the spell was too powerful. Fistandantilus could not control it. The spell shattered the fortress of Zhaman. It collapsed in upon itself and was now known as Skullcap. Thousands of his own army died in the blast, including the wizard who had cast it.

That is what the minstrels sang, and that is what most people believed. Raistlin had always imagined there was more to the story than that. Fistandantilus had gained his power over hundreds of years. He was not elven, but human. He had, so it was rumored, found a way to cheat death. He extended his life by murdering his young apprentices, drawing out their life-force by means of a magical bloodstone. He had not been able to survive the shattering effects of his own magic, however. At least, that's what the world supposed. Evidently Fistandantilus had once again cheated death. Yet he would not do so for long.

"Fistandantilus—the greatest of all magi," Raistlin said. "The most powerful wizard who has ever lived."

"I am," said Fistandantilus.

"And you are dying," Raistlin observed.

The old man did not like this. His brows contracted, the lines of his face drew together in a dagger point of anger, his outrage bubbled beneath the surface. But every breath was a struggle. He was expending an enormous amount of magical energy merely to hold this form together. The fury ceased to boil, a pot under which the fire was put out.

"You speak the truth. I am dying," he muttered, frustrated, impotent. "I am nearly finished. They tell you that my goal was to take over Thorbardin." He smiled disdainfully. "What rot! I played for far greater stakes than the acquisition of some stinking, filthy dwarven hole in the ground. My plan was to enter the Abyss. To overthrow the Dark Queen, remove Takhisis from her throne. I sought godhood!"

Raistlin was awed listening to this, awed and amazed. Awed, amazed, and sympathetic.

"Beneath Skullcap is . . . or shall we say was, for it is gone now"—Fistandantilus paused, looked extremely cunning—"a means of entering the Abyss, that cruel netherworld. Takhisis was aware of me. She feared me and plotted my downfall. True my body died in the blast, but I had already planned my soul' retreat on another plane of existence. Takhisis could not slay me for she could not reach me, but she never ceases to try. I ar under constant assault and have been for centuries. I have littl energy left. The life-force I carried with me is almost gone."

"And so you contrive to enter the Test and lure young mage like me into your web," said Raistlin. "I would guess that I ar not the first. What has happened to those who came before me?"

Fistandantilus shrugged. "They died. I told you. They spok to me. The conclave fears that I will enter into the body of young mage, take him over and so return to the world to com plete what I began. They cannot allow that, and so each tim they see to it that the threat is eliminated."

Raistlin gazed steadily at the old man, the dying old man. ' don't believe you. The mages died, but it was not the conclav who killed them. It was you. That is how you've managed t live for so long—if you call it living."

"Call it what you will, it is preferable to the great nothing ness I see reaching out for me," Fistandantilus said with hideous grin. "The same nothingness that is reaching out fo you, young mage."

"I have little choice, it seems," Raistlin replied bitterly. "E ther I die at the hands of three wizards or I am to be sucked dr by a lich."

"It was your decision to come down here," Fistandantilu replied.

Raistlin lowered his gaze, refused to allow the old man' probing hawk eyes to gain admittance to his soul. He stared the wooden table and was reminded of the table in his master' laboratory, the table on which the child Raistlin had written, s triumphantly, *I, Magus.* He considered the odds he faced thought about the dark elves, wondered at their magic, won dered if what the old man had said about them was true or if was all lies, lies intended to trap him. He wondered about hi own ability to survive, wondered if the conclave would kill hir simply because he had spoken to Fistandantilus.

Raistlin lifted his gaze, met the hawk eyes. "I accept you offer."

Fistandantilus's thin lips parted in a smile that was like th grin of a skull. "I thought you might. Show me your spellbook.

5

aistlin stood at the bottom of the cellar stairs, waiting for the old man to release the trapdoor from the enchantment that held it shut. He wondered that he felt no fear, only the razor-edged pain of anticipation.

The elves had halted their assault on the cellar doors; they had figured out that magic held them. He allowed himself the hope that perhaps they had gone. The next moment he laughed at himself for his foolishness. This was his Test. He would be required to prove his ability to use magic in battle.

Now! came a voice in Raistlin's head.

Fistandantilus had disappeared. The physical form the old man had taken had been illusory, conjured up for Raistlin's benefit. Now that the form was no longer required, the old man had abandoned it.

The cellar doors swung violently open, falling with a resounding boom on the stone-flagoned floor.

Raistlin trusted that the elves would be caught off guard by the sudden opening of the door. He planned to use these few moments of confusion to launch his own attack.

To his dismay, he discovered that the dark elves had been prepared for just such an occurrence. They were waiting for him.

An elven voice spoke the language of magic. Light blazed, a globe of fire illuminated Liam's face. The instant the door flew open, the flaming ball, trailing sparks like the blazing tail of a comet, hurtled through the air.

Raistlin was not prepared for this attack; he had not imagined the dark elves would react so quickly. There was no escape. The flaming ball would fill the room with fiery death. Instinctively he flung his left arm up to protect his face, knowing all the while there could be no protection.

The fireball burst on him, over him, around him. It burst harmlessly, its effects dissipated, showering him with sparks and globs of flame that struck his hands and his astonished face and then vanished in a sizzle, as if they were falling into standing water.

"Your spell! Quickly!" came the command.

Raistlin had already recovered from his startlement and his fear; the spell came immediately to his lips. His hand performed the motions, tracing the symbol of a sun in the air. Sparks from the fireball still glimmered on the cellar floor at his feet. He noticed, as he moved his hand, that his skin had a golden cast to it, but he did not let himself do more than remark upon this as a curiosity. He dared not lose his concentration.

Symbol drawn, he spoke the words of magic. The symbol flashed brightly in the air; he had spoken the words correctly, accurately. From the fingers of his outstretched right hand streaked five small flaming projectiles, a puny response to the deadly weapons of the powerful archmages.

Raistlin was not surprised to hear the dark elves laughing at him. He might as well have been tossing gnome crackers at them.

He waited, holding his breath, praying that the old man kept his promise, praying to the gods of magic to see to it that the old man kept his promise. Raistlin had the satisfaction, the deep abiding satisfaction, of hearing elven laughter sucked away by indrawn breaths of astonishment and alarm.

The five streaks of flame were now ten, now twenty. No longer smidgens of flame, they were crackling, sparkling white-hot stars, stars shooting up the stairs, shooting with unerring accuracy for Raistlin's three foes.

Now it was the dark elves who had no escape, no defensive spells powerful enough to protect them. The deadly stars struck with a concussive force that knocked Raistlin off his feet, and he was standing some distance from the center of the blast. He felt the heat of the flames all the way down the cellar steps. He smelled burning flesh. There were no screams. There had not been time for screams.

Raistlin picked himself up. He wiped dirt from his hands, noting once more the peculiar golden color of his skin. The realization came to him that this golden patina had protected him from the fireball. It was like a knight's armor, only much more effective than armor; a plate and chain-mail clad knight would have fried to death if that fiery ball had struck him, whereas Raistlin had suffered no ill effects.

"And if that is true," he said to himself, "if this is armor or a shield of some magical type, then it could aid me considerably in the future."

The storage room was ablaze. Raistlin waited until the worst of the flames had died down, taking his time, recovering his strength, bringing his next spell to mind. Holding the sleeve of his robe over his nose against the stench of charred elf, Raistlin mounted the stairs, prepared to face his next foe.

Two bodies lay at the top of the cellar stairs, black lumps burned beyond recognition. A third body was not visible, perhaps it had been vaporized. Of course, this is all illusion, Raistlin reminded himself. Perhaps the conclave had simply miscounted.

Emerging from the cellar, he gathered up the skirt of his robes, stepped over the body of one of the elves. He cast a swift glance around the storage room. The table was a pile of ash, the mops and brooms were wisps of smoke. The image of Fistandantilus hovered amidst the ruins. His illusory form was thin and translucent, almost indistinguishable from the smoke. A good stiff puff of breath could blow him away.

Raistlin smiled.

The old man stretched out his arm. It was cloaked in black. The hand was shriveled, wasted, the fingers little more than bare bones.

"I will take my payment now," said Fistandantilus.

His hand reached for Raistlin's heart.

Raistlin took a step backward. He raised his own hand protectively, palm out. "I thank you for your assistance, Archmagus, but I rescind my part of the bargain."

"What did you say?"

The words, sibilant, lethal, coiled around inside Raistlin's brain like a viper in a basket. The viper's head lifted; eyes, cruel, malignant, merciless, stared at him.

Raistlin's resolve shook, his heart quailed. The old man's rage crackled around him with flames more fierce than those of the fireball.

I killed the elves, Raistlin reminded himself, seizing hold of his fast-fleeing courage. The spell belonged to Fistandantilus, but the magic, the power behind the spell, was my own. He is weak, drained; he is not a threat.

"Our bargain is rescinded," Raistlin repeated. "Return to the plane from which you've come and there wait for your next victim."

"You break your promise!" Fistandantilus snarled. "What honor is this?"

"Am I a Solamnic knight, to concern myself with honor?" Raistlin asked, adding, "If it comes to that, what honor is there in luring flies to your web, where you entangle and devour them? If I am not mistaken, your own spell protects me from any magic you may try to cast. This time the fly escapes you."

Raistlin bowed to the shadowy image of the old man. Deliberately he turned his back, began to walk toward the door. If he could make it to the door, escape this charnel room, this room of death, he would be safe. The way was not far, and though part of him kept expecting to feel the touch of that dread hand, his confidence grew with each step he took nearer the exit.

He reached the doorway.

When the old man's voice spoke, it seemed to come from a great distance away. Raistlin could barely hear it.

"You are strong and you are clever. You are protected by armor of your own making, not mine. Yet your Test is not concluded. More struggles await you. If your armor is made of steel, true and fine, then you will survive. If your armor is made of dross, it will crack at the first blow, and when that happens, I will slip inside and take what is mine."

A voice could not harm him. Raistlin paid no heed to it. He continued walking, reached the door, and the voice drifted away like the smoke in the air.

6

Raistlin walked through the doorway of Lemuel's storage room and stepped into a dark corridor made of stone. At first he was startled, taken aback. He should have been standing inside Lemuel's kitchen. Then he recalled Lemuel's house had never truly existed except in his mind and the minds of those who had conjured it.

Light gleamed on the wall near him. A sconce in the shape of a silver hand held a globe of white light, akin to the light of Solinari. Next to that, a hand made of brass held a globe of red light, and beside that hand, a hand of carven ebony held nothing—in Raistlin's eyes, at least. Those mages dedicated to Nuitari would see their way clearly.

Raistlin deduced from these lights that he was back in the Tower of Wayreth, walking one of the many corridors of that magical building. Fistandantilus had lied. Raistlin's Test was over. He had only to find his way back to the Hall of Mages, there to receive congratulations.

A breath of air touched the back of his neck. Raistlin started to turn. Burning pain and the nerve-jarring sensation of metal scraping against bone, his own bone, caused his body to jerk with agony.

"This is for Micah and Renet!" hissed Liam's vicious voice.

Liam's arm, thin, strong, tried to encircle Raistlin's neck. A blade flashed.

The elf had intended his first blow to be his last. He had tried to sever Raistlin's spinal cord. That breath of air on his neck had been enough to alert Raistlin. When he turned, the blade missed its mark, slid along his ribs. Liam was going to make another try, this time going for the throat.

Raistlin's panic-stripped mind could not come up with the

words of a spell. He had no weapon other than his magic. He was reduced to fighting like an animal, with tooth and claw. His fear was his most powerful tool, if he did not let it debilitate him. He remembered vaguely watching Sturm and his brother in hand-to-hand combat.

Clasping his hands together, Raistlin drove his right elbow with all the force his adrenaline-pumping body could manage into Liam's midriff.

The dark elf grunted and fell back. But he was not injured, just short of breath. He leapt back to the fight, his knife slashing.

Frantic and terrified, Raistlin grabbed hold of his attacker's knife hand. The two grappled, Liam trying to stab Raistlin, Raistlin struggling to wrench the knife from the dark elf's grip.

They lurched about the narrow corridor. Raistlin's strength was ebbing fast. He could not hope to keep up this deadly contest for long. Staking his hopes on one desperate move, Raistlin concentrated his remaining energy, smashed the elf's hand—the hand holding the knife—against the stone.

Bones cracked, the elf gasped in pain, but he clung tenaciously to his weapon.

Panic seized hold. Again and again Raistlin struck Liam's hand against the hard stone. The knife's handle was slippery with blood. Liam could not hold on to it. The knife slipped from his grip and fell to the floor.

Liam made a lunge to try to recover his weapon. He lost it in the shadows, apparently, for he was down on all fours, frantically searching the floor.

Raistlin saw the knife. The blade burned with red fire in Lunitari's bright light. The elf saw it at the same time, made a lunge for it. Snatching the knife from beneath the elf's grasping fingers, Raistlin drove the blade into Liam's stomach.

The dark elf screamed, doubled over.

Raistlin yanked the blade free. Liam tumbled to his knees, his hand pressed over his stomach. Blood poured from his mouth. He pitched forward, dead, at Raistlin's feet.

Gasping, each breath causing him wrenching agony, Raistlin started to turn, to flee. He could not make his legs work properly and collapsed to the stone floor. A burning sensation spread from the knife wound throughout his nerve endings. He was nauseated, sick.

Liam would have his revenge after all, Raistlin realized in bitter despair. The dark elf's knife blade had been tipped with poison.

The lights of Solinari and Lunitari wavered in his sight, blurred together, and then darkness overtook him.

* * * * *

Raistlin woke to find himself lying in the same corridor. Liam's body was still there, beside him, the elf's dead hand touching him. The body was still warm. Raistlin had not been unconscious long.

He dragged himself away from the dead body of the dark elf. Wounded and weak, he crawled into a shadowy corridor and slumped against a wall. Pain coiled around his bowels. Clutching his stomach, he retched and heaved. When the vomiting subsided, he lay back on the stone floor and waited to die.

"Why are you doing this to me?" he demanded through a haze of sickness.

He knew the answer. Because he had dared to bargain with a wizard so powerful that he had once thought of overthrowing Takhisis, a wizard so powerful that the conclave feared his power even after he was dead.

If your armor is made of dross, it will crack at the first blow, and when that happens, I will slip inside and take what is mine.

Raistlin almost laughed. "What little life I have left, you are welcome to, archmagus!"

He lay on the floor, his cheek pressed against the stone. Did he want to survive? The Test had taken a terrible toll, one from which he might never recover. His health had always been precarious. If he survived, his body would be like a shattered crystal, held together by the force of his own will. How would he live? Who would take care of him?

Caramon. Caramon would care for his weak twin.

Raistlin stared into Lunitari's red, flickering light. He couldn't imagine such a life, a life of dependency on his brother. Death was preferable.

A figure materialized out of the shadowy darkness of the corridor, a figure illuminated by Solinari's white light.

"This is it," Raistlin said to himself. "This is my final test. The one I won't survive."

He felt almost grateful to the wizards for ending his suffering. He lay helpless, watching the dark shadow as it drew closer and closer. It came to stand next to him. He could sense its living presence, hear its breathing. It bent over him. Involuntarily, he closed his eyes.

"Raist?"

Gentle fingers touched his feverish flesh.

"Raist!" The voice sobbed. "What have they done to you?"

"Caramon," Raistlin spoke, but he couldn't hear his own words. His throat was raw from the smoke, the retching.

"I'm taking you out of here," his brother said.

Strong arms slipped under Raistlin's body. He smelled Caramon's familiar smell of sweat and leather, heard the familiar sound of creaking armor, his broadsword clanking against the stone.

"No!" Raistlin tried to free himself. He pushed against his brother's massive chest with his frail, fragile hand. "Leave me, Caramon! My Test is not finished! Leave me!" His voice was an intelligible croak. He gagged, coughed.

Caramon lifted his brother, cradled him in his arms. "Nothing is worth this, Raist. Rest easy."

They walked beneath the silver hand, holding the white light. Raistlin saw tears, wet and glistening, on his brother's cheeks. He made one last attempt.

"They won't permit me to leave, Caramon!" He fought for breath enough to speak. "They'll try to stop us. You're only putting yourself in danger."

"Let them come," Caramon said grimly. He walked with firm, unhurried steps down the corridor.

Raistlin sank back, helpless, his head resting on Caramon's shoulder. For an instant, he allowed himself to feel comforted by his brother's strength. The next moment he cursed his weakness, cursed his twin.

"You fool!" Raistlin said silently, lacking the strength to speak the words aloud. "You great, stubborn fool! Now we'll both die. And, of course, you will die protecting me. Even in death, I will be indebted to you. . . ."

"Ah!"

Raistlin heard and felt the sharp intake of breath into his brother's body. Caramon's pace slowed. Raistlin raised his head.

At the end of the corridor floated the disembodied head of an old man. Raistlin heard whispered words.

If your armor is made of dross . . .

"Mmmmm . . ." Caramon rumbled deeply in his chest—his battle cry.

"My magic can destroy it!" Raistlin protested as Caramon laid his brother gently on the stone floor. That was a lie. Raistlin did not have energy enough to pull a rabbit from a hat. But he'd be damned if Caramon was going to fight his battles, especially against the old man. Raistlin had made the bargain, he had been the one to benefit, he must pay.

"Get out of my way, Caramon!"

Caramon did not respond. He walked toward Fistandantilus, blocked Raistlin's view.

Raistlin put his hands to the wall. Propping his body against the stone, he pushed himself to a standing position. He was about to expend his strength in one last shout, hoping to warn off his brother. Raistlin's shout was never uttered. His warning died in a rattle of disbelief.

Caramon had dropped his weapons. Now, in place of his sword, he held a rod of amber. In the other hand, his shield hand, he clasped a bit of fur. He rubbed the two together, spoke the magic. Lightning streaked from the amber, sizzled down the corridor, struck the head of Fistandantilus.

The head laughed and hurtled straight at Caramon. He did not blench, but kept his hands raised. He spoke the magic again. Another bolt flashed.

The old man's head exploded in blue fire. A thin cry of thwarted anger screamed from some far distant plane, but it died away to nothing.

The corridor was empty.

"Now we'll get out of here," Caramon said with satisfaction. He tucked the rod and the fur into a pouch he wore at his belt. "The door is just ahead."

"How—how did you do that?" Raistlin gasped, sagging against the wall.

Caramon stopped, alarmed by his brother's wild, frenzied stare.

"Do what, Raist?"

"The magic!" Raistlin cried in fury. "The magic!"

"Oh, that." Caramon shrugged, gave a shy, deprecating smile. "I've always been able to." He grew solemn, stern. "Most of the time I don't need the magic, what with my sword and all, but you're hurt really bad, and I didn't want to take the time fighting that lich. Don't worry about it, Raist. Magic can still be your little specialty. Like I said, most of the time I don't need it."

"This is not possible," Raistlin said to himself, struggling to think clearly. "Caramon could not have acquired in moments what it took me years of study to attain. This doesn't make sense! Something's not right. . . . Think, damn it! Think!"

It wasn't the physical pain that clouded his mind. It was the old inner pain clawing at him, tearing at him with poisoned talons. Caramon, strong and cheerful, good and kind, open and honest. Caramon, everyone's friend.

Not like Raistlin—the runt, the Sly One.

"All I ever had was my magic," Raistlin said, speaking clearly, thinking clearly for the first time in his life. "And now you have that, too."

Using the wall for support, Raistlin raised both his hands, put his thumbs together. He began speaking the words, the words that would summon the magic.

"Raist!" Caramon started to back away. "Raist, what are you doing? C'mon! You need me! I'll take care of you—just like always. Raist! I'm your brother!"

"I have no brother!"

Beneath the layer of cold, hard rock, jealousy bubbled and seethed. Tremors split the rock. Jealousy, red and molten, coursed through Raistlin's body and flamed out of his hands. The fire flared, billowed, and engulfed Caramon.

Caramon screamed, tried to beat out the flames, but there was no escaping the magic. His body withered, dwindled in the fire, became the body of a wizened old man. An old man wearing black robes, whose hair and beard were trailing wisps of fire.

Fistandantilus, his hand outstretched, walked toward Raistlin.

"If your armor is dross," said the old man softly. "I will find the crack."

Raistlin could not move, could not defend himself. The magic had sapped the last of his strength.

Fistandantilus stood before Raistlin. The old man's black robes were tattered shreds of night, his flesh was rotting and decayed, the bones were visible through the skin. His nails were long and pointed, as long as those of a corpse, his eyes gleamed with the radiant heat that had been in Raistlin's soul, the warmth that had brought the dead to life. A bloodstone hung from a pendant around the fleshless neck.

The old man's hand touched Raistlin's breast, caressed his flesh, teasing and tormenting. Fistandantilus plunged his hand into Raistlin's chest and seized hold of his heart.

The dying soldier clasps his hands around the haft of the spear that has torn through his body. Raistlin seized hold of the old man's wrist, clamped his fingers around it in a grip that death would not have relaxed.

Caught, trapped, Fistandantilus fought to break Raistlin's grip, but he could not free himself and retain his hold on the young man's heart.

The white light of Solinari, the red light of Lunitari, and the black, empty light of Nuitari—light that Raistlin could now see—merged in his fainting vision, stared down at him, an unwinking eye.

"You may take my life," Raistlin said, keeping fast hold of the old man's wrist, as Fistandantilus kept hold of young man's heart. "But you will serve me in return."

The eye winked, and blinked out.

7

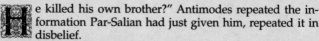 e killed his own brother?" Antimodes repeated the information Par-Salian had just given him, repeated it in disbelief.

Antimodes had not been involved in Raistlin's Test. Neither teacher nor mentor of an initiate is allowed to participate. Antimodes had handled the testing of several of the other young magi. Most had gone quite well, all had passed, though none had been as dramatic as Raistlin's. Antimodes had been sorry he missed it. He had been until he heard this. Now he was shocked and deeply disturbed.

"And the young man was given the Red Robes? My friend, are you in your right mind? I cannot conceive of an act more evil!"

"He killed an illusion of his brother," Par-Salian emphasized. "You have siblings of your own, I believe?" he asked, with a meaningful smile.

"I know what you're saying, and, yes, there have been times I would have been glad to see my brother engulfed in flames, but the thought is a long way from the deed. Did Raistlin know it was an illusion?"

"When I asked him that question," Par-Salian replied, "he looked straight at me and said in a tone that I shall never forget, 'Does it matter?' "

"Poor young man," Antimodes said, sighing. "Poor young men, I should say, since the other twin was a witness to his own fratricide. Was that truly necessary?"

"I deemed it so. Odd as it may seem, though he is the stronger of the two physically, Caramon is far more dependent on his brother than Raistlin is on him. By this demonstration, I had hoped to sever that unhealthy connection, to convince

Caramon that he needs to build a life of his own. But I fear that my plan did not succeed. Caramon has fully exonerated his brother. Raistlin was ill, not in his right mind, not to be held responsible for his own actions. And now, to complicate matters, Raistlin is more dependent upon his brother than ever."

"How is the young man's health?"

"Not good. He will live, but only because his spirit is strong, stronger than his body."

"So there was a meeting between Raistlin and Fistandantilus. And Raistlin agreed to the bargain. He has given his life's energy to feed that foul lich!"

"There was a meeting and a bargain," Par-Salian reiterated cautiously. "But I believe that this time Fistandantilus may have got more than he bargained for."

"Raistlin remembers nothing?"

"Nothing whatsoever. Fistandantilus has seen to that. I do not believe that he wants the young man to remember. Raistlin may have agreed to the bargain, but he did not die, as did the others. Something kept him alive and defiant. If Raistlin ever does remember, I think it is Fistandantilus who might be in considerable danger."

"What does the young man believe happened to him?"

"The Test itself shattered his health, left him with a weakness in his heart and lungs that will plague him the remainder of his life. He attributes that to the battle with the dark elf. I did not disabuse him of the notion. Were I to tell him the truth, he would not believe me."

"Do you suppose he will ever come to know the truth?"

"Only if and when he comes to know the truth about himself," Par-Salian answered. "He has to confront and admit the darkness within. I have given him the eyes to see with, if he will: the hourglass eyes of the sorceress Raelana. Thus he will view time's passing in all he looks upon. Youth withers before those eyes, beauty fades, mountains crumble to dust."

"And what do you hope to accomplish by this torture?" Antimodes demanded angrily. He truly thought the head of the conclave had gone too far.

"To pierce his arrogance. To teach him patience. And as I said, to give him the ability to see inside himself, should he turn his gaze inward. There will be little joy in his life," Par-Salian admitted, adding, "but then I foresee little joy for anyone in Ansalon. I did compensate for what you deem my cruelty, however."

"I never said—"

"You didn't need to, my friend. I know how you feel. I have given Raistlin the Staff of Magius, one of our most powerful artifacts. Though it will be a long time before he knows its true power."

Antimodes was bitter, refusing to be mollified. "And now you have your sword."

"The metal withstood the fire," Par-Salian replied gravely, "and came out tempered and true, with a fine cutting edge. Now the young man must practice, he must hone the skills he will need in the future and learn new ones."

"None of the conclave will apprentice him, not if they think he is somehow tied to Fistandantilus. Not even the Black Robes. They would not trust him. How, then, will he learn?"

"I believe he will find a master. A lady has taken an interest in him, a very great interest."

"Not Ladonna?" Antimodes frowned.

"No, no. Another lady, far greater and more powerful." Par-Salian cast a glance out the window, where the red moon shone with a ruby's glittering brilliance.

"Ah, indeed?" Antimodes said, impressed. "Well, if that's the case, I suppose I need not worry about him. Still, he's very young and very frail, and we don't have much time."

"As you said, it will be some years before the Dark Queen can muster her forces, before she is prepared to launch her attack."

"Yet already the clouds of war gather," Antimodes remarked ominously. "We stand alone in the last rays of the setting sun. And I ask again, where are the true gods now that we need them?"

"Where they have always been," Par-Salian replied complacently.

8

Raistlin sat in a chair before a desk in the Tower of High Sorcery. He had been a resident of the tower for several days, Par-Salian having given the young man permission to remain in the tower for as long as he deemed necessary to recover from the effects of the Test.

Not that Raistlin would ever truly recover. He had never before been physically strong or healthy, but in comparison to what he was today, he looked back upon his former self with envy. He spent a moment recalling the days of his youth, realized regretfully that he had never fully appreciated them, never fully appreciated his energy and vigor. But would he go back? Would he trade his shattered body for a whole one?

Raistlin's hand touched the wood of the Staff of Magius, which stood at his side, was never far from his side. The wood was smooth and warm, the enchantment within the staff tingled through his fingers, an exhilarating sensation. He had only the vaguest idea what magic the staff could perform. It was requisite that any mage coming into possession of a magical artifact search out such power himself. But he was aware of the staff's immense magical power, and he reveled in it.

Not much information on the staff existed in the tower; many of the old manuscripts concerning Magius, which had been kept in the Tower of Palanthas, had been lost when the magi evacuated to the tower at Wayreth. The staff itself had been retained, as being of far more value, though it had—according to Par-Salian—remained unused all these centuries.

The time had not been right for the staff's return to the world, Par-Salian had said evasively in answer to Raistlin's question. Until now the staff had not been needed. Raistlin wondered what made the time right now, right for a staff that had purportedly been used to help fight dragons. He was not likely to find out. Par-Salian kept his own counsel. He would tell Raistlin nothing about the staff, beyond where to find the books that might provide him with knowledge.

One of those books was before him now, a smallish quarto written by some scribe attached to Huma's retinue. The book was more frustrating than helpful. Raistlin learned a great deal about manning battlements and posting guards, information that would be useful to a war mage, but very little about the staff. What he had learned had been inadvertent. The scribe, writing an account of Magius, described the mage leaping from the topmost tower of the besieged castle to land unharmed among us, much to our great astonishment and wonder. He claimed to have used the magic of his staff. . . .

Raistlin wrote in his own small volume: *It appears that the staff has the ability to allow its owner to float through the air as lightly as a feather. Is this spell inherent in the staff? Must magical words be recited in order to activate this spell? Is there a limit to its usage? Will the spell work for anyone other than the magus who is in possession of the staff?*

All these were questions that must be answered, and that was just for one of the staff's enchantments. Raistlin guessed there must be many more bound within the wood. In one sense, it was frustrating not to know. He would have liked to have had them delineated. Yet if the nature of the staff's powers had been presented to him, he still would have pursued his studies. The old manuscripts might be lying. They might be deliberately withholding information. He trusted no one but himself.

His studies might take him years, but . . .

A spasm of coughing interrupted his work. The cough was painful, debilitating, frightening. His windpipe closed, he could not breathe, and when the paroxysms were very bad, he had the terrible feeling that he would never be able to breathe again, that he would suffocate and die.

This was one of the bad ones. He fought, struggled to breathe. He grew faint and dizzy from lack of air, and when at last he was able to draw a breath with a certain amount of ease, he was so exhausted from the effort that he was forced to rest his head on his arms on the table. He lay there, almost sobbing. His injured ribs hurt him cruelly, his diaphragm burned from coughing.

A gentle hand touched his shoulder.

"Raist? Are . . . are you all right?"

Raistlin sat upright, thrust aside his brother's hand.

"What a stupid question! Even for you. Of course I am not all right, Caramon!" Raistlin dabbed at his lips with a handkerchief, drew it back stained with blood. He swiftly concealed the handkerchief in a secret pocket of his new red robes.

"Is there anything I can do to help?" Caramon asked, patiently ignoring his brother's ill humor.

"You can leave me alone and quit interrupting my work!" Raistlin returned. "Are you packed? We leave within the hour, you know."

"If you're sure you're well enough . . ." Caramon began. Catching his brother's irritated and baleful gaze, he bit his tongue. "I'll . . . go pack," he said, though he was already packed and had been for the past three hours.

Caramon started to leave, tiptoeing out of the room. He fondly imagined that he was being extremely quiet. In reality, with his rattling, jingling, clanking, and creaking, he made more noise than a legion of mountain dwarves on parade.

Reaching into the pocket, Raistlin drew forth the handkerchief, wet with his own blood. He gazed at it for a dark, brooding moment.

"Caramon," he called.

"Yes, Raist?" Caramon turned around, pathetically anxious. "Is there something I can do for you?"

They would have many years together, years of working together, living together, eating together, fighting together. Caramon had seen his twin kill him. Raistlin had seen himself kill.

Hammer blows. One after the other.

Raistlin sighed deeply. "Yes, my brother. There is something you can do for me. Par-Salian gave me a recipe for a tisane that he believes will help ease my cough. You will find the recipe and the ingredients in my pouch, there on the chair. If you could mix it for me . . ."

"I will, Raist!" Caramon said excitedly. He couldn't have looked more pleased if his twin had bestowed a wealth of jewels and steel coins upon him. "I haven't noticed a teakettle, but I'm sure there must be one around here somewhere. . . . Oh, here it is. I guess I didn't see it before. You keep working. I'll just measure out these leaves. . . . Whew! This smells awful! Are you sure? . . . Never mind," Caramon amended hurriedly. "I'll make the tea. Maybe it'll taste better than it smells."

He put on the kettle, then bent over the teapot, mixing and

measuring the leaves with as much care as a gnome would take on a Life Quest.

Raistlin returned to his reading.

Magius struck the ogre on the head with his staff. I charged in to save him, for ogre's are notoriously thick-skulled, and I could not see that the wizard's walking staff would inflict much damage. To my surprise, however, the ogre keeled over dead, as if it had been struck by a thunderbolt.

Raistlin carefully noted the occurrence, writing: *The staff apparently increases the force of a blow.*

"Raist," said Caramon, turning from watching for the teapot to boil, "I just want you to know. About what happened . . . I understand . . ."

Raistlin lifted his head, paused in his writing. He did not look at his brother, but gazed out the window. The Forest of Wayreth surrounded the tower. He looked out upon withering leaves, leafless branches, rotted and decayed stumps.

"You are never to mention that incident to me or to anyone else, my brother, so long as you live. Do you understand?"

"Sure, Raist," Caramon said softly, "I understand." He turned back to his task. "Your tea's almost ready."

Raistlin closed the book he had been reading. His eyes burned from the strain of trying to decipher the scribe's old-fashioned handwriting, he was weary from the effort involved in translating the mixture of archaic Common and the military slang spoken among soldiers and mercenaries.

Flexing his hand, which ached from gripping the pen, Raistlin slid the volume about Magius into his belt for perusal during their long journey north. They were not returning to Solace. Antimodes had given the twins the name of a nobleman who was hiring warriors and who would, Antimodes said, be glad to hire a war mage as well. Antimodes was heading in that direction. He would be glad to have the young men ride with him.

Raistlin had readily agreed. He planned to learn all he could from the archmagus before they parted. He had hoped that Antimodes would apprentice him, and had even been bold enough to make the request. Antimodes had refused, however. He never took apprentices, or so he said. He lacked the patience. He added that there was little opportunity in the way of apprenticeships open these days. Raistlin would be far better studying on his own.

This was a prevarication (one could not say that a White

Robe lied). The other mages who had taken the Tests had all been apprenticed. Raistlin wondered why he was the exception. He decided, after considerable thought, that it must have something to do with Caramon.

His brother was rattling the teapot, making a most ungodly racket, slopping boiling water all over the floor and spilling the herbs.

Would I go back to the days of my youth?

Then my body had seemed frail, but it was strong in comparison to this fragile assembly of bones and flesh that I now inhabit, held together only by my will. Would I go back?

Then I looked on beauty and I saw beauty. Now I look on beauty and I see it drowned, bloated, and disfigured, carried downstream by the river of time. Would I go back?

Then we were twins. Together in the womb, together after birth, still together but now separate. The silken cords of brotherhood, cut, dangle between us, never to be restrung. Would I go back?

Closing the volume of his precious notations, Raistlin picked up a pen and wrote on the cover:

I, *Magus*.

And, with a swift, firm stroke, he underlined it.

Coda

One evening, while I was absorbed in my usual task of chronicling the history of the world, Bertram, my loyal but occasionally inept assistant, crept into my study and begged leave to interrupt my work.

"Whatever is the matter, Bertram?" I demanded, for the man was as pale as if he'd encountered a gnome bringing an incendiary device into the Great Library.

"This, Master!" he said, his voice quavering. He held in his trembling hands a small scroll of parchment, tied with a black ribbon and sealed with black ink. Stamped upon the ink was the imprint of an eye.

"Where did this come from?" I demanded, though I knew immediately who must have sent it.

"That's just it, Master, " Bertram said, holding the scroll balanced on the tips of his fingers. "I don't know! One minute it wasn't there. And the next minute it was."

Knowing I would get nothing more intelligent from Bertram than this, I told him to place the scroll on the desk and to leave. I would peruse it at my leisure. He was clearly reluctant to leave the missive, thinking no doubt that it would burst into flame or some other such nonsense. He did as I requested, however, and left with many a backward glance. Even then, he waited, hovering outside my door with—as I learned later—a bucket of water nearby, intending, no doubt, to fling it on me at the first puff of smoke.

Breaking the seal and untying the ribbon, I found this letter, of which I have included a portion.

To Astinus,
It may be that I am about to undertake a daring enterprise. [1] *It*

is highly probable that I will not return from this undertaking (should I decide to undertake it) or if I do, it will be an altered state. If it should occur that I meet my demise upon this quest, then I give you leave to publish the true account of my early life, including that which has always been kept most secret, my Test in the Tower of High Sorcery. I do this in response to the many wild tales and untruths being circulated regarding me and my family. I grant you permission on the condition that Caramon also agrees with my decision. . . .

I did not forget about Raistlin's charge to me, as some have implied. Neither Caramon nor I deemed the time right for publication of his book. Now that his nephew Palin has grown to manhood and has taken his own Test in the Tower, Caramon has given his permission for the book to be published.

This is the true account of Raistlin's early life. Astute readers will note discrepancies between this account and others which have come before. I trust those readers will take into consideration the fact that the name of Raistlin Majere had become legend over the years. A great deal that has been written, told, and sung about the great mage is either false or a distortion of the truth.

I am guilty of some of this myself, for I deliberately misled people in regard to certain aspects of Raistlin's life. The Test in the Tower of High Sorcery—the Test that proved to have such a devastating and fateful influence on him—is one of the most important. Other accounts exist of his Test, but this is the first time the true account has been written.

The Conclave of Wizards has long decreed that the nature of the Test be kept secret. Following Raistlin's "death," certain wild and destructive rumors began to circulate regarding him. Caramon asked for permission from Par-Salian to lay these rumors to rest. Since the rumors appeared likely to damage the reputations of all magic-users on Krynn, the Conclave granted permission for the story to be told, but only if certain of the facts were altered.

Thus Caramon caused to be written an abbreviated story of Raistlin's Test, which came to be known as the *Test of the Twins*. In essence, the story is true, though you will see that the actual events are a great deal different form those earlier portrayed.

I finish with the conclusion of Raistlin's letter.

Margaret Weis

. . . I break the silence now because I want the facts known. If I am to be judged by those who come after me, let me be judged for the truth. I dedicate this book to the one who gave me life.

Raistlin Majere

[1] The enterprise to which he refers is his attempt to enter the Abyss and overthrow Takhisis. Those interested may find this tale in the Great Library, in the books marked "Dragonlance Legends."

Collections of the best of the DRAGONLANCE® saga

From *New York Times* best-selling authors Margaret Weis & Tracy Hickman.

THE ANNOTATED LEGENDS

A striking new three-in-one hardcover collection that complements *The Annotated Chronicles*. Includes *Time of the Twins*, *War of the Twins*, and *Test of the Twins*.

For the first time, DRAGONLANCE saga co-creators Weis & Hickman share their insights, inspirations, and memories of the writing of this epic trilogy. Follow their thoughts as they craft a story of ambition, pride, and sacrifice, told through the annals of time and beyond the edge of the world.

September 2003

THE WAR OF SOULS Boxed Set

Copies of the *New York Times* best-selling War of Souls trilogy paperbacks in a beautiful slipcover case. Includes *Dragons of a Fallen Sun*, *Dragons of a Lost Star*, and *Dragons of a Vanished Moon*.

The gods have abandoned Krynn. An army of the dead marches under the leadership of a strange and mystical warrior. A kender holds the key to the vanishing of time. Through it all, an epic struggle for the past and future unfolds.

September 2003

The Minotaur Wars

From *New York Times* best-selling author Richard A. Knaak comes a powerful new chapter in the DRAGONLANCE® saga.

The continent of Ansalon, reeling from the destruction of the War of Souls, slowly crawls from beneath the rubble to rebuild – but the fires of war, once stirred, are difficult to quench. Another war comes to Ansalon, one that will change the balance of power throughout Krynn.

NIGHT OF BLOOD
Volume I

Change comes violently to the land of the minotaurs. Usurpers overthrow the emperor, murder all rivals, and dishonor minotaur tradition. The new emperor's wife presides over a cult of the dead, while the new government makes a secret pact with a deadly enemy. But betrayal is never easy, and rebellion lurks in the shadows.

The Minotaur Wars begin June 2003.